Destiny waits for all... especially a headstrong princess.

Royal blood can take a princess only so far in life. Sooner or later destiny will sweep her off her feet.

If she's lucky, he's tall, blond, fun to push around, and helps her save their ice ball planet from a killer comet.

I0672458

Books by Morgan Q. O'Reilly

Frozen
Chinook, Wine and Sink Her

Open Window Series
Til Death Undo Us
Courage to Live
Weathering the Storm

Published by Kensington Publishing Corporation

Frozen

Morgan Q. O'Reilly

LYRICAL PRESS
Kensington Publishing Corp.
www.kensingtonbooks.com

Lyrical Press books are published by
Kensington Publishing Corp. 119 West 40th Street New York, NY 10018

First Electronic Edition: June 2008
eISBN-13: 978-1-61650-000-9
eISBN-10: 1-61650-000-X

First Print Edition: June 2008
ISBN-13: 978-1-61650-898-2
ISBN-10: 1-61650-898-1

Printed in the United States of America

To my good friend Marcy for proposing the idea that got me started. The original challenge was to write 100 pages of a story "From Hell." It became my 2006 NaNoWriMo project and went just a bit past 100 pages.

We loves ya, Misty!

Chapter 1

"No one will ever be able to convince me that Hell never freezes over," Noreen muttered as she looked over the flat, frozen vista on the far side of the thick window before her.

Blinking travel fatigue from her eyes, she focused past the reflected images of the people behind her in the large Ryadstholm Depot, many rushing in from the huge inter-galaxy cruiser on the launch pad. Even more were lining up to board it. Instead, all she saw was white landscape against a midnight-black sky. Outdoor lighting obscured the stars.

Just before opening the doors to let her disembark, the captain had said the early morning temperature was fifty degrees below zero, Celsius. Her guess would put it down around minus sixty. Not that it mattered much. Cold was cold.

"This isn't Hell," a deep voice replied from behind her shoulder. As she shivered, she saw a blond man's reflection in the window. "Noreen Tibbetts?" The voice was slightly hesitant, as if reading from a slip of paper. A different kind of shiver traveled down her spine. One that made her feel a little warmer.

Turning to face the speaker, she didn't appreciate the look of amused condescension before his eyes traveled the length of her body and returned to her face. Their gazes met, and she found herself mesmerized by the deepening of his already dark blue eyes. Dimly aware of a faint ringing in her ears, much like the sound of two pieces of heavy steel colliding, she fought for control as his stare fanned a tiny spark of heat deep inside. Shaking her head slightly to break the heat wave rising between them, she purposely ignored the shocked look he wore as she stepped back until a row of connected chairs stopped her retreat.

She wasn't staying long enough to dally with the locals. Especially not these locals. Still, had they been this magnificent before she left? After all, Hans, her bodyguard, was a very fine specimen of manhood, but this man made him look like a thug. *Oh Freya,* don't think about such things. This man was an escort, nothing more. A transport driver. Chauffer. Hired help.

"Fine, have it your way. *Helvete.*" She gave him an insincerely sweet smile to cover her sudden lack of breath and wildly beating heart. No need for panic attacks!

His gaze had just wandered to her secretary, Fiona, obviously waiting with her, but cut immediately back to Noreen at her use of the local term. Let him figure out how she knew the old Nordic word for Hell. She knew the word in more languages than he was probably even aware existed.

Before he could question her, she regained control of her emotions and nodded to the bulky bundle in his hands. "Is that for me?"

"Yes. I wasn't told there were two of you, though." Uncertainly he set down a pair of boots and held out an insulated parka and high-waisted pants that matched the outerwear he wore. His unzipped parka showed a thin, white silk undershirt clinging to what looked like a muscular chest. "They'll be more comfortable without the jeans and sweater you're wearing."

Ignoring the lift of his eyebrow and the challenge in his eyes, she squared her shoulders, took the outerwear from him and set it on a chair. "My secretary has accommodations here and will see to the bulk of my luggage. That pile will go with me now." With a wave of her hand she indicated half a dozen soft and hard cases, then grasped the bottom of her wool sweater and lifted it over her head. Hans, with the help of Sophie, her personal maid, had control of the trunks and suitcases that made this pile look like luggage for a day trip.

The blond man's gulp was loud enough for her to hear as she carefully pulled the sweater over her neatly coiled hair. Bet he wasn't expecting her to strip down in the public lounge to the clinging fire-red silk shirt she wore under a bright blue wool sweater. Handing the discarded garment to Fiona, Noreen quickly toed off her woolen shoes and shimmied out of her jeans.

Lust flared in his eyes as his gaze swept her lower body encased by clinging silk leggings to match the top. Disregarding the sudden pebbling of her nipples in response to the nearly physical caress of his perusal, Noreen glanced at Fiona and saw her secretary smirking at the man's reaction. So he noticed she only wore the long silk underwear and no other under items?

Knowing she'd be in tight quarters for a few days, she'd opted out of wearing additional under things. Stepping into the thick cold-weather pants, Noreen added an extra wiggle as they slid up over her hips. When she felt her unbound breasts jiggle in response, she glanced up in time to see his jaw tighten. Yup, he noticed. Not laughing was a strain as she watched him shuffle his feet and make a point of looking away.

"So, handsome escort, what might your name be?" A quick tug tightened the shoulder straps that held up the garment. Through the silk of her leggings, the soft fur lining was a lover's caress against her body. Fur seal, a distant cousin to the seals of Earth, highly prized for its deep sable softness. Per local custom, she mentally sent a sigh of thanks to the spirit of the animal who'd given up its life to feed the tribesmen, and its skin to keep her warm. One of the very rare luxuries of living on the iceball, known to the universe as Nordia.

After a startled frown, a slow smile spread across his face at her impertinent tone. It was almost too easy to bet no one usually talked to him so casually. Liked a sassy female, did he? Maybe the trip would be entertaining after all.

"Gunnar. Gunnar Zaren. Princess Coreen personally asked me to make sure you arrived in Stravicsholm safe and whole."

"I'm honored." It was hard keeping the sarcastic tone from her voice, and she muffled it further by turning to pick up the parka after stomping her feet into the tribal-made fur-lined boots he'd also brought along. Thankfully they were broken in and the waterproof tanned skin soles molded softly to her feet.

Yeah, I just bet Cory asked you personally, the cynical thought crept into her mind and she swiftly kicked it away as well. No lusting after locals and no trashing royalty. Even if she did outrank Cory. Gunnar didn't know that and didn't need to. Let him find out in a couple weeks when she was six star systems away.

Fiona finished folding her discarded clothes, and zipped them into the nearest case.

"How long will it take to reach Stravicsholm?" her secretary asked her escort, as the last piece of luggage was grabbed by a porter and loaded onto a trolley.

Noreen watched the porter head out the door toward a bright orange transport as she searched the pockets of the parka for mittens. Compact and boxy, the cab of the snow crawler rode high over articulated tracks instead of wheels. She'd have to climb a short ladder into the vehicle.

Right, in this bulky gear. Was it too much to hope the cab would be warm enough to unzip the parka? She suppressed a frown when her luggage was stored in the cargo bay at the back. If it froze, there'd be hell to pay long before they reached their destination.

"Three days if the weather holds. A storm could delay us by a day or more."

Noreen glanced back in time to see Gunnar's eyes assess the cool blonde who nodded sharply. Yeah, he could see Fiona had the local look and the questions were beginning to rise in his mind.

"I'll try to check in along the way." Noreen turned to her secretary, eager to dispatch her before he started asking those questions. "Leave word at the palace in care of Princess Coreen's name when you get settled, just to make sure there hasn't been a change since we made the reservations."

"Yes, of course. Travel safe."

Noreen felt an extra squeeze as Fiona embraced her. Fi knew how hard this visit would be. "Look after the other two," Noreen added with a whisper.

Fiona kissed her cheek then stepped back. "I'll see to everything. You just enjoy the trip. As much as possible, anyway," she added in an undertone.

For the first time in more than ten years, Noreen was heading off without at least one of her staff of three in attendance. Stepping, unchaperoned, into a small transport, with a man who looked like he wanted to spend the trip in bed with her. Why had she agreed to leave Hans in Ryadstholm? After quelling the sudden knot of nervousness in her stomach, it also occurred to her it was her first visit home since her sixteenth birthday. The very day she'd grabbed Fiona and left the planet in an attempt to avoid her fate. Fate, it seemed, had more ways than one to skin the proverbial cat. She tried to ignore the little voice that said one more life had just slipped away.

* * * *

Four hours later, Noreen caught herself shifting in her seat with impatience as the snow crawler lived up to its name. Reasonably insulated from the harsh elements, she huddled in the soft luxury of her parka and stared out of the large cab windows. The grinding pace of the tracks was perfectly designed to travel across the many layers of white crystals covering Nordia's frozen tundra. She struggled to ignore the muffled, but steady clanking of the transport, which grated further on her already irritated nerves. Her mind was occupied trying to figure out whether

Cory's frantic plea for her to return home really meant Fader was deathly ill. Knowing Cory, it could have just been one last desperate ruse to get her home at last.

Shivering, Noreen glanced at the blue glow of the clock on the control panel, which emitted beeps and small flashes from various lights finally agree to come home. Was Fader sick or not? Was it a trumped-up cold or was it serious? Cory's silence on the matter was enough to make her want to scream.

"Where are we stopping tonight?" Noreen scanned the map in her head. One thousand very long kilometers, over frozen ground, at this tedious speed seemed endless. Just six days ago she'd been dancing in the sun, many light years away from this frozen Hell. And now...now...she was slowly crawling the last thousand klicks.

"We aren't stopping tonight. We're joining a convoy in a few hours. Once that happens we'll connect to the vehicle in front and then it's easy for the next two days."

And nights. The unspoken words shimmered almost visibly in the frigid air between them.

"What do you mean?" An odd chill settled in deeper than anything this cold place and this disturbing man had already done to her. She pulled the hood of her parka up around her ears and wrapped the coat tighter about her body.

"I won't have to steer." He shot her another smile that said he thought she was cute in her ignorance. "Then we can talk, or find other ways to amuse ourselves."

Ignorant. Yes, she was ignorant of peasant ways. When she'd left this place ten years earlier she'd done it in style in a galaxy cruising-rocket. Only peasants traveled by these slow transports, and in convoys, taking days to reach their destinations.

By normal transport, in three days, she could be several star systems away. On a world without one spot of snow. A world where white was from time to time. Nearly noon, the sun was just barely peeking above the horizon to the south, far behind them. The elongated rays sent even longer-looking shadows out in front of them, like misshapen fingers pointing north, pushing them further into the dark chill. Another day or two, and the sun wouldn't rise at all for six weeks, only providing a glowing red spot on the southern horizon for a few minutes each day.

Folding her arms as best she could, Noreen rubbed her cheek against the hood pushed back from her face but still warming her head. The heater of the transport worked only well enough to keep the front and side windows clear of frost. A glance at the digital readouts for the interior and exterior temperatures showed her it was seven degrees Celsius inside, with a midday high of minus fifty outside. Gunnar didn't seem bothered by it. He wore his parka unzipped and had tossed his heavy outer mitts aside in favor of thin, woolen, knit gloves.

With a heavy sigh, she once again cursed the communication last week. Damn Coreen for dragging her back to the one planet she never wanted to see again! Not even in pictures. A place she hated so much, anything white was banished from her sight, lest it remind her of where she'd been born. Leave it to her sister to be the one to drag her back. Only by hinting at Fader's failing health did Coreen get Noreen to banned. Not even the sea foam dared appear white. Beaches were gold, sea foam was aquamarine, and every cabana boy was tanned a deep, golden brown.

"What I don't understand," she spoke slowly, so he wouldn't miss a single word, "is why we have to travel this way at all. Why can't we fly in? Why couldn't the inter-galaxy land closer to Stravicsholm?" At the very least she should have been able to catch an intercontinental express rocket, which should have been able to land within a half-day's ride of the main capital, not three.

"Weather. This point in the season, it isn't safe to blast in and out so far north. It's barely safe enough to land near Ryadstholm. Besides, the reindeer and musk oxen herds don't like the racket so we've returned to the old ways. Slower, but life is so much better. Relax, princess, and enjoy the ride."

Noreen merely glared at the implied insult of the princess remark. She also wasn't sure she liked the grin on Gunnar's face. Handsome enough that he knew it all too well, his smile bordered on lecherous in her mind, his tone too smooth. Blond hair, nearly as white as the snow outside, brushed his shoulders, and he had the traditional blue eyes of the Nordian people. Traditional in that they were blue. Not so traditional in that they were a deep blue, sparkling with tiny flecks of what looked like silver. Fey eyes. The eyes of a spirit man. The rest of him was remarkable as well. Square chin, square jaw, providing an aristocratic frame for smooth skin the color of bleached maple, a very light golden brown. Warm vanilla. From what she could tell, under his outer clothing he seemed to have a body to match. Not that it mattered. She wasn't going to be checking out his body close up.

"Wait. We're not stopping?" She frowned. "Where will we sleep?"

When Gunnar shot another tolerant smile at her, she had the urge to slap it off his face. The man's arrogance apparently knew no bounds. He reached over his shoulder and pushed a button. A thin panel slid open to reveal a cabin behind them. She turned to get a better look. Behind Gunnar's seat was a plastic, half-height, open-topped cabinet with a showerhead over it. Inside, sat a self contained toilet. One step away, behind her seat, was a small fridge under a single radiant burner next to an equally small counter, barely big enough to assemble a sandwich on. Along the back wall was another low cabinet, presumably holding other necessities. Where were the beds? Was there enough room for stacked bunks?

"See the panel on the back wall?"

"Yes." It looked like a painting. White landscape with the night sky striped by the polar lights. How typically Nordian.

"It swings down to make a platform bed."

"A bed," she repeated, not wanting to comprehend. It would come down to rest on the half-height cabinets and span the entire depth and width of the cabin.

"The bed," he emphasized, with a note of laughter in his voice. "Big enough for two, I assure you. Cozy, but still comfortable."

"I'm not sleeping with you!" The words burst from her before she had a chance to think.

"Why not? Shared body heat is the best way to stay warm while sleeping."

She stared at him in horror as he calmly steered the transport around an ice boulder.

"I'll sleep here, or after you've had your rest, I'll take the bed. We can sleep in stages." She was not sleeping with a Nordian. She'd purposely stayed far away from genetically compatible humanoids in her travels, preferring partners who couldn't accidentally impregnate her. Men who catered to her, begged for her favor. Partners who would leave the most fragile part of her intact. Each one carefully investigated and researched over several months, seduction allowed only when she was ready to leave a planet.

No ties. No commitments. Usually only two nights were allowed, a week at the absolute maximum and only if the man in question was seriously hot. The last man had been hot enough, but Cory's communication hadn't allowed the week she'd been working up to.

"No, it doesn't work that way." She watched him shake his head to underline his statement while steering around a deep drift sweeping across their path.

"I am not sleeping with you," she repeated with more heat, tossing him a good glare for emphasis.

"If you're worried about your virtue, don't be." He openly laughed at her now.

"Excuse me?" She dropped her voice to its lowest register and regarded him with a finely-waxed arched brow. Freshly waxed, and not just the eyebrows. Knowing she'd be far from civilization, she'd indulged in a full day in the ship-board spa. She was set for at least four weeks, six if she couldn't get things wrapped up quickly. Hopefully her hair color would last that long. Anything to hide her true appearance. Almost anything.

"I'm promised already. I've sworn to remain pure until the right one comes into my life."

Noreen felt the blood drain from her face. "The Promised One?" she blurted out.

Staring at Gunnar's face, she caught his sharp questioning look before a bleep from the control panel drew his attention back to his driving.

"You've heard of *The Profetia?* The Prophecy?" he asked harshly.

She forced herself to snort and turn to look out the window again. "Who hasn't?"

"I thought you weren't of this land?"

"Even off-worlders hear things."

"Not about The Profetia," he said with a frown.

That was a mistake. She shrugged carelessly as if it were no big deal. He was right. The Profetia was never spoken of beyond the planet they traveled across, and never with off-worlders.

"Where did you hear of it?" he pressed, his voice far from amused. Enough that she almost laughed at his commanding tone even though she felt a tremor run down her spine.

"I don't remember." She lifted her nose in the air, as if his question were boring her to tears.

"I don't believe you. Only those born to the land know of The Profetia."

"I have an aunt from here," she muttered. "So who are you, again?"

"Gunnar Zaren. Why? Have you heard of me?"

"Didn't the male half of The Profetia have a title or some other royal designation?" she asked casually, with a dismissive wave of her hand. Did she come across as only mildly curious? Good thing her thick mittens covered the sudden shaking of her hand. *Must be time to eat.*

"Yes. I'm a Duke." His reply sounded reluctant.

"Am I supposed to kiss your ring, or something, now?" She gave her voice a teasing quality.

"Or something," he muttered, with a lifted brow that silenced her.

Oh *dritt!* she silently cursed. No, the local swear words were out. They would tip him off for sure. *Shit.* There, the old Earth word would work.

A duke, he'd said. But which one? If he was The One, he could only be… oh shit, what was the name Cory'd used? Damn Cory!

An uneasy silence fell as he steered around another mound of white in the darkening landscape. No, not darkening. Never dark. The minute frozen crystals around them caught and reflected every little spark of light from every possible source no matter how remote. Transport headlights lit up the landscape, as would the moonlight and starlight in a short while.

Trying to find her calm center, Noreen listened to the crunching of the vehicle treads rolling over the snow. Not soft like the flakes the sky produced, the snow on the ground was packed and dry. Dry because the extreme cold sucked all moisture from the air. They followed a track, which shifted and changed as the snow blew and drifted across the relatively flat land. The convoy would be a relief to Gunnar, allowing him to rest from his constant vigilance. Unfortunately, it would free him up to concentrate on her.

Ten, long galactic years seemed as if they'd passed in only a few days the farther she traveled north. Ten years of seeking out every warm and colorful world she could find. Ten years of warmth, of never wearing anything heavier than jeans and a cotton sweater. Usually she wore no more than a length of cloth wrapped around her. Knotted over a breast, it often slipped off when least expected, and more often when desired. A small smile lifted the corner of her lips as she thought of the last time her colorful wrap had slipped. The hands which had pulled it away had belonged to a man as dark as Gunnar was fair. Black hair, black skin, black eyes. Never a man with skin whiter than hers.

For a moment she forgot her predicament and fell into a daydream, remembering the feel of large, warm hands on her body, the lovely contrast of dark skin against hers, a tanned, golden brown. Chocolate and caramel. A very lovely contrast, indeed.

"Where are you from?"

Gunnar's voice broke into her reverie and she closed her eyes as the daydream faded, leaving behind a very familiar hollow ache between her legs. She squeezed her thighs together, and let the fantasy go with a sigh.

"I'm from no place in particular. I travel a lot."

"But where were you born? Where are your people from? If you have an aunt from here, are you related by your mother or father?"

She felt his eyes on her profile. If he looked close enough he'd see the signs. She hadn't quite convinced herself to alter her appearance permanently with any of the surgeries available across the universe. So far, she'd stuck to superficial means with the help of skilled technicians.

Hair, naturally every bit as white blonde as Gunnar's, now was a hot red. Not sweet, golden red. Cherry red that glowed like the clouds burning from the last ray of the sun. Deep blue eyes were hidden under even deeper brown artificial lenses. Skin as pale as his was naturally disguised after years under every sun she could find. At first she'd burned as bright red as her hair color, but special creams had helped her brown until she was almost the shade of the warm furs caressing her body through the silk. A color that, even now, she could feel fading, despite spending the last hours on the inter-galaxy ship under sun lights. Hopefully the sun light she had packed in her luggage would arrive unharmed.

"My people were wanderers." She evaded the direct question. Even under torture she wouldn't admit she'd been born within a hundred light years of this iceball.

"Humanoid."

"Obviously," she scoffed.

"Where were you born? Your accent almost sounds as if you're from here."

Great. A speech specialist was he? "My accent reflects many places. What about you? Do you travel far?"

"Only as far as this transport can carry me," he said tightly.

Peasant, she thought again, despite his own speech and the admission of a noble title. "You've never been off the planet surface? Not even to cross the continent or ocean?"

"I've had no reason to leave the planet surface or my home. Everything I need is here, including boats to cross the sea."

"Except your Promised One," she muttered.

"Yes," he answered shortly.

Damn, he had good ears to have heard that over the sounds of the vehicle and the instruments on the consol. She'd have to be careful. A bad habit, she often blurted out her thoughts without realizing it. Good thing she'd decided to never be a politician. "So what is your mission in life, Duke Gunnar Zaren? Who are your people?"

Glancing toward him, she saw his jaw clench slightly. Didn't like her bored tone of voice, did he? Maybe, if she used it more, he'd leave her in silence.

"Who wants to know?"

"I do."

"But who are you?"

"I'm Noreen Tibbetts, just as your communication said."

"That's just a name. Who are you?"

"I'm a humanoid woman of mysterious origins. I arrange travel across the universe for adventurous beings." And travel even more just for fun when not working.

"What is a travel agent doing on Nordia?"

Travel agent. It worked. It was either that or pose as a reporter or research scientist. "I've been invited to write an article."

"Tourists are few and far between."

"Someone wants to change that." Certainly not her. There was little to recommend here, and the best features could be found on more pleasant planets.

"Nobody wants more tourists."

Noreen shrugged. She couldn't agree with him more, but for now she had a role to play. "Tourists bring in revenue."

"We don't need money."

True, the planet was quite well-off for an iceball. Mining for rare minerals brought in huge sums for tiny amounts. Not to mention the market for rare furs and exotic wools. Many companies also leased acreage for deep cold research. Poverty was not a problem on Nordia.

"Look, I was invited to come and write an article. I'm not even sure I can recommend this place with a good conscience, so don't get your nappies in a knot."

"Nappies?"

There was that arched brow again.

"Absorbent underwear. For infants."

Gunnar snorted. "Diapers? You think I wear diapers?"

"If they fit..." she let the comment drift away.

"Is this common off-world?" He scowled in her direction.

"Is what common?"

"This...sarcasm."

"You've never heard sarcasm before?" No, he didn't like the astonished tone of voice, if his deep frown and flush were a good indication.

"It isn't common here."

It would be if she still lived here. "A pity. I find sarcasm helps one to laugh in situations that would normally make one cry or shoot something."

"Shoot?"

"As in to use a firestick to inflict great injury, possibly even death, upon another being," she explained as politely as she could.

"Ah, use of a gun."

"Exactly." Give him points for a little education. Guns weren't permitted on Nordia, even for research. She'd found them fascinating the first time she'd seen one in use. Until she'd seen the carnage they could wreak on living things.

"You must think I'm an idiot," he accused her.

"Only depends which planet you're standing on at the time." She sighed and looked out the side window again. A lesson she'd learned well after blasting off this particular iceball. And here she was, trapped in this damn transport for three long days with the very man she'd left this planet to avoid. The One, waiting for his female equivalent to appear. *Dritt.*

Was this some elaborate plan of Odin? Thor? Freya? One of Loki's pranks?

Which brought her back to the problem of sleeping arrangements. There was no way in Hell, or on this frozen version of it, she would sleep next to this man. Not all versions of Hell were hot. In fact, the cold could burn just a badly as fire. Given a choice, she'd take flames over ice any day.

Chapter 2

Gunnar looked at the woman beside him. She huddled in her parka as if she'd never get warm, though how she could be cold with the red-hot, silk underwear she wore... Just let him touch her and she'd be warm. His fingers clenched tightly around the steering wheel.

No, don't think about touching this woman. She's not The One. Couldn't be. The noise he'd heard at the depot had been the sound of a child dropping a toy. Possibly even luggage trolleys colliding. Thor's Hammer was just a legend anyway.

Too bad. Bleach her long, braided hair white, give her blue lenses for her eyes, and she'd almost look like the princess. Crown Princess Coreen Ileana Adelaide Elizabeth Audelhuk, Duchess of NyUppland and NyDalarna, first in line to the throne upon which sat an aging king, was the very essence of Nordian womanhood, but she wasn't The One. As her loyal subject, and even more loyal friend, he'd been unable to deny the special request of the princess to pick up this woman. This woman who could be the twin sister of the princess, if one didn't pay attention to her coloring. Or her attitude.

Then again, many of the women inhabiting the palace could very well serve as a double for the princess. It didn't help that all nine of the king's daughters had similar names, all ending in 'oreen'. King Bjorn had been a busy man in his prime. Just not busy enough to produce sons. And only one daughter from his official wife, Queen Elke, or so the stories said. Rumor included tales of a twin who'd died at birth, but he'd never been able to find proof. Coreen merely laughed it off as palace intrigue. Daughters from the concubines didn't count in the line of succession. Coreen was the duly acknowledged heiress-apparent to the throne, followed by a male cousin with a duchy.

Hence the confusing point of the damn Profetia.

If his grandfather's ability to interpret the ancient document hadn't already been proven fifty times over as genuine, he would have thought the old man had cooked up this scheme with either the king or Coreen. So here Gunnar was, in the prime of his life, traveling from city to city to attend boring social functions, all in name of searching for a woman who would, according to The Profetia, produce the first male heir in fifty years.

Which made no sense at all. Gunnar was twelfth in the line of succession. How could he father the next king? Especially if the Crown Princess wasn't The One, destined to be his bride? He would have gladly married Coreen, but it just wasn't to be. While he was fond of her and admired her, she'd never rocked his soul like the ringing of Thor's Hammer. Or at least that was the feeling he was supposed to have upon discovering his Promised One, according to his grandfather and the king.

Gunnar shook his head and turned his attention back to Noreen, the mystery woman from beyond the galaxy.

How did she get her skin so brown? Was it naturally that way? Somehow he didn't think her red hair was a natural color. Even though he didn't travel off-world, he did read and study the news and had never seen a being with hair such a color. At least not with that skin and eye color combined. Or in humanoid form come to think of it. And what a form. She was of a height and shape to mold perfectly to him. Long legs curved into hips just wide enough and rounded enough to fit his hands. A narrow waist curved up into a lean torso, which presented breasts perfect for holding and suckling. All attributes he knew would make her a fine mother. Motherhood be damned, they were all perfect attributes to take to his bed. He wanted to suckle on the perfectly shaped breasts he'd seen outlined under the red silk just before she'd pulled on the heavy outer gear.

Trying to shift to a more comfortable position, he had to content himself with looking at her large, thick-lashed eyes, pert nose and lush lips. Red cream colored her lips at the moment, as much to protect from the elements as to emphasize their shape. Lips he could imagine wrapped around a certain part of his body which was uncomfortably throbbing at the moment. Lips he longed to taste.

He swallowed a groan at the sex-drenched thoughts overrunning his head and body.

Where were these thoughts coming from? Sure, he appreciated a beautiful female, but he didn't spend time dreaming of peeling off their clothes to see if their skin color was the same over every inch of their bodies. Granted, with the women of his planet, he already knew the answer to that particular mystery. He'd seen photos of people who lounged in the sunlight with the express purpose of changing their skin color. Often times they covered one part of their body so it remained its natural color. Did Noreen do that? Or was she the same all over?

No, there was no point dreaming about the strange woman beside him. He knew who his mate was. He just hadn't met her yet. Which was damn perplexing, because he'd traveled to nearly every city on the planet, and attended more tedious court functions than he could count, in an effort to find his Promised One. He was sure he'd met every Nordian woman of the right age. All in the name of finding The One. The Profetia said he'd know her the moment they met. The Profetia also said she'd be one of his people, not an off-world stranger.

So why did this woman, Noreen, intrigue him so?

"You never said where you were born," he reminded her.

"You're right. I don't see how it's pertinent. I'm here to find out about your world. Why don't you tell me what makes all this cold and snow special?"

Sharp, this one was. He wasn't used to women with tongues this fast. Most tended to go tongue-tied in his presence. Between his title and the mystique of The Profetia, it was if the gods had placed an aura around him, elevating him on a pedestal. Though he found her reluctance to talk about herself frustrating, in a way it was refreshing. A challenge. And the bed thing. There was a question there. What concerned her? His word was good. Mostly. Well, usually in that area at least. She might tempt him otherwise. In the close quarters of the cabin her soft scent teased him, pushing away the usual odor of hot metal and fuel.

"What makes snow special?" He repeated her words to refocus and mentally rolled his eyes. Now he sounded like an imbecile who couldn't string two thoughts together. So much for the fancy education, or the years of running a duchy and the king's intelligence network.

"Yes. What makes your world so wonderful you've never left it?"

"Good question. I'm not sure you'd believe me. You'll have to see it for yourself."

"Well then, it seems we don't have much to discuss, do we?"

"You don't want to come clean about something as simple as where you come from, why should I share the intimate details of a world I love? You give every appearance of not wanting to like this place. How can you call that objective reporting?"

"Tell me about these herds you mentioned earlier?"

"Know what a caribou is?"

"Yes."

"Well, they aren't caribou."

"Really."

"Reindeer. Domesticated caribou. The first herds were brought with the original colonists from Earth five hundred some-odd years ago." Just as the gods and people had been imported.

"So I've read. What makes them special?"

"You don't want to talk about reindeer."

"It seemed like a neutral topic. What else is there? I believe I read something about thermal pools. Tourists would find those interesting. People have been known to spend their whole lives in search of the perfect hot springs and mineral waters."

"Ah yes, the thermal pools. Very nice places." Especially since people bathed naked. As a general rule, Nordians were a fit and beautiful race, so it was a pleasant way to pass the time. None of those swimsuits he'd seen in travel articles. There were thermal pools on their route.

"Really? Care to elaborate?" she pressed, as he scanned the weather dials.

"I'd rather talk about what you know of The Profetia and The One."

"Tell me about your connection to the royal family. Princess Coreen Audelhuk? Where does she fit into all of this?" she countered, with a little wave of her mittened hand.

It wasn't that cold in the transport, so why did she wear them still?

"Good question," he shot back at her. "How do you know the princess?"

The woman shrugged and rubbed her forehead. "I got a message one day," she said wearily.

He wasn't buying the act. Coreen used the very same gesture and tone on him when she wanted to avoid certain subjects. He'd seen the Queen and all the other palace women do it, as well as women across the planet. Were the more annoying habits of women universal?

"She's the one who asked you to come here?"

The shrug, as an answer, was growing tiresome. Something didn't mesh and, with most of his attention centered on driving the transport, he didn't have time to figure it out. Once they connected with the convoy he'd have two nights and days to untangle the knot. And maybe a few other things. How long was her hair when released from the braid coiled at the back of her head?

"Look, it's mid-day. There are some food packs in the cabinet under the bed. Do you mind picking out something for us to eat?" he suggested, instead of carrying the verbal hide-and-seek further.

"What kind of food packs?"

"For now, there are some self-heating ones. Easier to ingest while driving. Later, when we've connected to the convoy, I'll put together something more appetizing."

"Any special requests?" She loosened her restraint and spun her chair sideways.

"Surprise me, Noreen. That is your name, right?"

"Yes."

Her short tone made him raise a brow. She brushed against his shoulder as she moved into the tiny space behind him. Even through the thick layers of clothing between them, he felt the electric shock. Noreen? She was an off-worlder. She shouldn't have this effect on him. He shifted in his seat again. Would this arousal not ease?

"Which cabinet?" Her husky voice seemed to reach down into his very soul with her simple question.

He shook himself enough to tell her, then turned on the overhead light for her to see better. It also turned the windshield into a mirror, allowing him to watch her crouch to look through the cabinet. A few minutes later she handed him a foil pack radiating warmth and the scent of meatballs and noodles. She set another pack with hot tea in the holder near the steering wheel.

Though convenient, nourishing, and ultimately satisfying, the foil packs left a void in the dining experience. Sucking mashed meat in sauce through a tube was unnatural. It was just one more reason he looked forward to meeting up with the convoy. They'd have a real dinner tonight. Or, at least, as real as he could manage in these quarters.

"Not bad," she pronounced after taking the empty packs to the trash. He watched her sit back and sip hot chocolate, her seat once again facing forward. "A dram of Lidarian mint brandy wouldn't go astray here." He wondered at the ever so fleeting wince that followed her statement.

"Is that one of the places you've traveled?"

"Lidaria? Yes, as a matter of fact. Lovely world. Fabulous beaches. Just left there before coming here."

"Beaches? As in real sand and warm water?"

"Yes." He wondered at the far away dreamy look in her eyes. What memory did she relive? He watched a flush warm her skin when her eyes cut back to his.

"Tell me about the beaches." He wanted to hear her voice and felt nearly desperate for a safe topic to discuss. One where she'd do most of the talking. After the high-pitched simpers he'd had to listen to from hopeful women, her soft throaty tone was a balm to his ears. The mixed accent and slightly foreign cadence of her voice made him think of faraway places he'd only been mildly curious about before.

"Soft, pale gray sand, deep green waters, fruit trees every other step, flowers so bright and sweet-smelling it is difficult to believe they're real. And the mint, well, it's just everywhere."

Another memory that brought a small smile to her face, followed by the hint of a frown quickly smoothed into a neutral expression.

"What did you do there?" he prompted.

"I enjoyed myself." Her simple statement, made with small, wry smile made him want to grind his teeth. Must every word be pulled from her?

"What does that mean? What did you do to enjoy yourself?"

"I lounged on the beaches, swam in warm seas, and sailed across the waves. I drank sweet juices, ate all the fresh fruit I could stand and I enjoyed. The Lidarians are very friendly people."

"Men?"

"Beautiful men," she agreed, with another cryptic smile, and a stab of vicious jealousy slashed through his gut.

"I see."

She looked at him with those distinctive eyes. "What do you see?"

"Nothing. None of my business anyway." Purely to see how she'd react, he steered the transport toward a snow drift. Just enough to tilt the vehicle a little and tip her from her seat into his arms.

"Hey!" The moment the transport settled down again, she pushed away from him.

It hadn't been long, but long enough for him to wrap his arm around her waist. That oh-so-very-slender, curvy waist he'd seen when she'd changed. Unexpected, the nearly paralyzing heat boiling his blood made it hard for him to breathe. Suddenly he had visions of pulling her into the bunk without the heavy outer clothing. The bunk was a cozy nest with a feather mattress and thick alpaca wool blanket. Often he'd wondered what it would feel like to spend a long, dark night there with The One in his arms.

"You did that on purpose," she accused him safe on her side of the cab.

He merely grinned at her.

"I thought you were holding yourself pure?" Those disturbing dark brown eyes narrowed as she glared at him. He wanted to see the look in her eyes as he conquered her.

"I am, but that doesn't mean I don't like a warm armful every now and again."

"Just exactly what do you mean?"

The heat of her glare spiked a feeling through him he'd never felt before. He'd had all the normal urges, and had even indulged in self pleasure while dreaming of his woman, but never had he felt the need so fast, so strong, and so absolutely intense.

"It means I enjoy the company of a beautiful woman as much as the next guy. Probably as much as you enjoy the company of a beautiful man." He returned her stare, until the transport glanced off the side of a snow drift and nearly tipped him into her arms. Too bad he wore his safety harness.

As if reminded, she fastened her harness again and he felt a sense of loss. He'd been hoping to lay the transport over and give her no excuse to crawl off again.

"Will the ride be this tippy once we join the convoy?" Annoyance was transmitted by her glare and snippy tone. Cute. It made him want to smile more.

"No, it will be nice and smooth." Except for the uphill and downhill portions. Now that could be fun while sleeping.

Judging by her glare she was beginning to question his definition of pure, and her definition of Hell.

Chapter 3

So this wasn't Hell, eh? Could have fooled her.

Never say never. The words from the old man came back to haunt her again.

Had Coreen planned this? Had she set up this particular conveyance? Probably.

Noreen wiggled in her seat and laid her head against the shoulder strap of the harness holding her in place. At least she wouldn't be tumbled into Duke Zaren's arms again. She'd bet her next case of Lidarian mint brandy he'd tipped the transport on purpose. So much for remaining pure until he met The One. And she only had half a case left anyway.

Biting her lip in annoyance, she closed her eyes against the darkening sky. Barely past mid-day, it was already black as night elsewhere and would remain so for the next nineteen hours and fifty-five minutes. Not bad for a planet with twenty hour days. Winter. Why, if she had to come back at all, why did it have to be in the deepest part of winter? Ruthlessly she tamped down on the panic wailing to break away from her tight control.

With her eyes still closed, she thought back to that day, oh so long ago, when her world had tilted, only to land her in her current circumstances. She'd been sliding for ten years, fighting and clawing to avoid the destiny thrust upon her by the old man with the wild, silver eyes.

She'd been at the summer house, enjoying the very short season when the sun provided warmth to the frozen world of Nordia. The small island on the equator, where the house was located, was only suitable to inhabit during the three months of warmth. The ocean around it was never warm enough for swimming. Not for her anyway, although others braved it and teased her for preferring the thermal pool. Nevertheless, she'd enjoyed the gardens with the tall trees, the green a blessed relief from the stark white she lived with the rest of the year.

Her sisters all teased her about her quest for warmth, but that was their way, everyone joining in and no one immune. With names all similar, Noreen often led the teasing of Coreen, Loreen, Doreen, Moreen, Toreen, Boreen, Soreen, Zoreen, and Joreen.

What had her father been thinking? Ten daughters, all named the same except for the first letter and the copious middle names. It was madness. At least he hadn't named them alphabetically. That would have made them all so much easier to track. Although all their mothers hated the chaos of it, the girls had grown to love it, and all answered to the call of *Reen* when the dinner bell rang.

But there must have been a method to his madness. None of Bjorn's lesser subjects, and damn few of the nobility, could remember who was the true crown princess. Indeed, it worked to Noreen's advantage that Fader had purposely never been clear on that subject at all. At least, not until they'd all started reaching the age of majority. She may not have hung around, but she'd sporadically stayed in touch and remained aware of the current status.

Coreen was the better princess anyway. She'd been the one who'd excelled in political studies, while Noreen had stared out the window and daydreamed of ways to stay warm year round. While Coreen argued political policy with their father, Noreen had buried her nose in every travel brochure or picture book she could wheedle her father into getting for her. Planets with warm seas had drawn her attention like no others. If the ocean water wasn't at least body temperature, she shunned it completely. By age fourteen, she'd had a list nearly as long as she was tall of all the worlds she wanted to visit. She even had a few picked out as possible permanent residences.

While Coreen strode the halls of Parliament, absorbing the laws of the land, their father had indulged Noreen by letting her decorate her apartments with sun lights and potted trees from exotic worlds. He'd even let her turn the vast thermal pool room into her vision of a tropical paradise, complete with an imported-sand beach and brightly painted murals for all to enjoy. Ancient stone columns had become the trunks of palms and banana trees, each surrounded by bushes of sweet flowers that bloomed year round. Colorful birds had brought music to the air with their sweet songs and a small team of gardeners had kept it perfect.

Was it still like that? Were her rooms untouched? Or had Fader completely disowned her as threatened? No, he would have cut off her allowance if she'd been disowned. Besides, it wasn't as if she'd done nothing to help Nordia while she was away. Just six months ago, the latest in planet-wide communications had been installed because she'd seen it demonstrated on Earth's most recently-colonized planet the year before.

She felt a small wave of shame as she thought of the trouble she'd put her family through. It had all started at a summer party to celebrate the sixteenth birthday of the crown princess, and she'd been wandering amongst the birch trees at the edge of the gardens.

It caused her father no small amount of pain that his eldest daughter shunned the spotlight of society and royal obligation. Noreen had argued endlessly, not only with her parents but Coreen as well, that it wasn't her fault she'd been born five minutes earlier than her sister. It wasn't her fault she wasn't suited to rule. Because of her tearful pleas, the ceremony naming her crown princess on their sixteenth birthday had been held in secret, with only the old bishop, her parents and Coreen in attendance. To the rest of the world Coreen was the crown princess, and Noreen had no intention of ever spoiling the perception. Why couldn't Coreen and Fader play along? Moder had long ago thrown up her hands and refused to discuss the old argument at all.

Identical twins. It had been a good joke from the beginning. Fader had been more than happy to let the world believe one daughter had died. Only one was ever presented to the people at a time and she was always called simply The Princess. Never were their names used. Noreen suspected half the time, at least until they passed the age of five, her father couldn't tell them apart. By then they'd developed distinct personalities and very individual traits were making themselves well known. Enough to confuse the few correspondents allowed into the palace. The growing collection of sisters just made the confusion worse. In effect, the young princesses became invisible to anyone outside the private household. The queen also insisted on keeping her daughters, and the daughters of the two concubines, secluded as much as possible. In truth, Noreen wondered if the people knew just how many children the king had and they supported.

While her half sisters might not be eligible to be called Princess, they were given their own titles upon their age of majority. Loreen and Doreen were Duchesses and the others were Countesses, each with their own properties and incomes. And all were married now, with the exception of herself and Coreen.

Which brought her back to the reason she was here under protest. Fader was dying, or so Cory had implied, and she wanted to marry. The old bishop insisted Noreen come home and fulfill her destiny as The One. Nordia had a right to know the true princess.

Like bloody Hell would she let them make *that* announcement. She was home to renounce her title once and for all. Let Coreen carry on as next in line, as she was born to do.

Noreen's eyes grew heavier, the constant grinding groan of the transport lulling her into sleep. She pulled the hood of the parka up around her head to further block out the noise and the lights from the panels. Might as well get some sleep now, because she sure wasn't going to share that man's bed tonight, destiny or no. If he was too stupid to put the name clues together then so be it. But, in his defense, since half the girl children born on Nordia over the last twenty-six years were similarly named, maybe the resemblance of her name to Coreen's didn't stand out so much. How to hide in plain sight. Maybe her father had done her a favor after all. He certainly hadn't done himself one.

She settled into a restless doze, segments of dreams mixing with her thoughts. Once again she wandered the birch grove behind the summer palace.

The ceremony had taken place early that morning, the crown of gold, encrusted with every gem known to man, rested heavily on her head as she bowed to the bishop. She'd tried three or four times to remove the crown and put it on Coreen's head until her father had held her shoulders as she knelt to accept the benediction sealing her to the throne of Nordia for all time. The only reason she repeated the vows was a deal she'd made with her father. She'd have to serve as Queen for one full year before she could abdicate in favor of her sister. And then it would be done quietly, Coreen stepping in as if she'd been queen all along. The twin thing again. It didn't make sense to her. If they could do it then, why not now? At least the world now knew the Crown Princess as Coreen. Another sign to Noreen they were catching on she had no intention of ever ruling.

Both her father and sister had rolled their eyes and tried to explain, once again, why having two appear as one was good for keeping the monarchy safe. Like there'd ever been death threats.

A quelling look from the old bishop had silenced her protests—whines he'd called them—and she'd repeated her vows as he sprinkled sacred water from the heart of the planet on her and recited old chants. For a brief moment she'd had a vision of the gods, Odin, Thor and Freya in the forefront, smiling down on her, welcoming her to the ranks of royalty, soft melodic tunes wafting like a dream through the chamber. The vision faded with the sound of Thor's Hammer ringing in her ears. Later she told herself it was merely a hallucination. One she could never seem to talk about with Coreen, oddly enough, even to this day. Her father understood, and even then it was difficult to speak of with him. He'd merely patted her on the head, told her it was the proper order of things and to get used to the idea.

While the others gathered for cake and the specially-hoarded champagne to celebrate, the heavy crown once again locked in the vault, she'd snuck off to walk the groves. Something profound had happened and she didn't understand. It was then she came upon the old bishop looking as if he'd been waiting for her.

"You are The One," he'd told her, his ancient eyes sparkling like silver stardust. "You have been chosen and anointed personally by the gods."

"What?" She stopped in her tracks and stared up at the old man with the wild, bushy, white beard.

"'Tis a great honor, Princess, one you would do well to heed. Your consort is on his way to meet you as we speak."

"Consort? Who is he? I have no choice?" Horror at the very thought chilled what little warmth the sun had imparted. It felt as if they were in the dead of winter and not high summer. "I'm only sixteen! I can't marry now!"

"He doesn't yet know he is The One for you. The blessing will soon be revealed to him. For now, he thinks he is coming only to claim his duchy."

"He is coming here?" She looked around wildly, thinking he might leap from the trees.

"He will arrive within the fortnight depending on weather. He travels by traditional means."

"Slow boat, in other words," she'd muttered. Was his duchy so impoverished he couldn't afford a proper transport? "Who is he?" she demanded.

"I cannot tell you, Your Highness, you two will have to discover each other on your own. I only know he travels to be here. You will be married within the year."

Noreen's jaw had dropped in a most undignified manner. Married within the year? She was just sixteen! Her mother had been twenty when she married the king ten years her senior. "Never!" she shouted as she backed away. "I won't! I won't do it!"

The old man had merely gazed at her with those mystical eyes. "Never say never, Your Highness. Your fate was sealed today. You have no choice but to fulfill your destiny."

With those dreadful words he'd turned and disappeared into the grove.

She'd returned and pretended to mix in the celebration, before fleeing to her rooms. By midnight, she'd packed a bag and bribed a footman into finding transport back to Ryadstholm for her and her newly hired personal secretary, Fiona. Ryadstholm was the largest city near Summer Island. From there, Fiona had found them an outbound luxury cruiser and, by morning, they'd been on their way to anywhere warm.

Thinking she'd get over her temper tantrum sooner, her mother had talked her father into calling off the royal security service he'd sent out to haul her back. Instead, he'd sent a maid and bodyguard to complete her small entourage, and to provide security as she traveled from world to world.

The entire entourage was currently cooling their heels in Ryadstholm, while she traveled north in anonymity. To keep busy, they were seeing to her residence there, though it was a waste of effort. In a matter of days she'd abdicate, spend some quality time with her father and mother, maybe see her half-sisters, and then it was back off to the stars for her.

Nope. No controlling husband, babies, or government for her and no more Nordia. Let Coreen fulfill The Profetia.

As half consciousness slipped away into sweet blackness, she could swear she heard the sound of Thor's Hammer and a deep chuckle against the background of sweet voices singing with joy.

* * * *

Gunnar glanced over at Noreen and saw her head loll off to the side. Amazed she'd been able to sleep the last couple hours, he figured she really was an experienced traveler who could probably sleep standing up. Still, with her head rolling around, she looked uncomfortable. Thinking to make her more comfortable, he gently pushed her back against the safety harness. They were approaching the convoy so he tapped a few keys into his onboard computer. Reluctant to wake her just yet, he sent ahead the message to connect them up smoothly and quietly. The rapid reply from his convoy commander pleased him.

As he drove the small transport into view of the slow-moving line of larger transports, he once again considered his plan for accommodations.

He could move the both of them to a larger transport, more like a mobile dwelling, but decided not to. The smaller quarters gave her less room to avoid him. He may have sworn an oath to remain pure until he met The One, but there were many degrees of purity.

The only promise his grandfather had extracted from him was that he'd always use a barrier. If the flesh of his cock didn't directly touch the flesh of his partner, then he was holding himself true to The Profetia.

He'd been all of eighteen, and recently educated in the sport of enjoying a woman, when he'd arrived in Ryadstholm to take control of his duchy. At the ceremony he'd vowed to get no children on any woman until he had at least two children by The One. He was, in effect, to remain pure.

Later, talking with the king, he'd defined the boundaries of what was considered pure. A man with a wife, two concubines and several children, the king had been reassuringly sympathetic to his plight. The king had also loaned him several books and disks of visuals on the subject of how to enjoy a woman and avoid unexpected offspring. That summer had been the most informative and educational of his young life. Several maids in the royal household had been most willing to further his book learning with practical lessons. With no small appreciation for the irony, Gunnar figured he owed the king many years of loyalty for the particularly illuminating education.

His grandfather, the bishop, had merely rolled his eyes in resignation and explained it was the child that was the important point. Use a barrier and save his seed for The One.

A gentle bump indicated their connection to the line of larger freight transports. One in front and one behind. In the middle of the convoy, they were well protected should a storm blow up. The larger transports would push and pull the smaller one along and keep them from being lost in the white-out conditions common this time of year. They also had more power to draw on from the larger transports and he didn't have to be so stingy with the heat. Checking the settings for heat and communications, Gunnar eased out of his unzipped parka. It would be easier to prepare dinner without the bulk, and the heat from the small burner would warm the cabin nicely. Maybe then Noreen would take off at least the parka and mittens. He wanted a long look at what lay under her thin top.

Years of practice lent economy to his moves. With less effort than it had taken her to choose lunch, he pulled a pot from the small fridge and set it on the burner. Transport stew, the best he'd ever tasted. Rich gravy with large chunks of reindeer and plenty of wine. A few tubers and vegetables grown deep in thermal caves and they had a meal in a pot. But the real prize was the bread, baked fresh this morning. He pulled it from the food locker and set it on the small counter space. Too bad he didn't have a real radiant-heat oven to warm it in. What he sacrificed in conveniences, he hoped to make up for with female companionship.

Besides, he didn't think the show of wealth on the larger transport would impress her much. And, if it did, he didn't want to spend time with her. No, better to let her assume he was a simple transport operator. Titled, but humble in origins. Not uncommon on Nordia. People didn't have much use for nobility who put on false airs. Everyone worked on this planet. Their very survival in the harsh elements depended on it.

Truly, seduction hadn't been on his mind until he'd watched her shimmy out of her jeans and sweater. The wiggle of her ass had made him drool like he hadn't since that sensuous summer so long ago. Easy women had long since lost their appeal, and it had been many months since he'd sought one out to ease the frustration of not finding his destined mate. Neither his grandfather nor old King Bjorn had been of any help in guiding him to the right woman. Noble or common, he had no idea where to even look anymore.

For the next two nights, he wouldn't worry about it. Moving at this pace, it would be late the day after tomorrow before they arrived in Stravicsholm, where he'd deliver her to Princess Coreen. Whoever she was, she had to be of some level of importance, because the palace had never made such a request before. At least not for a live person. Goods, yes, but a living, breathing being was usually flown directly to the nearest depot.

Noreen. Was it a coincidence? Certainly there were enough females with similar names. The king's daughters, all nine of them, for starters. In addition, the daughters of nearly every common and noble family had at least one daughter with similar if not the same names. He'd even seen such variations as Foreen, Koreen, Goreen, Horeen, Roreen and Voreen. Multiple times over. Reen was the most common female nickname on the planet. She'd mentioned an aunt. Maybe her name came from there. She was about the same age as the king's eldest daughter, so it could be a coincidence. Would she like being called Nory, just to be different?

He stirred the stew and inhaled the heating aroma. Good and thick, it should warm her nicely. A quick twist of his wrist and he pulled the cork on a bottle of the best red wine he could find. Mugs would have to do. He set one in the cup holder near her chair and bent over her to look at her face framed by the hood. Asleep, she looked like an angel. It was a shame to wake her.

"Nory?" he spoke softly.

"Hmmm?" she moaned, luxurious eyelashes fluttering against her cheeks.

"Nory, time to wake up, *älskling*."

"Cory?" she murmured.

Cory? Who was Cory? Coreen?

"Nory, time to wake up. Dinner is ready."

"Doan wanna eat. G'way, Cory," she muttered and turned her head away.

He put a hand on her shoulder and shook her gently.

"*Dritt*, Cory, g'way. Just like you to wake me up when I haven't slept in days, *rot op, teef*."

Gunnar straightened and stared down at the woman now blinking her eyes in an attempt to wake up. Did she just tell the Crown Princess to drop dead… and call her a bitch?

"Noreen?" He tried again, this time using a deep authoritative voice. "Time to wake up."

"Blow it out your ear, Bjorn," she giggled. "Oops, I mean Fader, *Your Majesty*." She giggled some more and then her eyes popped open.

Gunnar felt his jaw drop as he watched her eyes widen in horror. If he understood correctly, she'd just cussed out the two top members of the royal family…as if they were…her family.

"Who are you?" he asked more harshly than intended.

"What is it to you?" She pushed her hood back irritably. "What's burning?"

"*Dritt!*" he cursed and stepped behind her seat. "Lean forward!" he told her. "You just pushed your hood into the stew."

"Wha?"

It took him a minute to clean up the mess and stir the stew again. Needing a moment, he turned the burner on low then sat down with his cup of wine. He nodded to hers in the holder and watched as she lifted it and inhaled before tasting.

"Very nice," she said quietly.

"Now, let's try this again. Exactly, for the record, who are you?" He pinned her with his hardest stare and she didn't look away.

"My name is Noreen Tibbetts."

"I might believe Noreen, but I don't buy Tibbetts. Try again. Where is your family from, and this time I want the name of a planet."

"Noreen Elke Josephina Angelica Tibbetts...Audelhuk." Her eyes widened even further as if she couldn't believe what she'd just said.

"Audelhuk? As in Bjorn Audelhuk, His Royal Majesty, the King of Nordia?" Gunnar narrowed his eyes further as he gazed into hers, now wide open in her pale face as her chin trembled.

Slowly she nodded as if fighting to keep from doing it. "What... are you doing to me?"

She tore her gaze from him to glance at the wine for just a bare moment before looking back at him as if compelled.

Well, she was. One of his more subtle talents, eyes that compelled people to not lie to him. Useful when it came to protecting the monarchy.

"There's nothing unusual in the wine," he spoke soothingly to cover his shock. "Are you the missing twin?"

Again she slowly nodded. "How did you know?"

"I've heard rumors for years. Especially the first summer I came to court. Ten years ago. I stumbled over many whispered conversations in the halls of the palace."

"I left that summer...ten years ago..." she spoke slowly.

"Why? Why is your name never spoken? Why are you coming back now? And in disguise?" He fired the questions at her and bit back more when she shook her head slowly.

"Release me," she ordered him, speaking slowly and deliberately.

She was fighting his talent! And winning! He sat back feeling stunned.

With a decided snap, she closed her eyes and drew in a deep breath.

"Don't you *ever* do that to me again," she growled.

"I'm responsible for security and intelligence about any possible threat to the royal family. If you don't give me some answers, I'll use whatever means necessary to get them."

Fascinated, Gunnar watched as without opening her eyes, she pursed her lips, set down the wine then pulled off her mittens and tucked them into her parka pockets. No one had ever shaken off his talent before. Yet, as he watched, she held her hands apart then brought the flattened palms together in a clap before her face. The sound he heard wasn't the slap of flesh he expected. The sound rocked the small transport and sounded like... a steel hammer of immense size landing on an anvil of equally immense size. Just like the sound he'd heard this morning, only louder. Much louder.

He clapped his hands over his ears, his eyes squeezing closed as if they could shut out the ringing sound that shook his very bones.

A full minute later he lowered his hands from his ears and stared at the woman in front of him.

"What the Hell was that?" he demanded as his communications center lit up with lights and beeps.

Noreen's face relaxed into a smile as she reached for her wine. She smiled more as she sipped and looked mighty pleased with herself.

"You didn't recognize it?" she asked sweetly.

"Thor's Hammer, woman!" he snarled out the common curse and turned to the console.

"Exactly," she replied calmly.

His hand holding the communications handset froze half way to his mouth. It couldn't be... the loud squawk of his communicator made him shake his head.

"Duke Nordenskiold?" He heard the voice of Wilton Leebrick, his convoy commander, come from the small speaker. "You okay, Zaren?"

"Yeah, Wil, yeah, we're fine. Did we upset the connection?" He ran a hand through his hair. It was long and needed cutting. Right after he figured out why this woman could call on Thor's Hammer with her little hands. Only Bjorn, the King, and Coreen...no, the Crown...Princess...

The communicator squawked, jolting him again as Wil's voice came over the speaker. "No, the connections are fine. That was some kinda rocking going on. Sounded like you got hit with a bolt of lightning but no one saw any."

"Must have been a stray bolt. Freak storm. Keep an eye on the weather monitors," Gunnar snapped into the mic then disconnected and turned back to the woman with impossibly red hair and brown eyes. "I'm going to ask again, just who the Hell are you?"

"I told you, I'm Noreen Tibbetts."

"No," he shook his head. "How do you fit into the royal family?"

"Oh, that. I'm the soon-to-be ex-Crown Princess."

Chapter 4

It was rather funny, actually, watching Gunnar's face as he digested the information. First his amazingly deep blue eyes sparked with a flash of silver glitter, so eerily similar to the old bishop's, she shivered. Then his pale skin warmed to a mottled red before fading again. If he clenched his jaw any tighter he'd probably break some teeth. It only took a minute for him to draw in a deep breath and regain control. It usually took her father much longer. Just one detail she'd noticed about him the times they'd communicated by vid-com over the last few years. Once, she'd timed Fader at three minutes.

She sipped the rather excellent wine but, if he was a duke, as the man over the communicator had confirmed, then it was only to be expected. A nice touch. Had he been planning on seducing her? Now there was something to laugh about. Instead she smiled as sweetly as possible and took another sip of wine.

"Did you say we're having stew for dinner? It smells delicious," she cooed, and smirked when his jaw clenched again.

"Yes, Your Highness. Let me get you a bowl. Would you like bread with that?"

"Why thank you, Duke Zaren, that would be lovely."

His movements were stiff as he held out the bowl and spoon to her. "It might be easier to eat if you shrug off the parka," he suggested. "Your Highness."

She paused for a moment, testing the warmth of the air with her nose. It did feel warmer. She nodded and unzipped the coat before sliding her arms from the sleeves. Leaving it behind her was enough to keep her cozy and allow her movement as she took the bowl from him.

"Thank you, kind sir." See? She still remembered her manners.

Apparently he did as well and executed a short, sharp bow in response. It only took a moment for him to hand her a hunk of soft fresh bread before he returned to his seat with his own dinner.

Hungry, she didn't feel a need to fill the silence with inane chatter. With her eyes closed she savored a bite of the bread dipped in the gravy. One more little thing she'd missed without realizing it. Ryadstholm bakers were the best, next to the palace kitchen staff. Must have been baked this morning.

"Reindeer?" she asked. "Northern herd?"

He nodded in response, his mouth full.

"Delicious." She returned to her meal stopping only to drink the wine. He refilled her mug without prompting and she gave him her sweetest smile in thanks. It was damn awkward, now he knew who she was. A real conversation killer. Not that they'd had any good conversation yet. Now he'd be even more close-mouthed. A pity. Then again, maybe she'd get some more sleep. Maybe now her cover was blown she could call for a real transport to get home sooner.

His rough voice and sharply asked question broke into her thoughts. "Why?"

"Why what?"

"Why did you leave? Why is your name never spoken? Why is it no one knows about you?"

She gazed at his eyes cautiously. No silver glitter now. Ah, the silver indicated his power to squeeze information? Good to know. Now he only looked curious, possibly even a little hurt. Because he wasn't privy to the state secret?

"Well." She set down her empty bowl and picked up the wine. "I suppose it started out innocently enough. I'm the elder by just a few minutes, but Coreen should have been born first. She loves this place and she's a born politician. Fader's true daughter. Me, I'm just an accident of birth and birth order." She looked away from his frown.

"But why? Why did they let people believe you didn't exist at all?"

"I actually prefer it that way. And with all those silly names running around—can you imagine ten Oreens?—it was just easier for me to hide away. Also, Fader kept muttering something about the perfect security setup."

Gunnar nodded. "I can see that," he admitted grudgingly. "Does that explain why there's only one of you in the family portraits?"

She nodded. "And why one of us was always kept in the nursery. They swapped us out, but Coreen did better in public than I did."

Gunnar gave her an odd grin. Good thing he didn't keep her wondering about it for long.

"I saw a news piece on the vid-com. I must have been about six and I remember seeing your father pick you up during a parade. You were in tears. It was you, not your sister, right?"

She felt the flush burn across her cheeks. "Oh my, I was four at the time and it was so very noisy. I was terrified."

"But instead of handing you off to a nanny or a bodyguard, your father picked you up and held you."

Noreen smiled. "Yes, he did. I remember it very well. He promised me I'd never have to attend another noisy parade if I quit crying. He made me feel so safe."

"I remember. He held you close and then you turned around, arms around his neck, legs around his waist and rested your head against his. The camera zoomed in on your smile as you tried to look so brave."

She ducked her head. While embarrassing to say the least, it was one of many times she remembered her father protecting and comforting her and only her. There was a tiny catch in her breath as her heart swelled for a moment, only to crash a moment later heavy with guilt. "He's a good father," she said quietly.

"He's a good monarch."

She nodded in agreement. All the more reason for her to abdicate. Only Cory could take his place. When Gunnar didn't speak she looked up and was surprised to see anger in his face.

"What?" she asked.

"Why did you leave?"

"Why does that make you angry," she countered.

"Because…it has to be…you…you're…The One."

Damn, he put that together fast. Then again, the Thor's Hammer thing had just, well, *hammered* that little fact into place. A flash of ice raced through her veins and she felt a moment of fear as she gulped. His eyes flashed angrily and hands clenched around the empty bowl he still held.

"It hasn't been proven. Just a silly legend." She tried to laugh off her discomfort.

Gunnar set down his bowl with careful deliberation. "No. It isn't a silly legend. My grandfather told me…" his voice faded out.

"Your grandfather told you what?" She leaned back in her seat as his burning eyes rose to hers. She could only stare back as he took the mug of wine from her numb fingers and set it aside. He didn't need to use the silver glitter to compel her to rise from her seat, leaving the parka to fall from her shoulders.

She only felt the cool air for a moment before he pulled her into his arms and lowered his mouth to hers. Too shocked to protest, she gripped his shoulders as he bent her backward ever so gently, his lips warm against hers. Soft. And the perfect fullness. His long fingered hand slid up her back and into her hair at the base of her thick braid coiled at her nape. Moving with far more experience than she expected, he yanked out the pins holding her hair in place. Pulling the final pin, his lips took advantage of her distraction and opened her mouth.

A tiny squeak of surprise escaped her throat and she dug her fingernails into his biceps when he pulled her closer, his tongue plundering her mouth. *How dare he?* It was the last thought she had as his hand stroked her back, something tugging on the end of her braid. Hungry for more, she leaned into him, slid her arms around his neck and pulled him closer yet.

Breathing hard by the time he broke the kiss, she abstractly felt his fingers weave through her hair, smoothing the waist length tresses as if he'd never touched hair before. His lips on her cheek, then jaw, then earlobe were doing amazing things to her blood. The small cabin, which had been so cold before, now felt as if it were the very center of a blazing furnace.

Hands smoothly unclasped the shoulder straps of her overalls and they slid down her silk encased body.

"Nory," he murmured against her throat.

It was on her lips to answer with a yes when the com-link squawked again.

"Duke Nordenskiold?" The disembodied voice cut through the haze of desire.

Gunnar pulled her close and rested his chin on her head for a moment.

"Your Grace, come in?" The voice enquired again.

"Remind me to smash this thing," he muttered to her, then grabbed the handset.

"This better be good," he growled at the poor person on the other end.

"Sorry, sir, but there's a communication coming through from the palace, sir. The king himself."

Noreen felt her heart flop over at the words and rested her head against Gunnar's chest. She smiled weakly when he kissed the top of her head.

"Put it through." There were a few clicks then he spoke again, "Zaren here."

"Gunnar, my boy? Is that you?"

Noreen followed Gunnar's urging when he sank down onto his seat and tugged her along. She stopped just long enough to pull her overalls up again then sat on his lap.

"Yes, sir, it's me. What can I do for you, sir?"

"I understand you picked up an important package today. Is the package in good condition?"

Noreen grabbed the handset and answered for herself. "So much for the surprise," she snorted. "Package indeed."

"Princess." The relief was clear in his voice.

"Hiya, King," she joked back.

"You're home. Your moder will be so pleased."

Noreen glanced at Gunnar and rolled her eyes. She was only surprised she didn't get the royal *We*.

"I see you arranged the nice weather to really make me feel as if I never left," she commented, glancing out the window. The large transport in front blocked the view but they could still see to either side and it didn't look good. The wind had picked up and snow was blowing horizontally. Fast. She shivered as if each burning snowflake pelted her, each howl of the wind like the screeching of a poorly tuned Ooorodian harp.

"Only for you, *älskling*," he chuckled.

"How did you find out?"

"There are certain people who can't keep a state secret to save their lives, which is why we usually don't include them on the need-to-know list."

"You caught Moder getting my rooms ready, didn't you?"

"Yep!" he chortled, then coughed. "Among other little clues."

"What was that?" she asked him sharply.

"Just a little cough, nothing to worry about, Princess."

She glanced at Gunnar who gave her a little shrug. "I understand this little trip will take three days, so you'll see the brown of my eyes day after tomorrow."

"Brown?"

"I changed my eye color."

"Lenses, right? They'd better be temporary. What else did you do?"

"I'm not going to spoil the surprise. You won't recognize me. Nobody else did."

"Don't be too sure about that," her father warned.

"Yeah, yeah, you've had me followed since the day I left. I know all about your spies. I bribed them to keep quiet."

"I pay them better," he laughed. "Just tell Zaren to be careful, there's a storm blowing in and you all might want to circle up the convoy and let it blow over. Too bad you aren't thirty klicks further along, there's a spot where you could pull over and keep toasty warm."

"Speaking of the good duke, what is your opinion of the man? Is he to be trusted?"

"I trust him with my most precious treasure."

Noreen felt a rush of warmth as Gunnar squeezed her waist. "You let Cory date him?"

"Funny. Let's just say I trust him far more than I trust someone calling himself the Lidarian Minister of Agriculture who's been banging on the Ryadstholm office doors since early this morning wanting to know where you are. Prince Somebody or other."

"Hollis Traxelgard is here?" She swallowed the squeak that snuck out and ignored Gunnar's sharp glance.

"Do you know him?"

"Yes, but I didn't expect to see him again so soon. I mean, we have a date, but not for eight weeks. And then I'm supposed to be back on Lidaria. I had no idea he'd ever follow me here."

"Well it seems he's under the impression you wanted to see him much sooner. He's all but threatened an invasion to find you."

"Oh. Well, I'm sorry about that. I don't know what lit a fire under his tail." Actually, she did, but she wasn't about to tell her father, or Gunnar, about *that*. She hadn't known until too late that certain...acts...were the equivalent of a marriage ceremony on Lidaria. "I thought he understood," she sighed. Men. Always hearing only what they wanted to hear.

"Apparently he didn't. Does he know your bodyguard on sight?"

"Yes."

"I'll have Hans convince him you're safe and sound."

That sounded ominous. "If it doesn't work I'll talk to him by vid-com when I reach home."

"*Älskling...*" Her father drew in a deep breath. "I have to ask but, did you, call upon... you know, a little while ago?"

"Um, you mean the clap thingy?"

"That's the one."

"Yeah, dukey here was trying to compel me into revealing state secrets."

"Ah, then that explains things."

"What things?" She'd never heard of a side effect of using the clap. In fact, she'd never used it before.

"Well, the storm for starters. There's also been a little excitement in the palace."

Noreen frowned. "What kind of excitement?"

"I'll tell you when you get home. Call when the storm blows over. Oh, and Princess, you remember The Profetia, right?"

She heaved a heavy sigh. "Yes. How could I ever forget? What about it?"

"Let's just say your destiny is at hand. Trust your heart to keep you warm."

"More riddles." She snorted in disgust. "Yes, Pappa."

"Oh, Gunnar? Make the most of the storm," her father chuckled. "Check in when you can to let us know you're okay. We have your current position noted."

"Fader? What do you mean?" she asked using her most imperial voice. The one most often used for over-eager cabana boys who thought she was an easy target. And over-zealous Princes of Lidaria.

"It's time to fulfill your part of *The Profetia*, sweetling."

"*Pappa*? It sounded suspiciously like you just *gave* me away."

"Not me, Princess." Her father laughed while her veins frosted over. "Odin. Your union has been heaven-blessed from the beginning. The gods are tired of waiting for the next heir. And, frankly, so am I. As are a few other people. We'll have a formal ceremony in a few weeks, but for all intents and purposes, I now pronounce you married."

"To whom?" She had to try one last time even though she knew the answer.

"Why Gunnar there, of course! Which adds another Duchess title to your name, but, for all legal purposes, that now makes him Prince Consort Audelhuk. We'll deal with the particulars and official paperwork later."

"Fader," she growled in the tone that usually made him back down. The shock invading her system was all the more unsettling because of his next words.

"Gunnar, don't hold it against her. It isn't her fault. Please keep that in mind. I know you know what you have to do, but temper your actions with the knowledge that I created this problem. She's only living up to how she was raised. She doesn't know anything else."

Before she could ask what he was talking about Gunnar took the handset from her and replied, "Yes, sir. I need to check in with my convoy so we're ready when the storm really hits. It's building up a good blow as we speak."

"Make the gods happy, you two." With a final crackle of static, the king was gone.

"Sweetheart, *älskling*," Gunnar murmured, his lips on her throat again. "Would you, please, put the stew pot in the fridge and then get ready for bed? It's the safest spot to ride out a blow."

"Excuse me?" Heart pounding in her throat, she tried to lean away from him but he just held her closer.

"We need to prepare for the storm. Once the hatches are battened down, we'll talk. Okay?"

She nodded numbly. It wasn't the chore she objected to, but rather the ever-so-very-clear implication he was about to bed her.

He gave her a brief kiss and a squeeze, then turned to the com-link.

Chapter 5

Noreen listened with half an ear as she gathered up their bowls with icy fingers. Gunnar spoke rapidly, repeating instructions his people probably knew by heart. She found a tiny sink, just big enough for the two bowls, by lifting the counter to the side of the burner. There was still half a pot of stew, which she slid into the fridge, taking up the only empty spot. It looked as if they had a few eggs, some milk and butter. The fresh items would stretch out the dried rations, of which she'd seen plenty in the cabinet. She decided to leave their mugs out, then looked at the shower stall. There was no privacy for using the privy other than the half high wall. Was this a time for modesty? Could she slide the panel shut?

The transport came to a stop, something made it jolt, and then it moved forward again, this time going up an incline. She turned to see what was happening.

Gunnar spoke to her over his shoulder. "We're moving into the empty trailer. Our weight will help keep it steady and it will give us more shelter." He turned his attention back to driving the smaller transport into the space men in bright orange parkas indicated.

She just nodded.

"Nory?" His concerned tone made her look down at him as he pulled to a stop and turned off the main engine. The rear trailer door clanged behind them, immediately muffling the sounds of the storm and, from the corner of her eyes, she noted people running to connect cables to the transport now nestled in the cargo bay.

"There's a larger, more luxurious transport a few trailers up. We still have time to get there if you want to make a run..." his voice trailed off as she shook her head. "You want to stay here?"

"Yes. I'll be fine. Go ahead. There's plenty here to keep me just fine." She'd sleep in a camel stall before she stepped into a blowing storm like the one raging outside.

"No, that's not the point. If I go, you go. If you stay, I stay." He turned and stood.

"Oh," she said, staring at him.

"What's wrong?" He took her hands in his warm ones.

"Nothing." Well, other than a little privacy. Her father's final words. And really cold wind. Really strong, cold wind. She squeezed her eyes closed briefly as a gust shook the transport.

"Really, Duke Nordenskiold, I'll be fine here. You have your crew to take care of. I'm sure they need your leadership during this storm." She pulled away from him and bent to look out the window. It appeared there were thick cables holding their little vehicle to the floor of the transport. And now the crew members were plugging in what looked like power cables.

She felt Gunnar's hands on her waist before he put his arms around her and pulled her to a standing position.

"Nory, we'll be fine here. A little close quarters, but warm and safe. We have plenty of power for heat and lights. We also have plenty of food, and water for washing. What we don't have are luxury accommodations."

"I've lived in worse places." She lifted shoulder. He hadn't spent three weeks on a tramp cruiser. "At least this is designed for humanoid use." She supposed her nearly suppressed shudder spoke for itself.

"I'm guessing you have some stories to tell."

She felt laughter bubble up inside as he turned her around in his arms. "Stories? I could keep you up for three days or more with all the stories I have to tell."

"I'd rather you keep me up for three days another way, with stories in between," he said, his voice shooting a spark of thrill through her body. "The One…" He sounded dazed as he lifted a lock of her hair and rubbed it between his fingers. "At last."

"Um, Gunnar." She swallowed hard, her eyes on his as he moved closer.

"Yes, Nory?"

"We really need to talk."

"About?"

His hands reached the overall clasps she'd reattached.

"Gods, fathers, and prophesying old priests aside, I feel funny about this." Her eyes searched his deep blue ones. Only a hint of silver flecks remained. Low lights glowing from near the ceiling made the color deeper, and cast an intimate glow in the small space.

"About what?"

"This… thing… everyone says is between us."

"You mean the destiny thing?"

Her breath caught as the clasps were undone again. It didn't take anything for the insulated pants to slide down her legs. The material was stiff enough they didn't pool in a sexy manner at her feet. So unlike a soft, thin sarong. Before she could think, Gunnar's lips brushed hers, his hands warm and firm on her back.

"It's okay, Nory. It's meant to be. You and me. I have it on good authority."

"Gunnar—" her weak protest was cut off when he pulled her body tight against his, their tongues meeting in that oh-so-sexy dance. This time it was slow and heat-building as his tongue leisurely explored the inside of her mouth, stroking and tasting every surface. With a groan she sucked his tongue in and gently pulsed her mouth around it.

His response was all she could have hoped for as he crushed her to him. She felt him, hard against the soft swell of her stomach. It reminded her of other pressing needs and she pulled away, breaking the kiss.

"Gunnar," she tried again only to catch her breath at the feel of his lips on her earlobe. "I need a minute," she gasped.

"For?"

"Can I just have a minute? Please?"

"What's wrong?"

She avoided his eyes when he stepped back to look at her.

"Why don't you go check the tires or something?" she suggested

"We don't have tires on this thing."

"Gunnar! Please. Just give me a few minutes, okay?"

Understanding dawned in his eyes. "We're not going to be able to avoid this the next few days." The man had the nerve to laugh at her.

"Don't make me pull rank on you," she growled.

An odd light entered his eye. "Noreen, this can't be avoided without great discomfort. Take care of business while I cover the windows. And don't lower the bed until I go."

He pulled her close and kissed her nose. There was no getting around it. With as much dignity as she could muster, she pulled off her boots and overalls, then braved the half stall. At least the floor seemed warm. Probably from the engines. Thankfully he waited until he heard the flush before turning back.

"We're alone now," he told her. "The crew is lining up the transports and we're going to get a few more klicks behind us. Might even reach the nearest thermal pools."

"Great." She busied herself by folding up her parka and overalls, trying not to listen as he washed up. How did she get here?

"Would you like a shower first?"

"Um, no, that's okay. I washed up already." It wasn't a proper bidet, but a wet cloth worked just fine in a pinch.

In a matter of a few minutes the panel was pulled down and the feather bed fluffed. Gunnar's attention to the corners puzzled her for just a moment before she was distracted by the cold.

"Come on, you're shivering." Gunnar pulled her over and held up the covers for her.

The bed was soft, she'd give him points for luxury linens, but even with extra fine Kookorian cotton flannel sheets and a thickly woven alpaca and silk blanket, it was damn cold. Hadn't he ever heard of bed warmers? She rolled to her left side, facing the back wall trying to give him room in the narrow bed. Comfortable for two, sure, if the two were very thin and very small. Like children. He was probably one of those sprawler types who took up the entire bed with his wide shoulders. She heard the rustle of clothing before she felt him climb in the bed and wrap himself around her back. She pulled the covers up around her ears.

"You're cold?"

"This ain't Sandy Topiary," she quipped.

"Where's that?"

"It's about three hundred light years from here. And a thousand degrees warmer." A slight exaggeration, but damn it was cold! Why had she come during the winter?

"You know what's wrong here, don't you?"

"I took off my parka," she said through chattering teeth.

His chuckle was low and warm in her ear. "You didn't take off your silk undies."

He slipped his hand under her top and before she could protest, the warmth of his hand began to seep into her back.

"Silk is warm," she retorted.

"Flesh is warmer." Lips teasing the skin behind her ear demonstrated the flesh on flesh theory. "Smart of you not to wear a bra."

She shivered more, but guessed it wasn't entirely from cold. "The undies aren't coming off, so get any wild ideas out of your head right now."

"What ideas?"

Noreen swallowed heavily as a shudder wracked her frame. This was insane! Her father had *given* her to this man and practically ordered them to bed. If that wasn't a mood killer she didn't know what was. Besides, it was damn cold in here still.

"I thought you were going to turn up the heat a little." Did that sound like whining?

"I did. It's practically roasting in here."

"N...n...no...it...isn't." Her teeth chattered more forcefully. Her nose and ears were cold and now her unbound hair was caught under him. Should have cut it like she wanted to. Fiona had talked her out of it. Nosy, bossy servants. "W-why...d-did...you...undo...m-my...hair?"

"Because, it's very sexy and I wanted to feel it and see it loose. Now I want to see it hanging down, creating a curtain enclosing just the two of us."

His hand slid from her back around to her abdomen. She could feel the warm skin of his stomach against her back where he'd left her shirt pulled up. Shaking too hard, she couldn't reach around to pull it down. Warmth followed the hand slowly moving across her body.

"First chance I get, I'm cutting it. It's too hard to take care of if you're going to unbraid it on me."

"No."

Where did he get off telling her how to style her hair? His audacity rendered her speechless.

"Why did you dye your hair?" he asked.

"Don't like white." There, her voice was coming back as her space in the bed began to warm. "Too cold."

"This red is awful."

"It makes me feel warmer. I like red."

"Well I like your red undies. Wish they were a little more brief though," his chuckle was warm in her ear and a shiver ran down her body. "Still cold?"

"A little."

"And the brown lenses for your eyes? More disguise?"

"Yep."

"So what was this about you soon being the ex-Crown Princess?"

His body was a far more subtle seductive force than his eyes. Dangerously close to cupping her breast, his hand spanned the plane of her stomach, his fingers touching the beginning swell of flesh. In an attempt to preserve what remained of her modesty, she placed her hand over his to hold it from moving more.

"I came home to abdicate in favor of Coreen so she can marry you and do the royal princess stuff she was born to do."

That apparently struck a nerve.

Gunnar's hand stopped moving. He stopped moving. Not even a breath. It was as if the man froze.

A second later Noreen was on her back staring up into blue eyes flashing with angry silver sparks.

"What?" he demanded.

"I'm a horrible princess," the words tumbled from her in a rush. "Cory's the one interested in politics and ruling. She'll be the better queen. That's why we can't make love. You're meant for the Crown Princess and I'm abdicating. Since you're going to be my brother-in-law, I'm not going to have sex with you now. Or ever. That's why you should have gone to the other transport while you had the chance." Ooh, he didn't look happy.

"I have enough trouble with the gods messing with my destiny. I don't need you doing it any more than you already have," he growled at her.

"What are you talking about? I'm freeing you. It's obvious you're in love with Cory. You don't even know me." She tried to wiggle out from under him but he just pressed his body more firmly against hers. How'd he get between her legs? Why did he have to come to bed naked?

"Y-you..." he stuttered, as if he were choking on the words. "You spoiled little brat! You ran away ten years ago and put me through hell waiting for you to show up. You dumped your responsibilities on your sister and left your entire family to cover for you. I've never heard of a more selfish act. That's what your father was talking about."

Noreen put her hands on his chest and tried to push him off her. "How dare you!" When that didn't make him move she thought about trying the clap again. "I was just getting out of Cory's way!"

Gunnar's eyes sparked even more and he grabbed her hands, pinning them to the bed on either side of her head. "Oh, no, you don't. Not again. You won't call down Thor's Hammer on me again. Ever."

Angry, she bucked her hips trying to dislodge him. Damn, he was heavier than her. She wasn't tiny, but he had nearly double the raw muscle mass she had.

"Oh, yes, there you go, *älskling*," he crooned. "A woman with spirit, that's what I like."

"Of all the insufferable... You arrogant... Egotistical... Maniacal... goat! I thought you were pure!"

"My flesh has never touched another woman's flesh. At least not like this."

Noreen gasped when he thrust against her. He felt... huge.

"No!" she shouted. "Not like this. You can't!"

Panic clawed at her heart and she felt the start of burning tears sting the back of her eyes. She'd never been forced before, each lover treating her like a precious jewel, never taking more than she allowed. Always the one in control, she'd never had so much as a bruise unlike the ones most likely forming on her wrists right now. Fear made her gasp and fight against him.

"I can... but I won't." He was unmovable as he stared down at her. "I won't rape you, even though I'd probably have not only your father's blessing for doing it, but Odin's as well. You're right. I'm arrogant enough that I want you willing and begging for me."

Her mouth dropped open to let loose another barrage of insults, but his mouth stopped her. Pinned beneath him, with his hands easily holding her wrists, she was no match for him when he kissed her. Before she could even think, he sucked her tongue into his mouth and used his to stroke it. A mad, sensuous clash erupted as she fought to push him away and he used subtle strength to hold her in place. The ease with which he restrained her was frustrating. And his kiss... *Moder Freya*... she'd never experienced anything like it.

All thoughts of cold flew right out of her head. Heat, delicious and consuming, flashed though her, starting where his cock pressed against her and seared her to her fingertips and toes. Burning, she surrendered to the kiss and melted into the feather bed. His grip on her wrists loosened, but he didn't release her even as his kiss gentled. Now straining to get closer, she writhed beneath him, her hardened nipples pressing against his hard chest through the silk.

Intent on the kiss and the feel of his body against hers, she didn't pay attention when he slid her hands to the corners of the bed, spreading them wide. All she wanted was his hands on her body, his lips covering her skin. Cold clicks took her by surprise. Something both soft and hard replaced his hands around her wrists. With a squeal of protest she tried to pull her hands away and found them trapped, the rattle of metal grating to her ears.

Lips on her earlobe stole the heat of her protest.

"Gunnar," she moaned as a wave of fire rolled down her body, directly through her nipples to deep in her center. "What did you do?"

"Just playing," he murmured, his tongue hot against the skin of her neck just above the high neck of her shirt.

She pulled against the restraints as he kissed a spot right behind her ear. Oh, she'd never felt *that* before and turned her head to let him reach it better. Funny, instead of feeling cold, now she felt hot. She'd never felt this hot on this planet.

"Don't fight it, baby," he told her.

As long as he kept his lips on her body she wouldn't argue.

"Why?"

"I've heard it's fun this way."

"But…"

"Shhh. I won't hurt you. I promise."

He kissed her again and her head spun. The man was a genius. Where did he learn…?

Whimpering, she twisted away from the kiss. "I thought you were pure?" she gasped.

He pushed up on his elbows and looked down at her with a tiny smile. "I am. I've never made love to a woman without a barrier. Not even when she used her mouth."

"What?" Stunned at his revelation, she couldn't complete the thought. "I…I…I thought…"

"I was a virgin?" He smiled down at her as he stroked her cheek. "Oh sweetheart, ten years is a very long time to wait for your true love to show up. I've never spilled my seed in or on another woman. I saved that all for you. But that didn't mean I didn't do some studying. The way I see it, this is my final exam, sort of like the test to get my transporter's license. Everything up until now has been training for this moment. If you aren't both satisfied and pregnant by the time we pull into Stravicsholm, we'll just run off to your apartment and lock ourselves in until I get it right."

Chapter 6

Gunnar watched, holding back his laughter as her mouth gaped open and closed like a goldfish. No sound came out initially as she worked her mouth. Eventually she worked up to indignant splutters.

"You— I— Outrageous... Intolerable— How dare you!" She finally got the words out as a shout. "Release me!" she ordered in a truly imperious tone. Too bad she'd forgotten one little thing.

"I dare?" He regarded her with his best arched brow. "You've kept us apart for the last ten years. We should have at least five children by now. There is so much lost time to make up for, my princess. And we start tonight. Here. Now." He leaned over her and punctuated each declaration with a kiss. *Moder Freya*, but she tasted good.

And felt good too. Her breasts were every bit as full as he'd glimpsed this morning and her nipples poked against the thin silk covering her. Resting on his elbows over her, he couldn't see her whole body like he wanted to. The question, now, was: did he remove her clothing the civilized way, or the more fun way?

"Do you have more of these long underwear items in your luggage?"

"Why?" she snapped her question back at him.

"That's not the response I'm looking for. Yes, or no?"

"Yes," she muttered.

"Good answer. Definitely the preferred one."

Alarm made her eyes sparkle, even through the ridiculous lenses. "Why?" she asked again.

"Because," he pushed back until he knelt between her legs, "I'm still trying to decide how to get these off of you."

He trailed his fingers down her body, brushing over her breasts, watching her nipples grow even harder. Her stomach quivered as he smoothed his hand over it.

"Ticklish?"

"A little."

No, she couldn't very well deny it.

He reached for the waistband of her leggings. She folded her legs up and pressed her feet against his chest. A moment before she put power into her legs to push him away, he grabbed her ankles and spread her legs apart.

"Still feisty, eh?" He chuckled in the face of her groan.

"I told you, I won't make love to you," she protested through clenched teeth.

"Oh, but you will, and you'll beg me for it," he promised her.

"Gunnar, this doesn't make sense! I'll make a lousy queen. I can't do this," she wailed.

"You can, and you will. The gods don't choose the unable."

A strong gust of wind hit the side of the van their transport was cocooned in.

"See? Odin agrees with me," he told her. "Well, I guess we'll have to do this the hard way."

Brown-tinted eyes flew open wide as he reached behind him. Before she could squeal, a lined cuff encased one ankle. It wasn't much of a struggle before he had her other ankle bound, the ankle cuffs just like the ones holding her wrists. She was securely spread on the bed before him like a five-point star.

Spluttering protests began to come from her again and he leaned over to kiss her deeply. Damn but she tasted, and kissed, wonderful. He felt each kiss right down to his throbbing shaft. Rubbing against the silk covering her sweet body only made him ache more. Maybe he would take her fast this first time. But first, he needed to know…

She wiggled against him when he touched her. Wet, she'd soaked the silk between her legs with her sweet-scented potion. The bucking of her hips became more pronounced as he lingered, stroking her, feeling every contour though the thin fabric. Without much effort he found the point where the seams came together. He was able to work a finger through, breaking the threads holding the pieces together.

Tongue sparring with tongue, he worked his finger through the seam, ripping the material when the thread held tight. Frustrated at the slow progress, he pushed back up to his knees, grabbed the edges and pulled. Her squeal of dismay nearly drowned out the sound of the ripping fabric.

Unable to keep from looking he had to know... ah, she was nearly as dark there as the rest of her body.

"Sun in the nude often?" he asked.

"Every chance I get."

Smooth. He reached out a tentative finger to touch her hairless folds. "Is this natural?"

"Waxed. Yesterday." She gasped as his fingers danced over her soft skin.

"I've heard of the technique. I think I like it." He bent and kissed where his fingers touched, his tongue lightly teasing and tasting. "Mmmm, I think I like it very much." Moaning and writhing indicated she agreed with him.

Still the big question... "Dare I ask? Are you...?"

"My maidenhead is intact," she whimpered as his finger slid into her. "Go gently. Only my physician has ever touched me there."

Heeding her plea, he worked his finger in slowly. "Tight. You are so very tight... ah, there it is. So you are a maiden still." *But how innocent?*

Fascinated by her smooth skin, he stroked her, watching the moisture seep from her. He used one finger to fondle her sacred passage, a thumb on the tiny bud of flesh nestled coyly at the apex of her thighs.

"So slick and wet, my love."

Her moan made him smile. Easing his thumb off her clit, he watched as she tried to follow, thrusting her hips toward him.

"Ah, so she knows what she likes. What else does she like?"

"What do you mean?"

"I know the boundaries of my purity, but what of yours? How has your body been used by others, my princess? Has the Lidarian lusting after you tasted your sweetness?"

"I... I don't know what you mean. I don't like your implication."

"There are other ways to fuck, Princess."

"I didn't give you leave to use crude language with me!"

He couldn't help the laugh. "Nory, my pet, you've completely missed the point here. You may be a princess to the people, The Crown Princess, but to me, you are my wife. My mate. That makes me your husband. Your Master."

He watched her eyes fly open wide. "Yes, that's right, Noreen. The Nordian marriage ceremony still requires you to swear obedience to me. Man and wife. In our household, I own you. Body and soul, my love."

The shaking of her body as the words sunk in was nearly laughable until he remembered the king's words. She didn't know any better and was merely responding to how she'd been raised. Since she was her father's precious treasure, everyone had catered to her from the moment she'd been conceived. Even during her travels, she'd had others to look out for her and do her bidding. She'd probably never seen the seedier side of the planets she traveled to. This woman was an unbroken thoroughbred mare who needed the benevolent hand of a Master to tame her. The books the king had given him those many years ago came back to him. Lessons he'd learned and practiced with the palace maids. How would she feel about the small stable of slaves he kept at the country estate? Each one a curvaceous morsel devoted to his pleasure. Did it matter?

"Mate, that means equal in the marriage," she spat back at him. "I'm no man's toy."

His grin made her shrink into the soft pillows under her, despite the fire of defiance in her eyes. The growl from low in her throat as she pulled against the fur-lined leather cuffs holding her was damn cute.

Grasping the fabric of her bottoms, he tugged on the two halves and separated the center seam completely from front to back, fully exposing her dazzling treasure, only the stretchy waistband holding the garment together around her middle.

"Very beautiful pussy, my wife. But I have to wonder how many other men have seen it? Touched it? How discriminating have you been? Obviously you saved your *fitte* for me, and I do thank you for that, but how about your *rompe*? Or your mouth?"

Struggling against her restraints caused her breasts to jiggle enticingly beneath her silk top. Ah yes, her very beautifully shaped breasts. He wanted to see those in the flesh. Were they brown too? So easy to push her top up and over those luscious mounds.

"Ah, so you do sun in the nude. I'm not sure I like this dark brown skin. We'll see over time, won't we?"

"Argh!" Her indignation could find no words and he smiled as he bent down to kiss first one tight nipple and then the other.

"Very nice. No artificial body shaping, just cosmetic surface changes. Good choice." He drew one nipple into his mouth, his hand grasping the other breast and massaging.

His stomach resting against the sweet damp cleft between her legs, he took his time suckling and laving attention to her very sensitive nipples. Dusky pink, it was hard to tell by color the defining line between her soft skin and the puckered sweetness of her nipple. In the low light, he took his time looking at her from all angles. The symmetry of her was perfect. Each curve, swell and line of her body was as if it'd been drawn by a master artist.

Good idea. He'd commission a painting of her at the first opportunity. A nude for their bedroom. Possibly one for his office. No doubt an official portrait would be commissioned for their wedding as demanded by tradition.

"What are you thinking?" she asked him.

He used his tongue to draw a wet line up her body, stopping only to circle her breasts one by one before traveling up her long slender throat to her mouth. Her breath came in pants by the time he claimed her mouth, his aching cock nestled against the liquid heat weeping from her.

One hand twined in her hair, the other traveled down her body stroking, touching, pinching and tweaking as he moved downward, each inch bringing him closer to his desire. Better to get to it and claim her. There was plenty of time for talking and training after. They had a marriage to consummate at the moment.

His hand skimmed the smooth skin of her flat stomach. Not hard, just softly, beautifully feminine. Used to seeking soft curls, his fingers were surprised to slide so easily into her slick heat, brushing over her hard little clitty. She liked that. Stopping to tease and learn the feel of her, he envisioned a small ring through the hood and felt his body surge in reaction. Yes, a small, private sign of his ownership of her body. When they reached home, he'd see to it immediately. An easy way to subtly remind her of her vow to him. He'd take care of it the night of their state wedding.

Moaning against his mouth, her whimpers indicated her rising desire. She was hot. Nearly hot enough to take with the least amount of discomfort to her. Renewing the ardor of his campaign, he sucked in her lower lip as his fingers slid down to the soft flesh between her legs. One finger slipped in easily and he explored the barrier within.

Firmly anchored on one side, small bridges of flesh adhered it to the other side, leaving a hole barely large enough for his finger to slide through. She bucked against him, the tone of her whimpers changing.

"I'm sorry, *älskling*. I can't spare you the pain," he murmured against her lips. "I can make it quick." He eased back and stroked the tender skin of her opening until she moaned with need again. Moisture coated his fingers as he positioned himself at her entrance.

Heaven, the smooth slick heat of her was better than he'd ever dreamed. Slowly he pressed in, savoring the tightness of her around him, the pleasing feeling of her flesh embracing his.

"Sweet Freya, you feel so good, Nory."

"Gunnar," she moaned.

"I want you, Nory, do you want me?"

"Yes," her reply was barely more than a whisper against his lips.

"You're mine, Nory. Mine for all time."

"You're mine, too, Gunnar."

"Yes." This was meant to be. "As I claim you, I acknowledge your claim on me." Poised for the perfect thrust, he rose up on his arms and stared into her eyes. "Do you agree?"

"Yes!" Brown eyes glittered back at him, her gaze locked with his.

With her cry, he put his power into thrusting forward, one fast surge to breach her maidenhead. Was it the rush of blood that made his ears ring or was it Thor's Hammer? He couldn't tell if the transport rocked or if it was just his soul. He threw back his head to let an ancient warrior's cry rip from his throat.

Filling her completely, he felt the soft entrance to her womb as the root of his shaft nestled between her nether lips. A more perfect fit he'd never imagined. From base to tip, she held him securely, pulsing around him as he kissed the tears from her cheeks.

"Don't move yet," he soothed her.

"It hurts!"

"I know. Give it a moment. The pain doesn't last long. Slowly now, can you work your muscles?"

"I... I..."

The squeeze of her around him nearly ripped away his control. Burying his head in her neck, soft hair caressing his face, he groaned. "Yes, just like that, *älskling*."

Her tears eased as she gripped him again. A wave of her moisture enveloped him as she shivered.

"Ah," she breathed, a new urgency claiming her voice.

"Does it still hurt?" He needed to move. Would die if he didn't move.

"I don't think... so," she moaned with his gentle movement.

A tiny pull back, then a tiny thrust in. "Freya's sweet *fitte*, Nory. This is heaven."

"Gunnar," she moaned. "Release me."

"I can't, not this time, Nory. I'll take care of you, love, I promise." He leaned over her and claimed her mouth as his body claimed hers. Words left him as instinct took over, the natural pulse of life driving him on as much as her body rising up to meet him. Even bound to the bed, she met his rhythm and he took every care to go slowly. It was a good idea until she started bucking against him, urging him on.

Wanting to watch her face, he pushed up on his arms. Had her legs been free, he had no doubt they would have been wrapped around him. No help for it now, he wasn't about to stop long enough to release her.

Gaze locked with hers, he watched her face as their passion built. She stared back at him, never flinching, a small grimace of need on her face. Glorious, with a look of intense desire in her eyes, she was beautiful, the blazing color of her hair burning like their mutual need. What would her face look like as she took flight? The tiny mews from her throat grew breathy and he longed to take her over. Using super human power he rested on one arm and reached down between their bodies to rub her button. A flush started between her breasts and began to bleed across her skin. With a cry, she threw her head back and thrust her hips up against him. She clenched down hard as her body spasmed, and he lost control.

With a shout, lightning burst from the base of his spine and, in hot spurts, he cemented his claim by filling her with what felt like every last drop of his soul.

Chapter 7

Cold cleansing air filled Noreen's lungs as she sought make sense of her world. Her head spun even as her body throbbed around Gunnar still embedded in her.

In her. In her *fitte*.

Her virginity... gone.

And not by her choice. Exactly.

Taken.

Married.

The reality was so very different from the dream she'd held so close not even her staff, her closest confidants, knew.

A tear trickled from the corner of her eye.

What happened to the sweet courting rituals? Where was the elaborate wedding gown? The champagne? The beautiful silk-draped bed? The bedroom open to a warm tropical night sweet with the scent of flowers on the breeze, the terrace leading down to a beach sliding into bathtub warm waters? Where had been her chance to whisper into her husband's mouth, those two tender words, *take me*? Where had been her turn to touch, explore and share in the taking?

Another tear welled up over the rim of her eyelid.

Gunnar's lips nuzzled aside the fabric of her top still wrapped around her neck and kissed the tender spot under her jaw, his mouth soft, even reverent. But where was the love in it?

She turned her head aside and tried to draw in a steady breath.

Somehow wearing torn and pushed aside red silk winter underwear while being tied to a cramped bed in a common transport had never entered her dreams of making love, much less her wedding night or the rending of her final barrier.

His hand cupped her breast as he lay on her body and all she could think about was how this wasn't right. Yes, the feeling had been wonderful, glorious even, the orgasm had been beautiful, magnificent, all she'd ever hoped for, but...

She swallowed against the disappointment aching to burst forth.

"Oh, Nory," his husky whisper against her ear was followed by lips teasing her earlobe.

Obviously she'd done something right. He seemed pleased.

Without warning, a sob bubbled out from between her compressed lips. She froze, her body tensing, doing her best to hold back the flood battering at her heart.

She felt him tense and then push up off her body. Now he'd move off her and... what? What did men like him do after sex?

Squeezing her eyes shut, she tried to wipe out the memory of another man and another place. Hollis Traxelgard. Just one night, she'd told herself as he wooed her. The week before Cory's demand to come home, Hollis had wined and dined Noreen. After meeting at an embassy dinner, they'd danced under a different moon each night, sunned at a different beach each day, and indulged in all the decadent pleasures of Lidaria. And then Cory's vid-link communication had come through, complete with the ever headache-producing twin-speak. It wasn't fair that Cory could pelt her mentally as well, especially over such a long distance. Even the gods couldn't touch her across the galaxy.

Irritated at having to leave, Noreen had made arrangements for the next luxury class galaxy-cruiser. Scheduled to depart the following day, she'd decided Hollis would have to hold her for a while. So she'd let him into her room that night, securing from him the promise not to breach her maidenhead. He'd fallen to his knees and made love to her with his mouth and she'd returned the favor, enjoying his deep, dark chocolate mint flavor. Did all Lidarians taste of mint? Most of their food incorporated the herb in some way, even if only as a garnish. Did they ingest so much of it they tasted of it too? Probably. It certainly enhanced the physical experience.

Her mistake had been letting him go one step beyond oral pleasures. She'd never considered it a big deal to let a man take her ass. It saved them from taking her virginity and it felt mighty nice. So when his ardor had increased after several mouth-numbing rounds, she'd knelt on the bed and presented her bottom. She'd been amused when he covered her posterior with worshipping kisses, spending long moments caressing her, oiling and preparing the way until she nearly cried out for him to just take her, dammit. His mutterings hadn't made sense at the time, after all, she was in a pleasant erotic haze, tired but still ready for more, a euphoric state where she could make love for hours or sleep deeply. Since he hadn't given her the impression of being ready for sleep or departure, to her it was the next logical step unless she wanted another mouthful of his sweetly flavored seed. She was full.

Her first hint at something unusual came as he'd plunged into her, all the while promising she'd never want for anything. Then, as he'd pumped in and out of her, the mutterings began to sound like words of love. It had felt great, but it wasn't love. Hoping she was mistaken, she let herself go with the moment and, after several very nice orgasms for her, he'd ejaculated into her with a shout very much like the warrior's cry Gunnar had emitted just a few minutes ago. She'd fallen asleep with Hollis still deep inside, his arms around her, his deep voice promising her the moons and stars and a life of luxury. No different than a dozen men over the years had spoken in the heat and afterglow of passion. She didn't think anything of it.

The next morning she'd awakened sluggishly to find him gone, a Lidarian Lily on the pillow beside her. No big deal. She had a rocket to catch and, with Fiona and Sophie prodding her, she'd flown through dressing, the final catches on her luggage fastened as Hans ushered the bulk of her bags out of the hotel. Her personal planetary communicator had bleeped on the way to the off-world transport depot. Hollis. He wanted to see her. Desperately. She'd promised to look him up as soon as she got back. Emergency at home and all that. Of course she had no such plans at all.

Arriving at the depot, she'd found Hollis waiting for her with a case of Lidarian brandy, a casket of jewelry and armfuls of the sweet green lilies. The flowers weren't allowed on board, but the captain had been most happy to accept half of the case of brandy as a bribe to delay take-off for ten extra minutes. Hollis had made her give him the date of when she'd be back. Eight galactic weeks was the earliest she could promise and with the rocket engines firing up, she'd given him a long goodbye kiss.

"I'll have the house prepared for you when you return," he'd said, his parting words carrying over the rocket engines.

"The house?" She'd turned back to him. "I don't understand?"

"Our house. Your family will be most welcome to come and visit us at any time. If I can get away, I'll follow you in a day or two. I should meet them as soon as possible," he'd declared, as if the brilliant idea had just jumped into his brain.

"Excuse me?" The lowered tones and raised eyebrow had been met with confusion.

"But of course, my darling." Hollis held her close and trailed his lips over her neck. "I'll also have your wedding ring with me. That casket is just a few trinkets to tide you over until I can have the perfect ring made. You caught me by surprise last night and I wasn't prepared. But not anymore! Everything will be perfect from here on out. I promise."

"Wedding ring?"

"Yes! When you gave me, what did you call it? Your so very beautiful and perfect," his hands cupped her bottom as he pulled her close, "*rompe* last night, it was the sealing of our marriage contract. I couldn't be happier, my little dove."

Stunned, to say the least, she'd stood there staring at him, not quite open mouthed, but speechless nonetheless.

"*M'lady*!" Fiona's urging and firm grip on her arm had saved her from erupting in a royal hissy fit right there on the ramp. Hans had gripped her other arm and she'd found herself on board and in the first class lounge with a glass of the captain's strongest spirits in her hand.

Once they were free of the planet's atmosphere and in her state rooms, she'd pinned a royal glare on her staff.

"Who is going to explain to me just how we missed this little detail pertaining to the marriage ceremony? Sexual practices? Legal contracts?"

Fiona had arched a brow at her then shrugged. "It isn't in writing anywhere, and I looked."

Noreen sighed and nodded. "I know. I know you searched. One of those little things never discussed."

Hans had sat down next to her and draped an arm around her shoulder. "M'lady, I too researched and questioned everyone. Never a whisper."

"I know, I know." She'd rested her head against his shoulder. Even Sophie had looked sad as she shook her head and knelt at her mistress's feet. In ten years it was the first time they'd failed to turn up every meaning of every part of the courtship dance on each world visited. Normally they stayed six months or more, so had time to ferret out these things thoroughly before Noreen indulged in a carefully orchestrated seduction. Cory pushing her to come home after being on Lidaria only a month had disrupted the routine. No, it wasn't her twin's fault. She'd made her own choice and the blame for the mistake fell on her head alone.

Noreen had rubbed her aching forehead wearily. "Fi, at the first opportunity please check the legal records pertaining to marriage. First, of course, for the things which bind and then for the things that dissolve. If need be, we'll use my father's counselors, but only as a last resort. You all did your best. Now I ask for your help to clean up my mess."

"Of course, Princess. We'll get it taken care of," her loyal secretary had assured her. "You're tired. Why don't you settle in and I'll have dinner served here tonight. I'm sure the captain will understand, and you may join him for dinner tomorrow night."

At her nod, Hans had lifted her in his arms and, with Sophie following, he'd taken her to the bedroom.

And now, here she was again, in another bed. And this time she was caught but good.

The sob ripped from her control and she couldn't hold back, couldn't gain control of herself. Her life was in shambles and she didn't know where she'd gone so very, very wrong.

"Nory, Nory, my love, there's no reason for tears."

His conciliatory tone and dismissive words made her cry all the harder. How could this be? How could this have happened?

"Ah, *älskling*."

She felt his weight settle on the bed next to her and he wrapped his legs around hers, his arm across her body. He'd chosen the side she'd turned to, so she turned her head the other way. The only means she had of rejecting his sympathy.

"Nory, did I hurt you?" Confusion and concern in his voice cut through her tears, but didn't make them lessen.

How could she tell him just how deeply she was wounded? Not her body, but her true self? Her heart and soul? Every dream of a romantic married life fled and she wept deep, body-wracking sobs. It wasn't for her, it seemed. Odin, Thor, Freya, Loki, her father, sister and the duke had all conspired to trap her at last.

She felt him shift, his weight leaving the bed. Torn and weeping, she felt the fluids seep from her body as he left her.

A moment later he returned and a warm damp cloth was gently applied to the sore flesh between her legs.

"Shh, *älskling*. I'm sure I didn't hurt you that much. You've bled a little, but it has stopped. It isn't pouring from you." He chuckled. "That would be the elixir from which our children will spring. The most miraculous cocktail in the universe."

Children! More sobs ripped from her throat. She didn't want children! Children who would be subjected to all the nonsense of royalty, never knowing a free moment of their lives.

Even though she'd nominally been on her own these past ten years, she'd never been truly alone. If it wasn't one of her small retinue hovering within eyesight, she knew there were at least two of her father's spies following at any given time. Depending on the planet, there could be more.

The disguise of travel writer and agent had not always held up under close scrutiny. At least not in the early days. The last few years she'd nearly perfected the art of disguise, and hiding had been easier. Still, how many travel agents traveled with a personal secretary, maid and bodyguard? Hans was a beautiful specimen of Nordian manhood but, with his bulging muscles, could never be mistaken for anything other than what he was. Hopefully, he and Fiona could calm Hollis's ardor and send him back to Lidaria with an annulment or whatever means of dissolution worked for his planet.

But children! No, she would not become a fertile field to be plowed for the sake of royal heirs. And yet, Duke Gunnar had just done that very thing.

Exhausted beyond caring about anything anymore, she couldn't dredge up another burst of sobs and, with a hiccup, tried to stop crying. But still the tears came, sliding from her eyes over her cheeks as she gulped and gasped, trying to calm her panic. *A Princess never cries*, her mother's quiet words came back to her.

Princesses must hold up their heads at all times, a smile at the ready, a graceful hand always available to extend to a loyal subject. By her mother's decree, nail polish wouldn't dare chip on her delicate hands, a stain never adhere to her teeth. Whining was not allowed and displays of temper were beneath her. At least while on Nordia. In that respect, it had been a relief to go undercover as much as possible. She still wasn't prone to tantrums, and she really didn't whine, despite whatever that vile old bishop had said so long ago. She just wasn't a public type of person. Usually. Okay, the kiss with Hollis at the depot hadn't been exactly retiring, but it had been meant to be farewell.

"There you go, my pet." Gunnar crooned soothingly in her ear as he gently dabbed at her tears and wiped her nose. "One good blow now." He held a tissue for her.

How humiliating.

"You may release me now," she hiccupped. "I... I won't do you bodily harm." It wasn't as if she could run away.

"Ah, no, *älskling*. You're there for a while. I'll let you up briefly in a few hours, but you will spend the rest of the trip in this bed, available for my pleasure."

Her burning and swollen eyes flew open as she whipped her head around to look at him. "You've had your fun, now I insist you release me. You've effectively trapped me here in this transport for the duration of the storm. That should be enough amusement for you."

"Amusement?" His dark blue eyes sparkled as he stared back at her. "No, my wife. This is not about amusement. I have slaves for that. No, this is about you learning your place, you learning to accept your fate as my wife, securing your devotion to me. This is the time when we will bind ourselves together, body and soul. The breaching of your maidenhead was just the beginning." He cupped her chin, his strong hand warm in the cool air of their tiny cabin.

His eyes flicked over her as a shiver ran through her, and she felt the goose flesh rise up on her skin.

"Ah, I see you are cold still. I'll raise the heat a little more, but I don't want to start sweating either. While we do have some water for washing, it isn't enough for multiple showers."

He leaned forward and pressed a warm kiss on her lips. Just long enough for her to melt a tiny bit, before he pulled away and turned to dispose of the cloth somehow.

"Slaves?" The word puzzled her. There were commoners on Nordia. Well remunerated servants certainly. But slaves?

"Consensual slaves. I suppose you might consider them sex slaves, but they do so much more. It isn't so much their livelihood, but rather, their lifestyle. I take very good care of them and they are well compensated for their service."

"B-but..." she stuttered.

"I know, and no, I never had sex with them without being properly shielded," his voice was soothing again. His deep eyes stared into hers as his hand slowly explored her body. "You're my first full flesh contact, just as I was the first man to claim your most sacred portal. Just as I am the only man who will ever do so."

His hand kneading her breast brought a small groan to her lips, but still she held his gaze.

"We need to talk, Nory. I need to know what you know about loving. This," his hand cupped her mound, fingers teasing her nether lips, "is mine and only I have been here. But this," a finger slid down to cover her puckered hole, "how many have entered through this door?"

Instinctively she clenched her muscles. It wasn't likely she'd willingly allow admission there again to anyone. Pity, because she liked it.

"How many, sweet Nory?" He watched her face closely.

"I didn't keep count," she whispered. Lying was pointless. She just couldn't do it. One more reason she'd make a lousy monarch.

"So more than one, eh?"

She gulped.

"No more, Nory. I mean to erase the memory of other men's touch on your body. I will be imprinted on you to the point you'll never desire another man."

"That hardly seems fair if you are allowed concubines and sl... slaves," she spat.

"Ah, the slaves. You don't like the idea of them. Well, I may retire them when we get to the country estate. I won't make that promise now. They were a means to keep me sane while you evaded your duty here at home."

She felt her jaw drop. Before she could utter a word he used a finger to push her mouth closed.

"In fact, I believe a thorough claiming is an excellent idea," he said.

Chapter 8

Perfect. Just the right swell of breast to fill his hand. Gunnar molded the flesh to fit his grip, her nipple peeking out from near the base of his thumb. It pebbled so nicely. Her eyes still held a deep mix of emotions, a profound sadness overshadowing all. Connected to the tears?

A deep shuddering shook the transport then all grew still. Ah. The weather must be such the convoy could no longer make headway. The computer bleeped discreetly to let him know Wil had sent an update. He'd given orders not to be disturbed by the audio communicator unless danger was imminent. Wil knew his job well, Gunnar wasn't needed to micro-manage.

He leaned down to press another kiss on his bride. "Let me check the update. Wil was going to try and get us to the nearest shelter so we could ride out the storm a little more pleasantly. The crew deserves a break to recreate if we made it."

At her small nod, he gave her a smile. If only all her training would be so easy... no, he expected more spirit from his princess. A deep and complicated woman, he'd have to stay on his toes until he knew her inside and out.

Not bothering to pull on clothes, he settled in his seat.

"Well, what do you know, Odin has been most kind. The worst of the storm is just now coming at us and we made it far enough to reach the back entrance of Dante's Grotta." Good choice. A popular resort area.

He picked up the handset of the communicator. "Wil."

"Your Gr...Highness?"

"Ah, the king announced it already, has he?"

"Yes, sir. Well, he passed word to me, but it hasn't made it to the news broadcasts yet. Congratulations on your marriage, sir."

"Thank you. I'll pass your wishes for happiness onto my wife. Now, about the resort. Do they have rooms to spare? I'd like a private suite for the princess and myself."

"I was just checking, sir...let's see...yes, in fact, the royal suite is available."

How perfect. "Are there enough accommodations for the crew?"

"Yes. A few will have to double up, but it sure beats sleeping in the transports. Sir."

"Wil, save it for in front of the king. This doesn't change our working relationship, okay?"

"Yes, sir...uh...Zaren."

"Better," he sighed. "While you're making arrangements, we'll want a cosmetic technician at the first opportunity. The princess will require someone skilled in hair and skin. Oh, and let's leave her true name and my new title out of the reservations. Use the name on the manifest, Noreen Tibbetts, if you must give one at all."

He heard the tapping of keys before Wil answered again. "Done. They're sending a transport to pick us all up and get us safely into the caves. I'll come by to help with your luggage."

"Five minutes?"

"Uh, make that ten."

"Right. See to the crew. We'll be ready."

"Yes, sir."

* * * *

"Your Grace, I'm sorry, but it just isn't possible. If I try to lighten her hair, it will merely turn pink." The small beautician stood before him wringing her hands.

"If I use enough bleach to remove all the color, you might as well shear off all her hair. The dye is so deeply ingrained it will ruin her hair to bleach it out. I can color over it, make it dark brown or black, but to lighten it is not recommended."

Gunnar glanced at his bride sitting in the chair with a carefully blank expression on her face. But her eyes, now free of the brown lenses, flashed back at him with blue fire and created an instant heat, an instant need in him. She stared at him a moment longer, before dropping her gaze to where her fingers drummed on the arm of the chair. The beautician had just repeated the very words Nory had said while dressing in the transport.

"I can give her a treatment to make her hair softer and scrub her body with sea salts, but there is nothing I can do at this time to adjust her skin coloring, sir."

"Then do what you can. I want her soft and glowing from head to toes."

"If you don't like my hair red, I would consent to black," Noreen spoke up.

"The opposite of white."

She shrugged. "I like red because it makes me feel warm. Black would merely cover it. Which do you find more pleasing?"

Her hooded gaze challenged him and he considered the options. He really didn't like the red. Turning to the smaller woman he said, "Make it black."

"Yes, sir."

Wil had the convoy crew in hand, so Gunnar chose a comfortable chair where he could watch as the spa personnel leaped into action. It didn't matter that it was after regular business hours. He'd promised to pay double.

"So, while I'm getting beautiful to your standards," Noreen's husky voice broke through his thoughts, "will you do the same for me?"

"And what is it you have in mind?"

"You could use a manicure yourself."

He put a hand to his chin. "And a shave as well as a hair cut."

"No, leave the hair long. Maybe shape it so it grows out better, but leave it long."

She returned his lifted brow with one of her own. He regarded her for a long moment then nodded and found himself in the chair next to hers, the staff doing their best to contain the curiosity burning in their eyes.

Three hours later, dressed only in long, soft toweling robes, he carried her over the threshold of their suite. Scrubbed, polished, petted and pampered, Gunnar found himself ready to spend the night loving his wife. He carried her to the bedroom and set her on her feet near the extra large bed.

"Thank you," she said daintily, then yawned. "It has been a most exhausting day. I will sleep now then we may talk in the morning."

He stood stunned for a moment then burst out laughing. "Nice try."

"Excuse me?"

The lowered voice and raised brow over flashing blue merely made him smile. Tugging on the cord holding her robe closed, he pulled her to him. The cord came loose and he pushed her robe from her shoulders. Her hands came up to cover herself and the white robe stopped at her elbows, leaving her still tanned shoulders enticingly bare.

"The black hair looks much nicer with your blue eyes and dark skin," he said, and pulled her hands away. The robe finished its journey to the floor and settled around her feet.

"Thank you, but what does that have to do with sleeping?"

"Who said you would sleep this night? We're here to enjoy ourselves."

"And I will find much enjoyment in sleep so, if you will excuse me…" She turned away.

His hand caught her arm. "No, I won't excuse you."

The imperial glower would have seared his skin had he been a lesser man.

"My dear, dear wife." He reached over her shoulder and pulled forth a long tress of her soft dark hair. "Now is when we truly begin getting to know one another. We need to set the rules of our life together and cover every intimate detail. I need to know your past and you need to understand how things will be from now on. You will be mine in every way before this night is over."

"My dear duke," her words were laced with disdain, "as much as I hate to remind you, I carry the higher rank here, and when I say I'm tired, I mean it and will go to bed. To sleep. I have several issues to sort out with not only you, but my father and sister as well. In order to do that with any degree of intelligence, I need sleep and time to think. So, for now, I will bid you good night." She turned away again.

He pulled her back and into his arms. "This is our wedding night."

For some reason the comment made her chin tremble ever so slightly and the sad look return to her eyes.

"No, this is not our wedding night," she countered, only a tiny waver in her voice giving away her emotion. "Despite the fact you have taken that which I've guarded all my life, I do not acknowledge this marriage." And this seemed to upset her for some reason.

"You acknowledged our mutual claim on each other."

"Words spoken in the heat of passion. They have no binding force."

"They do." He pulled her closer yet and dipped his head to hers. Only twelve or thirteen centimeters shorter than he, she was the perfect height, which made her tall for a woman. Her body curved and molded to his, breasts pressed against his chest, her softly rounded stomach and thighs a perfect cradle for holding him. "Our union was consecrated with the blow of Thor's Hammer, my love."

Fingers woven into the long loose hair at her nape ensured the proper positioning for his mouth to take hers in a deep, soul-blending kiss. Never had a simple kiss stolen his breath or made his head spin the way kissing her did. He didn't need to hear the crash of Thor's Hammer again to know this was right. The vibration sang through his body and he held her close as her body melted against him. Air to breathe, food to eat and wine to drink would all be meaningless without her kiss.

She pulled away with a softly uttered curse. "Enough, Thor! I'm sorry I ever called your attention to me," she muttered.

Gunnar pulled back and stared into her eyes as an odd sound echoed in the hollowed out space deep within the mountain. "Did I just hear...? I could swear I just heard a chuckle."

Avoiding his eyes, she pursed her lips and nodded briefly. "Thor having a little fun at our expense. Half the reason I ran from here. At least, beyond the star system, the gods couldn't reach me." She closed her eyes and murmured, "Damn you, Cory, for dragging me back here!"

Playing with her soft hair he had to ask, "How did she get you back here?"

"A vid-com and a twin-link. Told me Fader was dying and something evil was about to happen. If that were the case, then why wasn't there a cruiser at the depot to take me direct to Stravicsholm? Why the three-day trek through the wilderness?"

"Twin-link?"

"We can't exactly talk mentally, but we can send emotions and sometimes pictures to each other. She blasted me but hard and gave me a major headache."

He watched as she lifted a hand to rub her temples again.

Nory sighed wearily. "A rather effective means of underlining the urgency of her message."

"Ah. Rather handy I should think."

"Only if you're the one sending and not receiving." Clouded eyes blinked up at him. "How is my father? Is he truly ill?"

"He's getting on, but he's still hale as far as I can tell. It's probably more a matter of he'd like to retire. Not the usual arrangement, but as I'm sure you know, it isn't unheard of either."

"Olaf VI retired, or abdicated, to let his son take over during a period of economic uncertainty. Erik IX, or the Economist depending on how you like to remember him, wanted to put into practice all the fresh ideas from his brand new advanced degree in business from the university."

"Good thing they worked too."

Noreen nodded and tried to step away again.

Instead he rubbed the back of her neck and pulled her close again.

"Please, I meant it when I said I was tired," she said softly.

"And I meant it when I said this was our wedding night. We can sleep tomorrow. For now, we have a large room and space to become better acquainted."

Gunnar backed her up until the bed stopped their progress. "Your choice, Nory. Oral? Or anal?"

"Sounds rather clinical, dukey." The bored look on her face was cute, but she didn't fool him. A fine blush rushed across her skin like the swipe of a water color brush over paper.

"Not in the least. I don't plan to spend our wedding night sleeping. Either choice is just a starting point. Neither is the end."

Noreen shuddered as a yawn over took her. "Sorry, but I need some sleep. We'll talk, if I wake in a few hours."

Gunnar held her chin, humor adding to the pleasant hum in his blood. He could almost hear the thought in her head. *It had been worth a try.*

"I need you, Nory. I've wanted you for so long, just one taste isn't enough."

His softly spoken words must have touched something deep inside. She quivered in his arms. He cupped her buttocks and lifted her ever so slightly against his cock, which now parted the panels of the robe he still wore. Curiosity replaced the fatigue in her eyes.

"I think we'll start with a dessert of sweet woman," Gunnar murmured in her ear. "I want to taste you thoroughly."

What could a girl say to that? Her body softened, and he felt her surrender. This would be a night to remember. He'd make sure of it.

"Oral sounds just fine to me…"

She let him lay her back on the bed and watched as he discarded the robe. Oh ja, she would submit to this. He knelt on the bed and lifted her legs over his shoulders.

"Beautiful. Even better without the red underwear." He lay down, her thighs bracketing his head. "One serving of creaming Nordian wench coming up."

His lips touched her and he swore to himself, before the night was over, she'd find a new way to reach the stars. Over and over again.

Noreen didn't complain when, hours later, Gunnar lifted her and carried her to the bathroom. The man was talented and her exhaustion was the proof. He'd tongued her through two orgasms, then rested as she'd returned the favor. Unable to resist her cream, or so he said, he'd dived between her legs again, before flipping her over onto her knees. Showing great stamina, he'd taken her from behind, first vaginally and then, finally, anally. It was a night unlike any ever experienced before. She'd lost count of her orgasms, and had barely been able to rouse herself as he sat her down on the edge of the large tub in the bathroom. He smiled at her as he turned on the taps over the tile pool built out from the underground wall.

In the main cavern of the resort, a series of underground ponds formed terraced pools. Thermal springs came from deep within the porous rock and filled the upper pool with the hottest water, safe only for the most hardy of swimmers. Overflow cascaded down into the next pool, cooler by a few degrees. Minerals from the water formed a colored version of the ice formations found on the surface. Copper made the mineral deposits and water green, while iron tinged it with rust. Again, overflow cascaded down and formed other pools, each level cooler, until the lowest level was comfortable for small children and the elderly. Perfect for long soaks to ease sore bodies.

For those able to pay, in a select number of special suites such as the one they occupied, pipes had been run to allow even more control. Cool water from snowmelt could be mixed in with the hottest of the spring waters for a truly custom soaking experience. The tiled pools also allowed for other additions to the water, such as scented salts and oils adding to the therapeutic experience. Over the years Noreen had sent home gifts of exotic bath additives for her family and she saw a few of their favorites displayed on a shelf carved from the stone wall.

"In you go, Nory."

"Don't you ever get tired of ordering me around, dukey?" He was getting to her, but she couldn't let him know it. Maintaining the upper hand was necessary.

"Princess," he chuckled. "How well the name suits you."

Without warning he tossed her face down over his knees and his hand landed with a whoosh and sting on her bottom.

"What is my name?"

"Dukey works—" she replied, in her most disdainful tone, only to be cut off by another slap of his hand.

"Care to try again?"

"My father will hear of this," she snarled, then yelped.

"Your father is the one who gave me the books and visuals on how to train a wife properly."

"He what?" Noreen's screech echoed off the cavern walls as it turned into pained moan. Tears began to leak from her watering eyes as she tried to make sense of his words. "My…my father…?"

"Oh yes, my wayward princess. He knew I'd need to bring you into line someday. Now it all makes sense," Gunnar chuckled. "The fog has lifted, and now all is clear as crystal. You, my wife, need correction to help you focus on your duties to your world."

Closing her eyes, she wished she could shut out his chuckles and the throbbing of her aching sex. Despite her outrage and protests, she was most horrified to find her body reacting the way he apparently expected it to. Her heart stuttered—but was it with dread or excitement?—when his hand slipped down between her legs to stroke her quivering flesh.

"There we go," he murmured in approval. "The sooner you submit, the sooner life will be happy again for you."

"I won't submit. I outrank you." Her feeble reminder didn't carry the weight she'd wanted. In fact, she'd sounded downright wimpy.

"Let me remind you, you may be the Crown Princess, and outrank me in Parliament, but here, between us, as your husband I outrank you." His clever fingers found her vulnerable button and she whimpered.

"Please, stop. I'm too sensitive," she moaned.

"All you have to do is behave yourself. No backtalk for starters."

"You are so getting chained to the bed," she growled.

"Not," Gunnar laughed. "You'd need help, and they'd rather watch you being chained to the bed first.

Noreen stiffened. "You wouldn't…"

"No, I wouldn't bring in an audience. What we do is just for us to enjoy. Your subjects—I guess I should say our subjects—don't need to see their future queen that way."

"So…are we going to sit here all night or take a bath?"

Chapter 9

Two days later, Gunnar considered his options. The storm had kept them bound at the resort for a full day, providing a pleasant break for the convoy crew, but he'd had little sleep. The crew was now tired again, as it had taken nearly a full day to shovel the transports out from under the snow accumulated in the storm.

The worst they'd seen in thirty years, Ole and his wife Hedwig swore to anyone within hearing. Caretakers of this particular thermal pool resort for nearly forty years, Gunnar suspected they could very well be right. Then again, he assumed the storm had involved a little divine intervention.

Glancing toward the curtained-off bedroom, where his sleeping princess lay sprawled across the bed of the royal suite, he made the decision to stay one more night. Noreen, while enjoying the lovemaking, complained and strained against bondage of any kind, unless it was part of a love game. Pleasant though it was, he was tired from meeting her demands. He'd never experienced such exhilarating love play or lovemaking and, like a drug addict, he wanted more.

"We'll start out again in the morning," he told his convoy commander.

Wilton Leebrick nodded, his long Nordian hair braided in the ancient style. Shaggy brows hovered over ice blue eyes that had seen a dozen winters more than Gunnar, and carried that much more wisdom as far as Gunnar was concerned.

"Has the king made an announcement of any kind yet?" Gunnar asked. He'd been too deeply involved with his wife to pay attention to the news broadcasts.

"No, not yet. I've let the palace know our status from time to time and they seem most content with the updates. Not one word about the princess or your union."

Gunnar nodded. It was just as well. Better to get her home first. "And locally? What are the rumors flying about?"

"They're whispering that the lost princess has miraculously appeared and the next line of The Profetia has been fulfilled. The old timers apparently recognized the sound of Thor's Hammer battering the world."

Gunnar grinned. At last count, Thor's delicate hammer had rocked his soul no less than five times in the last three days.

"They say you've met your mate, claimed her, and have planted at least four children in her."

Gunnar laughed. "All we need is one. A male heir as predicted."

"The people hereabouts have been offering up devotions in unprecedented volume the last two days. I suspect there will be a baby boom come forty weeks from now." Wil's eyes sparkled with lusty humor and Gunnar wondered if he'd contributed to the coming population explosion. "The youngsters, whose belief in the gods was tenuous at best, are among the more devout. The stories of the old timers remembering when Bjorn claimed Elke, and the conception of the princess, have been retold more than once. A whole new air of romance is permeating the air. It is only a matter of time before it spreads to the entire planet."

Gunnar allowed himself another chuckle, then asked, "Any word about the Lidarian?"

"He's still making noises about invasion if she isn't brought back to him. Legal action has also been mentioned."

Gunnar grinned.

"That doesn't bode well for the off-worlder," Wil chuckled.

"No, it doesn't." Gunnar's grin widened, before he laughed. He now had the whole story on Traxelgard from Nory's point of view, or at least she swore it was the whole picture. At best, he figured the man had made up the ruse about the wedding. In any case, it didn't hold any water. Nory was his now. A surge of pride and protectiveness filled him with a desire to let loose the warrior in his soul. A dose of modern civilization forced the Viking berserker back under control for the time being.

"Well," Gunnar clapped his commander on the shoulder and escorted him to the door. "Get your well-earned rest tonight. We leave first thing in the morning."

"Six?"

"Better make it seven." Gunnar glanced back at the bedroom. "We'll steal one extra hour of sleep. I'm sure the king won't mind. Too much."

"Aye, sir." Wil clasped the hand Gunnar extended to him. "Get your own rest, sir."

"I'll do that tomorrow."

Wil returned his grin then left the suite.

Locking the door, Gunnar turned back toward the bedroom. Thick carpets woven from brightly-dyed, soft Nordian wool muffled his steps, and he slid past the curtains.

One more night here and she'd be docile enough to move to the transport vehicle. Two days and one night together in the tiny space and they'd be inseparable for all time. They were nearly there now, her deep blue eyes beginning to look at him with love and respect. It was a relief to see it replace the suspicion and distrust. There was no doubt the two of them were stronger together and the blending of their souls was all but complete. The final confirmation would come with the family reunion in Stravicsholm. Until she heard it from her father, face-to-face, she wasn't prepared to believe he'd given Gunnar the means with which to bind her to him. From there, hopefully, she'd see he was bound just as firmly to her. This wasn't a one sided union.

Black hair spread out across the pillows, providing stark contrast to the white silk sheets Hedwig had produced the day after they arrived.

Nory had grimaced at the white, but thanked the proprietress profusely for the luxury. Ever since, the older woman had been falling over herself to cater to every need and wish. Gunnar had seen Nory do her best to keep her requests gentle and understated, only to have Hedwig go far above and beyond in providing only the very best in terms of food, wine and other services. Holding her expressions of dismay at causing the woman and her staff more work, until they were alone, Nory made sure to thank each person who tended to them. Her style was simple and quiet, and all the more profound and sincere, resulting in redoubled efforts to please her.

And now, she slept. Thick lashes, also tinted a dark color to hide her blonde origins, lay like soft fans on her cheek. Even in rest she glowed with health and loving. Lots of good loving.

As much as Gunnar's goal was to addict her to him, he was caught in his own addiction to her. The scent of her, the sound of her breathy cries of pleasure, her sultry chuckle and soft husky voice. Her taste and the feel of her skin were all he craved now. He lived to feel her wrapped around him, pulsing, gripping, pulling every last drop of his essence from his body. It would be a miracle if she carried only one child.

Nory stirred against the fur lined cuffs holding her to the bed. Chains from the cuffs were attached to the four corners of the bed frame. In truth, he was the one chained to her. Did she even realize she'd enslaved him?

The thin sheet covered her body in a way that made his mouth water. Every curve of her was outlined beneath the soft silk, looking like a sexy landscape. He'd never be able to look across the plains, freshly blanketed in snow, without visualizing her like this. The woman he loved was one with the land he loved. But she hated the land.

No, it wasn't the land she hated, it was the snow and the cold. She'd admitted it was all very pretty, as long as she didn't have to step into it. Viewing from afar, preferably while standing under a hot sun sipping fruit juice, was the best way to appreciate Nordia, she'd said. She adored the people. It was just...well...did the world have to be so...*white*? If she had to live in snow, couldn't the gods at least make it green or orange? Lavender would be nice as well. Or, if they had to stick to blue tones, how about a hot turquoise?

He'd stared at her in amazement, even as he thought of the thermal pool rooms beneath each palace. Each one had been decorated in mosaic scenes, using the brightest colors available. It all made sense now. The arrival, every eight months or so, of mysterious off-world shipments containing plants, birds and small creatures from tropical worlds, along with a host of foods, appliances, entertainments and items such as cloth and lotions. She'd admitted to sending those as well. When he told her of the new imports gaining in popularity, especially the scented bath items, she'd smiled in pleasure.

She'd been making over her society, one shipment at a time. What would she think of the changes at the palace? Did she have any concept of how she'd affected her world?

Gunnar knelt at the foot of the bed and bent to kiss her thigh, nudging the sheet away with his mouth. He liked this waxed skin of hers. A new process the spa technicians had questioned her extensively about. They'd grimaced in horror as she gave them the blow by blow process, but were intrigued when she explained the benefits. No shaving with risk of cuts, no worrying about hair removal for weeks, no itchy stubble after only a few days, and improved hygiene. After all, what purpose did pubic hair serve? Granted, body hair provided an extra layer of warmth, which was good on a planet like Nordia, but how pleasing was it, really? Wear an extra layer of underwear and remove the hair, Nory had declared, while the women all nodded wide-eyed.

She was now committed to providing enough waxing supplies to denude roughly three hundred women. Another new trend, introduced by their travel-wise princess. Noreen would probably become the most popular name on the planet for the next sixty years, Gunnar thought with a sigh of resignation. At least she hadn't suggested *he* be waxed.

The sheet slipped from her lower half and he gazed upon her sweet cleft, the skin pink and glistening. Smooth, and so very sensitive. He lightly traced a finger down the edge of her outer lips, and was rewarded with a slight shifting of her hips and a soft sleepy moan. Still swollen from their last lovemaking, he found her sweet center irresistible. He took his time touching her, lightly exploring, and watching each quiver with fascination. What a wondrous world the female body was. To date he'd been fascinated with breasts and curvaceous asses, but this…this center held a whole universe of mystery. So very beautiful.

"Gunnar." She said his name in a breathy sigh.

He nipped her right where her thigh ended and she flinched.

"Why must I call you Master?" she asked, still sleepy.

"Because, Mistress of my Heart, it is fitting I be the Master of yours," he murmured against her tiny bud. He smiled when she gasped.

"Ahh," she moaned. "Are you saying you love me?"

"I do, and I am." He would not hold his breath waiting for her to say the same words. He wouldn't. That was childish, but even still his heart rate doubled and his head felt light.

"I think I am growing to love you too."

As his lips closed around her, he let out his pent-up breath. It was good enough for now.

"Oh!" Her cry was sweet and her hips rose up to meet him.

Several minutes later she cried out again as she pulsed around his tongue. Aching for all of her, he rose up and plunged into her, seating himself fully with one thrust. She surged around him as he took her ever harder and faster at her insistence, the waves of pleasure building within her.

"Nory!" he shouted her name as the jolt of energy pooled in his loins then burst from him. Each pulse sent another jet of hot essence deep inside her and she clasped him close the only way she could. Tugging at her chains, he knew she wanted to hold him. Instead he lay on her body and held her close, his lips worshipping her with kisses and declarations of love.

"Gunnar?"

"Hmmm?" He nipped the nipple near his mouth.

"Uh, I mean, Master?"

"Yes?"

"How long are you going to keep me chained?"

"I don't exactly know. I rather like seeing you wide open and ready for me." He pushed up to lean on an elbow and look down at her with a smile. "I might keep you chained to the nearest bed until your skin and hair fade to their natural colors."

She grimaced at the thought. "Oh. That could be a very long time indeed."

"Maybe I'll just keep you chained until I'm sure you won't run away from me. Ever."

"Oh."

He watched her face for a long moment. "See? You're still planning your next hop off-planet, aren't you?" The hot flush covering her face confirmed his suspicion. "Sorry, my love. I've got you here in my arms. You're not leaving me again."

"Why not come with me?"

"Oh that's clever," he had to admit. Impossible. But clever. "There're things which require attention here. Our world needs us."

"Seems to me, they've done just fine without me around these past ten years. Pappa and Cory have all in hand. I'm not needed."

"You are. I don't know all of the king's plans, but I do believe I've heard rumors of Princess Coreen wanting to see a bit of the universe. The queen as well. Time to step in and do your duty." He touched her pert nose that wrinkled at his assessment.

"Duty," she scoffed.

"Besides, according to The Profetia, we're now on the edge of something big. The heir must be brought forth. The text isn't entirely clear so, once we reach Stravicsholm, we'll have to see what the priests say now."

"Your grandfather?"

"Yes. He's still one of the primary scholars of The Profetia. He says, that as each line is fulfilled, the next becomes clearer. If that is true, then the last few days should have revealed quite a lot. I'm sure everyone is most anxious for us to arrive."

"When will we arrive?" Deep blue eyes looked up at him.

"We leave in the morning and, if Thor was accommodating enough to sweep most of the snow away into drifts alongside the road, then we'll make good time and arrive the day after tomorrow. If the snow is cumbersome, it may be the day after that. We'll have to see."

"Why don't we leave tonight?"

He leaned over to kiss her lips. "Because, unlike you, who have spent the day deliciously tied to this bed, the others spent eight hours shoveling snow and checking on the cargo. Thankfully, all of which is intact. The heaters held up. The fuel cells are being replenished, supplies refurbished and enhanced and, in the morning, we'll start out fresh and ready for anything."

"I feel guilty lying here while everyone else has worked so hard."

"You've been doing the most important job of all." He teased her with another kiss.

"Oh?"

"You, if the rumors are right, are incubating several candidates for the position of heir."

He grinned when she flushed a bright pink.

"Rumors?" she squeaked.

"Apparently the resort is agog with speculation and is convinced we've conceived at least four potential heirs right here." He placed a hand over her womb and felt a glow of warm pride. Had they really conceived? They wouldn't know for weeks yet.

"How do they know I'm here? I thought I was registered anonymously?"

"I hate to tell you this, but there are those who remember the sound of Thor's Hammer from when your parents met, married, conceived and then birthed you."

"Oh..." Her wide eyes would have reflected the stars had they been outside.

"I believe we're responsible for the renewal of faith in the gods."

"Oh..."

She couldn't seem to find a good response, but the flickering in her deep eyes told him her brain was working hard. The small O of her mouth was darn cute and distracted him from wondering what she might say next.

"So, is that my role in The Profetia?" The words burst from her. "To be the incubator for the next great king? Is that my sole contribution to this world?" Her tinted brows furrowed in the center of her forehead. "That makes me no better than a...a... brood mare!"

"I never thought of it that way before."

Her gasp and look of disbelief told him she found his comment outrageous. "How could you not think of me any other way? Look at my own mother. What has she done other than oversee a whole passel of children? Eight out of ten not her own? Sired by her own husband?"

He blinked at the heat of her glare.

"And that reminds me," she continued. "If you think you're going to keep concubines and fill the palace with children, think again. The people have enough to do supporting their own children without supporting a huge royal family as well. If, as my father says, we are indeed married, then you are married to me and will not seek out the beds of other women."

Surprised at the heat of her words, he drew an imaginary line down her body starting at her firm little chin. "What about bringing other women to our bed?" He lazily trailed his finger around one heaving breast.

"I... I hadn't thought of that."

He smiled when her breath hitched and her nipple tightened into a sweet pink bud. "I like women, you know. I'm rather attached to you already."

"Well I like men," she said with a hint of defiance and lifted her chin. "If we bring other women to our bed, then we bring other men as well. Would you risk another man impregnating me?"

He felt the teasing tone of their conversation drain from him and he frowned down at her. Her laugh and crooked smile didn't help his mood.

"I didn't think you'd like that idea much," she said quietly.

"You won't stand for the old double standard, will you?"

"Not a chance."

"Hmmm, more rules to think about."

"You and your rules," she sighed and rolled her eyes. "Speaking of which, I'd like to get up. It isn't comfortable staying in this position for hours on end."

He raised a brow at her forthright manner.

Lowering her eyelids, she heaved a sigh. "Please, Master, may I be released from the chains?"

"For what purpose?"

"To stretch and ease my muscles. Possibly even to eat dinner sitting up this evening."

He watched a smile tug at her lips. She was a spicy one to be sure. Tweaking a nipple to punish her sharp-tongued comment made him smile when she yelped then sighed. Just to see it again he tweaked the other nipple and was rewarded with a deeper sigh. His traveling finger continued down her body and teased around her rising button. He discovered sweet wetness in her secluded passage. She moaned and tilted her hips to better embrace him.

"You wish to get up?" he asked her.

"Yes."

"And what will you do for me if I let you up?" He was in the mood to negotiate.

"I'll pin you to the bed and ride you like my favorite rocking horse," she said, her eyes opening to stare into his.

"Deal."

Chapter 10

"Gunnar?"

"Hmmm?" He smiled at the soft voice in his ear. His world cruised on a plane far beyond the confines of this small planet.

Soft breasts pressed against his chest, heaving for air much like he did. Sweet lips, soft and kissable teased his ear. The weight of her on and around him was just right, a woman blanket held firmly in place with the anchoring spike he provided. The very same spike she now gripped and massaged using only her inner muscles.

"Might we go out and use the pools tonight?" she asked.

"You want to swim amongst the commoners?"

"They're our people, not animals. Besides, they won't recognize me. Maybe we can quiet some of the rumors you say are circulating."

The way she nuzzled his neck told him she was a fast learner. After her riding him to other end of the galaxy and back, he had no will to resist her request. Frankly, he was drained. Literally. He doubted he could produce another drop of semen if his life depended on it, and his muscles were beginning to protest the vigorous bed exercise of the last forty-some odd hours. The thermal pools would feel good. Of course he'd keep her to the cooler ones. No good to cook the embryo if she were indeed pregnant already. It would also mean the more populated pools.

Raising his arms to hug her close, he kissed her shoulder. "If it would please you, then, yes, let us go and float a while."

"Then have dinner sent here?"

"Hmmm, a good bottle of wine, a little bread and cheese, then sweet sleep until we brave the fierce elements again in the morning." He held her close when she shivered.

"Yes, cook me good so my bones stay warm long enough to get to the transport," she murmured in his ear.

"Yes, my love. A quick rinse before we go."

She bounded off him and sashayed to the bathing room. With a groan he followed. She hummed a happy little tune as she braided her thick long hair. Black was wrong for her, he decided.

"Are you sure removing the color would damage your hair?" He stood behind and watched as she pulled the length over her shoulder to finish the braid.

"Yes. I tried it once, in my early days off-world. I ended up nearly shaving my hair off. It took three years to grow it out again. Though I have been tempted to go back to a shorter style. So much easier to take care of while traveling. And with a baby or two hanging off my legs..." she said with a shrug.

"No. Please, don't cut your hair." He met her gaze in the mirror and returned her raised brow with a scowl. Who was the Master here? That should have been an order and not a request. Wait, did she just mention babies? He shrugged it off. "Come, a quick shower then we'll go out."

"Yes, Gunnar."

Later he recalled it hadn't even occurred to correct her use of his name. Her hands felt wonderful as they massaged a gentle cleanser into his skin, her body soft as they shared the soap. She rinsed him and quickly dried most of the dripping water off him, though truly it was only to keep the floor of their room dry. They'd be wet again in less than two minutes.

In a daze of self-satisfaction, he followed her along the mezzanine where their suite was located, until she reached the upper pool. Like everyone else, they were naked. Unlike everyone else, her figure was perfect. Silence fell as, group by group, people in the cascading pools caught sight of them. He looked out over the immense cavern and watched as face after face turned to look up at them. Noreen held a quick and quiet conversation with a young attendant as Gunnar watched all attention turn their way.

He heard her thank the young man before gripping his wrist.

"Ready?" she asked, and Gunnar turned to look into her smiling face.

"For what?"

"To get in, of course. Last one to the bottom is a rotten Garzootlian tritonator." She gave him a wink, then dove into the deep end of the hottest pool.

"Holy—" he exclaimed, then dove in after her.

The second he surfaced, he blinked the scorching water from his eyes in time to see her slide over the edge where the water fell into the next pool. No time to curse, he followed. He was in the pool barely long enough to appreciate the slightly cooler temperature before he followed her over the edge to the next pool. Five levels down he caught up with her in the lowest pool in an area other patrons had cleared for them. As his head broke the surface he watched her swim to, then rise from, the knee deep water and shake out her hair, which had lost the tie holding it in its braid.

If he hadn't seen it for himself, he wouldn't have believed it later.

A beam of light shone down from the roof of the cavern, like a spotlight, surrounding her. She raised her face to the source and he stood from the water to join her.

"Look." She pointed, as she gripped his shoulder to maintain her balance. "Where do you think the light is coming from? It's the middle of the night for crying out loud."

When he didn't answer, she looked at him, her eyes crinkled in puzzlement. "Are you okay? Was the water too hot for you?"

"No. It was too hot for you! I should tan your hide for that." Something was very different. "Your hair…and skin…" How could that be?

"What?"

He drew a handful of hair over her shoulder and held it in the light bathing them. It was white blonde. The color of Nordia. White blonde, but not white, it looked as if threads of sparkling gold were woven throughout. With his other hand, he reached for hers and held it against his chest. She was as pale as he was, her skin a milky white, smooth as silky satin, that glowed in the surreal light.

Stunned speechless, he wasn't prepared when she stamped her foot and yelled at the ceiling. "*Odin!* Freya! Make them stop messing with me!"

Echoing through the cavern, a manly gasp was followed by a long, soul-suffering sigh of the variety only a woman could produce.

"I told you," a dulcet tone filled the grotta, "didn't I? I told you not to mess with a woman's appearance." The voice sighed again. "I'm sorry, my precious Noreen. He really does have a point. Now listen closely."

Gunnar watched as Noreen glared at the source of the light with her lips pursed as if holding back a barrage of scoldings.

"Ahem!" The deep throat was cleared before the ringing tones of Thor's Hammer shook the very roots of the planet.

"We got the hammer thing already," Noreen shouted at the ceiling. "Stop knocking down poor innocent people and get to the point, would you?"

"Silence!"

Gunnar resisted the urge to drop to his knees when his little flower of a woman crossed her arms under her breasts and thrust out a hip, still glaring up.

"Oh for Loki's sake, how I am supposed to make a world-shaking pronouncement when she's got those things pointing at me?" the male voice muttered, then grunted.

Judging by Noreen's wicked grin, Gunnar guessed the god was talking about her nipples, and that Freya had most likely elbowed Odin in the ribs.

"People of Nordia, your True Princess has returned. She has been claimed by her True Mate, the man you know as the Duke of Nordenskiold. The two of them have joined in a union which cannot be rent asunder. Already from this union, Princess Noreen carries the next male heir. And a few others."

"What?" she shrieked.

"Quiet you. You may be The Promised One, but that doesn't give you the right to sass me. Oh, and no more hot pools for you."

"Get back to the subject, please," the softer voice interrupted.

"Right. In three weeks' time, on the Winter Solstice, all Nordia will be tested. The nobility is to gather in Ryadstholm. There you will be guided by your King, Princess, and her husband, the new Prince of Nordia. Those not of the nobility will also be needed on this day, and your leaders expect you to tune in to the world-wide communications systems already in place. They will tell you what is required of you. Every soul will be needed. Do not fail your gods or your leaders."

A deep silence fell on the caverns, broken only by the sound of falling water.

Noreen cleared her throat and continued to squint up into the light.

"Yes, Princess?" Odin inquired.

"Is that all?"

"It will do for now."

"Then do you mind killing the light?"

"Ah, sorry, I was just verifying the number of fetuses."

"And?"

"Privileged information," the voice chuckled. "That is all, you may return to your activities."

The light went out and Gunnar watched as his very proper princess-wife stuck her tongue out at the ceiling.

Thor's hammer rang out, and as it faded, a deep chuckle echoed in the cavern.

Noreen drew in a deep breath, hoping it covered her shaking. Thankfully Gunnar pulled her close so she could bury her head in his chest for just a moment.

Fetuses? Plural? More than one? Gunnar's warm hand shook as it rested over her abdomen. Her very bare abdomen exposed to the inhabitants of the caverns. Her very bare ass hanging out where they stood in the water only rising to their knees. And under his hand, their children nestled secure in her womb.

Babies.

She tilted her head back to look into Gunnar's smiling eyes. Pride and love shone there.

"Defying Odin again, eh?"

"He changed my hair and skin color." She gave him a pout then smiled.

A whisper brushed around the edges of the cavern and she sighed. "I guess we need to say something."

"At least acknowledge the loyal subjects of the realm."

"Kiss me first," she pleaded.

His eyes sparkled with humor as he wrapped his arms around her waist. "Of course, my wife."

"My husband," she said with wonder as his lips pressed to hers, their bodies entwined, as her arms slid around his neck. Damn Thor, she thought as the ringing sound of his Hammer rang out again, drowning out the cheers and whistles of approval that blessed their kiss.

Wanting a touch more privacy, Gunnar pulled Noreen down into the water, easing them over to a deeper part of the pool. They'd attracted enough attention. He wanted her body cloaked in water at the very least.

Breaking the kiss, he stared into her eyes. "I hope you believe me, because I really do love you. I'm excited for our future together."

The smile in her eyes struck his heart with an electric thrill. "I do believe I love you too," she murmured.

He rested his forehead against hers, and they shared a brief moment in their own little sphere before the cheers and whistles broke through.

Gunnar let her turn in his arms, so she could wave to the people now gathering around them. Those hanging from the pools overhead, playfully splashed water until he looked up and waved back. The crowd had doubled, at least, from when they'd left their suite not fifteen minutes earlier. It looked as if the entire complement of staff and guests were in the great cavern now.

One of the first people to make her way over to them was Hedwig, the grand dame of the resort. Without pausing, she cupped Noreen's cheeks then kissed each one.

"Ah lass, I knew you as a babe. Not many folks remember there being a set of twins born right off. Your father was brilliant in hiding you out all these years. He did a right fine job of bamboozling us." Her smile said she didn't really mind.

Gunnar's heart flopped when Noreen touched the older woman's cheek, then kissed it. "I remember you too, Heddy."

The older woman blushed and stammered. "A right fine queen you'll be when your day comes," she announced.

"So it's true?" a young woman said, from where she hovered shyly nearby. "You're the Crown Princess? And you married the Duke?"

Gunnar chuckled. "The state wedding is a little time off, but by the grace of the king and the blessing of the gods, we met and married two nights ago."

"Newlyweds and expecting already!" Ole exclaimed, a meaty fist pounding Gunnar on the back. "Well done, man! And it happened here!" he shouted to renewed cheers.

Feeling the need to protect her, Gunnar pulled Noreen's back against his chest and, hidden by the water, spread a hand over her womb.

"How d'we know she's the real princess? What about Coreen?"

Hedwig glared in the direction of the voice. "Noreen's the elder twin. Identicals were born, not five minutes apart, and the first one was marked," she called out. "My lady, if you'll forgive me?"

"Of course." Noreen smiled though Gunnar felt her tense slightly. She turned and put an arm around his neck then lifted a slender foot above the water.

Hedwig grasped her foot and lifted it to show a red mark, to the side of her big toe. It was shaped like a crown.

"Just as promised in The Profetia," Hedwig declared. "This be our right and proper heiress! As if Odin's visit wasn't enough to convince you. I saw each and every one of you cowering in the water when he spoke, but not our Princess and her Prince. Not them! She stood up to the gods for all of you. Not to mention Thor's Hammer's been shaking up the planet for the last few days. That hasn't happened since Bjorn married and the princesses were born."

Hedwig dropped Noreen's foot, then turned back to them and spoke quietly. "I was ladies' maid to your grandmother for many years and was at court when you were born. We'll be there again when you need us."

"Thank you. Nordia would not be the world it is without people like you."

The older woman's face creased in bashful smile as a pleased flush infused her face. Gunnar watched as Noreen gripped her hand and kissed it. Hedwig's eyes flew wide and she dropped in a quick curtsy in the water as she kissed Noreen's hand in return. Had Noreen not been holding her hand, he wouldn't have been surprised if Hedwig had bowed clear to the bottom of the pool.

Following his wife's lead, Gunnar gripped Hedwig's elbow and kissed the old woman's cheek. She nearly burst into tears. Ole was next with a bow and kiss for Noreen and Gunnar grabbed his hand in a firm shake.

"We've got your back," Wil's quiet voice was in his ear as the people began to surge forward to pay their respects.

Noreen held up her slender, pale hand, and it was as if the world froze. "Good people, we will gladly greet you all, but it is late, so we ask that we be allowed to greet the families with young children first. Those of you who will be in Ryadstholm in three weeks time please make way for those who will not. None of you are required to swear oaths of fealty. We merely wish to thank you, in advance, for your faith and support in the coming days. We know not what Odin has in store for our world, but for him to come out and speak so openly indicates the utmost urgency. Let us spend this night in celebration of the life we enjoy here."

She dropped her hand, and Gunnar watched in growing awe as the nobles who'd been rushing forward to claim their positions stepped back, and the couples with infant children were gently ushered forward.

Noreen held out her arms to the first young couple with an infant boy, and asked, "May I kiss your babe?"

With her mouth hanging open, the young mother nodded, and handed over her baby. Noreen took him with the gentlest of hands and gazed into his wide open eyes.

"And what is your name, brave young warrior?" she asked.

"He is Bjorn, for your father, Princess," the father said.

"Then Bjorn, we welcome you with open arms and pray you be a true and loyal friend to the young heir to follow in a few months time." Noreen carefully touched her nose to the nose of the infant then kissed his forehead. "May Odin's blessing be on you always."

The look on her face, as she cuddled the infant for a moment, melted Gunnar's heart and he could readily see their sons in her arms. He felt a suspicious dampness in his eye as the little sprite gripped his finger. "A strong one to be proud of," he said to the father and smiled at the mother.

Noreen handed back the baby as the parents curtsied and bowed, then stepped back for the next family. As she concentrated on the people approaching them, Gunnar noticed many of his convoy crew had formed themselves into an informal honor guard, while Ole and Hedwig sorted out the petitioners. Without looking organized, the flow was smoothly handled so he and Noreen were free to greet the people who wished to meet them. Babies and toddlers were cuddled, and anyone under the age of twelve had their foreheads kissed. Everyone else shook hands as they greeted their royal couple. And from the look on their faces as they turned away, each and every one felt as if a great honor had been bestowed on them, Noreen thanking each and every person for their loyalty and hard work that contributed to the success of Nordia.

What seemed like an hour later, Wil spoke quietly in his ear. "The king wants the two of you on your way post haste."

After Thor's dramatic pronouncement, it only made sense. "Can we get the personal transport out and ready to go?"

"The larger one is ready and fully stocked. I've got two drivers lined up for you so you can drive straight through. The larger luggage pieces have already been loaded."

He'd been hoping for the smaller transport vehicle, just large enough for the two of them, but the larger unit would be better. With a nod he accepted Wil's initiative. "Let us extricate ourselves from here and get dressed. We should be able to leave within the hour."

Ole came to his shoulder next. "If you two want to swim under the waterfall on the right, there's a passage leading to a lift up to your level. I'll send one of the girls to help the princess wash off the minerals and dress for the trip."

It was on the tip of his tongue to protest, but Wil's nudge let him know there were details he needed to see to while Noreen made ready. With reluctance, he nodded and Ole passed the message to Hedwig with a look and a sharp nod.

Noreen kissed the cheek of a blind and withered crone whose clouded eyes leaked with tears of joy. "Be well dear friend," she said to the older woman.

"Odin's and Freya's blessing on you, my Princess," the old woman responded and was led away by her daughter.

"Good people of Nordia," his wife's clear voice carried throughout the cavern. "It seems our distinguished visitor earlier stirred up the government and we are being called to the palace. Our short vacation here must be even shorter yet. We'll be in touch via the news broadcasts. Many thanks for letting us share our joy with you this evening."

To the cheers and whistles of the people, they turned and dove into the deeper waters of the pool behind them. Setting a leisurely pace, Noreen swam with the grace of a mermaid toward the waterfall indicated. Stopping for a brief moment to wave, they ducked through the curtain of water and into a secluded paradise. A ledge behind them formed steps up to a tunnel lined with a lighted rope.

Gunnar stopped on the lowest step and still stood chest deep in the water. Tugging on Noreen's hand he pulled her into his arms. Floating, and gently buffeted by the water, her body slid against his, all soft and smooth.

"Ten minutes," she said against his lips. "I just want to float here for ten minutes. Just the two of us."

"Five. A maid will be waiting to help you wash your hair and dress." His cock twitched as lust returned.

"I hate being recognized. No privacy and always on a schedule imposed by someone else." She pulled away and leaned back until she floated, her hair spreading out around her, half floating, half sinking in the water, a beautiful white nimbus-like cloud around her.

The curves of her body poking up through the water enticed him and he forgot about people waiting for them. Her breasts looked like soft hills rising above the surface. Water undulated across her stomach and into a small V at the top of her soft thighs. White, feminine thighs. Stroked by the warm water, he felt himself growing hard for her. With one hand under her, he traced the line where the water ended against her body.

"Tease," she softly scolded, her husky voice instantly solidifying his desire.

"Me a tease? How about you lying there, with those…things… pointing straight up at me?"

She giggled as he repeated Odin's complaint. "What *things* are you referring to, my lord?"

His finger traced the waterline around her breasts and he watched her nipples tighten into tempting peaks. Slowly, using only his fingertip, he trailed a spiral path up her breast. "I believe our god was referring to these." The groan issuing from her throat as he tortured her nipple was most satisfying.

Arching her back, she pushed her nipples closer to him. "Gunnar," she moaned.

"Hmm?"

"Just a quick one? I want to make love in the water. Who knows when we'll get the chance again?"

He couldn't very well argue when her hand traveled below the water and wrapped around him. *Dritt,* she had a way when it came to touching him. A stroke of her hand, a sigh against his lips, and a whisper in his ear, all had the effect of shooting every drop of his blood into his cock. With his own groan, he pulled her upright and then settled her body down on him, two puzzle pieces designed to fit perfectly. Trying to remember people waited on them, he took her fast and hard. Fingers digging into his shoulders, and heels into his buttocks, signaled her approval.

Letting her lean back in his arms, he watched the water tease her nipples while he pulled her tight against him. It seemed like only seconds before she convulsed around him, drawing his heated seed up from deep inside. Thrusting into her with a deep groan of satisfaction, he hoped the noise of the waterfall masked her cry. He pulled her up into his arms again and their lips had barely touched when a tentative call came down the tunnel.

"Prince Gunnar? Princess Noreen?"

"We're coming," Gunnar called, careful to bite back his impatience. Nory seemed to have a point about privacy.

Chapter 11

When it took an hour just to wash, dry, and braid her hair, Gunnar had to admit, maybe, she had another point about desiring a shorter, easier, style. He wasn't sold on the concept yet, he'd said, but he could admit she had a point.

Noreen counted it as a victory and shared a small wink with Tabitha who'd drawn the short straw to help her get ready. Little did Gunnar know, left to her own devices, Noreen would have braided it wet and coiled it in a tight bun against the back of her head. Once on the transport she would have taken it down and let it dry at its leisure. This worked better. Maybe he wouldn't be in such a rush to loosen her braid and she wouldn't end up spending half the morning brushing out the tangles.

Bundled deep into her outer gear, she dashed the half dozen meters from the resort entrance to the waiting transport. Resting high over tracks just like the ones on the smaller vehicle, this one was much longer and a little taller. Except for the blunt nose and the boxy driver's cab, it was rounded, almost like an inter-galaxy rocket tipped on its side. A short ladder had been dropped down for them to climb up into the body of the vehicle. While she stamped the snow off her boots, ground crews tossed the ladder up and slammed the door shut behind them.

"Oh man, oh man, oh man!" she exclaimed. "Isn't the heater turned on yet?"

She watched as Gunnar and the two men assigned to them exchanged glances.

"What would you like the temperature set at, m'lady?" the driver, identified as Leif, asked.

"Twenty-three degrees would be wonderful," she cooed in her most persuasive manner.

The three men choked. Leif and Nolan looked at Gunnar.

"Twenty-two?" she inquired, thinking she was being most accommodating.

"Nineteen," her husband said decisively. "I'll keep you warm," he promised with a grin.

"But...but...nineteen? Nineteen! That's a sleeping temperature. Can we compromise on twenty-one?"

"Nineteen *is* a compromise. We normally set it for fifteen or sixteen."

"*Fifteen?*" She didn't think her voice could squeak quite like that anymore. "It's amazing anyone will work for you at all."

She didn't think there was anything for the men to laugh about.

"Why? That's a good hot summer day around here. What do you consider too hot?"

"Thirty-seven is getting up there." She reluctantly lowered the hood on her parka, then pulled it back up as cold air bit her nose. "If you all will excuse me, I'll dig out something to keep me warm until the temperature is suitable."

She caught Gunnar rolling his eyes as she pushed past him toward the sleeping chamber at the back. On the way there, she passed through a lounge with a table for two across from a sofa. Next, kitchen counters lined both sides of the aisle and showed a sink, cooking surface, radiant oven and a tall cooler unit. Pausing to look, she noted it was full sized and well stocked. It even had a freezer compartment. Well done.

The tiny bathroom was at least fully enclosed, though not much larger than the unit on the other transport. Enclosed was acceptable. A folding door slid to the side to reveal a very acceptable bedroom, not too different from the last onboard one she'd had on the galaxy-cruiser. Though there was plenty of white—the sheets again—many other colors brightened up the room. A small desk to one side sported a vid-com port and a computer screen. Another screen filled the wall at the foot of the bed and she presumed it could be used for watching visual entertainment while cuddling in bed. Great idea, especially since the bed had a large and thick down feather comforter. Oh good, she'd sleep warm! Especially with Gunnar wrapped around her. The man put out the most amazing amount of body heat. A good thing in this climate.

Someone had thoughtfully unpacked one of her suitcases. Fortunately they'd chosen the one crammed with her warmest clothes, including a sleeping suit of the finest silk fleece she could find. In one piece, it fit loosely with soft stretchy ribbed fabric around the neck and wrists. There were mitts, of a sort, she could fold over her fingers to keep them warm, or fold them back if she needed to use her hands. She'd had feet with soft-grip treads sewn on, and had a hood she could cinch up around her head if needed, leaving only her eyes and nose poking out. The part that made her giggle the most, was the drop down flap in the back. She wouldn't have to undress to deal with business. Its melding of varying shades of bright red reminded her of the Kookorian sunset, and she pulled it from the closet, determined to slip into it right away.

But first the compartment needed warming up. She wasn't taking off her parka until the temperature reached twelve at least. That would be warm enough that she could quickly leap from her outer gear to the soft sleeper. Whether or not she kept on the hot turquoise-colored silk long underwear she currently wore was still up for debate. If he insisted on keeping the vehicle so cold, she'd keep it on. It wasn't like they'd have sex with the two other men on board anyway.

There had to be a temperature controller for this compartment somewhere. Every cruiser she'd ever booked passage on had controls in the First Class or, even better, Diplomat Class cabins. The captains had mildly complained about how much energy she used in heating her cabin, but her company at dinner and tales of her travels had helped soften the comments. It probably also didn't hurt that she usually carried a few cases of the best wines to be found anywhere and the most she'd ever had to bribe a captain with was a case and a half. But that had been a very long trip and every bottle of her Baudegeran red wine had been worth it. And the crews usually wore big smiles after spending a little time with Fiona and Sophia.

For a moment, she reminisced over those weeks on the cruisers. While the girls were out chatting up the officers, she'd dine with the captain or play cards in her stateroom with Hans. Dear Hans. He was mean player when it came to Sergrottian Strip Poker. He never let her win, and usually cheated without regret. They'd had some fun games.

The door to the bedroom opened and she looked up at Gunnar's face.

"There was an odd smile," he commented. "What were you thinking about?"

"Hmm? Oh, just remembering… never mind. It was nothing."

"Why are you still in your outer wear?"

"I was just looking for the temp adjuster in here. Where is it?"

"It's controlled at the main consol. You can't change it."

She wasn't so sure she liked his smile as he reached for the zipper on her parka. Hoping to stop him, she grabbed his hands. "Not until it warms up more."

"It's late. We'll climb into bed and get warm there."

"Sleep is a fabulous idea. Right after I change."

"I didn't say sleep."

She forgot to hold his hand and he tugged the zipper down.

"No!" She pushed his hand away as cool air whooshed into her coat. "I'm not undressing until it's warmer," she told him again.

"What's that?" He nodded at her fleece suit lying on the bed.

"My pajamas."

"Your what?"

She grinned when his brows nearly hit his hairline.

"My sleep suit," she repeated calmly. "Once it warms up in here, I'll change into that and wear it until we get close to Stravicsholm, and then I'll change into more proper clothing. Which reminds me, how long until we arrive there?"

"Um, oh, about thirty hours. We'll be about ten hours faster without the convoy." He shrugged out of his flannel shirt. Underneath he wore a silk shirt similar to hers but without the high collar.

"We really need to do something about your wardrobe," she commented. "The white has to go. Good thing the Kookorian textile merchants like me so well."

"We need to work on upping your metabolism, so you don't need sixteen layers of clothing." He pushed her parka off and tossed it out of the bedroom door. "Overalls next."

"Hey!" How'd he do that? She wrapped her arms across her chest to try and stop the shivers.

"The sooner you strip off the outer wear the sooner you get to leap into bed." He tossed back the covers then reached for the clasps. It only took a minute for him to release them, push them down to her hips, and then he grabbed her by the waist and lifted her onto the bed. Boots and pants were pulled off and tossed after her parka. "Hey Leif, do us a favor and hang those up, please. Good night."

Noreen scrambled under the covers, grabbing for her fleece suit while he pulled the door shut and secured it with a snap. Just as she wrapped her fingers around the sleeve of the pajamas he pulled them from her hand.

"No, no, no," he told her.

"But I'm cold!" She lunged for the pajamas again.

With an evil sounding laugh he tossed them to the floor then skimmed out of his pants. A heartbeat later he pulled off his shirt, slipped under the covers and pushed her onto her back.

"You won't be cold for long," he promised.

"But we have," she gasped as his cold nose touched her neck, "other people," she squealed as a cool hand slid up under her shirt, "out there!"

Come to think of it, she really liked a man who kept his word.

* * * *

She also liked a man who knew how to make the dull hours of travel more interesting. He particularly liked Sergrottian Strip Poker only he added his own twist. For each hand she lost, a new restraint was added. It wasn't long before he played her cards for her, dealing them out onto her stomach, and a new erotic torture was added.

"No, please, I need to sleep…Master," she moaned. His teeth tugged at her nipple again and she writhed as much as the cuffs holding her allowed. How many orgasms had she had? With the babies in mind he'd been very gentle, but still… quality and quantity combined until she was on the edge of consciousness. Her entire body vibrated. And still…

Gunnar smiled down at his wife as she slid into a trance, then sleep. She was a tough one. He hadn't known a woman could last that long. A glance at the clock said it was past dawn, or if they were near the equinox it would have been dawn. Tempted to wrap himself around her and sleep as well, he felt the need to at least review any new information that may have come through. Tucking the covers around her carefully, he dusted a kiss over her lips then pulled on a pair of pants and eased from the bedroom.

Leif was asleep on the sofa while Nolan guided the transport across the frozen plains.

"Any news?" he asked the young driver as he leaned into the cab.

Nolan nodded toward the computer display. "The gods really shook everyone up yesterday. The nobles are outraged the princess had been hidden from them. The scientists have just noticed a comet aimed right at the planet, the people want to know what else the government is hiding, and a retailer has announced a new line of mint products, including brandy, from Lidaria to arrive soon on a fleet headed our way. Oh, and the clothing merchants are raving about the new silk fleece for winter wear."

Gunnar cast a jaundiced eye at Nolan's droll tone. "Business as usual I see. Any specific word from the king?"

"I believe there are some encoded messages there for you."

"I need coffee first. What about you?"

"A cup would be great."

Gunnar made the hot beverages then settled into the passenger seat of the forward cab. Sipping from his steaming cup he began sorting out the messages.

Bjorn wanted to know why this Lidarian ass was so insistent about seeing Noreen. Her staff wasn't confessing anything yet. Good question, Gunnar wondered if she had indeed told him everything. They'd deal with it in Stravicsholm. It also appeared there was a fleet of starships, not cargo ships, headed their way. Mercenaries hired by the Lidarians to secure the princess? More questions to ask his wife. For a moment Gunnar mourned what appeared to be the loss of his quiet and routine-ordered life. Marrying the princess brought a whole new round of unanticipated complications with it. So much for the honeymoon.

Okay, Lidarian threat aside, what was this about a comet?

Leaning back in his seat, Gunnar held the warm coffee mug and tried to make sense of the particulars pointed out by the scientists. A comet was headed their way. A hunk of ice roughly the size of his convoy vehicles all lumped together could kill every man, woman, child and alien on the planet. The report was paralyzing. So far the information was restricted to the highest levels of the government. Presumably to avoid mass hysteria. Estimated impact date—six weeks out. There was no time to move the five million people inhabiting the planet, no guarantee they could get everyone off and no place to send them even if they could.

Where did the gods fit into all of this?

In the relative silence of the forward cab, Gunnar absorbed the familiar sounds of the transport as he tried to grapple with the enormity of the information. The crunch of snow under the smoothly rolling belted treads, the quiet whoosh of the heater circulating air warm enough he didn't need a shirt, the soft bleeps of the control panel monitoring everything from outside temperature to oil temperature and fuel reserves. Nolan had music quietly playing to keep him company over the long, silent, white miles. Hundreds of years away from Earth, and the echoes of twentieth century oldies still comforted Nordia.

And sleeping in the back was his Promised One, bearing his children. Why had the gods brought her back and almost certainly pushed the union if their world was on the eve of obliteration?

And what would the universe lose if Nordia were destroyed? A few million hardy souls? A lump of frozen rock? Would the Universe notice, or care? He'd care.

The rocks and even the ice of this planet were in his bones. The very minerals made his blood sing. The polar lights danced to his movements in the deepest part of the cold dark nights. Snow bears tracked him but held a respectful distance, seals rose up through their air holes to kiss him and sled dogs scampered after him when he strode through a village.

He held the economic lifelines in his hands and employed nearly one percent of the planet in hauling cargo in the exchange of minerals, metals, woolens and furs for off-world goods. Others bargained for them, but he moved them from place to place, and knew each roadway, each stop from city to the smallest village. From the highest noble to the simplest laborer, he carried the pulse of his people. Their goals, his goals, their cares also his. His commanders saw to it that those with sick children found extra food and blankets on their doorstep, like a gift from Freya. A disobedient son was given new purpose, with work to keep his hands busy and out of mischief. Willful daughters, straining at the bounds of village life, found themselves with opportunities to work for good families in the larger cities, or were drawn into trade. Many were encouraged to attend university and aid the various communities of researchers in their work.

Losing Nordia would leave a huge hole in the Universe. What plan did Odin have for saving his people?

"Sir?"

Gunnar shook off his moment of melancholy and glanced at the driver. "Hmm?"

Nolan held out a headset with mic to him. "The king."

He settled the headphones on his ear then spoke into the mic. "Sire?"

"Funny, Gunnar, real funny. I just noticed you checking your messages. Anything strike you as interesting?"

"The silk fleece, the Lidarian fleet or the comet?"

"Mint brandy aside, that Traxel-what's-his-face is claiming Noreen married him the night before she left Lidaria. He's not carrying shipments of brandy in those war-cruisers headed our way. He wants Noreen presented front and center to complete the marriage ceremony. Says it is merely a formality at this point as they've consummated the binding ritual already."

"Like Hell. I take it he wasn't pleased to hear Odin's little announcement last night then?" She was his. And would stay that way.

"He didn't hear it directly, only born and bred Nordians heard it. But the news people have been all over it and he heard about it that way." The king paused a moment and Gunnar let the silence settle. "What did Odin mean when he said she had those things pointing at him?"

Gunnar burst out laughing. "We were standing in the lower pool at the resort in a shaft of light."

"Oh."

Yup, the king got it.

"Okay then." A new energy filled the king's voice. "So, now the planet knows she's been in hiding, even though no one has been given the details about where she's been. Those savvy with computer research have managed to figure out most of the new imports finding their way to us over the past decade are the result of her travels. She's being lauded as the person who's most improved our economy and style of life since Erik the Economist."

"So they're able to convince themselves she was doing something noble for the planet, rather than running away from her duties?"

"Exactly. By the way…has she, did she…give you much… trouble?"

Laughter burst from him again. "Trouble? Sire, you raised yourself one strong-minded hellion. I'm exhausted trying to tame her. No, it won't be an overnight process, and with her new, pampered status as mother of the heir, it will take even longer. Still, she's sweet tempered, for the most part and, in all honesty, I'm not entirely sure your techniques are going to work with her. They may kill me first. Freya's heart, is she ever strong."

"Weak-minded women bore you, Gunnar," the king chuckled.

"True. Care to give me a heads-up on what we'll be walking into when we arrive?"

"Her mother and sisters are beside themselves preparing your chambers."

"And?"

"We'll try to sneak you into the palace as quietly as possible. You two are being hailed as holy people and the devout are gathering on the palace steps."

"In minus forty degree weather?"

"That never stopped a true Nordian."

"It would stop Noreen."

The king burst into a full laugh. "You have a point."

"Why is that exactly? Why does she crave the heat and sun so much?"

"I'm not sure. It was just the way she was wired, we figured. And then she took off, after your grandfather scared her."

"What happened there?"

Gunnar found himself nodding in sympathy by the end of the story. "I might have run too. He never told me I was on my way to get married."

"Well, at least she's home. Still, she did make a good ambassador when she couldn't hide the essence of her upbringing. You do realize she really is responsible for most of the trade agreements pouring in these past several years, right?"

"She negotiated them herself?" Why did that surprise him?

"Most of them. And on the planets where they don't talk to women, if the goods or technology were critical enough, I'd send Malcom Arildsen to do the negotiating with the details she and her retinue gathered. Quite the reconnaissance crew they were. They even managed to rat out the security details I had on her tail. Hans may look like he's all muscle, but he's remarkably street savvy as well. Sharp." The king made a noise of admiration, and Gunnar frowned against a small stab of envy.

"How does Coreen feel about being displaced as Crown Princess?"

"Thrilled. She's sick of being in the spotlight, and has been nagging her sister for years to return. The minute we have Odin's situation under control, I'm afraid she's going to take up where her sister left off. Well, she may stick around for the birth, but after that she's grabbing the nearest rocket across the galaxy." The king's deep sigh spoke volumes about his feelings for his headstrong daughters. "At least she'll concentrate more on practical items rather than the luxury items Noreen has been digging up to send our way."

Was Coreen really more practical? He wasn't so sure. "Has Odin spoken again? Given you more details?"

"He won't say a bloody word," the king growled. "He wants his Precious One here first. The priests are closeted with The Profetia and, even now, are trying to decipher the next lines. Looks like the clear weather should hold. You're making good time. Have your driver go to the usual spot, and we'll bring you in the back way."

Gunnar nodded. The king spoke of a warehouse that sat over a thermal tube, now used as a utility corridor. The underground maze of tunnels was vast but, if one knew where they were going, they could be used to get anywhere within the city without setting foot above ground.

"Thank you, sir."

"Thor's beard, man, you're my son now. I give you leave to call me Bjorn."

"Well, in private anyway. Let's see, our estimated arrival is," Gunnar looked over at Nolan, who pointed to a display on the control panel. "Look for us around the fourth hour."

"Even better, middle of the night. Safe journey to you."

"Aye, sir. Bjorn."

The king's chuckle could be heard before the communications went silent.

Chapter 12

Bundled in her parka, Noreen waited for the transport door to open.

"You don't need the parka," Gunnar said, exasperation clear on his face and in his voice.

"Easy for you to say. The last planet I was on had a mean temperature of thirty degrees, nicely modulated within two degrees either way, around the clock. It's nearly one hundred degrees the other direction out there." A deep shiver claimed her body and she pulled the hood down tighter.

Gunnar's sigh was nearly strong enough to blow the door open. "We're in a heated warehouse. You won't be out in the elements."

"And what is the warehouse temperature set to?"

"Seven degrees usually. Just for you, it is set to fourteen right now."

"Thanks, but still too cold for me. Just get me into the thermal tubes."

"Yes, Your Highness." His answer sounded a tad sarcastic to her, however, at Leif's signal, she watched as he pushed the outer door open. The ladder-like stairs unfolded next; he stepped down them and reached out a hand to help her.

While warmer than outside would have been, the cool air of the warehouse still bit her cheeks and nose. A man she recognized as one of her father's spies from a few years earlier, stood by what looked like a freight elevator door.

"Collin," she greeted him, extending a hand, "good to see you again and how is Marisa?"

Collin's grin split his face as he bent to kiss her hand. Why couldn't people just shake it? She quickly pulled it back into the sleeve of her parka.

"Marisa is just fine and says to let you know she'll be happy to talk babies with you anytime."

"Oh dear. How many in the past three years?" He'd left the detail watching over her because she'd spotted him and his wife was nearing term with their first child.

"Three, and one more on the way."

She shook her head. "Must be one set of twins there. Still, I can see we're going to have to start a new education program soon," she teased with a smile.

"Yes, Princess." He gestured to the elevator. "If you will? Your family is waiting. We'll have your luggage delivered as soon as possible."

"By all means, Collin, let us be on our way." She stepped into the lift with Gunnar at her side. "I presume you know the duke?"

"Yes, pleased to see you again, Prince Gunnar," Collin said with a short bow and sharp twinkle in his eye.

"I guess Gunnar is better with the title than Zaren, eh?" She laughed up at her husband. "Just what is your full name anyway?" The air warmed considerably as they went down, and she pushed back the hood and unzipped her parka.

"We don't have time for all that now," he responded. She wondered at the slight flush and the clearing of his throat. "Gunnar works."

"I still like Dukey better." She merely smirked at him when his hand tried to connect with her posterior. The long, thick parka provided protection from more than the cold.

The trip was made swiftly to the lowest level where a cart waited to smoothly convey them along the thermal tube on inflated rubber tires. So much quieter than the loud, clanking, metal tracks of the overland transports. It was also far warmer, and Noreen shrugged off the parka, setting it on the passenger seat next to Collin.

One thing was apparent from the moment they stepped from the lift. The thermal tube, left behind centuries ago after massive volcanic activity, was painted in bright and uplifting colors. When she'd left, all the underground passages had been in a natural state with only strings of lights or piping run along the ceilings and walls. In the more narrow tunnels the floor had been leveled as needed for easy passage. Now the walls had been smoothed and decorated.

"Wow," she softly exclaimed as they traveled along the tube covered with bright murals and swirling designs. "Who did all this?"

"Your remodeling of the palace thermal pools was so well received, your father set aside funds for the school children to beautify the tunnels.

One week a year, each fifth level class is given a section of tunnel to paint. A few budding artists have been discovered over the years, and the tunnels have been color coded to keep people from getting lost in them," Collin told her.

"Brilliant idea, Pappa," she said softly.

"No, brilliant idea, Princess Noreen," Gunnar replied.

She shrugged him off irritably. "I just took care of my personal spaces. He extended it."

"No one thought of it at all until you started the ball rolling," he pointed out.

With another shrug, she dropped the topic and amused herself by taking in the sights. Paintings of polar lights were in abundance, as were bears, seals, birds and many other wild and domesticated animals. Then there were panels of abstract blocks of color. Bright and cheerful colors that made her smile. Images of Odin and the gods followed images of the heroes and founding families of the original colony days. More landscapes, and then portraits telling the history of Nordia as they traveled from one tube to the next. Weaving all of them together, rows of colored stripes lined the floor with occasional stripes turning off down different tubes.

"Which one are we following?" she asked Collin.

"M'lady?"

"Which colored line are we following?"

"The gray one."

"Gray?" She squinted but didn't see it.

Collin removed his glasses and handed them over his shoulder to her. With a frown she held them up and clear as day, a light gray stripe ran down the center of the floor.

"Clever," she said and handed the glasses back. "When do I get my pair? And what do the colors mean?"

Gunnar answered. "Blue is generally East to West, red is North to South. Green will run you between the city center and outskirts, pink in the center directs people to public buildings such as the library or museum. Yellow is for the outer loops. The arrows point toward the center of the city. Purple indicates the air transport depot. The gray, which requires the glasses, leads us to the palace."

"And?"

"And... what?"

"When do I get my magic glasses?"

"You don't. They're for the security teams only. And since you won't be down here unescorted, ever, there's no need for you to have a pair."

She didn't care much for the level stare he directed into her eyes. His beautiful eyes, deep blue with the slightest flecks of silver, like glitter, or light hitting the angular ice crystals outside…

"Stop it!" She snapped her eyes shut and shook her head. "It doesn't work on me."

"It almost does," he muttered. "Why doesn't it work on you?"

"I don't know, maybe I'm impervious to your power of persuasion. Or maybe my powers are stronger, did you ever think of that?"

"Just what are your powers, by the way?"

"Good question. Other than the…" her mouth twisted around the words for Thor's hammer, "…noise…thingy, I'm not sure what I'm capable of." It wasn't generally something discussed in great detail. Everyone knew members of the nobility each had some sort of talent, or power. Those strongest in their talents were trained for leadership according to their skills and where they were needed most. Society was generally divided into four areas of career—Government, Business, Science and Medical, or the Church. Those with weaker talents were guided into supporting roles depending on what the exact talent was. Those with an ability to read minds were directed to the church whereas someone like Gunnar could be useful in both business and government, possibly as a liaison between both…

"You said you were responsible for security?" she asked, trying to remember their earlier conversation.

"In my role of transporter I'm able to pick up odds and ends of information. Gossip to most people, I tend to get wind of disturbances and can pass them on before they become trouble."

"People talk to you. Trust you."

"Yes."

"Because you compel them to?"

"Rarely. Mostly my charming personality just makes them want to talk to me," he laughed at her.

"Charming. Right. You really charmed me right off the bat."

"Sarcasm doesn't suit you." His censure was softened when he nuzzled her neck. What the man could do to her with just his lips and hands…and eyes…and…other body parts…the very thought made her sigh.

The cart turned into a narrower, darker tunnel, and she once again paid attention to their directions. "Are we getting closer?" The walls were painted a plain, pale yellow here, the lines on the floor fewer and fainter, almost as if the paint were fading, or, more likely, someone didn't want the tunnel to be obvious.

Soon, even the plain yellow paint faded and the lines disappeared, the floor underneath growing uneven.

"Yes, we're nearly under the palace now." Collin answered after they turned into a smaller tunnel, this one dark and unpainted. Another turn and he brought the cart to a halt. "From here we go on foot."

She grabbed up her parka but Gunnar took it from her with a small shake of his head. How he'd been able to get through the warehouse wearing only jeans and a lightweight wool sweater she'd never know. Even now, under her jeans and thick wool sweater, she wore another set of her silk underwear, complete with a warm turtleneck. This time she wore hot pink under a brilliant blue sweater, hand knitted with wool from Arquellian sheep, which was nearly as warm as the wool produced on Nordia. She felt very pale with her skin and hair returned to their native colors. One more thing to discuss with Odin, she decided.

Apparently her husband liked her jeans. As he guided her forward to follow Collin, his hand skimmed from her waist to her rear and patted lightly. A small noise of appreciation echoed in the tube as she followed the small light ahead of her. The smack echoed a little louder, when she let her hips sway just a tad wider than normal. Not that he'd spent much time walking behind her to know the difference. How much they had to learn about each other.

The tunnel continued to twist and turn, the path underfoot growing uneven with loose rock; the channel grew rougher and smaller. Several turns later, Collin stopped and turned off the light. In the complete dark, he knocked lightly on what had looked like a dead-end. The air pressure changed and, when Collin reached for her hand, she took it and extended one behind her to Gunnar. He squeezed her hand reassuringly and, a few steps later, they stopped. In the dark, she caught the whisper of a door shutting. Collin turned on his light again, glanced at her to make sure she was okay then, with a nod of approval, started off again. Two turns later, the process was repeated. Feeling hopelessly lost in the dark, she waited patiently as the process was repeated a third time. The third door shut and low lights came up in a cleaner tunnel.

"Just a few more steps, m'lady," Collin assured her with a grin.

She glanced back and saw the door had a danger sign on it, warning of active lava. Nice diversion. Gunnar just shook his head again and urged her forward with a pat.

Feeling warm from the tube and the exercise of walking, she slipped off the sweater as they walked. A sound like a strangled grunt came from behind. They turned into a larger tunnel and Gunnar moved to walk beside her. She glanced up to see his eyes staring at the bounce and sway of her breasts under the silk.

"You're not wearing a bra?" He leaned down to whisper in her ear.

"I'll put the sweater back on when we get above ground. They never keep the palace warm enough for me," she whispered back.

The tunnels became progressively cleaner, wider and brighter, the distance between turns shorter with short inclines. No bright murals here. Just smooth, pale yellow walls.

"Here we are." Collin at last stopped at an elevator door. Using his thumb, he was scanned for security access before a key pad popped out and he typed in a code. The door opened and they stepped on. Collin pushed a button for the top level. "Your father's study," he answered, at her look of inquiry.

"Handy escape route in case of coup attempt or alien invasion?" she asked.

"Exactly," Gunnar answered.

"Have many of those over the years have we?"

"You'd be surprised."

She turned to look at him and he shrugged.

"It's happened. Quietly, and not in the history books, but attempts have been made on the lives of the royal family. Nordia isn't without her radicals or mental cases."

"I see. I'd like to hear more about this later."

"Most assuredly you will."

She didn't have time to question further as the lift stopped and the door opened. Standing on the other side were many familiar faces. Arms outstretched, as if to hold everyone else back, King Bjorn of Nordia, was first in line to hug his daughter.

Looking at the mass of people gathered, Gunnar figured it would take nearly an hour for her to be properly welcomed home. He was somewhat gratified when someone took the parka from him, and he was included in the hugs and kisses from the queen, the concubines and all Noreen's sisters. Freya help him, all nine of them. Coreen's laughter warmed his ear and she told him just to ride out the storm. They had a few years to make up for.

"Okay, okay!" He heard Noreen call out with a laugh several minutes later. "I'm home now, apparently to stay, so I'm sure I'll have a chance to catch up with each one of you before long. It's the middle of the night for heaven's sake, and we have big business to see to, right?"

Gunnar liked the look of affection in her eyes as she turned back to her father.

"Yes, you star-hopping, galaxy-shopping, princess, we have serious business and Odin won't say a word to anyone, not even the priests." He watched as Bjorn wrapped an arm around his daughter and tweaked her nose.

The smile she bestowed on her father stole Gunnar's breath. Seeing them side by side, with Coreen inches away, the resemblance was staggering. The mutual affection was crystal clear as well. More than the other girls, the twins were the female replicas of their father. From the white blond hair to the exact shade of blue eyes, their features were more delicate, feminine models of the robust king.

As Bjorn positioned the twins side by side in front him, Gunnar moved to look over his shoulder. Nory had a few very faint laugh lines around her eyes but, other than their clothing, the two women were identical. Height, weight, body shape, coloring, and crooked smiles, they were perfect copies of each other. If they decided to 'twin' him, he was in trouble.

"If they dress alike, how do you tell them apart?" Gunnar murmured in the king's ear.

"Put a huge wedding ring on this one," he tweaked Nory's cheek, "and you won't have any trouble. But there's another way." He put his hand on the shoulders of the girls and made them turn around. Both women had their long hair braided and coiled, only Nory's was round and low on her neck. Coreen's was wound in a vertical oval. "Their maids have been trained to do their hair differently so we can all tell them apart from a distance. Up close, you can usually tell by how they talk. This one," he patted Nory's shoulder, "has a sharp tongue while her sister is much sweeter."

"Can't argue with that." Nory's laugh was husky soft when she turned around to kiss her father on the cheek.

"And since she's been living off-world, I'm guessing her wardrobe will be most unique as well," the king said as he looked his eldest daughter up and down and shook his head.

Gunnar glared at his wife, who shrugged. She hadn't put her sweater back on over the silk top.

"So, business first? Or a few hours of sleep?" Noreen asked.

"Breakfast in an hour. Your sisters have put some clothes in your room, and we dug up some fresh items for Gunnar as well," Queen Elke spoke up. Twining an arm through his and one around Nory's waist, Gunnar didn't resist when she started ushering them from the large study. "So freshen up from your trip. I'm sure you were horribly cramped in that transport and would love a decent bath."

Gunnar found they were skillfully escorted down the wide hall and into a wing where he knew the royal apartments were. The concubines were in another wing, and their daughters had rooms there and on the floor below.

"We've converted your rooms into a suite suitable for a married couple. I made sure most of your decorative touches were left as intact as possible. We moved some of your plants back up from the thermal pool where they've been tended during your absence," Elke cataloged the improvements as they walked. Coreen and the king followed, while the sisters dispersed. "You'll meet up with your staff when we return to Ryadstholm in a few days so, until then, we have a maid and a secretary for you." She barely paused in front of a double door, before it swung open and they continued through into a spacious sitting room.

Curious, Gunnar heard his wife sigh with contentment as he looked at the room filled with light and… vegetation. There was no other word for it. Pots were scattered everywhere. Large ones with trees, medium ones with flowering shrubs, smaller hanging ones with trailing vines and, scattered on nearly every flat surface, more potted greenery, many with spots of bright color. And not one white flower in the bunch, he noted. It smelled…fresh and cool, sweet and…wonderful. Like a summer day. Sun lights beamed down from tracks in the ceiling adding to the summer ambiance.

"Oh, Mamma," Nory breathed. "It's perfect." She turned to hug her mother and Gunnar saw a tiny glint of moisture at the corner of her eye.

Elke turned from her daughter and put a hand on his arm. "Gunnar, we have a study for you just across the hall. We figured you'd want a little more quiet than trying to conduct business in here."

Touched at the gesture, he smiled. "Thank you, Your—"

"You may call me either Elke or any variation of Moder you feel comfortable with."

He didn't resist when she cupped his face and pulled him down to kiss both his cheeks.

"Thank you. It will take a little getting used to." He gave her a small smile. A mother figure hadn't been a part of his life since he was sixteen. Bjorn had come closer as a father figure when Gunnar took over the duchy at age eighteen, after his own father's death. Family was a strange notion to him and now, it appeared, he had it in abundance.

"I know, Gunnar. It's all a little overwhelming, but we'll try to be gentle with you," the queen laughed, then looked around at the matching chuckles from Bjorn and Coreen.

"We'll leave you two to freshen up," Bjorn announced. "One hour."

"Yes, sir," Nory's voice was rich with laughter as she hugged her father and then sister.

A small woman shut the door to the hall then turned with a curtsy. "I'm Blanca, Sophia's sister, Ma'am, Sir. I'll be looking after you until you meet up with her again. Sir, your man, Lars, will be along later today. I hope I will be acceptable for both of you until then?"

"Oh thank the gods, a Nordian woman with a normal name. Thank you, Blanca," Nory replied for the both of them as he nodded. "We're happy to have you. We'll bathe first. If you could lay out whatever passes for every day fashion around here these days, in the dressing room…? Once we're out of the tub I'd appreciate your help with my hair."

"Yes, Your Highness," Blanca bobbed in another curtsy, and Gunnar found himself biting back a smile.

"Blanca," Nory said kindly. "We don't expect a curtsy every time you speak. Now, if you could find us a pot of tea to drink while dressing, it would be most welcome. Give us thirty minutes, and then we'll meet you in the dressing room, okay?"

"Yes, Ma'am," Blanca said, with another curtsy, then giggled with a small blush.

Noreen just smiled and turned toward a set of doors on the left of the sitting room. "This way, my dear husband."

Chapter 13

Throwing open the doors to her dressing room was an odd experience for Noreen. For the past ten years she'd had ample dressing rooms in the apartments and hotels she'd stayed in but, due to the transient nature of her lifestyle, she'd never seemed to fill one, despite the large amount of luggage she traveled with.

And now, to see it arranged to share with Gunnar... was just odd.

"I've heard my sisters all say, the day they truly realized they were married, was the day they had to share their dressing rooms with their husbands," she told Gunnar, as she glanced at the screen made of panels of silk strung on wooden frames bisecting the room. No matter it had more square meters than the transport they'd just come from, it seemed small and cramped.

"Is it such a big deal?"

"No, not really, but it was a truly personal retreat. In the palaces, no husband, besides my father, gets his own dressing room. Nor wife, other than my mother, I suppose."

Where there'd been a settee and a chaise before, now there were two settees, the second one placed on the far side of the screen with an additional three-fold mirror. Beyond, looked like male clothing.

"It looks like you get the left side," she said with a grand gesture. "I'm sure we can work out something better if you're not comfortable in here."

"Oh, this is fine for me."

"You're not thinking," she said as he pulled her close. "For formal functions at the very least, we'll have a maid and valet in here with us. Everyday will be easier to work around I suppose."

"Certainly. I don't take an hour just to wash and dry my hair."

"I told you I should have cut it." She kissed his chin and stepped back. "Speaking of which, we'd better jump in the tub unless we want just a quick shower."

"Does your hair need washing now?" he asked, following her into the bathroom.

"Oh!" she squealed in pleasure. "They even updated it!"

"It certainly is bright."

She looked over her shoulder to see Gunnar blinking.

"Isn't it wonderful?" She laughed at the look on his face as she unfastened her jeans and pushed off everything from the waist down. He'd get used to it. "Oh, feel that! They put in the radiant heat floor I found when I visited Earth. It feels so good under my feet!" The warm, golden-red, glazed tiles added to the sense of warmth. "I got to visit a region called New Mexico and they had the most wonderful bathroom in the home where I visited. They call this color adobe. And the tiles, see how beautifully colored they are? The people from that region worked the most beautiful art. So full of life and color."

Talking rapidly, she undressed and told Gunnar all about the place she'd stayed. Clothes were tossed to the corner and she started filling the large bath tub.

"You made it all the way back to Earth?"

She turned around at the awe in his voice. "Yeah, it was really cool." She laughed at the phrase.

"Cool?"

"It's a really old American way of saying fabulous, really neat, fantastic."

"Cool, huh? You didn't freeze there?"

"I was lucky enough to get there during summer in the northern hemisphere. I actually got to meet descendants of the Swedish Royal Family. Really distant cousins. You're probably related to them as well. I imagine most of the Nordians are. The Nordic countries are pretty in the summer with really long days, like here, but much warmer."

"Different orbits, right?"

"Right. Their orbit is closer to being circular around their sun where we do more of an oval and we're further away from our sun. I still liked the American southwest better. Much warmer. And the ocean near the equator, oh the ocean, Gunnar, warm enough to swim in and so clear!" She grasped his hands as he looked at her curiously.

"You mean like that bathtub about to overflow behind you?"

"Ooops!" She spun around and turned off the taps. "Ah, into the water now."

Gunnar put a foot in and immediately pulled it out. "Too hot."

"What?" She bent over to stick her hand in. "No, that's just perfect. About forty degrees."

"I'd say closer to forty-one or forty-two, but either way it is too hot for you and the babies."

She watched as he reached for the drain.

"What? Are you going to control my baths now?"

"I don't want our children boiled."

He pushed the plug back in and turned on the cold water tap.

She stood, stunned, then without a thought, whirled and stepped into the glass-enclosed shower. The door wasn't meant to slam shut. Really. However, the next thing she knew it slammed open, swinging back in a wide arc. The handle hit the glass wall and looking down she saw blood mixing in with the water running down the drain.

"Odin!" she heard Gunnar cry out. "*Dritt!* Don't move, Nory, not one muscle."

"What?" A wave of faintness made her sway and she braced a hand against the tile wall.

"The twin-speak thing...can you call to Coreen? For help?"

She closed her eyes and thought of her sister, then opened her eyes to show the pile of glass at her feet. And the thin stream of blood mixing with the water from the shower head. Why were they limited to images and emotions? It would be so much easier if they could use words too.

"It's safety glass, Nory," Gunnar said calmly. "You're a little cut, but nothing major."

Closing her eyes again, she concentrated on Cory. Something pushed at her brain but she wouldn't let it in.

"Nory, can you turn off the water?"

Gunnar's voice was right next to her. How did he get there? He was naked too. Looking down still, she opened her eyes. Smart man, he'd thrown down a thick towel. Very smart. The message pushed into her brain, a vision of people running. *Doctor?*

"*Yes, a doctor too, Nory.*"

"*Cory?*"

"*Yes, love.*"

"*I can hear you!*"

"*I think you broke whatever barrier was holding back the words.*" Cory's dry tone arrived in Noreen's mind a moment before Cory herself entered the bathroom.

"Have a little temper tantrum did we?"

"Funny, Cory." Gunnar didn't sound at all amused to her.

A towel wrapped around her, and then Gunnar's strong arms lifted her.

"Here, Gunnar, walk on these towels next."

Noreen rested her head against Gunnar's shoulder. Cory's voice had an edge of worry to it.

"Set her on the counter, I think it's far enough away from the glass."

"Can you get her a robe?"

Why did his voice shake?

"I'll get you one too." There, a hint of amusement in Cory's voice. Things couldn't be that bad. "Ah, Doctor, so glad you could join our little party."

"Looks like someone had a good time," a dry old voice wheezed.

Gunnar barely got the robe around Nory before she slumped in his arms. "Doctor?"

"Not bad, not bad at all." The old man opened a case. "A few damp cloths to wash away the worst of it would help."

Gunnar watched as Coreen shoved one into the doctor's claw-like hand.

"Thank you. Now we'll just pull out the magic wand and seal up these little cuts. There, that was the messy one. At least it was safety glass. Otherwise that one would have been a severed artery."

Gunnar didn't find the doctor's running commentary particularly comforting. Why had Nory slammed the shower door? Why had she stepped into the shower in the first place?

A warm robe settled around his shoulders.

"Here, put this on," Cory said quietly, as voices were heard coming through the dressing room.

"Thanks." Letting Nory rest against his chest, Coreen helped him slip the robe on. Great, now all his in-laws would see them naked.

The doctor sealed a long cut on Nory's hip, as her parents burst through the door, followed closely by the maid.

"Whoa!" Coreen held up her hands. "Slow down folks, we've got glass all over the place here. Blanca? Would you ring for a crew to come clean up? Thank you. Pappa, she's fine. Just a few cuts."

"Why is she passed out?" The king demanded.

"She may like red, but she doesn't like blood, remember?"

"Gunnar? What happened?" The king's temper was restrained, even as he tried to sound reasonable.

"We were discussing water temperature, I told her the bath water was too hot, then next thing I knew she slammed the shower door shut, it bounced back around and then she was surrounded by broken glass." Gunnar shrugged when everyone looked at him like he was mad. "I don't know what set her off, but she was…upset."

"Exactly, what did you say to her?" Coreen asked him.

"Um, I think I told her I didn't want the babies boiling and she needed to cool down the bath water a few degrees." He looked at the doctor who now regarded him with inscrutable eyes. "Can the babies be hurt by water that's too hot?"

"How far along is she?"

"Three, four days? I don't know for sure. Night before last all Odin said was she was carrying more than one. He didn't specify the number."

"You're sure they're yours?" The doctor sealed another small wound.

"She was whole when I took her. I'm her one and only."

The doctor nodded. "It is highly unusual to determine pregnancy so early, but let's get her to bed and I'll see what I can do to verify it for everyone's peace of mind. There, I believe I got all the cuts, certainly the worst ones. Lift her gently."

Gunnar saw Coreen give a hand signal and everyone cleared the doorway. Cradling Noreen in his arms, he carried her through another door and into her bedroom. He didn't stop to take it in, but a riot of colors and plants assaulted his senses. One thing was very clear, she didn't like clean and simple lines or muted colors.

He did note that the bed was a large four-poster model. It looked close to eight hundred years, or more, old. Later, he promised himself, later he would admire the intricate, hand-carved details. For the moment he set her down on the mattress, a riotous rainbow of colored linens covering it. Coreen brushed back a large leafy branch trying to reach out to Nory.

"Back, you beast," Coreen told the plant. "She'll say 'hello' to you later."

Momentarily stunned by the now pouting plant, Gunnar didn't object when the doctor gently pushed him aside. How the hell did a plant pout?

"Her husband may stay, but we'd like some privacy for the exam, if you all don't mind."

"Of course, Doctor," Elke demurred and took Bjorn's arm. "We'll be in the sitting room."

Gunnar watched while the doctor used a scanning device to verify Nory's physical health. It was strangely comforting as the noises he muttered sounded positive, the word 'good' mixed often with 'excellent'.

"Now for the physical part of the exam. There's no help for it, as good as the scanner is, there's no replacing the human touch," the doctor explained as he pulled Nory's robe open.

"What?"

"My dear prince, older than recorded history itself, long before man realized the stars didn't spin around the planet but the other way around, the best way to determine a pregnancy has been by physically examining the patient."

The old man's hands worked quickly making brisk circles around Nory's breasts.

"No lumps," he explained, and Gunnar nodded. Lumps were bad. He got that part.

"Now for the pelvic exam. This is much easier to do in the exam room, but if you will hold her legs apart and back, I think we can manage."

Gunnar numbly did as the doctor instructed. Women went through this for their physicals? He flinched with her as she stirred at the feeling of the doctor probing her from inside and out.

"Yes, the uterus is quickening. Very early in the process, but I concur that she is carrying."

Gunnar was relieved to lower her legs and cover her while the doctor pulled off his exam gloves.

"As to your earlier question about how hot of a bath is too hot, I'm not sure there's a good answer. Certainly the extreme heat of mineral water fresh from the spring is too hot. Anything that raises her blood pressure or pulse, again, I would consider too hot. A temperature that makes her turn bright red should be avoided, but a flush of pink should cause no harm. Does that help any?"

"I was hoping for an actual number," Gunnar grumbled.

"Forty degrees is just fine."

Both men turned to look at the source of the comment, a tired sounding voice from the bed.

"*Älskling.*" Gunnar couldn't help the relief sweeping through him. He sat on the side of the bed and gripped her hand. "How do you feel?"

"Silly. What am I doing in bed?"

"You passed out." He watched her face pale.

"I didn't dream about the shower shattering?"

"No, love, you didn't. All your cuts have been healed and the doctor has confirmed your pregnancy."

"Thank you, Doctor."

"I suggest you remain in bed until tomorrow morning. Let those embryos settle in good. No stress, eat some fresh, healthy food, plenty of fluids and no vigorous exercise or saunas. I'll send a note to the cook about an appropriate diet for you. And keep your bath water at thirty-nine degrees."

Gunnar found her pale blush quite endearing, though her eyes hardened at the order for the temperature. He'd make sure there was a thermometer in the bathroom, as soon as he could arrange it.

"Yes, Doctor. Will you pass the word to my father?"

"He's waiting in the sitting room. I'm sure I won't be able to keep him from coming in."

"Thank you, Doctor," she said again.

"Welcome home, Princess Noreen. We've missed you."

The old doctor gave her a wink and patted her shoulder before leaving the room. Gunnar felt a whoosh of air as the tree bent over his wife again. Large soft leaves with ruffled edges waved directly over Nory's head.

"Bertrand!" she exclaimed and reached up to stroke the plant. "You're looking very healthy there, young man!"

"Bertrand? You name your plants?"

"Bertrand is not just any plant, he's a Hundpflanze from Betelgeuse IX. He was one of my first tree pets. Isn't he a beauty? And he's grown so much!"

Only the entrance of Nory's family stopped him from voicing his true opinion. The plant would be moving before nightfall. Preferably out to the sitting room or back to the palace pool rooms. In deference to the queen, Gunnar stood and let her perch next to her daughter while the king pounded him on the back. Coreen smirked from the other side of the bed.

Rubbing his hands together, the king spoke. "That has to be a record in conception speed. Well done, you two. Guess we'd better move up the wedding date, eh?"

"Wedding?" Nory squeaked from her pillows. "Tell me we don't have to do the whole state wedding thing, Fader."

"Of course you do," her mother said gently. "You're the future queen, your people have a right to participate in your wedding."

"Moder!"

"No. You will not wiggle out of this. They were cheated out of your majority ceremony, the wedding is non-negotiable."

"*Mamma.*"

Gunnar couldn't believe his ears. His wife was whining at her mother.

"We were thinking of doing it on the Solstice, but we can pull it together faster than that. The nobility will be gathered in Ryadstholm anyway…" The queen had a far away look in her eyes, as she stared at her horrified daughter. "Let's do it two days prior to the Solstice. Everyone should be able to gather by then and it will be taken care of when Odin's appointment comes up. Yes, that will work."

Gunnar watched as Elke, the very quiet queen he'd barely noticed before, patted his wife's hand and took control of the wedding.

"Time is short so you can wear my gown, but we'll save alterations until just before. Don't know how much you'll expand by then. Good thing you're essentially my height. Well then, I guess I have my marching orders. Don't worry about a thing, *älskling*. I'll have Blanca pull the dress out of storage and get it cleaned. Tomorrow or the next day you can try it on. Well, you need to rest. Doctor's orders."

"Is my bathroom cleaned up? I never got my bath."

"Blanca will let you know when it is ready. We want to make sure every sliver of glass is picked up," Elke said as she stood.

"Oh, Your Maj… Uh, Elke," Gunnar couldn't believe he stuttered. "How would I go about getting a water thermometer?" He ignored his wife's gasp.

"We'll have one sent up this morning."

With a kind smile she pulled him down and kissed his cheek.

"Thank you," he murmured.

"Rest well, sweetling," the queen called out in a sing-song voice, sweeping her husband out of the room with her.

"Cory," Noreen called after her sister. "Don't let them do this to me!"

Coreen came back to sit on the far side of the bed. "Too late. Moder will not let you escape this one and I won't stand in for you anymore. I'm now officially retired. When you're rested, you can tell me how to be a good ambassador. Other than that, we don't have much to discuss."

"No! This isn't the way it is supposed to be. You're the better politician," Noreen insisted.

"Which is why it is time for me to planet hop. The position of Crown Princess is little more than being a pretty smiling face. You can do that with your eyes closed." Cory leaned over and lightly patted her sister's cheek. "And no mentally pelting me today. You need to get your rest."

"Oh, so I'm to be a breeding puppet, right?" Gunnar watched as Nory leaned back against her pillows with her arms folded. "Great. Bloody fantastic life. Thank you so much."

"Hey, it's your life by birth. You've managed to pawn it off on me for ten and a half years. It was fun for a while, but I want something different now. I want to be chased and wooed by foreign princes. I want to swim in warm waters, under full moons, and sip fermented juices."

Gunnar noticed Cory's wink didn't go over well at all with her sister.

"Has nothing I've done meant anything?"

Gunnar reached for Nory's hand and she batted him away before rolling over on her side.

"Oh, Nory." Cory tried to touch her sister's shoulder, but grimaced and placed a hand to her head. "Don't do that!"

"Just go away. I want to be left alone," the muffled reply came from deep under the comforter.

"Noreen, this is no way to behave." Gunnar sat down beside her again.

"You go away too. I don't want to see either of you. Just leave me alone!"

He glanced at Coreen, who merely shrugged then grimaced again.

"I'm leaving," she sighed heavily. "And no, you made the assumption Fader was dying all on your own. I never lied to you. You were the one in danger and now you're safe. Welcome home, dear sister."

Chapter 14

Numb, Noreen felt nothing. Numb. Her work meant nothing. The trade agreements, the new goods pouring in, the increased exports, and the latest technologies. It all came to nothing. She was home to breed and smile. For the rest of her meaningless life. Her sister had lied to her to get her home, she was in more danger here, and now she was stuck.

Her last contribution to Nordia's market? Waxing products. How glamorous. At least she'd placed that order while in transit between the grotta and here. Her last contribution to modernizing her backward world. Body waxing. How poetic.

She felt like a bad-tempered child as the tears began to leak out, but she couldn't help it. Her life was reduced to producing children and overseeing boring state functions.

The bed shifted and she cried even harder. Why wouldn't he just leave her alone? She hadn't been alone since she met him. Even her staff left her alone when she asked them to.

He tried to lay down behind her, but there wasn't room, she was too close to the edge of the bed.

"Scoot over, Nory."

"G'way."

"I'm not leaving you, now move over."

"No!"

She felt his sigh against her back a moment before the bed shifted again. Burrowing deeper in the bed, she hoped he finally got the idea he wasn't wanted and left. Thinking she was alone, she tried to quiet her sobs.

Several minutes later the covers were thrown back and she found herself on her face in the middle of the bed.

"Leave me alone!" she yelled at him.

"You need to stay calm, *älskling*," he said.

His maddening tranquility didn't do anything to help her stop crying and she beat the bed with her fist. Why wouldn't anyone listen to her anymore?

The bed bounced again and he grabbed her wrists.

"No!" she shouted. "No," she sobbed. "Please, don't tie me up, please, Gunnar, please don't tie me up!"

"Sorry, my love. You need to calm down. This way you won't hurt yourself."

"No," she sobbed into the bed as he put the cuffs around her wrists. He stretched them out and she heard the distinctive snap of the cuffs being attached to restraining chains.

"Nory, you need to relax. This isn't good for either you or the babies." He spoke softly in her ear, his body warm over the top of hers.

"Gunnar, please, I'll rest, I promise, please, take off the cuffs. This isn't the time for sex."

"This isn't about sex, Nory. This is about learning to trust. Learning to love me and to trust in my love for you. Learning to trust me to take care of you."

"Gunnar, please," she whispered as he kissed her neck.

"No. Not right now."

She felt him push down on the bed, leveraging himself up until he straddled her thighs. Slowly, he began to stroke her skin, pushing the robe up around her shoulders.

"Just relax, Nory. All I'm going to do is give you a massage. Go to sleep if you can."

"Please Gunnar," she begged. "Leave me alone for a while. I'll rest, I promise."

"I'm going to take care of you, *älskling*, just relax."

"Why? Why do you cuff me like this?"

"So you don't clap your hands again," he chuckled. "Thor has rocked my bones enough, I don't need you calling on him to do it any more."

"Oh."

Gunnar's big warm hands stroked her back, gently at first, then eased slowly into deeper massaging motions.

"We forgot to take your robe off," he murmured.

He'd taken his off. The weight of him settled between her legs, resting in the valley where her thighs came together, held together by his legs. It wasn't hard to tell he was enjoying this.

"Since when do you let a little thing like my clothing bother you?" she muttered and was rewarded with his chuckle.

"I can't rip all your clothes. I have a feeling your clothing budget is outrageous enough without me destroying everything you put on."

"Funny. I'll have you know, most of my wardrobe was free, or practically so," she murmured. He really did know how to give a good back rub.

"Why is that?"

"Merchant samples. They wanted orders from Nordia and, if I found their clothes easy to wear and care for, then I felt better about helping them find retailers to sell their goods."

"Do they really do that?"

"Sure," she sighed as he rubbed her lower back. "In truth, I would pick up a few formal items on each planet. I always had some jeans, but mostly I wore not much more than a simple body cloth. A sarong, they're called on some planets. I have several of those." She smiled for a moment, then it faded. Like she'd ever get to wear them here. A tear leaked from her eye again.

Trapped. In more ways than one. Monarch. Wife. Mother. All titles she never wanted.

"What's wrong?"

His question was softly asked. Concern laced his voice.

"I might as well be dead. My life is over."

Gunnar stopped rubbing her back. Pain lanced through him with terrifying swiftness at the flat tone of her voice. It took all his will power to continue the massage.

"Why do you say that?" *Dritt*, it was hard keeping his voice calm.

"Because," she yawned, her voice fading to a mumble. "I'm trapped on this planet. I'll never see a warm sun or feel a hot breeze on my skin again. If I put my toes in the ocean they'll freeze off. My decisions are no longer my own and will affect more than just me and my small staff. I have not only you to answer to but my father, the government, the people, and now babies to worry about too. Every minute of my days, and nights, will now be ruled by what other people want from me. At night you'll want to make love and talk about your day when we don't have official functions. During the day I'll have to juggle official commitments, the children, the household, and staff. Not one moment of my day will be just for me. Never again can I look around and say 'I'm bored with this planet. Let's try that one.' I'm stuck. I have no purpose other than to smile at the people and make heirs. Ta da."

"When you put it like that it sounds damn depressing."

"How would you put it?"

"Well, the obvious one I think of, you'll have me to watch out for you. Like now. Aren't I doing something for you? I'm listening to you talk about your worries and cares. And the babies. You'll have the opportunity to raise fine young people. Teach them the wonders of the Universe and expand their horizons. Teach them everything you've learned and guide them as they grow into the people they're meant to be. Kisses and hugs any time you want them. Cuddles and giggles, bedtime stories and watching them grow. That's pretty important work right there. You can't make a much better contribution to any world."

Tempting as it was to spank her when she shrugged despondently, he knew it wouldn't help her attitude any. "Then there's all the knowledge you bring back to Nordia. You've forged commercial and diplomatic links far beyond our galaxy. You can continue to nurture those and keep improving the lifestyle of the planet. All your travels won't be wasted. You have stories and experiences to share. You also bring back new ideas to update our government and keep it from stagnating any further. There are plenty of things you can do to shake this planet up. Mold it into a better place to be. Make it attractive to off-worlders."

"But nobody wants tourists here. You said it yourself," she yawned, her words nearly unintelligible.

"Maybe I was wrong." He bent forward to whisper in her ear. There that made her smile just a little.

"You? Wrong? Can't be," she mumbled.

"Even I have my moments, *älskling*."

He continued to rub and stroke her skin until she drifted off to sleep. Even the damn plant seemed calmer as it hovered over Noreen, one slim frond gently stroking her hair.

Wanting to be close, Gunnar released the cuffs from the ropes, removed her robe, and carefully shifted her into his arms. With a soft sigh, she melted against him, and they slept.

* * * *

Noreen stirred and stretched. It was a relief to roll out of bed. How many days had she spent prone since arriving on the planet? Too many. Who was the doctor to tell her to rest? She glanced over her shoulder to see Gunnar, sound asleep and… wrapped around her?

Hey… She looked at her hand. It looked solid enough. What was going on here?

"Princess Noreen, All Wise and Munificent," a deep voice intoned, *"Gracious Heir of Nordia, Savior of the ByalbOgBeLun, Light of the World, Lady of the Lord of Light, Mother of the New Gods, Founder of Peace and Joy, Bringer of Prosperity and—"*

"Whoa!! Hold it right there, buster. Who are you?" She threw her thoughts out to the void where the voice emanated.

"I am Odin."

The voice was familiar enough, she'd heard it all her life, but there'd never been a face to go with it. Neither had she ever had an out-of-body experience like this before.

"Sure you are. Now, really, who are you?" She folded her arms and stated her demand.

The loud sigh didn't faze her one bit. She could sigh better than that.

"Come to the thermal pool beneath the palace and all will be revealed to you."

"Now? In this form? Or awake and in my own body?"

"Which ever suits you best. If you leave your body there, your husband is less likely to wake and worry."

"Good point. Now, can I do this the easy way?" She pictured the pool room as she remembered it.

"Why must you fly before you crawl?"

The grumpy tone brought her up short.

"Excuse me?" She blinked and found herself in a cavern that felt vaguely familiar. "Did I do that or did you? Hey, is this the thermal pool?"

"It is and it isn't. And no, we did it."

She turned to look behind her. Ethereal beings, a transparent glowing white, stood in a semi-circle.

"Explain," she ordered.

"Princess, this is going to take a long time as it is. Suffice to say, this is your world, and yet, it is not. We coexist in the same space, but in different planes. You do understand the concept, right?"

She wrinkled her nose at the droll tone.

"Fine, you understand the concept. Because you chose to leave the planet for so long, there is little time to prepare. You know the history of this planet from your point of view. Let us show you the history from our point of view. Might as well get comfortable."

She found herself reclining as images began to flow like a rapid visual through her mind, complete with narration. It started with a planet-side view of a deep space probe landing on the surface.

"Twelve hundred years ago, in our method of counting time, six hundred years in yours, the first of your people arrived on this planet."

"Right, it took seventy-five years to research the planet for suitability and twenty-five to gather the colonists from the northern lands of Earth and travel here." In the passing visual, she witnessed the arrival of the first colony transport rockets. Images of humans building and making homes for themselves rolled along in rapid succession. The first structures had been fabricated on Earth to be reassembled upon arrival. Later, native stones quarried from the mineral mines were recycled into buildings. Before her eyes, the Ryadstholm Palace was built directly over a major thermal vent, just as the Stravicsholm Palace was later built over this thermal vent.

"Correct," the voice continued. "When your people arrived, we watched from our plane, never contacting your people, content to watch as you settled the surface. As beings who live deep in the planet, it mattered not to us that you brought animals, plants and technology. For five hundred of your years, your people have treated the planet with respect and made the upper reaches your home with only superficial invasion of the lower caverns. While we prefer the heat deep within, your people thrive in the colder temperatures near the surface."

Noreen shivered at the mention of temperature.

"Yes, we know, you prefer the warmer places."

She rolled her eyes. "Go on."

"The only reason you are comfortable here is because your physical body remained behind. The temperature here is far beyond what even you can tolerate," the deep male voice said.

"Yeah, so, go on," she repeated and gestured for them to continue.

"Yes, Your Highness."

Noreen raised her eyebrow at the tone bordering on sarcasm.

"I presume you have a purpose behind this history lesson? Let's get to the bottom line here."

"The bottom line?" The visual ceased. "Very well. On the day you call the Winter Solstice, you will marry. At the moment your vows are completed the alien fleet hovering above the planet will open fire and attempt to destroy you and the ruling class, all of whom must gather for the wedding."

"Well. Okay. Why and what do we do about it? And my mother has decided the wedding will be two days before Solstice."

"You'll need to change that. On the day your first explorers set foot on this planet, a vision came to us. For twelve hundred years we have worked toward this day. Every calculation has been run and rerun a thousand times. Each fact studied in depth, models run over and over again. When we were sure of it, we contacted the ruler of your people. We have worked together ever since. Only the ruler, the heir and the holy man are aware of us as we truly are."

"My father, myself and the scary old bishop." Is this why he cornered her in the grove that day? To clue her in to this future? He'd done a lousy job of it.

"Yes. But you've always been aware of us, just not this...boldly—is that the proper word?"

"The word will do. So, why?" She felt like a four-year-old answering each explanation with the same one word question. Why? To them, she probably had the mental age and comprehension of a toddler. How humbling.

"Because of the very precise timing required, it is not open to the debate of general government. There is no doubt, the firepower of the invading fleet is needed to save both of our worlds."

"Come again?" Save their worlds? What was that about?

"We need your disappointed suitor to apply concentrated fire power on the spot where your wedding will be held."

"Why?"

"To move the planet out of the comet's path."

"Ah. The comet. I take it someone else knows about this." Like Fader and Cory perhaps? Certainly the bishop, but Gunnar? "Okay. So, we draw his fire...and...? Then what?" Using her best powers of concentration, she focused on the gods.

"This is where your destiny will come to fruition. You've already conceived the leaders of the generation who will rule the planet in place of the deities your people have worshiped for eons."

"Aha! I knew it. You're not really Odin. You're not really the pantheon of gods from old Earth. You would have followed me across the galaxy and all along my travels otherwise." A sense of smug satisfaction filled her.

"Correct."

"So you are beings who share this planet, but on a different plane or dimension, we're meeting in your version of our palace thermal pool and you've been guiding us for five hundred years."

"Nice of you to boil it down to simple facts."

"I'm a simple kind of *flicka*. Okay, so, what is my role in all this? Why is Gunnar 'The One' for me? Did you write The Profetia?" And was it all going to go to Hell in smithereens in just a few weeks? Why hadn't they started evacuating the planet years ago?

"She isn't as slow as you assumed." The female voice Noreen had thought of as Freya, sounded amused.

"I'm not as dimwitted as many people think I am. So, please, give me the basics."

"Here's the bottom line, as you call it. Partly because of the economics involved, your leaders chose to work toward this goal rather than abandon the planet. We cannot leave at all, therefore your ancestors chose to align their fate with us. You and your mate are the two strongest powers of your generation, the product of hundreds of years of careful genetic mapping. Your children are even stronger yet. We apologize for the multiple fetuses, but you gave us no choice. Had you remained on the planet and married at the prescribed time, they would have been spaced out appropriately. The number is critical, therefore you carry the full complement at once. However, had you not left the planet, we could not have ensured the spaceships required to apply the firepower needed."

"That sounds ominous. Okay, so, how many children do I carry? And I get to have all my children at once? One pregnancy and I get my body back? By the way, unless you have something up your sleeve, I will still be carrying at the date you've mentioned."

"The gestational period of your children has been slightly enhanced so they will be the equivalent of thirteen week embryos at the time of your wedding. After that, their growth will resume a normal pace to be born on or about what you call the Summer Solstice. They are powerful within you, also more manageable than if they were toddlers. You are the mechanism to focus the power they, and all your people, carry."

"Okay, here is where you need to go into more detail." Noreen leaned forward and her invisible chair tilted accordingly until her feet rested on the ground again. She pulled her toweling robe closed around her body, though in truth, it probably meant nothing to them that she was nearly naked.

"For now, we will give you a task list." The voice of Freya picked up the instruction. "Arrange the ceremony for midday on the Solstice, the time when the planet will be furthest from the sun. Your scientists will confirm the calculations in the next week, or is it two? I always confuse our two time-keeping systems. In any case, the exact position of where the attack will need to be aimed will also be confirmed. This is where the wedding will be held."

Noreen smiled for a moment at the being speaking. So they had females who played ditzy too? "Thanks, I think. I'm guessing you already know the location? And what purpose does that serve?"

"You will draw in and focus the power of your people to form a shield. The fire from the warships will meet this shield and push the planet into a new orbit. An orbit out of the path of the comet."

"Ah. And how will I draw in and focus this power?"

"You will know when you need to know. You are well suited to the job."

"I'll take it on faith. So where is ground zero?"

"Ground zero?"

"The location of the wedding."

"The place you call the Summer Palace."

"Because it is on the equator?"

"Yes."

"And that part of the planet will be facing the sun? Or on the side furthest from it?"

There was a pause and she watched while the milky white shadows vibrated, a strange melody coming from them. Was this their language? Beautiful. It sounded much like music composed by Nordian musicians…

"It will be furthest from the sun," the voice of Odin spoke.

"Then it will not be midday at the Summer Palace. It will be mid*night*."

A dissonant tone indicated the ensuing discussion was not harmonious as it had been before.

"Is there a problem?" she asked calmly. Silence fell and she felt compelled to press onward. "What I want to know is...will you be trying to push the planet closer to the sun, or further away from it?"

Chapter 15

"Look," Noreen stood and spoke to the *ByalbOgBeLun,* "Obviously not all the questions have been answered here. If I have a choice in the matter, I would prefer the planet be nudged a little closer to the sun and into a less extreme orbit. Is it possible to make that choice?"

The melodic buzz started up again, a little less dissonant than before. It was haunting, beautiful, and all too familiar. Had the sound of their conversations been the background noise of her childhood?

"Well, while you all work it out, I'm going back to bed before Gunnar wakes up and tries to talk to me. All I need is for him to think I've fallen into a coma."

The entity floating towards her spoke with the voice of Freya. "Of course. While they sort it out, let me give you a crash course in one small part of your powers. Do not be frightened, I will not hurt you or your children."

A feeling of warmth and love melded with the ethereal form that was Noreen. Without words, only beautiful music like the wind pipes of Yannininipaloka, Noreen understood how to focus her energy and think her essence directly back into her body. While her body slept on, the music sang in her head and the history lesson continued.

Somewhere deep in the bowels of the planet, she was shown a glimpse of a chart of not only her family, but Gunnar's as well, laid out with the exact pairings made to strengthen the talents and powers each carried. Each mate predetermined to draw from the best of each family on the planet.

Gunnar's family leaned to the holy side, as shown by his grandfather. Noreen's powers were more general, more all-encompassing, like a jack of all trades. She could touch on each type of talent and enhance the talents around her. Freya showed her how to draw in the energy around her and focus it on a single point. A lesson to be used at the appointed time. She didn't need to practice; it would happen when it needed to.

Have faith.

The words echoed, soft on the melody weaving through her dreams. The *ByalbOgBeLun* felt confident it would all come together, just as planned. Trying to have faith in beings older than the human race, Noreen did her best to quell the feelings of unrest inside her and turned into Gunnar's arms. Maybe it was rather nice to have a big strong man to hold her when she felt overwhelmed. Could it be there was something to this institution of marriage after all?

In his sleep, Gunnar pulled her closer and she pressed her lips against his chest. Firm muscles under smooth skin twitched at the touch of her tongue. Liking the reaction, she let her tongue dart out again, just the tip, to tease a tiny spot of his skin. Since their first kiss, it had been him calling the sensual shots. Every last one of them. Even when she taken the top, it had been with his permission. What would happen...

Nuzzling closer to him, she slowly pushed him to his back. In his sleep, he didn't resist and her lips softly brushing his neck only made him relax more. Taking her time, she laced her hands with his, palm to palm, and cuddled on his chest. Resting for long moments between movements, she worked his arms up and to the sides. Reaching carefully, she was able remove the cuffs from her wrists, wrap them around his, then connect the chains.

Still moving with extremely slow movements, she calmed a restless shift from him with massaging movements and fingers exploring the defining bulges of his muscles. Pure male perfection. Her hands worshiped his arms, then neck, her lips and tongue working lightly to create a trail of sensual fire from his neck to his chest. Circling his flat pink nipples with her tongue caused him to moan and stir against the restraints. Not wanting him to awaken yet, she rested on his chest, head tucked under his chin and hands laced with his as she evened out her breath.

While she waited for him to settle back into sleep, she planned her next moves. How to get his ankles restrained before teasing him awake. One part of him was already awake and it pressed against her, seeking her heat. Instinct, she silently chuckled, thinking it was a good thing. How to make it work for her?

A soft snore blew against her hair and she waited for the next. He relaxed into deeper sleep and she moved slowly, easing her way down his body, turning sideways until she was reversed over him. Ever the accommodating male, he spread his legs without her urging. With soft hands she encircled one ankle with a chain already secured to the bed post.

He shifted against her and she froze. Straddling his waist, she watched as his cock rose steadily. Stopping to play, she wrapped her hands around him, holding him gently. That was all it took to make him still his movements. Taking her time, she teased, keeping her grip light, reaching down to cup his soft sac. What a handful he was. Unconsciously she licked her lips, and decided to get the last limb restrained.

Using a massaging touch, she found it easy to secure the second ankle. Now he was hers. Hopefully he wasn't strong enough to break free. The thin chains didn't look particularly strong compared to his wrists and ankles.

Turning around again, she knelt between his legs and spent a few long moments just gazing at him. He had long limbs, nicely muscled and corded with strong veins. Apparently he helped with the physical part of moving freight. She could see him moving bales and boxes of cargo, his muscles rippling as he hefted the bundles with ease. In the summer, did he work without a shirt? A light bronze color would suit him very well. Just enough to look sun-kissed.

Under her hands, his thighs were hard and solid, her fingers able to easily trace the muscles under warm skin. A coating of blond hair covered his legs and she knew it helped keep him warm by trapping air under his clothes. She still preferred an extra layer of silk to warm her, but his crisp hair tickled her skin most erotically. Wanting to feel it, she straddled one thigh and rocked back and forth, her denuded nether lips barely touching him.

A rush of heat ran through her and she let her head drop back, thrusting her breasts toward the chill air of the room. She felt the end of her braid slither down the valley between her ass cheeks and knew it brushed against his leg, probably just above his knee. He liked her long hair, had told her so many times. A wicked thought came to her and she smiled. Yes, the braid could come in most handy. Taking a moment to let it brush against his leg, she raised her hands to her breasts. A slight tenderness around her nipples made her squirm a little more, pressing closer against Gunnar's thigh. He twitched in response, lifting his thigh an inch to press against her. A wave of warmth trickled through her, centering where she pressed against him.

That would leave a wet spot. The thought widened her grin and she settled more firmly on his thigh. A growl rumbled from his chest as she rode his leg. A twitch from him nearly unseated her. Thinking to anchor herself and distract him, she wrapped a hand firmly around his fully hardened length. *Oh Freya,* she'd known he was big, but how big... she had long fingers but her thumb and middle finger didn't meet when gripping him. No wonder he felt so wonderful inside her *fitte* and *rompe.* And so hard to wrap her lips around.

She glanced at his face before looking at the item in her hand. He had his own wet spot. Another glance at his face showed he watched her through slitted eyes. A grin split her face and, without looking away, she bent forward, cock in hand, extended her tongue and paused. Ah, he held his breath. Feeling her power over him, with a surge of satisfaction she reached out and licked only the drop of fluid from the tip. Air rushed from his lungs, the breeze ruffling her hair before he sucked in another lungful.

"Why can't I move?" he demanded in a deadly soft voice.

"It's my turn to make you beg," she purred and tightened her grip.

"I don't beg."

"Really?" She grinned, then licked again. Another sucked-in breath from him. Pulling her braid over her shoulder, she wrapped it around him to be rewarded with a low groan. "Well we'll just test that statement. For now, you're at my mercy." A chuckle escaped as she opened her mouth and took just the tip of his cock inside. Closing her lips, she hooked them on the ridge of the head. Swirling her tongue around, she twisted to caress him with her mouth.

Freya's fitte! Pulling against his restraints, Gunnar also fought his instinct to free himself. Holding back the fierce desire to fill her mouth and holding back breaking free of the bonds took all his concentration as she pleasured him.

"Nory," he growled. In response she took more of him in, her head lowering over him, her braid falling away. Her *fitte* pressing against his leg was like a brand, searing him, sending more blood into his shaft. The feeling...what she did to him...he never wanted it to stop. He could stay restrained to feel this. The sheer wonder that she'd captured him in this manner astounded him. No woman had ever defied him like this.

And he liked it.

That thought alone started the firing sequence and a fiery tingle started at the base of his spine. He felt his sac drawing up, priming, gods, it was going to be so good, already he felt lightheaded.

It was there... and then it wasn't.

Confused he opened his eyes to see her smiling down at him, her hand wrapped tight around the base of his turgid length.

"Oh, no, you don't," she chuckled.

"What?"

"You don't get off that easy," she said calmly as he felt his release subside.

"No!" he yelled out.

"Not yet, my pet," she repeated his words to her, obviously enjoying herself too much.

"But!" he protested. "I'll lose it, don't leave me hanging."

"No, you won't lose it. Just a little break. I don't want you coming too soon. I expect you to last a while longer yet."

Her grip relaxed and he fought for air. The woman was a devil. Twice more she brought him to the edge then held him there, pulling back a little before bending to build the fire up again with her tongue.

"Nory," he heard himself plead. "I can't take much more. Try to hold me back again and I may very well do internal damage."

"Do I hear a please?"

Her tongue rasped across the head of his cock.

"Please, Nory, please…" A flush consumed him. He'd never begged before in his life.

"Please, what, Dukey?"

"Please, whatever you do, please, let me release." There. He'd been reduced to begging.

"Ah, was that so hard?"

He closed his eyes to her words as she shifted and slid her body down onto his.

"Yessss!" she hissed as she seated herself completely on him. "Yes! You fill me, Gunnar, you fill me perfectly."

"Stop talking and fuck me," he said roughly, and forcefully clenched his buttocks to thrust his hips upward, lifting her an inch.

"Oh yes, buck for me," she moaned, and ground against him, hands braced on his shoulders.

"This would work better if my arms and legs were free," he growled.

"No."

"Nory!"

She stopped moving, pressing all her weight down on his hips, forcing him to still. "What was that?"

"Please, Nory, please, don't stop," he softened his voice. "For Thor's sake, please…" He let out a sigh of relief when she started moving again. "Yes, baby, yes!"

She stopped again and he groaned. "Who is in control here?" she asked him.

"You are." He hated to admit it, but she had him.

"Very good," she purred, and lifted herself slowly, letting him feel every sweet, slick inch of her. She stopped just before pulling off and incredibly, she tightened around him.

As he groaned, he watched her smile. Watching him from beneath hooded eyes, her smile had a feral quality to it. Helpless, all he could do was watch while she lowered herself, one slow centimeter at a time. Halfway down, she reversed herself.

A protest was on his lips when she stopped and gave him the imperial look with lifted brow. Clamping his lips shut, he allowed himself a moan, and she smiled, then lowered herself fast and hard. Beautiful as poetry in motion, her breasts bounced and she followed his gaze to them.

"You like these?"

He wanted to replace her hands holding the generous swells tipped with pink marvels with his own. Not trusting his voice, he nodded.

"You want to suck on them?"

He nodded again.

"You look hungry."

"Ravenous," he whispered, watching as she leaned forward. His mouth was ready when she held one breast for him. With satisfaction he felt the quiver run through her body and into his. The wetness surrounding him heated and increased with her shudder.

"Oh yes," she moaned. "Suckle me!"

Only too happy to obey, he tongued her nipple, teasing the flesh reaching for him. She flexed strong inner muscles, her *fitte* throbbing around him, the pulse driving him mad.

"Wait for me," she ordered, her voice thin and breathy. Tension filled her body as she worked deep inside, his mouth still hungrily teasing her breast.

"Ooooohhhhhhh, Gunnar!" she shouted, her climax bursting upon them both. He released her nipple and thrust his hips up as far as he could, all the muscles in his body stiffened, his release ripping from him.

Time hung suspended, Nory's whole being a picture of perfect ecstasy, her pale skin glowing with a rosy flush, eyes shut tight, lines of concentration etched over the planes of her face. A long keening wail came from her throat, a lover's song of joy. Where their bodies joined, searing heat fused their flesh as their essences combined.

Faultless unification.

Heaven.

The moment of ultimate pleasure sounded like a heartbeat in his head, the pulsing rhythm all throughout his body timed with hers in the most seamless of all unions.

How many heartbeats did they float in perfection? There was no way to know. He didn't want to leave, but the demands of his body and hers broke through, and with a gasp for air, they returned to their world. Floating like a feather on a gentle breeze, Nory slowly collapsed on his body.

He was dimly aware of her rising and falling on his chest, her heaving lungs matching his in force.

Wanting to hold her, he pulled on the chains holding his arms and they broke free from the bedposts. His arms crushing her to him barely elicited a squeal of surprise from her. With perverse satisfaction, he noted she didn't have the strength for it. He shifted his legs and noted they moved more freely as well. If he'd any remaining strength, he would have rolled her under him. As it was, for now, he had to content himself with holding her, lips pressing sporadic kisses on her forehead.

"I think we need a new restraint system," she muttered.

"Don't worry, that was just the traveling set. I have a much better setup at home. Perfect for holding you at all hours of the day and night."

"That is not what I had in mind."

He smiled when she nipped at his skin.

Chapter 16

Gunnar at her side, holding her hand, Noreen drew in a steadying breath before gliding through the open door to the dining room. The skirt of her long gown swept the floor and her hair was piled elegantly high on her head.

Blanca assured her all the ladies dressed for dinner, the men in suits of fine wool. Noreen had spent a long moment admiring Gunnar in his suit of navy. It made his eyes shine even bluer, and the heat from his gaze sent a different kind of shiver shimmering through her.

Chatter ceased as all eyes turned to them.

It was fun taking them by surprise.

"Noreen!" Her mother was the first to speak. "The doctor said you should remain in bed until the morning."

"I feel fine, Moder." She bent slightly to kiss her mother's cheek. At age fifteen she and Coreen had passed their petite mother in height by a few centimeters. Her father had proudly taken photos he kept encrypted on his personal computer. No photographic proof of two princesses was ever allowed to go further. That would surely change now.

In the background there was a shuffle while servants added two more place settings and chairs to the long table.

"We should have let you know we'd be down," Gunnar said, ignoring the mild glare Noreen directed his way.

"Not a problem." Her mother waved away the inconvenience. "We're never quite sure who will or won't show for the evening meal around here."

Noreen knew better, but she kept quiet. She'd done this on purpose. Coreen's casual dismissal of her that morning still left a bitter taste in her mouth, and she was in the mood to shake things up. For starters, Coreen's place moved from Fader's right hand to his left. Her escort moved to

Moder's left as well. She glanced around the room and noted the Earl of NyDunfiddich watching the juggling of place settings from Coreen's side.

If she was being dragged home to serve her role as Crown Princess, then so be it. Let the family take notice, and then the nobility. Noreen was not in a mood to be shuffled into a corner. Smiling, breeding figurehead be damned. Odin's plans called for so much more, and so did hers.

It was easier to think of the beings she'd met this morning by the familiar names. She still had much to puzzle out and had, with great reluctance, revealed her adventure to Gunnar. Relief had been great when he nodded in acceptance. He said it made sense and brought greater purpose to his life. Their lives. Apparently, she wasn't the only one feeling powerless by the dictates of The Profetia.

So here they stood. A united front before her family. All eight of the half sisters in attendance with their husbands, their children still in the nursery. Coreen and the Earl. The old bishop and an equally old Countess who Noreen recognized as a former governess.

"Come, there are people you haven't seen in years," her mother said.

Elbow firmly in Moder's grip, she was led to greet the guests.

The old bishop bowed to her, his eyes sparkling with a softened look as he glanced at her stomach. "Congratulations, Princess, and welcome home. The reunion is much anticipated and today is a day of great joy."

"Thank you." She didn't know what else to say to him, and stepped aside to let Gunnar greet his grandfather. His attitude may have softened, but the old man still gave her feelings of unease.

She turned to Countess Waldemar next. A classic beauty, she had all the bearing of a faded rose. A little more wrinkled, a tad stooped, but still lovely, her blue eyes were as sharp as an icicle.

"Princess Noreen." The older woman made a brief curtsy, a fond smile in her eyes.

Noreen enfolded her in a gentle hug. "Aunt Alice."

"You little hellion, you. It has been entirely too quiet around here without your zest for fireworks," the older woman whispered in her ear.

It didn't matter that Aunt Alice was shorter than the queen. The princesses would always be little to her.

"Well, I hope you enjoyed the bath salts I sent home from Sargordat last winter."

"A poor replacement for you, but they do ease the arthritis. I appreciate the monthly shipments."

"A shop in Ryadstholm will be carrying them on a regular basis in another month. I'm sure it is just a matter of time before a merchant here catches wind of them."

"About time," Aunt Alice muttered, then smiled and turned to greet Gunnar with familiar affection.

Funny how she felt like the stranger here, while her husband acted like it was his family they were visiting.

No, she sighed deep in her heart. This was no visit. This was home once again. At least when they were in the city. If he had apartments elsewhere, it would be a moot point. Her rooms here, and in the other palaces, would need modification to accommodate him. Details to be dealt with when the impending emergency was over. Now, how to explain to the family the upcoming events?

Putting off the thought, she turned to greet Albert Moers, Earl of NyDunfiddich. Only a few years older than she and Coreen, Al had been a childhood friend. Rumor had it he was one of the monarchy's most loyal defenders in Parliament.

Not that Parliament had a whole lot to debate. Nordians were easy-going folks most of the time, too intent on carving out their livings and staying warm. Family time was guarded, and a social institution from the beginning. The government kept its hand light on the people, and politics provided amusement more than anything else.

There were a few bars and public social places, but they were generally marriage markets and geared toward singles. Still, most courting was done in school, and unions were decided on long before graduation. Social meetings involved families, loud music and lots of beer. Dancing occurred while the crowd was still sober. When she'd described the event on Earth, someone had snapped their fingers and said it sounded like the old German custom of Oktoberfest. Most curious, she'd been whisked away to Munich where the festival was held monthly.

She almost giggled, thinking of Gunnar still single at his advanced age, and mingling with the party crowds. He was right. Had they met on time, they'd have had a few children, born singly, by now. Marriage by twenty was very common, with young couples completing university together and starting families a year or so after. Not many marriages were formed with great age differences. Those that did occur were for political or economic gain. Some things never changed.

Well, Gunnar wasn't the only old maid. She and Cory, as well as Al, all fit that description.

Morgan Q. O'Reilly

"Al." She reached out a hand to her old playmate.

"Princess." He bowed over her hand and kissed the back of it.

"Oh forget that." She laughed and tugged on his hand. Strong arms enfolded her in a hug as she kissed his cheek.

Casual chitchat confirmed Al was still single. Cory's suitor? Waiting for the errant sister to return? Most likely. The stab of perverse satisfaction she felt didn't feel particularly good, and she made sure she kept her thoughts quiet on the matter. She could feel Cory subtly probing the edges of her mind and it took determination to keep her out. Mentally spatting with her sister was not on the agenda. Getting a few digs in this morning had been self-defense. Anything she said now would be all-out war. To be avoided. A period of adjustment was needed to soothe wounded feelings on both sides. Cory felt put out for being forced to play the role of Crown Princess, putting her personal life on hold, and Noreen was put out at being forced back home. Fair trade in her book. Mature? Probably not. Later.

Before she could do much more than nod at her sister, her father was there.

"Time to be seated, my girls." He took their arms while Gunnar offered their mother his arm.

"Of course, Fader," she replied, and ignored the glance he sent her.

Coreen was handed off to Al for seating, while the king escorted Noreen to her seat. Careful of the long silk dress she wore, Noreen sat while her father pushed the heavy wooden chair under her. She now recognized the antique dining table for fifty as a most valuable piece of pre-colonial history. The fact it had traveled from Earth spoke volumes. Large and carved, it would have taken up considerable cargo space at the expense of more needed items. She couldn't remember the story attached to it. Surely the butler would know, as it fell under his job title to see the household antiques were cared for.

"A toast!" Fader announced. "Welcome home to Noreen and Freya's blessings on her marriage to Gunnar. Welcome to the family, Prince of Nordia."

Heavy silver goblets were lifted, and she met Gunnar's eyes down the long length of the table. A quick count revealed the mothers of the other sisters were missing. That was odd, they usually attended dinner.

It occurred to Noreen her mother's acceptance of the two concubines didn't match her own views on the subject. Not unheard of, concubines were allowed in those cases where a woman would have been living alone. Not polygamy, but more along the lines of helping to grow the population. Old maids were rare, loving relationships the focus. Living alone was just too hard in the harsh environs of Nordia. Why the king had two was something she didn't understand. Why her mother had only carried one pregnancy was another subject never discussed. Not because it was forbidden, merely she hadn't considered the question before leaving. Traveling and talking by vid-com were not conducive to deep heart-to-heart mother-daughter confessions.

Gunnar's eyes twinkled at her as he lifted his goblet her direction. She flushed at the heat of his gaze and earned a smile. Seeking to calm the pounding of her heart, she sipped from her goblet, only to discover juice, and sat back to allow the servant to place a bowl of soup before her.

Sitting to her right was the old bishop, who seemed most pleased.

"Granddaughter, at last I may call you that," he said.

Noreen stared at him a moment, then nodded. "I guess that does make you my grandfather." Not that she'd known one before. Both her parents' parents had died, either before she was born or when she was very young. She had no memory of them.

"Am I correct in thinking you spoke with Odin this morning?" he asked quietly.

Answering with a short nod, she took a dainty taste of the clear soup before her. Chicken with fresh vegetables. From the summer or hydroponics caves? Tasty in either case.

"What did he say?" Her father leaned toward her eagerly.

She glanced from her father, to the bishop, and back again. "Do you really wish to discuss it here?"

"No, I suppose not." Her father sighed, and bent over his soup. "After dinner will be fine, but you might as well do it at the table. It involves everyone here."

Noreen eyed her father carefully, and searched out the *ByalbOgBeLun* in her thoughts, careful to keep Cory's subtle probing at bay.

"*Yes, Princess?*" The feminine voice whispered in her head.

"*Am I to speak in front of the family?*" she asked.

"*Yes. These are the strongest of your people. You will need their help to link with the rest of the noble class at the appointed time. Do not let them debate. You know what must happen. Command them, as is your duty.*"

Right. Command them. Sidestep her father's authority with his people and command them.

"He expects this. Do not be dismayed. He is prepared for you and your mate to take over. Time grows short and his pride is in knowing you will save the people. His pride does not demand he retain the throne to the end of his days. Indeed, he looks forward to retirement and a life of ease. Be not concerned. He will hold his head high with pride in you," the voice told her. It was soothing and she accepted with a sigh. Marriage and motherhood was one thing. Rising to the top of the monarchy was not something she was prepared to deal with as well.

"Everything okay?" the king inquired.

"I suppose."

His eye had a knowing look and he reached for her hand. She gave it to him and he squeezed it reassuringly. "Our friend has it right, you know. It will happen soon."

His smile widened at the look of alarm she felt sure was on her face. Had he heard the communication?

"Not tonight, but soon," he said.

She could only stare as he turned back to his soup.

"Nory?"

Coreen's tentative question snuck through her stunned mental defenses.

"What?" She steeled herself and kept her eyes aimed at her soup. Her mother was asking Gunnar about their stop at Dante's Grotta.

"I'm sorry. I didn't mean to sound so callous this morning."

"Damn you, Cory. You do this to me all the time. You get me mad, and then retreat with an apology. It isn't fair fighting that way." She swallowed a spoonful of soup. *"Thank you for bringing help,"* she added quietly.

"I saw the glass and blood, and even felt the pain of the cuts in your skin. It terrified me as much as you." The confession held a sheepish tone. An image of the cook butchering a pig came back to both of them. Only four at the time, they weren't supposed to be in that part of the kitchen, and then to see their favorite pig being butchered... Noreen felt herself sway at the memory and knew Cory did the same. *"Anyhow, I knew you were okay when...well...let's just say we both need to work on shielding during certain private times."*

Noreen glanced up at her sister across the table and caught her blush. She felt a matching flush burn across her cheeks, then she grinned. *"Might as well learn how to keep a man in line early, sis. Don't let them get the upper hand unless you want them too."*

"Just remember that, when facing down Parliament for the first time."

Noreen stared at her sister's coy smile, then burst out laughing. *"Good point. I'll remember that."*

A long soul-suffering sigh came from the far end of the table, and Noreen turned her head that way. Coreen did as well.

"Bjorn, you're not supposed to let them have private conversations during dinner," the queen gently admonished her spouse and daughters.

"Not much I can do other than remind them of their manners, my love," he chuckled.

"Sorry, Moder," Noreen said, and heard Cory's voice echo the apology.

Sitting back in her chair, the queen indicated the soup course was to be cleared away. "We may as well discuss wedding details. All the girls are prepared to stand up with you." A delicate wave encompassed all the sisters. "Your brothers-in-law will stand with Gunnar."

"With Cory as Maid of Honor, of course." There, that will shut her up for a bit. "Oh, and we wish it to be on the Solstice, not before."

"Oh?"

Noreen smiled at the raised eyebrow. "Yes. On the Solstice. Midnight I believe. I'll have the exact time in a day or two. Oh, and we'll hold it at the Summer Palace."

That did it. A piece of silverware hit the stone tiled floor with a ringing sound that echoed in the now silent dining room. She suppressed a chill her heavy damask silk dress couldn't quite keep out. Even the glowing, lemon-yellow color didn't impart much cheer at the moment.

"Now, Noreen, surely you can see the impracticality of that. There aren't enough rooms at the Summer Palace to house all the people who will attend the ceremony," her mother said.

"We have that worked out," she said, and nodded at Gunnar.

"Yes, Elke, Moder." He cleared his throat. "I have plenty of transports that will serve as housing. I've already asked my Convoy Commander to start calling them all in. Most families own one anyway. The ice is solid this year, and they will only need to park there for one night, two at the very most. Easy."

Noreen smiled at him. The plan was brilliant.

"But for the ceremony..." Her mother looked confused. "Where will we hold the ceremony? The ballroom is not large enough. Only the cathedral in Ryadstholm is large enough to seat the entire ruling class."

"Outside. In the gardens. We'll stand on the veranda and people may stand in the garden. It will be short and then we'll move inside for the reception." Noreen smiled down the table and all the shocked looks made her grin widen.

"But... how will people dress?"

"In their best long underwear, jeans, sweaters and parkas. We don't have much time, so let's keep it simple."

Not to mention, they'd probably never get to the reception. There'd be a few things to deal with such as earthquakes and possibly lava overflows. The *ByalbOgBeLun* had gathered data on all possible, and probable, natural disasters to be expected. At the very least, a shaken population would need their leading families to leap into action. After they'd saved the world, of course.

"Noreen," her mother tried again, a stern look on her face. "This simply will not do at all. The people deserve a royal wedding in the grandest tradition."

"You may make up for it with the coronation, which I'm hoping won't be for several years yet." Even as she said it she knew it was hopeless. Her mother shook her head.

"No. The *coronations*," she emphasized the plural, "will take place at the same time as the wedding. The moment your vows have been said, you and Gunnar will be crowned as the Queen and Prince Consort."

This time a plate shattered on the floor and made her flinch. There must a new footman being trained. The silverware, and now the plate, would earn him double duty at the kitchen sinks.

"Oh lovely, this is just a great day for news, isn't it?" Noreen leaned back in her chair with a mutter. What was that about sarcasm? She swiveled her head to look at her father. "Is there something you wish to tell me, *Sire?*"

"Don't get snippy with me young lady," he chuckled. "Nordia needs you and Gunnar at the helm. You have the recent off-world knowledge to make us a stronger force in the universal economy. I don't have the energy or drive for it. I have too many grandchildren to play with, and am expecting more next summer."

There was no misunderstanding the look he gave her.

"So I'm expected to carry multiple children and revive our economy all at once?" What happened to being a figurehead?

"You're an amazing woman, my daughter. All of my daughters are amazing women. It's time for the next generation to take over. I'm ready to spend my summers fishing and the winters teaching the grandbabies how to drive their parents crazy." He leaned back and grinned. With a small wave of his hand, plates of salad were placed in front of the diners at his table.

Chapter 17

Noreen spent the salad and main courses mulling thoughts over in her head, practicing her shield against Cory. While not completely unexpected, the coronations threw a twist in the plans. How long did a wedding and double coronation combined take anyway? Fifteen minutes? Twenty? How long could they keep the guests standing outside on the deepest night of winter? Even at the equator, temperatures would certainly dip well below zero, as much as forty to sixty degrees below zero, or more.

"*We have a plan,*" Freya's voice spoke to her.

"*Glad to hear it. Mind sharing? My mother is about to have a stroke worrying about turning her guests into frozen treats for the snow bears.*"

"*Hold the ceremonies in the thermal pool. It is large enough, warm, the sound carries well, and it will allow the skin to skin contact you require.*"

"*Hello? Skin to skin contact? For what?*" Keeping her face serene was difficult at best. A glance at Gunnar showed his eyebrow cocked in concern. She shook her head and smiled.

"*In order to draw the energy from your people you will need to have physical contact. Much like your electric cabling. The waters will help enhance the connection. All that will be needed will be to open up the roof of the grotta. The hot waters will also keep your people warm.*"

"*And what happens when the planet begins to move? Ground shakes? Lava flows? These are all concerns, remember?*"

"*Fear not, we can shelter one grotta. The trick will be getting the common people to move to safe ground. Those spots are mostly inhabited already. Your engineers have been working quietly for centuries to build safe housing according to the specifications researched. A few people live in unsafe areas, outside the influence of government officials. If they cannot be convinced to move for their own safety, you may have no choice but to leave them where they are,"* Freya continued. Yes, thinking of her as Freya was so much simpler.

A thought occurred to her and she lifted her cup to cover her shudder of fear. *"Will your people survive?"*

"We will survive. It may be our planes of existence will be further separated in the coming quakes. For now, the palaces are built over the places where the curtain is thinnest so we may communicate. There are so many variables, we don't know what will happen for certain, though we have calculated to the best of our abilities."

"I just found you, I don't want to lose you!" Panic gripped her heart but was soothed away by the sweet music of the *ByalbOgBeLun*.

"We will always be with you, even if you cannot contact us. Just as you will always be a part of us. It is to be, and better than the destruction a comet would rend upon us all."

"I wish I had your calm certainty," she made the mental equivalent of a mutter.

"And we wish we had your sense of humor and passion. What will be, will be. Do your best, as we'll do ours, and that is all anyone can hope for."

At last dessert was served, and Noreen stared at the hot fudge cake with green whipped cream on top. "The Lidarian mint brandy I brought back?" she asked her mother.

"Yes. Your communications indicated you loved this treat, so we thought you might like to share it with us."

"Of course," she murmured, and avoided Gunnar's gaze. All eyes on her, she cut off a small bite and lifted it to her mouth. The brandy had nothing to do with Hollis and his obsession. Had to deal with that and find out what his issue was for real. He also would serve Nordia unintentionally. Mint brandy was a good thing. Maybe Nordia could learn to grow and make its own. She hesitated a moment, then slid it into her mouth. Forcing a smile onto her face, she faked a sigh of contentment. Good thing there was herbal tea nearby to wash it down.

A moment later noises of approval arose around the table. She snuck a glance at Gunnar, who wore a bemused look. He smiled when he caught her gaze. His smile said everything would be okay.

Her mother made a gesture that sent the footmen and servants from the dining hall. When the door to the kitchen closed with a quiet thump, her father spoke.

"Now, naughty Noreen, it's time to come clean."

She set down her fork and rested her hands in her lap. The temptation to twist the fabric of her gown was strong. The napkin in her lap suffered instead.

"I've been in contact with…Odin, off and on today. There is a specific reason for the Solstice wedding. The scientists are verifying timing and such but, at midnight on the Solstice, the moment the Summer Palace is at the furthest point from the sun, we need Hollis to fire his ships' weapons upon that location to move Nordia out of the path of the comet headed our way."

She let her eyes wander the length of the table and back. Her father nodded at her encouragingly to continue speaking. She had the riveted attention of every person there.

"Odin tells me that all of us seated here are the strongest of our race. Our individual powers will make up the core group, who will draw in the energy produced by the talents of our nobility. He says I am to be the focal point for gathering the power and sending it outward to form a shield. This shield must be strong enough to protect the planet and hold while the fire power pushes us out of the path of danger." She lifted her tea cup and sipped. Surprisingly, her hand did not shake.

"It has come to me over the course of dinner that the wedding and coronation ceremonies can be held in the grotta of the thermal pool at the Summer Palace. This is the exact spot the warships need to hit for the proper orbit to be obtained. It is large enough and warm enough to gather everyone needed. It will also allow for the skin to skin contact needed to better draw and focus the energy, the water helping to enhance the effect."

The reactions were mixed. A few of her younger sisters giggled a little, her mother frowned. The brothers-in-law tried to hide grins. Aunt Alice looked curious. Al kept his reaction hidden. Ah, a true politician. The elder of the sisters looked mildly shocked. Her father and the priest nodded. Cory looked thoughtful.

"Odin suggests you get married in the pool? Nude?"

Had to admire Mamma. The queenly mantle barely rippled with shock.

"Yes. Fewer impediments to get in the way of directing the power. The minerals in the water will help conduct the energy and sustain the shield."

"I've never heard of a nude wedding ceremony," Mamma sighed.

"No big deal. I attended such a wedding on OmegaZed. Quite fun." Especially the pre-wedding pat down.

"Oh?"

"No place to hide weapons. The royals were rather paranoid there. Good thing they breed fast. Assassinations were fairly common."

"I see. And what about the children you carry?"

Noreen placed a hand over her womb. "They are the strongest generation yet. They're crucial to the success of the shield and will not be harmed as long as we save the planet."

"You have Odin's word on this?"

"I do."

"Well. I see."

Noreen watched her mother place another bite of the dessert in her mouth, and savor it thoughtfully.

"How many babies do you carry?" was Mamma's next question.

"I do not yet know. More than one. I've heard speculation of up to four."

"Four? At once?"

Her mother's face paled, and a soft twitter went around the table. Apparently Moder remembered what it was like to carry twins. Not much comfort.

"Yes, so if any of you are thinking of leaving the planet right after the wedding, think again." She directed a glare at Cory's open mouth. "For starters, moving the planet will change weather patterns and a few other things. We may very well have some natural disasters to deal with from massive snowmelt, resulting in flooding, cave-ins, quakes, destroyed villages, possibly even lava flows and fires. This isn't like moving a transport across the city. At the very least, our population will experience a few bumps and bruises. All of you will be called upon to make personal visits and deliver emergency supplies."

With satisfaction she sat back and watched as her words sank in. A few of the sisters who'd lived a life every bit as spoiled as she had, looked like owls with spotlights aimed at them. Others set their chins with determination to do their duty. Their husbands looked thoughtful, then nodded. They understood. Cory did as well, if the look of resignation on her face were anything to go by. Too bad she couldn't see Al's face from here.

She turned to gaze at her father and was pleased to see a smile on his face. "I can't let you run off either. Not yet," she said softly. "You still have a very large role to play in all of this."

"I'll be the first one on a transport out to offer supplies and solace to the people," he assured her. "You'll need to stick close to the palace and be the central communications hub. Those children are going to tie you up in knots for several years to come."

"And you're the first babysitter I'm calling when they're all crying in the middle of the night."

It was good to hear her father's robust laugh. "Not only will I gladly walk the floor at the second hour, I'll also be there to help Gunnar pull you to your feet when you're too ungainly to get off the sofa."

"*Freya, I better get my body back after the birth!*" she sent the thought deep. Hopefully she was still young enough to bounce back quickly. Everyone looked around at the musical laughter filling the dining room. It didn't make her feel good.

She gave her father a smile, then turned to the other end of the table. "So, Moder, I guess we'll be rewriting those wedding invitations, right?" Noreen watched her mother's startled eyes return to hers, then take on a new look of resolve.

"But of course, Noreen. We'll take care of it first thing in the morning."

Noreen met the laughing eyes of Loreen, the eldest of the half sisters, not even a year younger than her and Coreen. "I guess we'd better get organized then, hadn't we? A wedding and a double coronation, soon followed by a bursting nursery, alone are enough reason to keep us all busy. Throw in a little world rearranging, and it looks like all vacations are canceled. I will say this for you, Noreen, you sure know how to make an entrance."

A glance down the table showed Gunnar's eyes crinkling with laughter, and her lips curved into a grin. "You know me. I love a good scene."

"Fader?" Doreen spoke up next. "Is it too late to send her away again?"

With a laugh, Coreen answered. "Far too late. Better get used to it, folks."

"Well," her father pushed his chair back from the table, "there's no time like the present to get started. We'll leave the wedding plans to your mother and sisters. I need to speak with you, Bishop Zaren, and Gunnar. Once we get a few things coordinated we can start handing out specific assignments."

Left with no choice, she took the hand her father held out to her and stood.

* * * *

Noreen leaned back against Gunnar, settling under his arm. The world felt just right to him, with her cuddled up at his side. He took the tea cup from her hand and set it on the side table.

"So, does that take care of things for now?" Nory asked her father, and glanced at the bishop.

They'd just compared notes, and his grandfather's accounts of the beings who shared the planet matched the king's and Nory's. Gunnar still wasn't quite sure what to make of it, but these beings were as much a part of their world as the minerals and thermal waters. More so, because they'd been there first. In this study, he'd heard the musical sound of their language, an echo of the music he'd heard played at every gathering on Nordia. The plans were beginning to make sense with each scientific report handed to him.

"Yes, I believe it does. We have the media information campaign sketched out. Al can oversee that part of it," her father said. "Coreen is also quite the media star as well. She can fill you in on the particulars of working them to our advantage."

"How serious is Coreen about Al?" Nory asked her father.

Good question.

"They wish to get married."

"Does it fit in with the plan?"

"The plan?" her father chuckled. "Oh, the genetic plan? It works. Then again with you two repopulating the royalty in one shot, it moves her further down the line of succession, so it isn't that big of a deal."

"Which suits her just fine," Noreen muttered. "So, when will they marry?"

"When all the excitement dies down. Let's get you two installed, get the planet moved, clean it up, have a few babies, and then we'll take care of the next wedding. That will give your mother something to plan and the planet an event to look forward to."

Noreen rested for a moment then pinned her father with a glare. "Why?"

"Why, what *älskling*?"

"Why are you abdicating? There's no reason to."

"There's plenty of reason. We're heading into a new epoch. That calls for new leadership. I'm not abandoning you, *älskling*. I'll be your advisor, but the planet will look to you and Gunnar."

"Why is he only Prince Consort and not King?"

"Tradition. Laws. Precedent." The king shrugged with eloquence, a suspicious twinkle in his eye.

"Well if we're changing tradition with your early retirement, why not change this one as well?" she asked.

"Gunnar? Have you strong feelings on this issue? You're a popular fellow with the people. Of course we'd have to get Parliament's approval."

Gunnar looked at the king. Still fit and strong, he didn't look like he was ailing. A little more gray than the first time they'd met, but still far from infirm. "I don't think we need to decide now. Let's get through this first and then Nory can decide."

"Thanks, put all this stuff on my head," she muttered at his side. "Just what I asked for."

"Nory, if you wanted it, I wouldn't give it to you this soon," her father laughed. "You don't want the power, so you'll use it with more wisdom than someone who covets the position."

"Great. Just great."

Gunnar smiled as she yawned, a dainty hand over her mouth.

"Time for bed." He nuzzled her neck.

"When do we leave for Ryadstholm?" she asked.

"Day or two down the road. We go visit Parliament tomorrow, so rest up."

"Yes, Pappa."

"*Yes, Pappa*," Gunnar mimicked her, and earned a glare for his efforts. "Come, m'lady, off to bed with you."

"Your Majesty."

They all looked toward the door of the study at the man who interrupted. Gunnar recognized the king's secretary.

"Yes?"

"I'm sorry to disturb you, Sire, but that Lidarian is making noise again. He insists on speaking with you. The Prime Minister is not able to calm him."

"I'll talk to him," Noreen said.

"What will you say?" Gunnar wanted to know.

"I will merely tell him I'll be in Ryadstholm next week and I'll meet with him then. It should be enough for him to see me."

"Keep it vague and friendly," the king advised. "Okay, Olaf, put him through." He stood and moved behind his desk. "On second thought, let me try first."

Chapter 18

"Your Majesty, at last, I am so pleased to speak with you at long last."

Noreen stood just out of view of the camera, but where she could see the monitor of the vid-com. Hollis, wrapped in layers of sweaters, and what appeared to be a fur cloak, looked out from the screen. His black eyes held not only a measure of relief, but annoyance as well.

His skin, what she could see of it, was still black and shiny like tempered dark chocolate, his thick black hair cut short.

"Ah, yes, Minister Traxelgard is it?"

Noreen watched as her father slumped in his chair, appearing old and tired all of a sudden. The fraud! She put a hand over her mouth to keep from laughing.

"Yes, Your Majesty, I am Prince Hollis Traxelgard, Lidarian Minister of Commerce."

She had to bite her lip at Hollis's barely restrained impatience. He didn't like being treated so casually.

"Prince Hollis. Commerce. Of course. Are we involved in trade negotiations with your planet?"

"Not exactly, sire. I am seeking my bride. She said she was coming home because of a family emergency. Since we married the night before she left, I'm sure you can understand how I wish only to be with her. I told her I would follow so I could meet her family, but I've been unable to find her. When traveling she goes by the name Noreen Tibbetts, and I understand this is for security reasons."

"We have many Noreens on this planet, Minister."

"Our customs ministry took note of her full name. The Noreen I'm seeking is your daughter, sire."

"Oh! My Noreen. Such a beautiful girl. Yes, she came home because I'm not feeling in top form. Just made it in this morning. Got trapped by the storm. Time for her to stand by her family. She's been away for so long." His sigh would have been heartbreaking, if she hadn't seen him fall into his act. Instead it was slightly irritating. Why did they have to play these games?

"Yes, sire. Anyhow, she is my wife by Lidarian custom. I wish to see her and complete our vows according to Nordian custom. It has been nearly two weeks since I've seen her and I'm sure you can appreciate how difficult it is to be separated from my wife."

"Your wife? I don't recall her mentioning being married to an off-worlder. No, that just isn't possible. As Crown Princess she isn't allowed to make an off-world alliance of such intimacy. There must be some mistake. She's already promised to a local Duke. In fact, the final part of the wedding ceremony will take place in just a few weeks time. I'm sure there's a miscommunication somewhere."

"No, no mistake, Your Majesty."

Noreen frowned at the scowl on Hollis's face. She'd only ever seen him smiling. The scowl wasn't attractive, creasing his smooth forehead. Hoping to ease the building tension in her neck, she rolled her head a little, then shook her head at Gunnar's look of inquiry.

"Well, we'll be in Ryadstholm next week, weather permitting. I fear it would be a waste of your time to travel here so, if you will bear with us, we'll contact you when we get situated there." Her father wiped a hand across his face, as if overly wearied. "Forgive me, Minister, I have the head of the church here and we have some business to complete. Give my secretary the information of where you're staying and I assure you we'll work this out next week."

"Sire, if I could just speak with Noreen, we could clear this up. I miss her so, and only wish to assure her of my love and devotion."

"Well, sir, I'll pass your words on to her. I'm sure you can appreciate that I haven't had time with my daughter in more than ten years. We have a lot to catch up on."

"Yes, sire, and I don't wish to deprive you of your daughter. In fact, as her husband, I look forward to meeting not only you, but your wife and the rest of the family as well. I understand it is considerable."

"Yes," the king laughed softly, "yes, they are a lovely field of flowers. Well, we'll be in touch soon. Thank you for calling."

He pressed a button, and the monitor went black.

"I don't believe you just hung up like that!" Noreen exclaimed, watching her father perk up immediately.

"Why not? He was being pompous, wasn't he, Gunnar?"

"Absolutely."

She stared when Gunnar agreed with her father. His grandfather was also nodding. All three men wore wicked smiles.

"What is he guilty of? He thinks we're married and he wants to see me. Is that a crime?"

"I don't see you running to leap into his arms." Gunnar eyed her narrowly. "Come to think of it, what did you ever see in him anyway?"

"He was charming. And darker than me," she muttered.

"Charming?"

"Yes. Charming." She folded her arms and faced the three men. The small twinges of irritation became a twang. "He treated me with courtesy. We danced and dined. We laughed and spent long days enjoying all the sights and delights of Lidaria. We toured the premiere brandy distillery, farms, chocolate factories, swam from the best beaches, skied on the water, bathed under jungle waterfalls and toasted each sunset. It was romantic, and he doted on me. He made me feel like a princess, instead of a possession."

She glared especially hard at Gunnar. "And not once did he chain me, or ignore my requests. My slightest wish was his command." Come to think of it, Gunnar and Hollis were opposites in more ways than skin color.

"You chained her?" Her father's tone of respect increased her sense of irritation.

"And you!" She turned on her parent. "From what I understand you… you…you provided the learning materials that encouraged this perverse behavior!" Hands on hips she felt a righteous anger flare up. At least Hollis was honest about wanting to be with her. "You then had Cory manipulate me into coming home. She made me believe you were dying! And… and…what did I come home to? A set up! I wasn't even given a chance to choose! You all set it up so I was trapped with this…this…man. Not even of my choosing!" She waved a hand at Gunnar and began to pace.

"Now, Nory—" Gunnar started to say, but she cut him off.

"No! No, you may not call me Nory. I was coerced and forced into coming home and this…this relationship! It doesn't count," she growled. "I renounce this marriage. I don't want to be married and I don't want children. And more importantly, I don't want to be queen. I abdicate my title in deference to my sister! And I'll make sure Parliament knows it!" She whirled and ran toward the study door. Out, she had to get out. Away from them.

Gunnar caught her with her hand on the doorknob.

"No!" she screamed. With strength she didn't know she possessed, she pushed him away, and he staggered. She flung the door open and ran, not even stopping to see what made the loud crashing sound behind her.

"Noreen!" Gunnar called after her, but she kept running, tears blinding her.

She made it to her rooms and rushed inside, locking the door behind her. Leaning against the door, tears rolled down her cheeks as she listened to Gunnar pounding on the door.

"Noreen, open this door!"

"No! I won't! Go away. I don't need you, and I don't want you!" she shouted back. Gasping she tried to swallow back her panic and disgust. Looking up she saw Blanca staring at her, eyes wide.

"M'lady?"

"Blanca," she gasped. "Keep this door locked. No one gets in!" She gripped the younger woman's arms. "Do you understand? No one. Not the duke, not my fader, not my moder, and especially not my sister. Do you understand?" Judging by the terrified look on Blanca's face, she looked like a mad woman. It didn't matter, she just needed to be alone.

"Yes, yes." The young woman nodded. "I understand. It will be okay, m'lady. I'll make you some tea and keep everyone out. It's been a long day, Princess. Let me help you get ready for bed."

"Bed," Noreen repeated the single word, and slumped against the door now vibrating from the person, or persons, pounding on the other side. She let her maid pull her away from it. Reaction began to set in and she felt her hands start to shake. "Bed is good."

"Just this way, come into the dressing room." Blanca's calm voice soothed her and she went willingly. In the dressing room, the pounding faded, and she sank down onto the chaise.

"Here you go, m'lady, this nightgown should keep you cozy tonight. Let me get the zipper on your dress."

Before she knew it, a soft silk nightgown floated down over her head, the long sleeves and high neck designed for winter nights.

"There you go. Just rest here a moment while I start the tea, and then I'll brush out your hair."

"Yes." She leaned back, resting her head. Tired. She was so very tired. And Hollis had treated her so gently. So courtly. Like a rare jewel, never a rough touch or harsh word. He listened to her, and everything she wanted had fallen into her lap.

A cup and teapot appeared on the small table next to her. "There you go. Now we'll just let it brew."

Gentle hands tugged at the pins holding her coiled hair. It felt so good having her hair brushed. Blanca's hands were competent and gentle, the rhythm of the brushing smooth and soothing. She was on the edge of sleep when Blanca began braiding her hair again. Leaving it unbound at night was a disaster.

"A spot of tea?"

"Thank you, I know you made it special, but I think I should go to bed now."

"Of course, here let me help you." Blanca's strong arms helped her up and guided her to bed.

"There m'lady. Rest well, and I'll keep the troops at bay until morning."

The soft down-filled coverlet was pulled up under her chin, and she sighed as the bed seemed to embrace her.

"You warmed it," she whispered. "Thank you."

* * * *

"My lord, I promised her no one would be let in. I'm sorry. My word is my bond and, if I let you in, she'll sack me for sure. If it got out I didn't obey the orders of my employers, especially the princess, then I'd never find another job in good society."

Gunnar stared at the small maid standing guard at the door of the sitting room. "I'm her husband."

"I'm sorry, sir, I really am. I'm bound by her orders." She stood firm, her hand shaking on the door despite the determined set to her chin.

As furious as he was with Noreen, he didn't have it in him to compromise her maid. "Fine," he capitulated with an explosive sigh. "I'll be in my study across the hall. If she changes her mind, please come get me."

"Of course, sir. The moment she asks for you, I promise."

"Just don't let her leave the palace. She has a reputation for running away." A humorless smile twisted his lips.

"Sir," Blanca protested with worry creasing her forehead.

"Torn between two masters, eh?" It wasn't fair to the girl. "I'll have someone else watch the door. You're right. It isn't fair to put you in the middle. See to your mistress. She needs to remain calm for the sake of the babies."

"Thank you, sir." Relief lit up her eyes and he turned away.

His eyes fell on the king. "Looks like I get to spend my first night in the doghouse," he tried to joke.

"Good thing the sofa in your study opens into a comfortable bed." The king chuckled and slapped him on the shoulder. "Come on, I put a bottle of vodka in your liquor cabinet. I'll call for security to hang out in the hallway and keep an eye on all the exits. She won't run off this time."

"Will you be able to fix the door she ripped off the hinges?" Gunnar softly closed the door to his study, and took in the classically decorated room in an effort to reconcile the action with his wife. Floor to ceiling wooden shelves were filled with books and art treasures. He watched Bjorn open a cabinet and remove two glasses. From there he looked at the plush upholstered sofa.

"Oh don't worry, the door will fix. We need to fix the marriage first."

"What marriage?" He took the glass Bjorn held out to him.

"There's a marriage. Now you have a little space and time, we need to concentrate on romance. You didn't have time for the little details. I'm thinking we start with a nice big diamond ring. Still the best stone in the universe."

"No, not a diamond. Too much like ice. That much I've figured out. She even wants the snow to change color. Can you imagine green snow? Purple?"

Bjorn laughed and moved to the com unit on the desk. He pushed a button and was answered by the head of security. "Niall, we need the palace force on full alert."

"Sire?"

"Princess Noreen is upset."

"Ah. Yes, sir. We keep her in the palace, right?"

"Right. Watch the doors into her apartment, and all the exits to the palace. Use cameras to help."

"Understood. We'll stay on top of it."

"Good man."

Bjorn disconnected and wandered over to an over-stuffed chair near where Gunnar sat. "What we should do is put a locater on that girl. Then we can catch her faster."

"Bet she's always been handful." Gunnar watched the older man grimace.

"From the moment she was born. They put her in my arms, and I swear to Odin, honest, she smiled up at me and cooed. Not one whimper from her, not even when they put the tattoo on her foot. I looked into those little wise eyes and I fell head over heels in love."

"What about Coreen?"

"Her too, but you know what they say about your first love. Noreen had a five minute head start on my heart. All she ever had to do was look up at me with those big blue eyes, all soft and sweet, a little smile on those pouty lips and when I gave in, she made it painless by wrapping her arms around my neck and kissing my cheek." The king sighed and stared into the clear liquid in his glass as if it were a mirror to the past. "I could never deny her anything and since she was always a few steps ahead of her sister, poor Coreen got stuck with the harsher realities of life."

"So, Noreen learned how to work you early, and Coreen was left to do her sister's work." He could see now as clear as the sea ice.

"Yes. This is all my fault. I played favorites, and it's backfired horribly. Coreen is furious, rightly so, and Noreen still refuses to face her fate. I don't know what to do." He drank deeply. "To be fair, Noreen did excellent work for Nordia while she traveled. She found new markets and brought us new technologies. She's upgraded our standard of living by bringing in the small luxury items as well. It was one reason I let her stay away as long as I did."

"But now…"

"But now… Now we are facing the annihilation of our planet, with no time to evacuate, and no place to go if we did."

Gunnar nodded. Earth was overcrowded, and had made it clear her colonies weren't welcome home, at least not en masse. The products were welcome, which was good for Nordia's economy, but that was all. Visits such as Noreen's were rare. The other colonies, less established than Nordia, were in no position to take in the entire population of the planet. Do or die.

"What is her talent? The strength she's displayed today?"

Gunnar watched as the king shook his head. "We were never able to determine her exact talent. Coreen can tell when people are lying, and much like you, can compel them to be truthful. Noreen never revealed hers. Your grandfather can sense it, but even he cannot determine what it is. Strong. She's very strong at whatever it is she has within her. He also thinks the babies are strong as well, much like Odin has told us."

"Why do they call themselves by the names of the old Earth gods?"

"Easier for us." Bjorn shrugged, and held out his empty glass.

Gunnar stood and took it for refilling. "Can my grandfather tell how many children she carries?"

"If he can, he hasn't told me, and The Profetia isn't giving it up yet. What is clear," the king paused to take the drink, "is that she is critical to the success of diverting the comet."

"And where do I fit in?" he asked quietly.

"You are the force that will keep her here, my boy. Keep her pregnant and she'll be happy to let you fill the role of monarch and deal with Parliament."

Gunnar stared at the older man for a moment, then laughed. "I hate to tell you this, but your daughters don't take well to submission. She's okay with it as a game, but in real life? Forget it. Won't work. Not sure I want it to."

The king joined in with a chuckle. "Oh hell, it was worth a try, wasn't it?"

"Nearly lost my head over it, but sure, almost anything is worth a try. So, diamonds are too cold. Fire opal? Rubies? Beryllos black prisms?"

"Fire opal might work. A good symbol of the fire within her." Bjorn leaned across the table and pushed at button on the communicator unit. "Olaf? Get me the jeweler and tell him to bring a selection of women's jewelry. We want to see gems with fire. You know, opals, rubies, those black prism things. Let us know when he's available. If he can make it in the next little while, we'll see him tonight, otherwise early tomorrow." He didn't wait for his secretary's reply before disconnecting.

"I hate to ask, but I can't contain my curiosity anymore, so I hope you don't mind," Gunnar said slowly.

"Ask away." A royal hand waved to indicate the floor was open.

"Why two concubines?"

Gunnar wondered at Bjorn's chuckle. "You're the first man brave enough to ask."

"Nory's brought up the subject and has told me she won't allow me the same."

"Well, long story, but let me see if I can explain."

Gunnar settled back and watched the king sip from his glass, looking thoughtful.

"Personally, as much as I adore all my girls, I wouldn't really recommend it. Sigrud and Anica are distant cousins of the Queen. Elke had just given birth to the girls and had such a difficult time with it we nearly lost her. The doctor advised against future pregnancies, so we had her sterilized. No hope of a male heir that way, but I couldn't bear the thought of losing her. I adore Elke and, despite the pre-arranged match, she's the love of my life. So far the gods have been good at making love matches to fulfill The Profetia, so there's hope for you." The glass was used to gesture his direction.

"Anyhow, Sigrud and Anica were visiting to help with Elke's difficult pregnancy, serving as ladies in waiting, if you will. Their husbands were deep in opening up a new mine, and this way they were being looked after just as they were looking after us. It was a mutual convenience and a happy circumstance. Until the cave-in."

Gunnar nodded. Everyone knew of the mining disaster a month before the princesses were born. The birth had brought a note of joy to a community mourning the deaths of fifteen men.

"What made it more poignant, both women had found out they were pregnant only days before the accident."

"That means…" Gunnar's eyes narrowed on the king.

"Right. Loreen and Doreen are not my genetic daughters. They inherited their fathers' titles, which is why they hold higher ranks than their sisters. However, since we couldn't have two widows with newborn children out in the far reaches where their estates are, and Elke needed help, we invited them to stay. When we determined Elke would never be able to produce the required male heir, we reached an agreement. If either Sigrud or Anica could produce a male child, he would be the heir. Fate, it seems, had it in for me. Thirteen females in one household." The king groaned, and dropped his head against the back of his chair. "You might be tempted to take on a concubine, but don't do it. They all cycle together and it just isn't worth it. I spend one week a month sleeping in either my dressing room or my study. I was hoping they'd offset each other and I'd always have a comfortable companion. Not to be."

Gunnar chuckled into his own drink. "Well, she wasn't thrilled when I mentioned my little stable at home."

"Have I taught you nothing over the years?" The look of disbelief on the king's face made him laugh outright.

"You tried to teach me women were second class citizens of little brain power. I'm sure my own mother would have beaten that notion out of my head."

"And your wife will. You need a new strategy. Resist every attempt to make you king. It will drive her crazy, until she at last does it with

Parliament standing over you with a sword and forces you to take the crown. Then she can never take it away from you."

He laughed with the king, but shook his head. "Not sure I want it, to tell you the truth. You'll have to sell me on the position, much like Nory will need to be sold on the notion."

"Now wait just a minute," the king protested, hand in the air. "My only consolation in having all these girls is their husbands. At last the balance is swinging back toward male dominance in this house. I've waited a long time to even out the numbers. And that means balance of power in the home as well. She doesn't really want to rule. You're strong enough to do it quite competently. Let her brow beat you into it, and then she can turn her energies into raising the passel of kids you're having right off the bat. She'll be too busy to deal with Parliament, laws and all that icky crown business."

Gunnar had to laugh. 'Icky crown business' is just how Nory would have phrased it.

Chapter 19

Heaven. Heaven just had to be warm. Noreen knew it in her very soul. She lay back in the deep tub, the scent of roses rising on spiraling tendrils of steam. The water was up to her chin, and her freshly washed hair hung over the back edge of the tub. Blanca stood behind her, working out the tangles while the hot water, sprinkled liberally with sweet scented oil, relaxed every muscle in her body.

"Ah, this oil feels good. I can feel it rehydrating my skin. I'd forgotten how dry the air is here." She lifted a hand and watched the water dribble back into the tub.

"Would you like a touch of it combed into your hair, m'lady?"

"Wonderful idea," she sighed. "Blanca, I'm sorry for putting you in a spot last night. Was he very angry you wouldn't let him in?" She'd woken this morning feeling guilty, but the feeling was quickly overshadowed by a bout of queasiness. Thankfully Blanca had been on hand with herbal tea and toast. Relaxing in the tub helped ease the rest of the feeling away.

"Not so much angry as frustrated and bewildered, ma'am."

"Hmmm." Keep him off balance; that would work for bit. "That feels wonderful, Blanca. You have a nice touch when doing hair."

"Thank you, m'lady. Sophie taught me."

"You must have been very young the last time you saw her."

"We kept in touch."

Just one more example of her selfishness. Freya knew she'd heard plenty since arriving on planet about how spoiled she was. Sophie, like Fiona and Hans, had been with her every single day of her journey. Not one of them had ever taken more than a day or two off for personal business, never once traveling home for a visit with family. They'd been their own family unit. Certainly as close, if not closer, than most families. She needed to touch base with them today.

"Have you spoken with Sophie since we returned?"

"Yes, ma'am. Every day. It is a joy having her close again."

"Please help me remember to call today. I need to see if they are okay and make some arrangements."

"Right after breakfast?"

"What time does Parliament go into session each day?"

"After lunch, the eleventh hour."

"Yes, then after breakfast works. I'll make sure they don't drag me into more meetings."

"Would you like to get out, before I dry your hair?"

"It's so warm here, I'd rather stay put."

"Of course, ma'am. Excuse me a moment."

With reluctance, Noreen left the water a while later. It was cooling, and Blanca gently urged her into her day. People were waiting.

Dressed in warm woolens, trousers as soft as eiderdown and a high-necked thick sweater, she slipped her feet into felted woolen shoes.

"Do the shops not carry cloth with color?" she complained, looking at the warm ivory ensemble she wore. With luck the rest of her luggage would arrive today.

Blanca wisely ignored the whine, and tucked a final stray wisp of hair into her coiled braid.

"There, m'lady, you're perfect now. May I call for an escort?"

"No, I'm sure my father has every camera trained on me, and every guard looking out for me. Stray one inch from the path to the dining room and I'm sure I'll be clapped in irons and sent off to the dungeon."

"But we have no dungeons, m'lady," Blanca replied, blinking in confusion.

"I know. More's the pity. I could have had the duke locked up in one last night. Any word from him this morning?"

"No, ma'am."

"Thank you, Blanca. I'll see you later." She stepped through the door from her sitting room to the hall.

Blessedly empty, the corridor stretched in two directions. To the left, her parents' apartments, Coreen's across and down a little. Gunnar's new study across the way and a little to the right. Had he slept there last night? Or had he found more inviting quarters?

The thought left a bitter taste of gall in the back of her throat. Slaves. He'd mentioned having love slaves at his country estate. *Well, we'll just see about that.* Wonder what he'd think of her closeness to her staff? She sighed, thinking of the comfort she'd enjoyed with her three personal attendants. She missed them, and was anxious to return to Ryadstholm and the familiarity of their routines.

Choosing to move in the direction of the family dining room, she turned to her right and strolled toward the main section of the palace.

On the third floor, across the hall from her father's vast study, were the more intimate common rooms for the family. People could choose to have meals sent to their rooms, but most often that option was saved for illness. Gathering over meals was a tradition encouraged on Nordia, and the royal family adhered to it with near fanaticism. Half past the fifth hour was the gathering time for breakfast. She was only a few minutes late.

She approached the dining room, expecting to hear conversations as everyone caught up on their schedules for the day. With all the sisters in residence, surely there would have been a significant amount of noise coming from within. If nothing else the laughter of her sisters' children should have been spilling out to the hall.

Nothing. The room was silent, as if waiting.

Curious, yet concerned, she stopped at the open door and looked in.

Gunnar stood alone in the room, a cautious light in his eyes as he caught sight of her. For just a moment her heart seemed to stumble over itself, then resumed a normal beat. Behind Gunnar, the long table was set with only two places facing each other across the middle. Heated serving dishes were arranged around the two settings and the rest of the long table, with plenty of room to accommodate the large family, was filled with vase after vase of flower arrangements.

Small bowls overflowed with colorful blooms. Tall crystal and porcelain vases held towering arrangements. Not one of them held a spot of white. Every shade of red, orange, blue, pink, green, and purple was represented in flower and foliage. The fragrance reminded her of the many tropical planets she'd visited and a wave of longing swept over her.

"Good morning." Gunnar lifted a delicate Carminrad rose of deep velvet pink.

She watched him slowly approach her, his stride loose and easy. Dressed in dark trousers, his shirt of pressed Kookorian cotton was a deep hue of blue with threads of green woven in a pattern that made it shimmer like the summer seas she loved to swim in. Seas she'd love to swim in with him, she realized with a small jolt remembering the perfection of his body in the waters of the grotta. He stopped before her and held out the flower.

"I hope this pleases you. The fragrance reminds me of you, the blush a pale shadow of your cheek flushed with pleasure."

Slowly, she reached for the flower, finding it easier to look at than his eyes. "Thank you." She inhaled the scent, fresh and complimentary to the scented oil she'd used in her bath that morning.

"You smell better than the flowers."

She glanced up to find him only a step away, and found it hard to keep from stepping into his arms. "Yes, well, I'm fresh from the bath. Give me a few hours. Where is everyone?" She gestured around the room.

"They all had other plans for breakfast. We have the room to ourselves."

"I see." Yes, she saw, all right. Her father pulling his strings of manipulation again. A hint of irritation furrowed her brow for a moment, before she smoothed it away with a forced return to serenity.

"Breakfast is ready. Would you prefer coffee or tea?"

He held out an arm for her. More out of habit than anything, she took his arm and let him escort her to the table. So he found refuge in formality. So be it. She could act civilized when required.

"Tea is fine."

A movement from the corner of the room revealed a footman carrying a silver teapot.

"They tell me it is a superior herbal leaf, which has been known to promote healthy pregnancies. If you don't like it we can choose another."

"If it is the same as Blanca served this morning then it will be fine." She let him seat her, then he surprised her by leaning past her to lift a lid on a serving dish.

"We have what the kitchen assures me is your favorite breakfast. Reindeer sausage, eggs, muffins and fruit. Fresh fruit."

"Fresh fruit at this time of year?"

"The modifications to the hydroponics program have been immensely successful. The various plants you've sent back over the years are thriving."

"Wonderful." She watched as he served the portions onto her plate. "Whoa there. I'm not a mineworker."

"No, but you are a mother." He smoothly bent down and kissed to top of her head.

"Thank you so much for reminding me," she muttered. Was she touched, or annoyed, that he seemed to know how hungry she felt? Deciding to reserve judgment, she tried to focus on the conversation he seemed set on having.

"How are you feeling? Any morning sickness?"

"No, I'm fine," she answered shortly and watched as he moved around to his side of the table. No need to tell him of her bout of queasiness that morning. It was gone, for now.

The footman poured her tea, and another brought glasses of juice while Gunnar loaded his plate with the hot food. He put twice as much on his plate, and she had no doubt he'd eat it all. She did have doubts about finishing her portions.

Laying the flower down on the table, she shook out her napkin and reached for her fork. Eating would take care of the need for conversation. Then again, Gunnar seemed to have that problem under control as well. He didn't leave her much room for commenting beyond an occasional noncommittal murmur.

Still, she had to wonder at this new approach. So far, he'd been gentle and charming this morning. It was a change from the overbearing attitude he seemed to force himself into, usually when she was annoyed, and then he became all the more overbearing. But now...he was being...sweet.

The clank of silver against china drew her from her thoughts, and she looked down at her plate in surprise. Her fork, seeking another bite, had struck china. Empty china. Without noticing, she'd eaten everything he'd served up for her.

"More tea? Are you still hungry?" he asked her, reaching for the teapot.

Blinking, she looked up at him. "No, I'm fine. Thanks."

"You're done then?"

His plate was also empty, though how he'd managed to eat while keeping up a stream of conversation she didn't know. He'd done enough talking for the two of them, and yet, she couldn't really remember what he'd said.

"Yes, I'm done." She watched as he stood and walked around the long table. "What's with all the flowers?" Damn, hadn't meant to ask. His smile drove home the point.

"It occurred to me, we never had time for a courtship." He took her hand and helped her stand. "And until the state wedding, I would be honored if you'd wear this as a token of my love for you."

Puzzled, she took the small box he held out to her and lifted the lid. Inside, nestled in a bed of fluff, was an exquisite ring. The large center stone was a fiery orange, faceted in a square shape. It was set low in a band of gleaming gold, inset with squares of a multi colored stone that looked like fire against a dark night sky. The flaming warmth of the middle stone was picked up as flecks mixed with blues and greens in the side stones flush with the band.

"The big stone is a fire opal, just like the ones found on Earth. The others are called black opal," he said, and took the ring from the box. With a smooth movement he slid it over the third finger of her left hand. Another timeless tradition, most likely dating back to Earth. Not many people wore rings of such design. If they wore stones at all they were generally set low flush in the band, channel style. Big rings didn't work with gloves which were worn nearly year round.

"It... it is beautiful," she said, and meant it.

"I know it isn't a traditional ring, but this just seems to fit you better."

"It fits perfectly." She tested the comfort of it on her finger. A more perfect fit couldn't have been found, unless she'd chosen the ring herself. Even though she knew he meant the style and colors, she chose to play naïve.

"No, I meant the stones. I looked at diamonds, but they seemed too cold for you. I want you to feel warm when you look at this ring." His eyes gazed at her, deeply sincere. "I want you to feel warm when you think of me."

"Thank you," she said softly, his eyes igniting the feeling of heat deep inside. She was still annoyed over his heavy-handed attitudes of the last few days. He wasn't going to melt her this easily. It took more than pretty baubles to win her over, and she forced herself to straighten her spine.

"I...I have some business to attend to," she said quietly.

"We need to be on our way." He cupped her elbow.

"I need to call my secretary," she insisted calmly, but with a firm edge to her tone. Dismissing her was not the way to win her affections, and he needed to know that here and now.

Gunnar stopped and looked at her for a long moment. "Will it take long?"

"I don't know. I haven't spoken with her since I left Ryadstholm. I need to see how they're doing and give her some instructions. It appears my apartments in the palace will need to be prepared, and I want to find out if Hans spoke with Hollis. Who knows how long it could take. A minute? An hour? Anything in between? I don't know."

She watched as thoughts flitted across his mind. "Of course. I'm sorry for presuming. Would you like to use my study?" He turned with her back toward the residence wing.

"I have my own desk. I'll join you when I'm done with my call." She stopped outside her door and waited for him to nod. There was an odd tension around him as he kissed her hand, and then waited for her to enter her sitting room.

The call to her staff was quickly handled. Fiona, efficient as ever, and more so on her home turf, had everything in hand. Just seeing Fi again, over the vid-com unit, helped to calm Noreen's upset thoughts. The distraction of catching up helped diffuse her confusion over Gunnar.

"We've met with Hollis," Fiona said, her manner and appearance every bit the professional secretary. "I can find no precedence for the wedding according to Hollis's claims."

"Then take it to the family lawyers." Noreen found herself conceding, with a sigh of resignation. "We need to resolve this and move on to the real wedding." It took only a moment to pass on the details to date. Fiona agreed to work with the Ryadstholm Palace, as well as the Summer Palace staff to prepare the apartments.

"You didn't say, m'lady. Do I prepare your rooms for your new husband as well?"

"Make sure he has his own suite, complete with library. I believe his man is called Lars. I haven't met him yet." She rubbed a hand across her forehead, and ignored Fi's look of concern. "Coordinate with him. I'm sure the palace butlers will know who he is and how to reach him." She ignored the heavy silence on the other end of the line. "And be sure there's a competent doctor at hand. I'm pregnant, but with how many embryos I don't know. Find one well-versed in multiples and in dealing with the hoops necessary."

"Yes, m'lady."

"Is there anything else I need to be aware of? Anyone giving you trouble?"

"Just the Lidarian prince, ma'am." Fiona's chuckle came across the line. "No, we're a bit bored here if the truth be known. We miss you."

A pang of loneliness hit her heart and Noreen forced herself to smile. If the truth be known, a touch of jealously was mixed in as well. She missed the comfort of her staff. "I miss you too, though please do pass on to Sophie her sister is a doll. Almost like having Sophie here herself."

"She'll be pleased to hear it."

"Well, if you get too bored, take up knitting. My babies will need warm clothes and blankets." The joke felt flat and weak to her own ears.

In a gesture so familiar it brought tears to her eyes, Noreen watched as Fiona reached out to touch the screen of the vid-com. "We'll be with you soon, ma'am," Fiona soothed her. "It will all work out just fine."

"Yes, I know it will. Well, the duke is waiting for me. I'd best find a way to procrastinate a little more, and really annoy him, and then it's Parliament's turn. If something pops up with Hollis or the lawyers, don't hesitate to let me know."

"Yes, ma'am. I'll let you know immediately." With a smile and wave, Fiona disconnected, and Noreen turned away from her desk.

"M'lady?"

She looked up at Blanca.

"The Prince would like to know if you are ready. He says Parliament is waiting."

"I thought we'd meet with them after lunch?" She stood with a frown.

"It seems they called a special early session, so that you might rest this afternoon instead."

"I see. Well, tell him to give me ten more minutes, and then I'll be ready to go." He could wait just a little longer, while she freshened up.

* * * *

The door to his study was open, so Gunnar heard when the door to Noreen's sitting room opened. A half an hour she'd kept him waiting. She probably didn't realize he could tell when she was through with her call. He stood and straightened the sleeves of his shirt, before shrugging into the formal jacket Lars held for him. She came to the threshold just as he secured the last button.

"Ready?" he asked.

"Blanca tells me there's a special session of Parliament this morning."

"Yes, we'll be able to step in and announce our marriage, then slip out again." He took her hand, and tucked it under his arm with a smile. "I believe your father means to end the session today, so everyone can begin preparing for the Solstice. We have many people to get to the Summer Palace in just under three weeks."

He kept the conversation going as he guided her to the common elevator. Normally he'd use the staircase, but he didn't know how tired she'd grow. She looked peaked now. Was it the lack of color in her clothing? Only the ring and her eyes kept her from being completely washed out. Just as they had this morning, her eyes looked expressionless. Dull, if he had to put a word to it. The lack of life-enhancing sparkle concerned him.

Just as during breakfast, she didn't respond to his comment. At least she still wore the ring.

"Nory." He pulled her to a stop and turned to face her. "I hate seeing you like this."

"Like what?" she asked softly, her head cocked inquisitively.

"Are you still angry?"

"To be angry would indicate I actually had feelings over this whole situation." She pulled her hand from his arm and turned away to continue down the hall.

"Nory, please." He caught her in a stride.

"My name is Noreen. You may address me as such, or the more common Your Highness." She didn't look at him as she glided down the hall. "I suppose I'll have to allow the more familiar term, but I don't have to allow the nickname."

Like that, was it? He watched her saunter away from him, appreciating her gentle walk. Personal feelings aside, they needed to present a unified front. He strode forward to catch up to her, and tucked her arm through his again. With no more reaction than a rag doll, she didn't fight him. Silence reigned as they rode the elevator down to the main level, where the king, queen and Coreen waited.

"Ah, good morning," the king brightly greeted them, and embraced his daughter. Gunnar met his questioning look with a half-raised shoulder.

"Oh Noreen, the ring is beautiful," her mother gushed.

The admiration was met with a tiny shrug before she turned to accept the long coat a footman held for her. Another item in white, Gunnar noted. He hadn't noticed the preponderance of white in Nordian fashion before. It was something he could change.

An uneasy silence fell on the group, Nory's mood infecting them all. The short ride to Parliament was equally silent as he watched her stare out the window of the transport, her face perfectly blank. A more perfect ice princess he'd never seen. This wasn't his princess.

"What is expected of me, Your Majesty?" she asked her father while staring at the passing ice-encrusted landscape.

"A short speech about how happy you are to be at home would be nice. Is it too much to ask?"

"Whatever you'd like, Your Majesty," she answered quietly, seemingly ignoring the slightly sarcastic tone of her father, and Gunnar resisted the urge to roll his eyes.

"Noreen, just do what you did at the grotta, and they'll be eating out of your hands."

"Yes, Your Majesty."

"We'll issue a verbal proclamation for the wedding. Have you the time yet?" the queen asked.

Gunnar's eyes were drawn to Nory's face as she closed her eyes for a few moments. Consulting with the gods?

"Midnight."

"Solstice night, so that would be Wednesday, three weeks hence?" The queen pressed.

Noreen paused for a moment longer, then nodded. "Yes, that Wednesday."

"Very good." The king clapped his hands, then rubbed them together. "Here we go now. Just smile and say you're happy to be home, we'll take care of the rest."

Once inside the large blocky building, Gunnar was tempted to drag Nory into a nearby alcove and kiss her senseless. Even it if made her mad, it was better than this dull nothingness she exuded.

No stranger to Parliament, he'd sat through many a session. It was odd to be standing behind the podium where all eyes were directed. Normally, he sat off to the right, towards the back. Politics wasn't his great love, but he played the game well enough. Bjorn and his grandfather had encouraged him, and he'd gone along half heartedly, more interested in the freight business. More interested in intelligence gathering. It always amazed him how much information there was to gather on such a small planet.

The Prime Minister, an old windbag named Alden Marshall, made a small speech, then the royal family stepped forward. Bjorn said a few words, praising his beautiful and talented daughters, then confirmed the union of his eldest daughter Noreen, recently home from her latest round of trade negotiations, and Duke Nordenskiold, no longer the planet's most eligible bachelor.

Applause thundered from the four hundred and twenty-two members who stood to show their approval. Gunnar knew they were just glad to have a marriage announced. The wedding of the heiress was at least six years overdue, as far as they were concerned. Not that Bjorn was old, but there was a certain rhythm to life and Noreen's absence had upset the balance. The delayed marriage of the princess had been discussed often enough in the halls. Whispers had long since given way to open and frank discussions. A sense of relief flooded the main council chamber, and the volume of the approval grew to a roar.

Through it all, Noreen maintained a small smile, no change in her expression. Gunnar was tempted to pinch her, just to get a reaction. Anything to change the polished marble of her facade.

At Bjorn's urging, they stepped to the podium together, and Noreen gripped the edge of the wooden stand as he held her other hand.

"Thank you for the welcome home. I only hope you will be half as pleased with me as you are with my sister, Coreen, who has been here all along. I know you're used to her, and love her, and she will continue to work for the good of all Nordia." She paused and cocked her head, as if listening to something, then slid her eyes to her father. His nod was subtle, but there all the same, and Gunnar wondered if they'd both heard something from the gods.

"Speaking of the good of all Nordia, your help will be needed in just a few weeks. This is the time we all must stand together, as we always have. It has been revealed a comet is currently on a path to intersect with Nordia. Of such a size to create great destruction, the gods will help us avert this danger. Your presence, and the presence of your families, is required at the Summer Palace this coming Solstice. At this time the formal wedding will take place, and the gods will reveal the means by which we will save our planet. Details will be transmitted soon so preparations may begin. You all heard Odin's proclamation a few nights ago. Only death is an excuse to stay away, for should any of you not attend, death may very well come to us all."

Gunnar slipped his arm around Nory's waist as he looked out at the stunned faces staring back at him. He settled his mouth into a grim line to show this was no fantasy.

"And when the threat is passed, we'll celebrate not only the marriage, but the greater event of a new age for Nordia. This isn't my planet. This is *our* planet. *Our* home. Our families have invested lifetimes here, and it is up to us to carry on in the tradition of the explorers we are descended from."

Noreen fell silent, and Gunnar glanced out of the corner of his eye. Hers scanned the assembly representing the leaders. Every seat was filled, even his, where Wilton Leebrick sat in for him. A man near the front stood, and Nory watched him, her eyes neutral but sharp, taking in his puffed-out chest. Malcom Arildsen.

"Princess, Your Highness, on behalf of Parliament let me welcome you home. In case any here wonder where you've been," he turned to face the assembly, "I'd just like to take this opportunity to remind Nordia how much you've done on their behalf these past ten years. Probably the most notable is the new worldwide communications system circling the planet. The same system which allows instantaneous contact with the far lands. The same system which allows faster and clearer contact beyond the solar system. Her contributions to the planet are too numerous to count but be assured most of the new products in your homes and businesses are the result of the Princess's ability to conduct trade negotiations." The older man turned back to the podium and bowed deeply. "We thank you for your dedication to your people, Your Highness, and we extend our most sincere wish for all the blessings of the gods upon your marriage and the new members of the royal family, who will soon grace us with their presence."

Noreen returned the bow with a regal nod and Gunnar felt his heart swell with pride. She acknowledged the renewed applause gracefully, as his eyes scanned the nobles before him. Most wore expressions of awe and adoration. A few sported carefully blank faces, and one or two scowled. He made a mental note of who wore the scowls. Not necessarily a threat, but it would be interesting to sort out the source of their discontent.

Noreen's arm slipped around his waist. It felt as if she wrapped herself around his heart. Warmth stealing over him, he held her close to his side.

Chapter 20

"Well! That went very well!"

Noreen sent a mild glare in her father's direction. He was pleased. Guess that was what counted most. She settled back in her seat for the return ride to the palace. Gunnar's arm was around her, and she was too tired to protest. So much for a simple visit to the chambers of Parliament. At least the nobility was on notice for the wedding. Let others see to the details of putting everyone in place.

"Nory, dear," her mother spoke, and she looked that way. "Since we're doing this in the pool, we've decided to devise headpieces to take the place of gowns. There must be some form of decoration to distinguish the wedding party from the guests."

"Yes, Mamma. Whatever you think best," she quietly murmured. She'd already put her foot down on the date and time of the wedding. Moder could take care of everything else.

"I'm not quite sure how to handle the reception afterward." The queen sighed, a gloved finger resting against her lips.

It occurred to Noreen that the unending white of her planet reminded her of other planets where wet, gray days were considered dull and depressing. The only color decorating her mother and sister came from their makeup. Even their jewelry was icy and cold, either diamonds or ice blue gems set in platinum. As if she could see it through her thick mittens, she glanced at her left hand where the ring Gunnar gave her encircled her finger.

Gunnar had chosen color for her. Warm colors set in yellow gold to remind her of heat. The heat from the planets she so loved. The heat of their physical encounters. It occurred to her he wasn't trying to force her into the mold everyone else conformed to. What did it mean? She closed her eyes and rested against him. Even through the thick wool coats they both wore, his body heat seeped into hers and she felt warm. Almost absently his lips found her temple and a tingle of magic shimmered through her body.

"I was thinking we could do a white crystal and silver theme," the queen was saying.

"No." The single word she uttered stopped the flow of conversation that was just warming up.

"I'm sorry?"

"No cold colors. Yellow, orange, red, brown. Bright bold and vibrant. I want hot, electric colors. You may use any material you wish, but the colors will be hot." She gazed at her mother and sister, their expressions surprised. Well, Moder was surprised; Cory just looked resigned.

"But Noreena," her mother protested, using the childhood version of her name, "wedding colors are always cool and pastel."

"Not mine. If I have to hire off-world painters, I'm going to change this planet into one of color. I'll paint the damn snow if I have to, but I don't want anything to remind me of frozen water at my wedding. Afterwards, for the reception, if we get to have one, you can do as you please. I have a feeling we should be preparing emergency supplies instead."

"Not a bad idea," her father muttered. "Should have mentioned that in your speech."

"Yes, I should have. Well, you can work with your ministers and issue a statement later this afternoon or early tomorrow." Never mind he could have mentioned it in his speech.

Gunnar's arm tightened around her and she glanced up at him. His closeness startled her a little and his gaze sent a jolt of awareness through her.

Wait a minute—she was mad at him, wasn't she?

He bent his head and rested his forehead against hers.

Trying to hold the rush of desire at bay, she closed her eyes and swallowed deeply. Tender, and so very sweetly, he kissed her nose and pulled her closer. A part of her felt deep disgust, but that was all it took and she melted against him.

"We have a little time before lunch, would you like a tour of the hydroponics grottas?" Gunnar asked her quietly.

"That would be lovely."

"Would you like me to request lunch in your sitting room or shall we eat with the family?"

"We should eat with the family." It felt so good resting against him.

"We don't have to. What is best for you and the babies is what's important here."

Babies. That plural word again. Noreen's head felt light and she would have swayed if Gunnar's arm hadn't been around her.

"I am a little tired…"

"Then we'll eat alone. The afternoon is clear so you can rest. The doctor thinks daily naps will be good for you."

"I'm not that pregnant," she muttered, but his lips on her forehead soothed her again.

"Yes, you are. Remember, your first trimester will pass in just a few weeks. That has to put some kind of strain your body."

Their arrival at the palace cut off her response. Inside, the butler and footmen waited as coats and boots were exchanged for soft indoor shoes. Blowing on her hands to warm them, she then pressed them to her cheeks. Lotion. Needed lotion to counteract the inevitable chapping from even a few moments out in the minus fifty degree weather.

Warm hands covered hers and warm lips brushed over her mouth.

"I'll warm you up," Gunnar murmured his promise, and she felt her cheeks instantly flush.

"Thanks, I think I'm set for now." She stepped away.

"Just call the kitchen when you're ready for your lunch," Moder said, and Noreen nodded, careful to ignore the concerned light in her mother's eyes.

Gunnar's hand under her elbow, they turned toward the elevator. The ride down was silent and she was thankful he didn't press her for conversation. Stopping on the hydroponics level, she stepped from the car into a brightly lit cavern. Rows of troughs held plants thriving in the environment. The soft hum of pumps gently circulating the water around the roots provided background music. A gardener looked up surprised, and then greeted them with a smile.

"Will we be in the way if we wander around for a bit?" Gunnar asked the man.

"No, no, m'lord. Not at all. Wander where you like." The gardener bobbed a quick bow, and Noreen made an effort to give him her friendliest smile. With a blush, the young man stared at her a moment, then directed his gaze to the floor.

"Thank you," she said softly. "We'll try to stay out of your way."

"No worries, Your Highness," he whispered, then backed away. Noreen repressed a sigh of impatience when he nearly ran to the next cavern.

"I wish they wouldn't do that," she muttered as she strolled toward the back cavern.

"They don't usually. At least not for me," Gunnar chuckled, as he followed. "Probably because you look so especially pretty today. It's enough to tie the tongue of any man."

A few minutes later, they found a spot arranged to look like a secluded corner in a park. There was even a stone bench to rest on. Rising from the water, a large vine rose and was entwined on a lattice trellis. Small white flowers and bunches of ripening fruit hung from another vine that stretched along the back wall of grotta.

"The inability to speak doesn't seem to be a problem for you." She looked away, thinking he'd done nothing but talk all breakfast.

"On the other hand, I find myself unable to stop blathering when faced with exceptional beauty." Gunnar's arm wound around her waist and turned her to face him, their bodies close.

The moment felt very intimate where they stood beneath the trellised vine. Green leaves and spiraling tendrils formed a loose curtain screening them, the sound of gurgling water masking everything but their breathing. Gunnar's warmth and woody scent surrounded her, the muscles of his chest bunching under her fingers, where her hands rested, not sure if they wanted to push him away or pull him closer.

"I'm sorry, Nory, for whatever I said or did to upset you," he said softly, and she looked up to see the sincerity in his eyes. "I don't want us fighting. We have enough battles on our hands right now."

Unable to look away, she tried not to laugh at his understatement. However, faced with the situation, she had to stop and consider all the changes the last few days had brought. She'd returned home thinking to abdicate, only to find herself permanently anchored in the one place she didn't want to be. Married to a man she hardly knew. Pregnant with an unknown multiple of fetuses, all growing at an enhanced rate. Her world in the path of doom and she was the hope of the planet, the one to turn aside the disaster with little control or knowledge of her powers to do so. And if that weren't enough, an alien suitor was on hand insisting they were married.

"Battles." Her laugh was more of a soft choking sound. "Right. Good way to describe it." She pushed against Gunnar's chest, but he only pulled her closer, a hand at her nape cradling her head to his shoulder. Resisting for only a moment, she let her irritation fade away, and melted against him. His breath, released in relief, was audible where her ear pressed to his chest. She slid her arms around his waist, and he enfolded her deeper in his arms.

"Can we start again?" he asked, and she closed her eyes, leaning into him.

"Can we?" she repeated the question. "There's still so much we don't know about each other. I don't know. Considering I never wanted to marry, I don't know how to be married. I especially don't know how to be a mother. Most of all, I don't know how I'm going to pull off what we're supposed to do on the Solstice."

"One step at a time, *älskling*, one step at a time. The first one is you and I deciding to stand together to face everything else." Gunnar kissed her forehead. "I know we don't know each other well, but already I love you, and not because of The Profetia. I love you because of what I do know about you, your spirit and your great passion."

Noreen felt her heart melting at his declaration. The tone, the way he held her, the very words, all pushed past the ice she'd covered her heart with the night before. Shame filled her. "Oh Gunnar, I'm such an idiot." The words poured from her as tears gathered.

"Hey, hey, hey, hush there," he crooned, sinking to the bench and pulling her down on his lap. "Hush, *älskling*, hush. You're not an idiot. You're overwhelmed and have had great burdens thrust upon you without warning. That has to upset anyone, much less a woman with an unprecedented rush of pregnancy hormones running through her body."

"That must be it." She sniffed in an effort to stem the tears. "I don't normally cry at the drop of a hat."

Strong fingers were gentle against her cheek as Gunnar wiped the tears away. "Of course you don't. You're more likely to rip the head off the fool who tries to hurt you than cry at him."

From deep inside a tiny bubble of laughter rose. "You're right. People who annoy me are more likely to bleed than drown. Well, unless we happen to be in water and then I might hold their heads under."

"There's my princess," Gunnar chuckled with her. "Remind me never to annoy you while in water."

"You shouldn't be trying to annoy me anyway." She sniffed back the last tear.

"You're right, but since I'm just a man, I fear my best efforts may not be good enough." The smile he gave her was irresistible.

"Smart man." She stared into his eyes. Not a hint of the silver sparkle that indicated he used his power to compel.

"So I've been told," he murmured, and rested his hand over her stomach. "It is still so incredible to know, to believe, that here rests the next generation."

A warm glow infused her, radiating outward from his hand. "Truly a miracle. Well, one with a little divine help."

"How do they have the ability to facilitate such things?"

"I don't know. They haven't revealed all their secrets to me." She shrugged. "Some things you just have to take on faith."

"Can you take me on faith?"

Gunnar's eyes still held the expression of sincerity she'd seen moments before. Did she have a choice? Their union had already been god and father blessed. Parliament blessed. They'd even exchanged vows of a sort, acknowledging their mutual claims on each other. All that remained was the official ceremony to make their union church blessed.

"I guess I'll have to, as much as you have to take me on faith," she said slowly.

"I have faith, Nory, I know we'll be good together. This is meant to be, let's make it good." He smiled at her, then pulled her close to nuzzle her neck.

"Oh Freya," she sighed, his lips starting a chain reaction where they touched her skin.

"Ever make love in an arbor?" Gunnar's voice rumbled beneath her ear.

"What if someone walks by?" she gasped. Being naked in public didn't generally bother her. Mostly, because everyone around her was naked at the same time. But here? It felt wicked somehow. Forbidden.

"We're hidden."

Butterflies fluttered in her chest when his hand slid under the edge of her sweater to rest against her stomach.

"Nory?" he whispered urgently. "I need you, *älskling*. I'll die if I have to wait another minute."

She chuckled weakly, feeling his pressing need against her thigh. "Oh Gunnar," she sighed, turning to meet his lips with hers. "I do love you."

It was the last thought she had. Words were simply useless as Gunnar stood and reached for the fastening on her trousers, his mouth hot on hers. In less than a minute her pants were down around her knees and she was kneeling on the bench with him easing into her from behind.

Hungry for each other, he filled her hot and fast, the very size of him making her cry out softly. A bird, startled in the branches above them, chirped then flew away as Gunnar drove deep, touching her womb.

"So ready for me," he groaned. "How do you do it, Nory? So hot, so wet..." He slid out, then thrust in again. "Tell me if I'm too rough." He slammed against her.

"Harder!" She urged him on, their location making her nervous and extremely excited all at once.

"Freya's *fitte!*" He groaned and answered her command, stroking her deep.

Two more thrusts and she cried out her cataclysmic release, Gunnar's strangled shout matching hers.

Chapter 21

"Tomorrow we leave for Ryadstholm," her father announced two nights later.

"Good. I'm anxious to proceed," Noreen said.

It was about time. The past three days had been enough to test the patience of a saint. And she was no saint.

The mornings had passed in a mixture of queasy stomachs and trivial details. Afternoons had been slept away, and the evenings filled with official dinners. Tonight's had been the most tedious by far. The last diplomat had just been bundled out the door with his wife and daughter. Noreen watched Cory and Al share a smile of relief. Miss Stanton had done her very level best to catch the duke's attention and Cory was ready to rip her braid out if Noreen knew that look at all.

"So, tell me, Al, have you asked for Cory's hand yet?" Noreen asked casually as she removed the heavy earrings the occasion demanded. Ancient and solid, the gold and diamond heirlooms were difficult, at best, to wear for brief formal portraits. Torture for state dinners. She handed the jewelry to Blanca, then turned so her maid could remove the matching choker. If she had to wear it one more minute, she'd probably disgrace herself by gagging. The pressure of anything against the front of her throat was unbearable.

When Blanca curtsied and trundled off with the State jewelry, Noreen turned to look at the stunned faces pointed in her direction. Her father smirked, but Al and Cory blushed. How cute.

"Well? When are you going to marry the woman?" Noreen prodded some more.

"I...I'd planned on waiting until a respectable period had passed after your wedding." Al pulled himself together enough to respond with dignity.

"Oh fi. Pappa, really, you should give them permission to marry as soon as possible. If this shield thing doesn't work, it would be a shame for Cory to die unwed." Noreen calmly pulled off her elbow length gloves.

"We thought Coreen might like a more planned out and elaborate wedding," their mother said gently.

"I think it's more important that Cory at least experience the great mystery of life before the world ends. Don't you?" She calmly directed her gaze at first her mother, then father, then Cory's blush. Al wore a tiny smile of approval.

"*I can't believe you'd discuss such a thing so openly,*" Cory hissed in her mind, but Noreen only smiled back.

"*Dear sister, I've been privy to your dreams these past few nights. You, my dear, are one horny virgin. I should know. The sooner you get laid the better.*" Al had been the star of each and every one of those dreams. Gunnar, reinstalled in her bed, had been the lucky recipient of the feelings those dreams inspired. Her eye caught his, and he grinned. He knew.

"Well, Cory?" their father asked. "We know you two intend to marry eventually. Would you rather gamble on the successful outcome of our defenses and plan for the great wedding of the century? Or would you rather have a quiet ceremony and enjoy a honeymoon while we run around and try to save our world?"

"*I hate you for this.*" Cory's childish taunt echoed in her head, and Noreen just shrugged.

"*Go for the quiet wedding and extended honeymoon,*" she advised privately. "Call the bishop, Fader. Let's get them properly wedded. It will make the shield operation so much easier if she isn't distracted by all that male flesh on Solstice night."

"Noreen!" Cory gasped, and blushed.

"Besides, I want her to be pregnant at the same time. It's no fun being the only one puking in the mornings. My babies are going to need playmates."

"I'm all for it," the king said, and turned to his hovering secretary.

"Oh come on, Cory. Let's have a wedding tonight," she wheedled her sister. "What do you say, Al? Have you even properly proposed yet?"

"I've been most remiss," the other man responded as he wrapped his arms around Cory from behind. "I didn't know for sure if I had the approval of the family."

"Well, hell yes!" Noreen rolled her eyes. "Otherwise we'll have to marry her off to Malcolm Alridson. I'm sure his children would just love having her step in as stepmother. Old Malcolm would be giddy with joy." She laughed at Cory's shudder of horror.

Al was very spry as he turned Cory in his arms and then elegantly fell to one knee before her. "Coreen, I'd be honored and pleased to call you my wife. Will you make me the happiest man on Nordia?"

Noreen nearly laughed as she pictured the older Malcolm attempting the same gesture. It would take two footmen to help the elder statesman to his feet. Al was more than able to sweep Cory into his arms and carry her off to bed.

The family waited in silence as Coreen blushed and spluttered.

"Oh please, go on. This is what you want," Noreen nudged her sister mentally. *"Do we need to have the talk about what will happen in the bedroom tonight?"*

"No!" Cory shouted. "I mean, yes, Al, I'll marry you. I was telling Nory to leave me alone," she explained.

"Oh good, we have that settled." The king made his pronouncement while Al swept Cory into a hug and kissed her soundly.

Noreen bit back a grin as her father told Olaf to call for the bishop.

"Oh, and Olaf? Have someone run down and grab a large bouquet for the bride," Noreen added her own little instruction.

"I'll call the jeweler while I'm at it." He bowed and left the room.

Noreen found herself pulled into a comforting hug, after Gunnar shook Al's hand and pounded him on the back.

"Good call. Wonder how twin-speak will work tonight," he murmured in her ear, while her mother and sisters made a fuss over Coreen.

"Oh Freya, I do not want to be a part of my sister's deflowering. You'd best keep me busy."

"I can do that." His grin sent a spike of warmth through her, his hands warm and comforting on her back.

"Nory, can we hold the ceremony in your sitting room? You have all the plants," Coreen stated.

"Sure." She stepped out to tell the footmen already rushing to set up.

The better part of an hour was spent assembling the impromptu wedding, the women pulling Coreen off to her dressing room. Coreen was helped into their mother's wedding gown. It was a perfect fit. At least one of them got to wear it. The queen could die happy.

Cory's eyes met hers while she was being fussed over.

"*Why?*" The question shimmered in the air between them.

"*Because, if the world does end on the Solstice, I want you to be with your love. To die alone would be a bad thing.*"

"*You have doubts of your success?*"

"*Our success. I can't do it alone, and I'm terrified of failing. How would you feel knowing the fate of the world flowed through your body? If timing isn't perfect, disaster will strike and only a handful of people will make it off planet in time. 'Tis an awful burden.*"

"*Thank you.*"

"*Wait until he passes gas in bed. You won't thank me then,*" she couldn't help the chuckle in her head, and laughed out loud at Cory's snort of disgust.

"If you aren't going to help, why don't you go supervise the arrangement of your sitting room," her mother said evenly, with a hooded glare aimed her way.

"Yes, Moder," Noreen said obediently, and kissed her mother's cheek. She even yelped for effect when Moder swatted her behind. Not that she could feel anything under the formal dress and two layers of petticoats.

"Go on. We'll be there in a few minutes. Send word when all is ready."

"Yes, Moder." In a swirl of pink silk, she swept from the room and down the hall.

Footmen and maids were bustling in and out of the door to her sitting room with chairs and armfuls of flowers. She stepped back to let a footman with flowers go in ahead of her. As she told him, his load was heavier.

The doorway clear, she tried to go through again and found herself in Al's arms.

"Oh, Noreen! I'm so sorry," he laughed as he set her straight on her feet. "Didn't mean to run you down."

"No harm. Where are you rushing off to?" Noticing his tie was crooked, she reached out and put it right. He stood patiently and let her fuss, pale blue eyes sparkling with a hint of humor and panic.

"I'm not exactly sure where I was going. Air. I needed air," he chuckled.

Rolling her eyes, Noreen slid an arm through his and steered him a few steps down the hall. "We'll go have a seat over there and talk for a minute. If you escape now, someone will be in trouble, and since I pushed the issue, I guess that makes me responsible."

Al waited until her skirts were arranged just so, then sat beside her on a padded bench. "I'm glad you did. I've wanted to marry her for years now, but…" his voice trailed off, and he looked away.

"But with me off and running around the galaxy and beyond, it wasn't possible, right?"

Al gave her a crooked grin. "Right. Not that I blame you for running. Given half a chance, I might have done the same were I in your position."

Noreen let her eyes search his face. Like most Nordians, he was blond with blue eyes and strong features that hinted at the distant Viking ancestry. Like Gunnar, he was tall, but his hair was cut short and perfectly combed. Well groomed. A man who strode the halls of government with ease and authority.

"I'm sorry for all the turmoil I've thrown into everyone's lives. There was no reason you and Cory could not have wed sooner."

"Noreen." Al picked up her hand and looked at it, rather than meet her eyes. "I understand the game your father played. Yes, he had choices, but he did what he felt was right to protect you. If the planet had known their Crown Princess was out gallivanting around the stars instead of staying here to do her duty, his position would have been in jeopardy. There have been many times over the course of our history here, the people have questioned the purpose of the monarchy. These secrets being revealed lately are calling that into question again. If the government has been hiding a princess and a comet, what else are they hiding?"

With the last sentence he looked up, his eyes questioning as he met her gaze.

"I think I see your point," she sighed. "I don't know everything, I just know we need to get past this comet threat and, once the planet is safe again, we can deal with anything else."

Al nodded. "That is the plan, and most of the members of Parliament are on track with it. There are one or two agitators, but then we always have them, so what's new? We're actually very well prepared for any disaster, natural or otherwise, as long as the comet doesn't actually hit the planet. I've been one of your father's closer confidants and have led the emergency preparedness movement these last five years. We can deal with volcanoes coming to life, ground quakes, fire, flood and general mayhem. What we can't deal with are the effects of a large direct hit. Look what it did to Earth a few million years ago? Wiped out entire life forms."

"And who are we to think we can save one little spinning ball of ice?" She felt no humor as she laughed.

"Well, at least I'll get to experience a little bit of heaven first," he said, and squeezed her hand.

"Just remind Cory to shut down her outside thoughts. I really don't want to be there when you two..." She cleared her throat. "As her husband, you should know, she and I can speak telepathically. Until a few days ago it was just images and emotions, but now we can use words. We're still learning to shield, so dreams are sometimes shared when we don't want them to be. Strong emotional outbursts are also transmitted because we forget to maintain the mindblock. It was how Cory got to us so quickly when the shower shattered."

Al's eyes sobered, then he nodded with a grin. "I'll remind her. I agree. I want it to be just the two of us tonight."

A footman coming to the door and looking around the hallway caught Noreen's attention. "Looks like they may be in search of the groom." Her suspicion was confirmed by the look of relief on the man's face.

Al nodded to the man and stood, handing her up from the seat. She swayed a little, a wave of exhaustion making itself known. Al put an arm around her waist.

"Are you all right? Can you hold up for just a few more minutes?"

"I'm fine. I want to witness this grand event," she assured him with a smile and let him lead her back to the room.

Blanca was there, as was Cory's assistant, Astrid.

"M'lady, sir, if you would take your places up near the bishop, we'll send for the bride."

"I'll send... *Cory, it's time.*"

"*Right.*"

"*Send Mamma and the sisters over. Is Pappa there?*"

"*He is. The others are on their way.*"

"They're coming," she told those watching her.

"Handy," Al muttered, then let Gunnar push him into his place near the bishop. Gunnar stood at his side, Best Man, and the husbands of Loreen and Doreen, as the eldest of the concubines, stood as well. The rest made up the gathered audience.

Less than fifteen minutes later, Al lifted the veil over Coreen's face and pulled her into his arms for a deep and breath-taking kiss.

The large, diamond encrusted band on Coreen's finger didn't shine half so brightly as the smile on her face. Champagne was poured, toasts were made, then Al lifted his wife in his arms and carried her from the room.

"Well that went well. Brilliant idea, Noreena," her father said, and tossed down the rest of his champagne. "Now if only your wedding could go so easily."

"Yes, well, we don't all have Coreen's luck." She sank wearily into the nearest chair and waved for Blanca.

"Yes, m'lady?"

"Please, tell the staff that clean up may wait until tomorrow. Just have them clear away the food and dishes, but the chairs and the rest," she waved at the room, "can wait. I know they're tired, too, and we still have to finish preparing for the trip."

"Thank you, ma'am, I'll pass the word then come back and help you prepare for bed. You're all done in."

"Yes, Blanca, and you're right. I'm ready for sleep."

"I can tell when we're being dismissed," her father chuckled, and bent to kiss her cheek. "We'll finish packing in the morning and leave right after lunch."

"Good night, Pappa."

After kissing her parents, and wishing her sisters goodnight, Noreen at last turned to her dressing room with Gunnar's arm around her.

"You're overtired," he said.

"Yes. But Cory is happy, so that is what matters most."

Blanca bustled into the room behind them, firmly shutting out the noise of last-minute clean-up in the sitting room.

Noreen stood still while Blanca began to unfasten the formal gown and Gunnar retreated behind his screen.

"What did you and Al discuss out in the hall?" Gunnar asked, while his man, Lars, helped him remove the formal apparel.

"Nothing much. It was more a matter of helping him calm his nerves. I wanted to make sure he didn't try to bolt."

Gunnar chuckled, and she caught Blanca's tiny smile.

"That's funny, coming from you," her husband said.

"Yes, well, as one who has bolted, I could identify the look of panic on his face. He only needed a moment of quiet to remember what he really wanted in life. I believe he'll be a good husband to her."

"He will."

The long nightgown floated down over her body, and she sighed with relief. Now just to wash her face, brush out her hair and then she could go to bed.

"Sit, m'lady. I'll bring the wet cloths here," Blanca told her.

Gratefully, she sank onto the chaise and waited. Now past the midnight hour, it had been a long day. Eyes closed, she didn't see Gunnar approach, but she felt his hands in her hair, pulling the pins holding it in place. By the time Blanca returned and draped the cleansing cloths on her face, Gunnar had her hair unbound. It felt good to have the weight of it off her neck.

"Leave it unbound tonight," Gunnar said.

"But—" she started to protest.

"I'd like it if you did."

Noreen sighed. Yes, he very much liked the feel of it on his body. She didn't like him rolling on top of it and trapping her at night.

"Very well. Just brush it well. And you may get the job of brushing it out in the morning." Her reply through the steaming cloths was muffled.

He only chuckled at her threat. It wasn't much of a threat. He liked brushing her hair as much as she liked letting him do it.

The cooling cloths were removed, then Blanca patted her face with a dry cloth. Lotion was efficiently applied while Gunnar slowly ran the brush through her tresses.

"Will that be all, m'lady?" Blanca asked.

"Yes, we're set for the night, Blanca, Lars. Thank you," Gunnar answered for her. Good thing, too. She was nearly asleep right there on the chaise.

Listening, she heard the rustle of her dress as Blanca put it in the closet, the petticoats next, then the door slid closed. Footsteps on the deep carpeting, then a softly uttered, "Good night," from the two servants, and the door to the sitting room snicked shut.

"Ah," Gunnar sighed. "Alone at last."

She couldn't help the little chuckle. "I warned you early on we'd find little privacy in our own dressing room."

"So you did, but we have it now. Off to bed Duchess Zaren."

"What if I'm too tired to move?"

"I might have to use this hairbrush for its other purpose." Gunnar's voice, deep and warm, was soft next to her ear.

She dropped her head back, and looked up to see him bent over her. "We can't have that. Help me to bed. The mother of your children needs her sleep. Those little darlings have sucked out all my energy for today."

"Imagine what they'll do to you when they're actually born."

A shudder went through her body at the very thought. "I think I may get a headache and go to bed for eighteen years or so," she told him, and let him pull her to her feet.

"Bed for eighteen or more years, yes, but not with a headache," he chuckled.

"Just make sure we have a really good nanny."

"Right."

Gunnar held the covers up for her and she rolled between them.

"Ahhhhh... Warm." She burrowed under the thick down comforter and soft flannel sheets. The bed dipped and Gunnar rolled up behind her.

"You don't need this anymore." He began tugging up her long nightgown.

"Yes, I do."

"Nory," he whispered in her ear, his hot breath making her heart beat just a little faster. "It's been an awfully long day, and I've had to go all those hours without touching you."

"You're touching me now."

His hand was under the hem of her gown, fingers stroking her hip.

"I'm just starting to touch you the way I want to touch you."

"You said it yourself, it's been an aw-aw-ful-ly long day." She yawned through the words. "I'm tired."

His hand cupped the back of her thigh, his fingers touching the seam where her legs pressed together. Moving slowly, he started behind her knee and slid backward, toward her center.

"You don't feel tired to me," he said. "You feel soft, warm," his finger brushed against the tiny bit of tender skin he could touch, "and wet." Lips teased her earlobe.

A shiver turned her blood into molten gold, warming her extremities and drenching his teasing fingers.

"I can feel how tired you aren't," his voice rumbled against the skin behind her ear.

"I'm exhausted," she tried to explain, as all her muscles contracted making her arch back against him.

His knee wedged between her thighs, lifting the upper one so he could slip his hand under to lift it higher. "Sure you are. Just lay there. I'll take care of you."

She reached down to help, guiding him into her. A hiss of pleasure escaped, harmonizing with his moan.

"Gunnar…"

"I've got you, baby."

Yeah, he had her. How could the man do this to her? She'd all but been asleep and now she burned for him, craved the release he promised, wanted nothing more than to be joined with him, like this, for always.

"Touch yourself, Nory. It makes me hot just thinking of you rubbing your clitty."

His lips and breath on her neck made her hot. Tugging on her nightgown, she lifted it, letting it bunch around her waist.

"Touch yourself," he urged her again.

Why did she listen to him? Why did she do as he told her to? She, who usually did the opposite of whatever anyone tried to command her to do? Reaching down, her finger brushed the top of her button, and she melted against Gunnar's chest. He had her. Right where he wanted her.

"Yes, *älskling*. Doesn't that feel good? I can't reach you, so you'll have to do what I want to do to you." Gunnar continued whispering instructions in her ear, describing what he felt, how her body wrapped around him.

Ever spiraling, her need grew and her body demanded satisfaction.

"Not yet," his voice wove a spell around her.

"I…I…"

"Not yet," he panted in her ear.

"But…"

"Keep rubbing, *älskling*, keep rubbing. Don't give in until I tell you to."

"Gunnar!" Shaking, it took all her concentration to hold back, her body growing hot, a light film of sweat engulfing her. "Please," she cried.

"Just…a…little…"

He moved faster, thrust harder, her fingers madly rubbing her clit, she felt him begin to shake in time with her…

"Now!"

Like a match set to gunpowder, his command set off her orgasm, the power of it ripping through every muscle in her body. She threw her head back and cried out as his arms wrapped tight around her. Tossed together, they clung to each other, riding out the erotic storm.

In the deep recesses of her mind she heard another cry of ecstasy and felt a deep contentment embrace her.

Chapter 22

"Would someone please explain to me, why these underground passages aren't used more regularly? We've been on this rock for five hundred years. There has to be some reason why we don't have a complete underground transportation system." Noreen barely blinked when her father's sigh carried over the hum of the electric carts they rode on in response to her question.

Eight hours, riding in small open carts, cruising along what passed for an underground highway on Nordia, left a lot of time for contemplating such questions. All small talk exhausted, she examined the roads they traveled. Mostly lava tubes with a few old mine shafts connecting them, the floors had been smoothed for easy travel. Once past the city limits, the tunnels reverted to rough walls with sporadic lighting for several kilometers, then slowly improved.

Four carts, in single file, ran on inflated tires over the underground road marked with the nearly invisible gray line. Now that she knew what to look for, Noreen could see a faint shadow of it without the special glasses everyone else seemed to need. The glasses just brought it into sharp relief for her.

"I don't know what you're getting all excited about," she muttered. "I can see it, that's all. Must be part of my talent." She took the bottle of water Gunnar handed her.

Riding in the third cart, they were behind her father, who rode in the second one with a driver and the bishop. She had trouble thinking of him as a grandfather. She still found him intimidating.

"Gunnar," her father called back, "you explain it to her."

Gunnar gave her a sidelong look, then shrugged. Without a word, he'd conveyed the message very clearly that, if she'd remained where she belonged, she'd know this. He'd just learned of the plans a few days ago.

"The plans to develop an underground system are pretty much in place. We haven't implemented them yet, because we don't know what moving the planet will do to it, exactly."

"You mean, by moving the planet closer to the sun, we increase the gravity and that could impact the planet?"

"Exactly. Will the tunnels collapse? Will the planet expand or compress? These tunnels could run with lava for all we know. Odin and the scientists have predicted all sorts of dire consequences."

"So, instead of investing years and money into the construction of something which surely would be destroyed, even if the planet is kind, isn't it better to wait until the event has happened? And only a few within the government have worked on this and kept the secret all these years?"

"Right, again. This way, to recover from the event, we'll begin a huge public works project. The work will improve planet-wide transportation, give people something to do, and help them feel as if they're contributing to the revitalization. Making it better, so to speak."

"Brilliant plan. Give the people a focus to recover from the event. Makes sense. So what are we looking at? Most of the tunnels aren't much larger than this one, if our path is any indication."

"Our mining heritage will come in handy there. The tunnels will need to be enlarged but, according to your father, we have the supply lines in place for the equipment we'll need."

"Hence the reason the crown has been saving money like crazy for centuries."

"And you just thought your ancestors were all tight fisted with their credits." Gunnar's tone said he was teasing her.

"I have noticed our palaces aren't gilded or studded with jewels. Our abodes are very humble when compared with the ostentatious displays of wealth I've seen elsewhere. We don't have priceless works of art hanging on the walls. In fact, there is almost nothing frivolous about living on Nordia."

"We are a sturdy, practical, people." He paused and she saw him looking at her with a solemn light in his eye. "Most of us anyway."

"What does that mean?" She told herself he wasn't trying to criticize her. Not really.

"It means most people work very hard for the wellbeing of the planet."

"Are you trying to say I haven't?" She dropped her voice an octave and spoke quietly.

Apparently he got the message he was treading on dangerous ground, because he immediately shook his head. "No, that's not what I'm saying. Nevertheless, you have started a trend where people are now looking for more comfort in their everyday lives. An upgrading of the things they gather around them. Our people haven't been poor, just practical in how they build and furnish their homes. You've created a new market."

"Why should people not enjoy the rewards of their hard work? There is more to life than plain food and white walls. I'm not suggesting we gild every surface in the palaces, but what is wrong with a coat of gold colored paint here and there? Why not import a few things which provide pleasure and have no practical use? The people work hard, they should play hard as well."

"Interesting thoughts," Gunnar said, and pulled her close under his arm.

The discussion was cut off when the carts slowed.

"We're stopping for a few hours," their guard and driver said.

Good. Noreen wanted to stretch her legs. While warmer, traveling underground wasn't as comfortable as Gunnar's full sized transport would have been. Visions of underground luxury transport almost made her swoon.

"Tell me more about these plans for the underground transport," she ordered Gunnar. "What types of vehicles are planned?"

"It is modeled on the underground systems on Earth. Cars, or trains I suppose they were called, linked together and pulled along. They'll ride on rails to keep them sorted out. Two sets so two trains can run at once."

She nodded her head. "I actually have some ideas there. I've been on similar systems, but engineered differently. It depends on the power source, but there are ways to make it very efficient."

Stepping from the now stopped cart, she saw the men all exchange looks. "What?" she demanded.

"I should have known." Her father pulled her into a hug. "Of course you have more experience, and I know the engineers would very much love to hear your ideas. We may even send them to the planets you recommend and let them study the latest in technology."

She kissed his cheek. "Such a wise king you are."

"Soon to be ex-king."

"Don't." Panic hit her stomach again. He just couldn't retire and dump all this on her. "Please, Pappa, don't abdicate. Please? You're still too vital and too strong. Don't duck out so soon."

She didn't like the look in his eyes. A little sad, a little mischievous, a lot determined.

"You can do this Noreena." He said the name gently, and pulled her closer. "You're the only one with the knowledge and experience to do it. You have the ideas. Just like with the underground transportation system. You have the fresh ideas that will bring us into step with the universe at large. Gunnar has the knowledge of the land and the people. It will take the two of you to guide us into this new age. You have the energy to do it. I've spent my whole life planning for a disaster. It is time for you to pick up the reins and pull this world into a new future."

"But, Pappa, you're talking like you think you're obsolete! You aren't!" She blinked rapidly to keep tears from spilling.

"No, I'm not obsolete," he chuckled. "By stepping aside to let you take control, I can travel the planet and help spread the new ideas. By stepping aside I'll be showing the world I have every confidence in you and your leadership. It is to build your support base that I'm doing this. You're already older than I was when I took the crown. It's a good age for stepping in."

"But the babies..."

"Their birth will help propel you further into popularity. As you're raising the next generation, you're building the world to be worthy of your children. If The Profetia is correct, and it always has been, your children will take the world much further than you will into the new age. It will fall to you to know when to pass on the crown to them. I'll be around to help you, but you need to be the leader. You and Gunnar. You should consider making him king by the way."

Sniffling her tears under control, Noreen pulled back. "I'll think about it. I don't know what to think yet, and I barely know him."

"Fair enough, and a decision for later. Come, let's get some dinner, then we'll press on again. Only a few more hours until we reach a resting spot where we can sleep for a while."

* * * *

Three very long days later, Noreen numbly stumbled into an elevator that lifted the travelers to the top floor of the Ryadstholm Palace. "We really need to talk about planetary transportation. For such a small planet, this is ridiculous."

She ignored her father's I-told-you-so look.

"When do the others arrive?" she asked instead. Her mother, Coreen and Al had all traveled in the royal overland transport, with the rest of the royal household following in a variety of vehicles, including Gunnar's transport.

"In the morning," her father replied.

"Which is how far away?"

"Five hours," Gunnar answered.

She sagged against him, just as she had the past several hours, while trying to sleep in his arms.

"Come, to bed now."

The lift door slid open. Fiona and Hans were there to greet them.

"M'lady!" Fiona gave a quick curtsy. "Your Majesty, Your Highness," she acknowledged the men with two more short curtsies.

"Fi, Hans," Noreen sighed in relief. "Straight to bed for us."

"Of course, Sophie has a bath waiting for you. Your apartment is ready and we have a light meal for you. You look exhausted," Fiona said, a slight admonishment in her tone.

"I am. Lead on, I can't remember the way." Noreen reached out and put a hand on Hans's arm. "Thanks for keeping an eye on the girls, Hans."

He smiled, even as his eyes cut to Gunnar. "Are you well, m'lady?"

"I'm well. Just pregnant." There was an awkward moment as the two men sized each other up. Impatient with the whole thing, she slipped a hand through an arm on each man. "I'm so tired I need the two of you to hold me up," she said, and tugged them after Fiona.

"Have me notified when you wake up," her father called after them.

"Will do!" she called over her shoulder. "All right, you two. Gunnar, this is Hans, my bodyguard and generally my big brother. Hans, this is my husband. You two will get along or I'll get rid of both of you. Any questions?"

"No, m'lady," Hans answered properly.

Gunnar's answer lagged until she pinched him. "No, I understand. You'll forgive me if Hans and I have a discussion about how his duties might change."

"They'd best not change too much. We have a working team here and I'll not have you tear it apart. My staff has been my family for the last ten years and they will remain so." Best get that idea clear right now.

"Of course, my love. Now that you're home, Hans won't need to concentrate so strenuously on bodyguard detail, and I'm sure he has many other talents that will help round out your expanded responsibilities."

She glanced at Gunnar, and saw only sincerity as he continued speaking. "Hans has necessarily been restricted in his duties to you, first and foremost keeping you safe in foreign surroundings. The king has told me he has many qualities beyond those of a muscle man. I'm sure he will be able to contribute greatly to the changes coming soon. For example, the transportation systems you want to improve."

She glanced at Hans, and saw his eyes sparkle a little. Gunnar was right. Hans had done much of the technology reconnaissance in their travels. He had all the technical know-how of a structural engineer and an astro-physicist. No formal studies beyond his initial college degree, he'd learned at a much vaster university than was available on just one planet—the universe in general.

"Very well. Hans is brilliant when it comes to those details. But I still want him close."

"Of course, *älskling*," Gunnar replied.

"Hans, where is Hollis now?" She moved on to the next business item bothering her.

"The Lidarian is in the guest wing. We felt it prudent to put him there. His warships are less likely to fire upon the palace if he is staying in it."

"Good plan. He is kept away from the family apartments?"

"Yes. We have guards on the doors into the family wing. Not to mention, he is always escorted in the palace."

"Excellent. We'll probably let him stew a day or two longer." How to keep him simmering until they needed him was the next concern. Just thinking of it made her head swim.

"Here we are, m'lady," Hans said gently, as she swayed.

Fiona opened the door where Sophie waited just inside.

"M'lady!" the maid cried and rushed to her.

Releasing her escorts, Noreen let herself be folded into the comforting embrace of her maid. She was so happy to see her staff together again she blinked back tears. It wasn't like her to be so emotional.

"Come, my sweetling, your bath is ready. You may drink your tea there, and I have a small snack for you. I'm sure you haven't eaten in hours, and you look like you're ready to fall over." Sophie's motherly clucking was like balm to her soul.

Younger than her staff, Noreen was sure Gunnar was getting a good chuckle over them treating her like a young child. Hans was the eldest of the four, at ten years older than Noreen. Fiona fell almost in the middle, at seven years older, and Sophie was two years older. Noreen's father had hoped their influence would help curb some of her more headstrong ideas.

Indeed, Hans had taken on not only the role of older brother, but he'd grounded her sexual experimentation by tutoring her first-hand, letting her know where things could get out of control. He'd been more protective of her vaginal virginity than she had. When her teenage hormones had got the better of her and she couldn't concentrate, he usually arranged a game of strip poker for the four of them and Noreen always lost. Rather, she always felt she'd won, but that was their secret. She, Gunnar and all Nordia, owed her mostly pure state to Hans's diligence.

"My lord," Sophie gave Gunnar a short curtsy, "Hans will see to your needs until your man, Lars, can meet up with us. We moved your things from your apartment over here." Noreen saw her glance toward Hans.

"Your Highness." Hans gestured to the other side of the sitting room. "Your dressing room and bathroom are over here."

"Poor Lars, always getting left behind." Noreen watched the battle of emotions waver across Gunnar's face, before he smiled and nodded.

"I'll meet you in bed," he told her, with a brief kiss on her lips.

"Yes, of course," she murmured, then let Sophie lead her away.

Once behind the closed door of the spacious bathroom Sophie began to coo. "Oh ma'am, he's a handsome devil! Those eyes, downright mysterious they are."

"Yes, and watch yourself. If they ever start to look more silver than blue, look away immediately." Noreen laughed, and pulled her sweater off. "Oh Sophie, how I've missed all of you!"

"We missed you too. How did my baby sister do for you?"

"She's wonderful, Sophie, but she just isn't you. Nobody could ever replace you. Ah, that feels good." She peeled off the last of her clothes, dropping them to the floor.

"The bath is just the temperature you like, m'lady."

"Freya's blessing on you." With a sigh she sank into the hot water, thick with citrus-scented bubbles. "I must warn you now, if Gunnar bathes with me, he won't let the water be so hot. He insists on nearly cold water." She settled in the tub, bubbles up to her nose. Leaning her head back, her feet rose to float above the bottom of the very large tub sunken into the floor.

"Why is that, m'lady?" Sophie draped her dress over the back of a chair and eased into the water, a natural fiber scrub brush in hand.

"He's afraid of over-heating the babies."

"Oh la. So tis true? You be pregnant?"

Noreen closed her eyes and murmured an affirmative. It was good to hear Sophie's accent again. Originally from the other side of Nordia, Sophie's people had more in common with the region of Earth where the people known as the Brits had come from. Mostly fair, her hair held a tint of strawberry and her cheeks were prone to the cutest freckles. Though Fiona and Hans had worked on their accents, Noreen had practically forbidden Sophie to change hers. Blanca had already erased her accent, and adopted the tone of the nobility. Sophie remained unspoiled in Noreen's estimation.

"Well, I'll have a word with the midwife m'self and check the old wives tales. I can't see how doing something the way you always have will have much effect on the wee bairns. D'ye know how many as yet?"

"No. Odin won't say and it's too soon for the doctor to tell. A couple of weeks more and we should know."

"You spoke to Odin?" Awe hushed Sophie's voice as she scrubbed one foot and then the other before working up Noreen's leg.

"Yes. More than once." She wanted to say more, but it felt as if her mouth froze. Must be part of the compulsion that would only let her discuss conversations with her father and the priest. Gunnar too. Not even with Cory could she talk about it.

"M'lady, it's been two weeks since you waxed?"

"Nearly, why?"

"Oh dear."

"What?" Noreen ran a hand down her thigh. "No...no way!" The beginning of soft hair could be felt on her leg. She moved to her mons, and felt it there as well. "Sophie!"

"Relax, miss, I don't have the means to wax you tonight, but I'll dig up the supplies and take care of it tomorrow."

"You have supplies?" Noreen sat up and created a small wave of bubbles.

"I had a feeling you wouldn't escape as easily as you wanted to, so I got some from the spa on the ship."

"Oh la," Noreen quoted Sophie's favorite phrase for all situations. "I wonder if it's the pregnancy. Or is it being back in the cold?" She fell back against the tub headrest and let Sophie resume scrubbing.

"Most likely the pregnancy. I'll ask me midwife friend. Still, it seems a bit early."

"Hmm, by Solstice it will be as if I'm three months gone, or so Odin says. Slightly time enhanced."

"Oh? Why's that?"

Noreen parted her legs so Sophie could clean there as well. Three days of quick sponge baths had done little to make her feel clean. She closed her eyes and relaxed. Sophie had a fine touch for giving baths.

"Odin says the babies are the key for the event to come. They need to be a certain stage of development. Afterward they'll resume a normal growth and be born near Summer Solstice."

"Oh my, those gods have it all worked out, do they?"

"What they can."

"Would you be wantin' your hair washed this evening?"

"Let's leave it until morning. I want to get some sleep and it will take too long to dry."

"Oh, aye. Morning it is."

Sophie worked up her body, and Noreen flinched at the tenderness of her breasts.

"Oh miss! I'm sorry."

"No worries, Sophie. Just normal from what I understand."

"What about the morning sickness?"

"Just have tea and toast on hand when you wake me, please. A little something in my stomach helps keep it settled."

"Aye, ma'am."

"Ah, Sophie, I've missed you so."

The maid's strong hands and gentle brush worked on the tension of her shoulders, wiping it away.

"I'll give you a quick rubdown with some lotion before sending you to bed. You have some dry spots. I'll have to have word with Blanca."

"Not her fault. The traveling. The air was dry and I slept in my clothes. We were traveling fast and quiet, so we didn't stop in the *grottas* along the way. We stopped in bare bones travelers' quarters and facilities were limited. I was lucky they cleared out the bathrooms long enough so I could brush my teeth and pee."

"M'lady! How awful! To treat you that way on your own planet. I'm appalled."

"Me too." Which was why the long distance transportation issues would be dealt with as early as possible. "Remember the old trains on Earth? The ones we saw in the museums?"

"Ja?" Sophie scrubbed her face and she had to wait to finish speaking.

"What do you think of traveling by train, underground, on Nordia?"

"Oh la! T'would be most wondrous."

"Well, you just may see it in your lifetime." We just have to survive the Solstice.

"Now that would be a sight to behold."

Noreen stood when Sophie pulled the drain plug and reached for the hand held shower head. It only took a moment for the water to reach the right temperature and her maid began to rinse off the bubbles.

"I'm thinking that will be one of the first new public works projects we start. After we get these babies born, that is."

"A fine goal, m'lady. A very fine goal. Nordia needs to come current with the universe."

"Yes, my Sophie, yes she does."

Chapter 23

Gunnar clenched his fists in diplomatic frustration. At his side, Hans wasn't in a much better state. The source of their frustration was the same.

If that black oil swab touched his woman one more time... Gunnar made himself release the thought. No, they had to keep Hollis Traxelgard, Prince of Lidaria, placated for now. It didn't help Gunnar accept Nory's flirting with the man any. Indeed, she gave every impression of being attracted to the man.

Gunnar stood and paced the formal drawing room in the public part of the palace. This was the third meeting with the man, and Nory was doing her best to keep him happy with vague promises of secretaries checking with the lawyers and reviewing marriage laws. She was sorry, she told him, with a look of regret in her eyes but, as Crown Princess, these things had to be negotiated at the state level, and not at the heart level.

Gunnar's pacing caught her attention and, for a moment, she was distracted from her conversation with the other man. That earned him a dark glare. Biting the inside of his cheek was the only way he could keep from grinning in response. The man was an ass, and Hans agreed.

Now there was another puzzle to ponder. Nory and her staff. Their first night in Ryadstholm, he'd walked into her bathroom in time to see her maid massaging lotion into her. Specifically, between his wife's legs. And she'd been moaning with pleasure! Neither woman had acted like anything was out of the ordinary. While he sat and watched, the maid had finished rubbing lotion into every inch of Nory's body then dressed her in a gown and brushed out her hair before braiding it again.

Confused and bemused, the feelings had only grown when she'd turned to him in bed, before the covers had even settled down around them. Warm and soft, sweet smelling and eager, she'd cuddled close and lifted her lips to be kissed. Wet and ready, she'd even let him remove her gown completely instead of just pushing it up and out of the way. Had the maid merely started her for him? Or had he interrupted something?

The next morning, she'd been just as eager, after sipping the hot tea and nibbling on the toast Sophie had brought. Slow, sweet lovemaking had left her glowing as she told him to leave her for a bit. There were womanly beauty secrets to attend to, and she didn't need him around for at least an hour. Two might be better. She'd make her presence known when she was ready to face the world in general. Sated but confused, he'd headed for his dressing room where Hans waited to assist him.

"Honestly," he'd told the other man, "I can see to myself."

"And my princess would have my head if I let you shave and dress yourself. I beg your pardon sir, but I answer to her direction."

It had been the only word on the matter he'd gotten out of the large bodyguard. Not a small man himself, Hans was the second person to ever make Gunnar feel average in height. Only his father had ever made him feel that way before.

It didn't take long for him to see the great affection Nory's staff held for her, and he knew each one would guard her with their lives. Odin forbid it ever came to that here on Nordia. However, it did make him wonder how often it had come to that during her travels. For example, what had Hollis Traxelgard looked like on his home world?

Gunnar glanced at his watch. Lunch time.

"Noreen," he interrupted, not caring if it came across rudely. "It is time for your meeting with the Minister of Transportation. We must go now."

If looks could kill, the black eyes of the black man would have roasted him alive. Gunnar returned the glare with his own icy one.

Noreen sighed and shook her head. "I'm so sorry, Hollis, but he's right. They want to hear about some of the planetary transportation systems I've experienced during my travels."

"Yes, you need a system that works better in the bitter cold," the Lidarian said with a deep shudder, making Gunnar wonder how warm his planet was. Nory had avoided planets where temperatures dropped below twenty degrees, even at night. If it went anywhere near zero, it was crossed off her list of places to visit.

"Well, we've had bigger concerns to deal with since colonization. We're ready to move forward now, into a new era." She stood, forcing the other man to stand, and held out her hand for him to kiss. "I must run along. My secretary will contact yours about when I'm free to visit again. Are you sure you don't want me to set you up with a tour guide?"

"No, no. I'll just make use of the thermal pools again, and I have some business to attend to myself. I must commend you on the off-planet communications system. It is one of the better ones I've come across anywhere. The translation software is nearly perfect."

Gunnar watched his wife smile in genuine pleasure.

"Why thank you, Hollis. I'm so glad to see it work so well for you. I had a bit of a time getting the government to put it in."

"They are most fortunate to have a princess such as yourself. Beautiful, clever, and extremely intelligent, your people are very lucky indeed." The man bowed over her hand, his shaved head shining in the low light of the drawing room, and Gunnar found himself wanting to put a fist in that smiling face. Could his fist make the man's lips swell even more?

"You're so sweet, Hollis," his wife simpered, and Gunnar nearly laughed. It was a move that belonged to one of her half sisters. Coreen never would have stooped to it, however, it seemed to be what the man expected, and keeping him happy at the moment was what mattered.

"Come, Your Highness," Gunnar pulled her hand from Hollis's. "We must leave. We'll be in touch, Minister." He gave the man the barest of bows, and left the room with Nory's hand tucked under his arm, Hans on their heels. He nodded to the security detail waiting to escort the Lidarian back to his apartments.

Once beyond hearing and sight of the drawing room, Nory pulled her hand from his arm.

"How dare you!" she hissed at him.

"How dare I what?"

"I'm having a hard enough time pretending to still be attracted to him to keep him on the hook. It is even more difficult with the two of you hovering and glaring at us while we talk!"

Gunnar watched as she turned and included Hans in her tirade. For once, he actually felt a kindred spirit, a sense of true brotherhood, with the big man. Hans didn't pay her any mind and merely gave her a tight grin.

"The man may have been charming on his own dance floor, but here he stands out like an oily rag in a pile of white silk. He isn't for you, Princess," Hans declared. Yup, Gunnar liked this man.

"I never said he was!" She threw her hands in the air. "He was a charming companion, a sophisticated tour guide, with the best wine cellar and the largest budget. Nothing more. He kept me entertained and let me in on some of the secrets of his planet. It was a spying mission, you dolt! I was doing my job! Is it my fault he fell in love? How did he find out my true position anyway?" Gunnar nearly laughed as she turned, arms folded across her bulging breasts, and narrowed her glare on Hans.

"Apparently they have a few secrets we weren't privy to. Such as surveillance and intelligence gathering. I'm still trying to figure out how they discovered your rank. It isn't on the papers we used for embarking on the planet."

"No, the only time I made the mistake of flaunting my rank was on Nefflerhein." She turned to Gunnar to explain. "My first off-planet stop. Only Fiona was with me then. We were two babies, off-world for the first time. We didn't know any better. Hans and Sophie caught up with us a couple weeks later. We left a trail a blind man could follow." Her lips twisted without humor, while Hans smiled affectionately.

"I don't even remember who all we ran into then. I was just so scared that by the time Hans showed up, I fell into his arms and he made everything safe for us. He also talked my father into letting me travel. With a little help from Moder."

"Yes, and it was your father's idea to groom you into a diplomat," Hans added, and gestured for her to continue down the hallway. "Like any of us knew what it took to be a diplomat."

Gunnar could see it now. Picturing Noreen as a sixteen-year-old girl, with poise to be sure, but facing down foreign ambassadors... Nory must have suffered a few hard knocks. "Was it difficult?"

The question earned him gales of laughter from both Nory and Hans. At one point she grabbed his arm and clung to him, halting their progress again. Wiping tears from her eyes she gasped. "Difficult? What a word. It was bloody awful! That's why we started working our way towards Earth. We figured at least we could meet up with some relatives. They, at least, were kind enough to give me some lessons in diplomacy. We faked it from there. It only took three years to refine our routine. How many times did I nearly cave and come home then?" She looked to Hans who just shook his head.

"I didn't keep count, my princess."

"Probably a good thing. Thank you for never throwing it in my face."

"Had I done that, it would have been rubbing in my own failures," Hans said quietly, and once again started them on their path.

"Are we really meeting with the Transportation Minister over lunch?"

Gunnar glanced over to see she'd directed the question to him. "Yes, we really are. We're also meeting with Emergency Services to find out where we stand on being prepared for anything."

"Oh la," she sighed.

"Isn't that your maid's phrase?" Gunnar asked.

"Yes, dear Sophie," she said with a smile.

Gunnar really had some questions about her relations with her staff. The only privacy they'd had since arriving Ryadstholm had been in bed. Even then, each morning, the maid was likely to show up with Nory's tea and toast just as Gunnar was feeling amorous. If he didn't know better, he'd wonder if she timed it just to interrupt the action or maybe catch a glimpse. Either seemed to be a likely possibility. Tonight he was locking the door.

* * * *

"Okay, Princess, let's see what we can see."

At the doctor's direction Noreen rested back on the exam table and looked up at Gunnar. One week until the Solstice, she was technically two weeks pregnant. Two months by Odin's reckoning. Still early, but the doctor thought they might be able to see something by ultrasound. It was silly to feel so nervous.

Gunnar's blue eyes held a hint of excited sparkle. He was looking forward to being a father. She still wasn't sure how she felt about being a mother. With luck, they'd know how many children in a few minutes. That part was the worst. Knowing there was more than one, but not knowing how many more than one.

The doctor in Ryadstholm was a century younger than the old doctor in Stravicsholm. Too old to travel, they'd left the doctor behind. This one, Doctor Bettina, was only a few years out of school and a popular obstetrician. She also had warm soft hands, unlike the old scary doctor, and she had attended many of Noreen's half sisters.

The wand moved over Noreen's stomach and all eyes were fixed on the monitor.

"Here we go, there's one little heart beating, two, three." The doctor pointed to the screen at each little pulsing spot. "There's number four... let's just be sure." She moved the wand around. "Don't forget to breathe, Your Highness."

Noreen swallowed and gripped Gunnar's hand. Four? Four babies? Too many!

"Let's try that count again." The doctor pointed at the screen once more. "One, two, three...four...ah! There she is, number five."

"Five!" Noreen squeaked, a strange emotion wrapping around her heart nearly as tight as Gunnar's hand squeezing the blood from her fingers.

"Five?" Gunnar echoed her.

She glanced at his face before staring at the monitor screen again. A little shocked, but happy too.

"Five," the doctor said firmly. "Five little heartbeats, all looking normal."

Well, the doctor sounded pleased.

"Don't they call those quintuplets?" Noreen gasped. It was probably a good thing she was laying down already, otherwise she would have fallen over.

"Yes. Quintuplets. Very rare to happen naturally."

"As if," she muttered. *Odin! Freya!* A hint of godly laughter answered her, so very faintly. "Five," she whispered, and Gunnar's grip doubled in strength.

"I told you we should have had five children by now," Gunnar said. He sounded entirely too smug to her liking.

"But...but...five? All at once?" Tears formed in her eyes as she looked back at the monitor while the doctor made measurements and captured screen shots.

"No problem," the doctor said smoothly. "We can do amazing things these days, even out here in the hinterlands of space."

"I know we aren't backwards, but five is still five," she insisted. "The human body wasn't designed to stretch that far."

"Oh yes it was. No worries, Princess," the doctor said, and turned to give her a smile. "They look like they're about two months along. Just as you predicted. If I hadn't seen it for myself, I wouldn't believe it. You say Odin has a hand in this?"

Noreen nodded, Gunnar's head bobbing along with hers.

"Amazing. Never would have believed it possible. We'll check again in six days." The doctor pulled the ultrasound wand away and wiped up the gel on Noreen's slightly bulging stomach. "I'll give you some lotion to help with the stretch marks and expanding skin. That will be the most uncomfortable part of this for you, I imagine. Especially this time of year when the air is so ultra dry. Use it liberally a couple times of day. Odin says the growth will resume a normal pace after next week?"

Noreen nodded again. What could she say? The entire situation was out of her hands. The gods and the babies were in control.

"I suppose," Gunnar said, "it's too soon to determine the genders?"

"Far too soon," the doctor said. "Because of the situation, we'll most likely be doing weekly ultrasounds just to keep an eye on the little darlings. We want our heirs to be healthy."

Heirs. Was that all these children represented to Nordia?

"They are so much more." Freya's voice was soothing in her head. *"You are so much more. Just rest and care for yourself and the children. Prepare for what you need to do."*

Right. Rest and prepare. The two words seemed mutually exclusive to her. *Faith.* She needed to have faith in the gods. They'd been studying this situation so much longer than she had.

Closing her eyes, Noreen rested a hand on her stomach and tried to connect with the children inside her. She knew it was too soon to feel movement, and yet, she had an image of five little beating hearts, each one doing a somersault. A warm glow seemed to start in her womb and spread outward, filling her with a sense of peace. Gunnar's hand cupped her cheek and she opened her eyes to see him staring down at her.

"You're so beautiful. Our children are the luckiest ones ever, to have such a mother as you," he said.

The tears won over her control, and one by one, spilled over her lashes and slid down her cheek.

Gunnar smiled, and bent to kiss the tears away.

* * * *

"Ma'am," Sophie gave Noreen a good glare. "You're supposed to be resting."

"And I will, I promise. I just want to do it while floating in warm water. If you want to keep an eye on me, you're welcome to come along, otherwise send Hans." Noreen dropped the last of her clothes and pulled on a thick robe made from toweling. Wrapping it around her, she tied the belt, and slipped her feet into the soft wool indoor shoes.

Sophie pulled Noreen's braid out of the robe, and shook her head. "I'll come with you, and then we'll rub you down with the lotion afterward. You do know the prince will have our heads if he catches us, right? He expects you to rest here."

"I'll rest. I just want to do it under sun lights and in hot water and pretend I'm on a tropical beach."

Stepping into the sitting room she met Hans's raised eyebrow with one of her own. He shrugged and lifted himself from the chair to follow.

"Can't stand it anymore, eh?" was his only comment.

She ignored him and turned to Fiona. "Ready for a break? Or is my father pelting you with work?"

"A break sounds like a wonderful idea," Fiona answered with a grin.

"Good, we're taking an afternoon holiday in the thermal pools. Hopefully we'll have them to ourselves."

She started to head for the stairs, but Hans redirected her to the elevator.

"I'm not an invalid. I do need *some* exercise," she protested.

"And if you're trying to do this without drawing attention to flaunting your disregard for your husband's orders, the elevator is more discreet."

"Good point." She let him usher her onto the waiting car.

She didn't bother hiding her smile when her three companions all inhaled the warm, moist air of the grotta beneath the palace. The underground spring provided so much more than just hot water to soothe sore bodies. The main source of heat for the palace, the springs formed the center of Ryadstholm, and spread outward to heat much of the city. Like the palace, many of the buildings had their own grotta beneath and provided a communal gathering place for the population. Apartment and housing complexes were built over the larger caverns to provide ready heat. They were also a social place, where both young and old gathered to see out the long winter nights. Come summer, people moved above ground to enjoy natural light and fresh air.

"Down by the cooler end of the pool, if you will m'lady." Sophie tugged on her arm. "That's one battle I'll not fight with the prince."

Noreen supposed she had to be grateful just for escaping her bedroom. "Fine."

The grotta instantly soothed her. Waterfalls created a musical trickle accented by the trills of colorful birds flitting from tree to tree, the sun lights adding to the illusion of a tropical world. Only a soft salt breeze was missing. She also heard the music of the *ByalbOgBeLun* and felt a sense of coming home she hadn't felt since stepping onto the planet. Could she move her study down here? The nursery?

Sophie led them to a secluded corner, where the pool formed a small cove. A few potted trees provided moderate screening. "Just in case someone comes looking, we'll be a bit more hidden here."

It would also make a good corner for other sport, Noreen thought with a grin.

She shed her shoes and robe, letting Sophie take them while she stepped into the water. The edge gently sloped, providing an easy descent into the water. One of her points of pride—a carefully designed sand beach. The thought made her smile. What a good landscape designer she'd fancied herself. The beach was a poor replacement for the real thing, but it would do. Knee deep, she executed a shallow dive and slowly swam the width of the pool. Only ten meters, it wasn't much exercise, but it was enough to stretch a little. She drifted back to the little cove, and turned over to float on her back.

Familiar strong hands cradled her from underneath.

"Hans," she murmured, already feeling sleepy.

"Rest, little one," he replied. "I won't let you float away."

Chapter 24

Gunnar excused himself from the planning session. Already restless and edgy, sitting in long debates didn't help. He was used to being on the move with his freight convoys and the inactivity of meeting with government officials was tedious at best.

Thinking to steal an hour or two with Nory, he headed for their apartment. All he wanted to do was hold her while she slept and drink in the beauty and wonder of her. Him, a father. Five children in one shot. She'd need extra special care. Just one child could be hard to carry, five had to be monumental. Finding their rooms empty, even of her secretary and maid, he felt a moment's panic and turned to the com-link.

"Security." A deep male voice answered his call.

"Can you tell me where Princess Noreen is at the moment?" If Coreen were in Ryadstholm he could have asked her. She'd know.

"She and her staff are in the grotta, sir."

"*Takk.*"

"Yes, sir." The guard acknowledged the thanks just before he disconnected.

What was she thinking? With five babies growing in her at an enhanced rate, she needed rest. She didn't see the tired shadows under her eyes or how she drooped with exhaustion each afternoon. Heading for the stairs, he made an effort to tamp down his irritation and worry. It hadn't taken the doctor's warning about carrying so many to heighten his concerns. Pregnancy, in general, was a terrifying concept to him. His mother and sister had died together during childbirth and he could still see the pale mask of his mother lying on her bed, the dead infant in her arms, his father prostate in grief, sobbing beside them. His father had never been quite the same afterwards and had slowly declined. Gunnar was convinced he'd died of a broken heart.

Alarm thrummed along his nerves and Gunnar took the stairs two at a time, running by the time he reached the door to the grotta. He forced himself to slow down. Security hadn't seemed overly concerned. *No danger.* Stopping to catch his breath, he paused for a moment. Feeling calm again, he opened the door and stepped through to the steamy heat of the grotta.

Noreen and her entourage weren't immediately visible in the large cavern. Nearly as large as the footprint of the palace itself, the grotta was at least one hundred meters long and close to thirty meters wide. Long and narrow, the pools were a natural shape, three falling below the hot spring at the top. Cold water was piped in to mix in the lowest level to provide a comfortable temperature for children and those who were advised against the higher temperatures. Like Nory. Deciding she was smart enough not to defy him there, he turned toward the lower end of the cavern.

The heat was such that he pulled off the sweater he wore, then unbuttoned his shirt. Maybe an hour or two lazing in the cooler pool wasn't such a bad idea. Rounding a corner, he saw the bright sun lights over a certain little corner. Look for the bright lights, of course. Hoping she was alone, wishing she wasn't, he quickened his steps until he could see a gathering of blond heads. They drew apart as he closed the distance and he saw Hans lifting a woman from the water. Nory. His heart leapt, then calmed again when Fiona and Sophie slowly followed. If anything were wrong, they wouldn't have been so tranquil. Shielding himself behind a leafy tree, he watched the small group.

Feeling like an outsider the three days they'd been in Ryadstholm, he was curious about the dynamics of the four. Reminding himself how close they'd had to be while on strange worlds didn't help—the jealousy still gripped him. He should have been by her side. Watching Hans carefully lay Nory on cushions pushed together on the sand and draped with soft towels didn't ease the feeling. The love her staff had for her was obvious in each gesture, each movement showing how they cared for her. He'd seen doting looks pass between them as they'd eased back into their routines and worked together to adapt to the new environment.

The sound of water and birds was just loud enough that Gunnar couldn't hear the question Hans asked of Sophie, who squinted up at the sun lights above them. Guessing it was about the intensity of light when the maid dimmed the artificial sun, Gunnar thought they would let her sleep on the make-shift bed on the pretend beach. Would they cover her? No, Hans lay down with her, enfolding her in his strong arms.

Swift and hard, jealousy like he'd never known before ripped through Gunnar. Nory was his wife. How dare Hans, a servant, a bodyguard, take such liberties? Before he could move toward them, first Sophie and then Fiona lay down on her other side, the four of them cuddling together.

Stunned, Gunnar stood in the shadow cast by the screening tree and tried to think through the implication of the vignette before him. He'd been told her story in bits and pieces, now he needed to put it all together.

He found a ledge of rock where he could sit and watch them, still screened by the imported flora.

Just sixteen when she'd left with only her secretary, Noreen had fled on the first galaxy cruiser she could find. Destination didn't matter. Off-world did. Away from him. Away from her life and into the great unknown. Just eighteen himself at that time, he tried to remember what Coreen had been like at the time, as he hadn't known Nory then. So young. So very young and as sheltered as the princesses had been, the loneliness and fear must have been overwhelming. Babies, she'd called herself and Fiona. Hans, big and strong, must have looked like Thor himself come to save and protect her.

Ten and a half years these four had traveled together, relying on each other in strange lands. Maybe it wasn't so incredible they were unusually close.

Aware that she was clearly sound asleep, he watched as Nory unconsciously burrowed deeper into the embraces of her staff. Their comfort at being so close, without wearing clothing of any kind, spoke clearly of a relationship far beyond that of workmates. These were lifemates who filled her need for love and companionship.

So where did that leave him?

Odin had decreed him to be her mate but, if he understood correctly, it was a genetic match the so-called gods had planned. A mating beyond her control, not of her choosing. The seeds had been planted and fertilized. He'd done his part and now she rested in the arms of the lifemates she'd chosen. The relationship she had control of.

She'd called herself a brood mare. What did that make him? Stud for hire?

His heart sinking, he saw Nory roll to her side and wiggle her bottom against Hans's groin. The man pillowed her head with one arm, the other wrapped around her waist, entwined with the arms and hands of the other two women, also wrapped around her.

Loving them had been her choice.

She'd had no choice about being his wife or carrying his children.

Did that mean he'd raped her on the small transport?

The memory of her tears came back to him. He'd callously brushed them away, telling himself they didn't matter, that she was just a female used to having her own way putting up a show. Playing games.

But in truth, had it been...rape? The thought staggered him. Feeling faint and sick with self-loathing, he moved as quietly as he could, retracing his steps until he stood outside the grotta.

Tears had come to Nory at other times. Their first night in Stravicsholm. He'd cuffed and restrained her then as well. The pressure in his head and stomach grew.

Nordia had one week to save itself from a killer comet. If they failed, their world was doomed. In that moment, it meant nothing to Gunnar. His world was already destroyed. Nordia could survive without him. He couldn't survive without Noreen's love. What had he done to earn it? Nothing. He'd been overbearing, rude, and insensitive. Physical love had been forced upon her, his presence in her life a somewhat unwelcome intrusion, as she'd shown him by locking him out of her bedroom, their first night in Stravicsholm.

Numbly, he turned away, and stumbled for a security door with a lava warning emblazoned on it. It was locked, but he had a passkey to open it. All the royal family did. An escape route in times of danger. Not caring where he ended up, he stumbled through the door, letting it clang shut behind him. If only there really was a tunnel of molten rock beyond the door.

* * * *

"M'lady, you must wake up."

Noreen turned into the broad chest of the man holding her. "G'way," she muttered.

"Noreen Elke—" Sophie began the list of horrid names.

"Stop!" she moaned. "I'll wake up, just give me minute."

"The prince will be anxious when he returns to your rooms and finds you not there. It is time to wash and dress for dinner. If he isn't there already, he will be very soon."

"Sophie, you are such a nag." She cuddled closer to Hans and felt the rumble of his chuckle.

"And if she weren't such a nag, you'd never be dressed on time for anything," Hans reminded her with a kiss on the forehead.

"Henpecked, that's what I am. I'm henpecked," she muttered and rolled away with a stretch and yawn.

"Your sister and new brother-in-law will be at dinner tonight. I know you wish to see them, so up now. Don't make me ask Hans to carry you."

"Okay, okay, I'm moving, see?" She rolled to her stomach to push herself up on her hands and knees. The cushions felt so good under her, the towels so soft and fresh, maybe she could rest just a moment longer...

The smack on her bottom jolted her awake. Not hard, it made more noise than it had stung.

"Hey!"

"Up you go," Hans laughed.

"Who is the princess here?"

"You are, but who will get chewed out by the king? We will. His bite is much worse than yours." Hans stood and lifted her hips until she rested on her knees and elbows. "A perfect position for another smack," he threatened and she quickly pushed herself upright.

"I'm up, I'm up." No more smacks. It was bad enough Gunnar liked her bottom pink. Little did he know, Hans like girls with pink bottoms, too. Don't go there. There were some things she didn't think Gunnar was ready to deal with just yet. Besides, that was her old life. She was on to a new one now.

With a chuckle, Hans lifted her to her feet then held her robe for her.

"Shoes on." Sophie knelt at her feet. "We need to go. I'm amazed he hasn't sent palace security after you. He should have been out of his cabinet meetings an hour ago," she clucked.

"Meetings I should be attending." Noreen sighed and felt the joy of her afternoon drain away. It was her inheritance and Gunnar was carrying the load of it. She needed to take part in the contingency plans and the planning for how to proceed once the crisis passed.

If it passed and left survivors.

If there was a planet left to even care about.

"All right, I'm ready. Let's go get me beautiful for dinner."

Rising from the pool level by elevator, they encountered a footman with cases of luggage on the first level.

"I'll take the next," he assured them.

"Looks like Coreen has arrived," she observed and mentally reached out tentatively. Ever since Cory's wedding night she'd carefully shielded herself from her sister so as not to intrude.

"Cory?"

"Nory! There you are! Is Gunnar with you?"

"Gunnar? No. I haven't seen him since lunch."

"You don't know where he was going then?"

"What do you mean? Going where? When?"

"Security shows he went through an emergency exit about an hour and a half ago. They lost track of him soon after on the monitoring equipment."

Noreen felt something nudging at her, a tug of alarm. *"What do you mean? Last I saw he was headed into a cabinet meeting after lunch. He ordered me to take a nap."* Why would he go out an emergency exit?

"They say he left after about an hour. Security says he called from your room looking for you and was told you were in the thermal pool. About twenty minutes later the emergency exit was opened and he hasn't been seen since. Did something happen down in the grotta?"

"No. He didn't join us." Where could he be?

The lift opened, but it took Hans grasping her arm to get her moving.

"Something wrong, m'lady?" he asked calmly.

"Gunnar appears to be missing. Hold on, I'm talking with Cory."

"He didn't join you?" Cory repeated in her head as Hans and the girls hustled her into her apartment.

"No. I would have remembered, because he probably would have yelled at me for taking my nap down in the grotta. Or one of the other three would have mentioned he was there. He never showed up." Noreen chewed on her lip.

"Where are you now?"

"Heading into a shower and then getting dressed. I'll be out in thirty minutes. Has anyone from security gone through the door after him?"

"The search teams left twenty minutes ago."

"When did you get in?"

"About fifteen minutes ago."

"All right. Thirty minutes will give security time to find him and you time to get organized. I'll meet you in Fader's study."

Ending the conversation with Cory, she stepped into the shower with Sophie on her heels. "Hans!" she called him into the bathroom and, with Sophie scrubbing and washing her hair, she told him what she knew.

Fiona ran back to the desk in the sitting room and, when Noreen emerged from the dressing room, twenty-five minutes later, wet hair braided, and dressed in warm woolens, there was no information other than the security team had only found what looked like one set of foot prints in the dust. They were following the tracks, but had moved beyond easy communicator range. The perils of mineral and metal laden rock.

Practically running, Noreen burst through the door of her father's study before the footman could stop her. The head of security, the old bishop, Cory, Al, and a half dozen security men were there. She glared back at her father's frown.

"What happened today?" she demanded.

"I was about to ask you the same thing," he snapped back.

"I haven't seen him since lunch. He kissed me when we parted and then he wandered off with you. What happened in the meeting?"

"He got restless and left. Said we were just going over the same ground over and over again. Said we were just trying to make ourselves feel better about the plans that have been put in place, and there's nothing wrong, and that we should start moving to the Summer Palace to get ready." Her father steepled his fingers together under his chin and leaned back in his armchair. "He had a certain look about him that said he was in need of female comfort."

Noreen rolled her eyes. Leave it to Fader to bring up mating practices. "Well we weren't hiding. If he'd come far enough into the grotta he would have seen us."

"You two didn't fight?"

"Not recently." After the morning's meeting with the doctor, Gunnar had been deliriously happy. She was the one who had felt like throwing herself off a cliff.

"Well, we need to find him. Can you reach out to him telepathically?"

Noreen eased into the overstuffed chair near her father. Hans was there, shoving an ottoman under her feet. She spared him a small smile, then returned her gaze to her father. "I don't know. I haven't tried before."

"Your connection with him should be nearly as strong as with your sister. Try."

Nodding at the order, she closed her eyes and relaxed in the chair. Her mind turned to the passengers in her womb and instinctively she rested a hand over them.

"*Gunnar,*" she sent the thought out with an image of him held in her mind's eye. "*Gunnar, come to me. Talk to me.*"

She sharpened the mental image of his eyes, the tiny silver sparkle, a smile, his possessive hold on her at night, the union of their bodies... *"Gunnar, if you can hear me, feel me, answer. Maybe I'm strong enough to connect us this way. Please, Gunnar, Master, return to me."*

Time hovered in suspension, all sound faded from the room around her, all was quiet, so quiet she wondered if she could hear the world breathe.

"Gunnar," she pleaded and searched for his essence, the spark of life that was him. *"Odin? Thor? Freya? Where is Gunnar?"* Not a sound entered her head. She felt a slight nudge. Cory. Cory's hand slipped into hers. Maybe... she latched onto Cory's energy and felt a surge from within.

"Gunnar," she called out again. Another surge, a familiar presence with no name... *"Fader?"*

"Yes, söt nos," his answer contained a tiny shiver of affectionate humor at the silly nickname as he picked up her hand and gave it a light squeeze. Their link brought a stronger surge of more power. *"Try again, sweet nose."*

She tried again, and again, gathering in weaker pulses of energy until the sizzling of it grew too strong and, with a yelp, she released those adding their powers to hers. Gasping she lay back against the soft chair and felt a hand rubbing hers, strong hands rubbing her feet, hands softly probing her abdomen.

"I can't...feel...no trace...no hint..." She couldn't even lift her head when someone held a glass to her lips. Gentle hands helped her and she swallowed a few drops of mint brandy. Weak tears burned at the back of her eyes, but even they took too much effort.

"Where's Odin? Thor? Freya? They didn't answer when I called..." A tiny hiccup escaped. It couldn't be a sob. She didn't cry in front of people.

There was silence, then her father answered. "I don't know where they are. It's as if... they're gone."

Chapter 25

Gunnar moved slowly. He couldn't see a thing and his entire body hurt, from the throbbing lump on his head down to his aching arms and legs. Come to think of it, his jaw felt like it was swollen or dislocated. Moving it back and forth made it hurt, but at least it moved. Thor's hammer, where was he and what had happened?

Heartache. Nory. Pain. Pushing through the locked door and into the black tunnel beyond. Wandering in the tunnels, then... more blackness. Soul deep despair. Nothing. He had no idea what had happened to him. Survival instinct cautioned him to stay still while he figured out he was lying on something hard. No sound. Neither hot nor cold. His head throbbed. *Nory.* Pain squeezed his heart to the point he thought he'd never breathe again. If only he could tell her how sorry he was and how much he loved her. The rest of his life would be devoted to worshipping her and showing her how much he loved her and their children.

Rape. Sweet Freya, he had to find a way to earn her forgiveness. She must hate him for it. First he'd raped her and then he'd called it their wedding night. No wonder she'd burst into tears. A quick kiss and then... No, he hadn't meant it to be that way.

Whispers of music brushed around him. Soft music he'd heard all his life. The music of Nordia that seemed to live within the rock that made up the planet. Music that caressed the mind and soul. So faint, he wasn't sure if it were his imagination, a hallucination, or real. In any case, it didn't matter. Wherever he was, it was Hell. Nory wasn't here with her sweet breath puffing across his chest, warm full breast filling his hand or her round *rompe* fitting into the bend of his body, soft curves cradling his rising erection. Where she wasn't, *Helvete* reigned.

"So." The voice was like a physical presence, the deep vibration of it felt in his bones. "You really love her?"

Gunnar held his silence, evening his breath to feign sleep.

"Nice try, but I know you are awake. Your brain waves are rocketing all over the place," the voice continued. "I'll take that last leap of heart rate to indicate an affirmative response. It is most fascinating how you humans obsess over love and other feelings. Emotions. So very primitive."

A light came up around him, showing the rough walls of an undiscovered cavern or tube. Possibly one that didn't go anywhere. The source of the light was indeterminate, but it filled the space where he lay. As he blinked, the black face of the Lidarian came into view.

"Ah, see? I knew you were awake."

"What do you want?" Gunnar asked as if talking about the weather.

"I want your princess." White teeth showed clearly against the gleaming black skin. A scent of mint teased Gunnar's nostrils.

"For what purpose?" He thought about moving, sitting up even, but his body didn't seem to want to work.

"She's a most extraordinary creature. So sweet, so entertaining. I have great plans for training her."

"Training? Noreen? You must be joking," Gunnar laughed, the sound feeling harsh against his dry throat. "What kind of training did you have in mind?"

"Why as a pet of course. Humans aren't good for much else. She's so full of energy, and so willing in so many ways. Of course, now you have breached that which she denied me, so maybe we'll bring you along so you two can perform together from time to time, though I very much like having her perform on me."

"You're not making sense." Gunnar tried to move again, but his body just didn't listen to the signals from his brain.

"Did she not confess to you how she spent her last evening on Lidaria?" The black man laughed, making Gunnar grit his teeth. "Ah, I guess not. Well, it was sweet, really. She invited me to her lodging and we engaged in all sorts of entertainments. I must say she is very talented with her… ah…what is your word? Mouth. There it is. The oral opening. Mouth. Tongue. It really is most amazing how she can open up her throat. Most of my humans have required months and months of very harsh training and never yet have any reached her proficiency level. Ah, that information upsets you? Interesting. I find it amazing how proprietary you human males get with your females. Still, with one as talented as she is, I suppose it is most understandable."

Gunnar watched the other man pace around him.

"You must be getting neck strain. Here…" Gunnar found himself sitting up. "That should be more comfortable."

"What are you?"

"Alien." The word hissed from Hollis's mouth, before he chuckled. "I just love doing that. The look on your faces in general is rather hilarious. Still, this is not my normal form or color, but it works when hunting humans. In Noreen's case, it wasn't hard to tell she preferred coloring as far from—well, yours, I suppose—as possible. I chose all black to provide her the contrast she sought. And, since we're on a humanoid planet, it suits me to remain in this form."

"So, why did you let her leave your planet, if you wished to own her?"

"I didn't expect her to dash off the way she did. She's the first one to not be swayed by brandy and jewels. Most of my pets were putty in my arms once I penetrated them. Something about the Lidarian mint plant makes my bodily fluid like a drug to most biologically compatible specimens. I have many humans with ancestries reaching back to your Earth and it worked the same with them. I still don't understand the difference. At least a half dozen emissions into her and still she escaped, when the others were stuporous after only two. I wonder if she has unusual powers or her pets were able to exert some influence on her?" Hollis spoke the last as if to himself.

"Her pets?"

"Hmm?" Hollis turned back to him then waved dismissively. "Oh, the three she calls her staff. Those who tend her. She has them very well trained. I had intended to absorb them into my menagerie as well, but now I don't know…I think it is better to separate her from them."

"So, now what?" Hollis seemed like he was in a mood to talk, so Gunnar thought he might as well keep the conversation going.

"Now? I use you to lure her away. It really is time to end this game and take her home to enjoy. She's led me on an exhilarating journey to be sure. Ten of your years. For one so oblivious to being stalked, it is amazing she's kept away from me this long." The being stopped his pacing and sat down, seemingly in midair.

Before he could speak again, Gunnar interrupted with his own question. "I'm curious. I don't believe we know much about the Lidarians. Mind indulging me?"

Hollis laughed. "Why not? We have time. They're searching for you, but I have this chamber shielded. They can't feel you, though they've made a damn fine attempt at it. Nearly broke through the shield before I had it fully functional."

Interesting. What kind of being was this? "How long have I been missing?"

"Four of your days. Your princess is nearly weak enough for me to snatch away. She's expended most of her energy searching for you."

"Searching? In what way?"

"You really aren't aware of her mental powers, are you? Noreen is like a high-powered telescope lens. Actually, more along the lines of laser optics really. The energy she gathers is like light waves. Signals come at her in varying wave lengths and strengths, but she absorbs them all," Gunnar watched as Hollis used his hands to illustrate the process, "melds them together, then sends them out, unified. Telepathy is only one small part of her power. I haven't figured out the rest, but she's been using the people around her to boost her powers and search out every nook and cranny of this frigid rock, trying to sense your mental signature."

Nory? Looking for him? A tiny wisp of hope unfurled deep within. Guarding that unbelievable thought close, he used all his control to keep his reaction buried. Hollis, in all his arrogance, didn't seem to notice now that he was on roll.

"You became aware of her about the time she went off-planet?"

"Hmmm?" Hollis returned from some thought. "Oh yes. I was deep in another hunt at the time, and she was so young there would have been no sport in capturing her then. Naïve, and unprepared for the universe at large. But adorable. Like a young lioness cub. I flirted with her a little. Enough that she ran straight into the arms of her bodyguard the moment he arrived. I decided to let her finish growing up, so continued with the hunt I already had in progress."

"How did you find her again?"

"I left a spotter on her. Each world where she stopped, I had someone watching her, if I wasn't already there myself. Sometimes they'd approach her for a mild flirtation. She never recognized them, because, like me, they can change to suit their environment," Hollis chuckled. "A wily prey though, she did give us the slip a couple times."

"How did she do that?"

"She, too, likes to disguise. For example, I know she arrived here with brown skin and red hair. It is easy to understand the change of hair color, but for her skin color to change so fast? If the whispers are correct it happened over a matter of a few minutes. Must be something in the water…" The other man faded into his musings again. "You were there, weren't you?"

Gunnar found black eyes watching him intently. "I was, but I can't explain it. She dove in with black hair and brown skin and emerged in the lower pool with white skin and white hair."

"Must be the water then." Hollis apparently decided and let the matter drop. "She learned the art of camouflage quite well, still, each being has a distinctive scent, or mental signature, one little item that makes them unique. A personality quirk, a finger twitch, verbal expression, that sort of thing. Even those who are identical in the womb, their individual experiences outside of it make them unique, though I am eager to meet her sister. If the twin could pass for her all these years, they must be extraordinary together."

Gunnar made a noncommittal grunt. Two people more different he couldn't imagine. "I'm curious about your world. Lidaria? Or someplace else?"

"Lidaria is my world. I've populated it with many humanoids on one continent, other beings on other continents. Noreen only saw what I wanted her to see. I was able, over the years, to gather information on what she likes, so was able to create environments where she'd be most content. I nearly had her, too. Another few days and she never would have heard the summons from home. She would have been completely under my spell."

A look of regret crossed the other man's face then was replaced by a light of anticipation.

"Still, it does make the capture so much more rewarding. I was right to let her go the first time. I can't recall a more invigorating hunt in the last thirty years."

"What will you do when the hunt is over?"

"Do? Take her back to my lair and enjoy her of course. The hunt is just the first part. Training comes next. I anticipate much enjoyment in the training as well. Is it true she carries cubs?"

"Cubs?"

"What is the human equivalent? Babies?"

"Does it matter?"

"It changes the temperament. She will either become more aggressive to protect her offspring, or she'll melt into motherhood. It's hard to tell until it actually happens. I'd hoped she wouldn't breed quite so soon. It changes the whole package, but again, with her talents, I'll take the risk."

Burning anger churned Gunnar's gut. Like hell would this thing get his hands on Noreen. His Nory.

"I see you don't like that idea either." Black eyes peered closely at him, a sparkle of amusement deep inside. "I suppose the cubs are yours. Then that makes my decision easy. You'll come along to care for them once they are weaned. That should ease her mind enough she can concentrate on pleasing me." Traxelgard chuckled deeply. "Now I just need to separate her from her bodyguards. You're safe here. I'll leave you to ponder your future. You'll get to experience the beaches and sun she loves so much. You'll like that part I'm sure, clothing is most sparse on Lidaria. Life is easy once you settle in. Anyhow, I have an appointment with her in a few minutes. I may steal her away this time. If that is the case, we'll be on our way very soon."

Unable to do anything for the moment, Gunnar held his silence and watched Traxelgard snap his fingers and vanish, an echo of his laughter the only hint he'd even been there.

Alone a moment later, he leaned his head back and dropped to the ground. The force holding him left, and he lay for a moment to still the spinning of his head and get his breath back. Eyes closed, he concentrated on Noreen's image in his mind.

Nory.

All he heard was the faint hum of Nordian music, eerie and haunting. No voices in his head. No sense of a presence or images like she tried to describe for him. Just the music that lived within the very bedrock of the planet.

Pushing up to his elbows, he looked around his cell. A bubble in the rock of the planet, the walls were smooth and there appeared to be no possible exit. High enough to be dark, the ceiling wasn't visible, but a hint of fresh air seemed to come from there. Much good it would do him, the walls provided no useful hand holds.

A meter away stood a bottle and what looked like a bundle of food. His stomach rumbled and he recalled he'd been here four days, according to the alien. Food would be a good idea. Keep the strength up.

Bread and water. How original. Eating for sustenance, not pleasure, Gunnar let his mind wander while chewing. Water had never tasted so good, as far as he could remember.

Four days lost. They should be moving to the Summer Palace now, to prepare for the Solstice. Would they travel without him? Noreen would be vulnerable outside the Ryadstholm Palace. Where was he now? Close would be his guess.

Shaking his head, he realized the music had grown louder. What did it mean?

"Gunnar?"

His name, spoken softly, like a whispered breeze.

"Gunnar, where are you?" A hint of anguish.

"Nory?"

"Gunnar? Gunnar! Is that you?"

Was that relief he heard? Or did he feel it? Did it matter? It was her.

"Nory?" he whispered, his heart hardly daring to beat.

"Gunnar, oh Gunnar! Where are you? Where have you been? Why haven't you answered?" The questions poured from her, almost too fast to understand.

"Nory, slow down. I don't think we have much time. Älskling, beware of Hollis."

"I know, we know. Details later."

He listened as she spoke to someone else. *"Thor, where is he? Is he near?"*

Gunnar didn't hear the answer, but Nory's panic eased. He drew in a shaky breath, feeling as if she did the same.

"Älskling," she said to him. *"Thor has your location. You'll be out soon. I need to distract Hollis. Trust... they'll get you out. Faith, my älskling, faith, follow the music. I must go now. Trust the music,"* she urged and, as she faded from his mind, it felt as if she caressed him.

Älskling. It was the first time he recalled her using the endearment. The band around his heart eased and he felt lightheaded. Did it mean... did she...could she...? *Thor*, if only it meant she loved him.

The music of Nordia grew progressively louder, until he sensed a presence in the cell with him. A wraith appeared as if from the rock. At first he was alarmed, and then he remembered Nory talking about them. Follow the music. He rose to his feet, and moved toward the wraith.

Chapter 26

"I'm sorry Hollis, what did you say?" Noreen found it hard to concentrate on him, all the while pretending to be open to his courting.

The last four days had been excruciating. Gunnar missing had been more than enough to send her into a panic, the *ByalbOgBeLun* going silent on her had just about made it a permanent condition. Freya's quick return assured her they were searching just as diligently for Gunnar. Without their searching she never could have found him on her own. Hollis had somehow shielded the chamber he'd been in, but now he was free. Or so Freya's soothing voice whispered over and over again.

As painful as the previous days had been, the next three weren't looking much better. At least she'd finally been able to link with Gunnar. Another wave of relief swept through her, making her feel faint. From the moment she'd discovered him missing, she'd hardly slept, only doing so when one of her staff bodily pinned her to the bed and held her through fitful dreams and nightmares. Eating had been forced on her too. The last two days, the only time she'd risen from her bed was to meet with Hollis. The rest of the time the doctor, and at least one of her staff, had hovered, while members of the family circulated through her room, lending her their energy to keep up the search for Gunnar.

Hollis leaned closer from his chair across the tea table. "Princess, you appear to be very tired. More so than the past few days. Are you feeling well? Are they treating you well here? You should come back to Lidaria with me. I'll make sure your every wish is catered to. You'd never be stressed or tired. Only rested and loved."

She took in his concerned expression, and found it hard not to shudder. He was so charming and attentive, but his very presence, once welcome, now made her skin crawl.

"I'm afraid I'm a bit under the weather. Solstice preparations are in full swing, and Moder expects me to take a hand this year." She smiled to ease her rejection of his plans. This was the part of political games she hated the most. Playing nice with someone who didn't deserve it.

"Ah, yes, the big welcome home, eh?" He leaned back and Noreen felt a measure of relief. What was it about his body language that set her on edge?

"Something along those lines. Will you forgive me, Hollis? I very much need to rest. I know this is time we've set aside to be together, but I'm just not good company today."

"Instead of sitting here, why don't we go for a walk? I understand you designed the landscaping in the thermal pool cavern to resemble tropical locations. I'm much impressed by your artistry. Would you give me a tour?"

"May we do it after dinner? Let me get a nap and I'll be a better guide this evening." She gave him her best smile. The smile widened when Hans stood close behind her. Hollis's eyes shifted to Hans and she could almost see his thoughts. If what she'd figured out in the last day and a half was true, Hollis was growing impatient to see his plans through. Exactly what his plans were, she wasn't sure, but they involved her in a way she didn't want to be involved.

With obvious reluctance, he nodded.

Success in hand, for the moment, she set down her tea cup with a sigh. "Dear Hollis," she simpered and hated herself for it. "You're such a patient man with all these official negotiations. A footman will come for you and escort you to dinner. We dine at the fifteenth hour, so expect him a few minutes before."

He stood when she did. *A proper gentleman*, she thought sarcastically. So proper he'd stolen Gunnar away. The *ByalbOgBeLun* had finally been able to follow Hollis to the cavern where they said he'd hidden Gunnar these past four days. If they hadn't had this appointment, Hollis might still be there, guarding Gunnar and doing... she suppressed a shudder at the thought. Gunnar. She had to see him, even though Cory said he was in good shape. A little hungry, a little dehydrated, but otherwise unharmed, she wanted to see for herself. She needed to touch him.

With a jolt she realized Hollis held her hand.

"I look forward to this evening," he said. He looked as if he wanted to kiss her, but a low growl from Hans made him step back and kiss the back of her hand instead.

"This evening, then," she repeated, extracted her hand, and turned to take the arm Hans offered her for support. It took all her will to walk sedately from the chamber and down the hall until they turned a corner.

"Hans?" she whispered urgently. "Where is he?"

"In your chambers, m'lady." Hans ushered her onto the lift.

Two minutes later, she burst through the door of her sitting room to see Gunnar sitting on an antique settee, drinking from a ridiculously delicate teacup. Cory hovered nearby with a teapot in hand, her mother with a tray of small sandwiches.

"Gunnar!"

He looked so haggard, dark circles under his eyes, cheeks slightly sunken. His hair was mussed and his clothes were a little dirty, but otherwise he just looked tired and hungry. It was all she had time to notice because she ran across the room and into the arms he barely had time to open as he stood.

"Nory, Nory, Nory." He murmured her name over and over again, his arms strong and tight around her.

Unable to help it any longer, she burst into tears, which drew gasps from the others in the room. Gunnar was back, it didn't matter if she cried or not and she wanted to, so there. Through the waterworks she pressed kisses anywhere she could reach and felt him kissing her cheeks, drying the salty drops.

His hands roamed her body, spanning her back, pressing her against him. So hard and strong, his body felt right against her and, when his lips touched hers, she heard the world sing out as if harmonizing in her joy. Sob- and breath-stealing, he kissed her hungrily, his mouth plundering hers as she rose up to meet him. On tiptoe she strained to be closer, and it felt as if he'd pull her right under his skin.

"All right, you two," her father growled beside them, "come up for air. *Uff-da*, my mother was right. Each generation thinks they invented sex. You can rip each other apart later."

Gunnar pulled back with a little chuckle and kissed her cheeks.

"Any minute now, what's-his-face is going to realize Gunnar is gone. We need to get you two out of here."

"No." Noreen shook her head. "Gunnar is well guarded here, and I promised to have dinner with Hollis tonight. We slip him a mickey in his dinner drink, then we bundle him off to the Summer Palace with us."

"Absolutely not."

She stopped in the middle of taking a breath to speak again. Gunnar's tone had never sounded more firm.

"Excuse me?"

"You," he gripped her shoulders, "will not go anywhere near that man, ever again. You will not touch him, you will not be alone with him, you will not be within three meters of him. He is a shapeshifter and a teleporter."

"What?"

"This humanoid shape is not his true form. I don't know what is, but this isn't it."

"Then how do we fight him?"

"I don't know yet, but you are his prey. He's been stalking you ever since you landed on your first foreign planet."

Gunnar stared into her eyes, the intense blue sparkling with tiny flickers of silver. The feeling of compulsion wasn't there, just his love for her.

"Stalking me? What did he tell you?"

"He said he'd first come across you on Nefflerhein, young, naïve and terrified. Said he flirted with you and, as soon as Hans arrived, you fled straight into his protection."

"Um, that would have been…Count Drexalsan of the Tevlarkakan System. Handsome, suave, entirely too polished, and he's right. His attention did scare me. But you say he's been following me ever since?"

"He knows you, Nory," Gunnar said solemnly as he stared into her eyes, but he wasn't seeing her.

"What do you mean?" she asked again with a sinking feeling in her stomach.

Gunnar ignored her and looked over her shoulder. "Hans, thinking back, can you see a pattern to the men she attracted?"

"Now that you mention it…"

Noreen turned around to stare at her bodyguard. He had the same far away, thinking look Gunnar had a few moments earlier.

"Yes, there was a pattern. Wealthy men. Merchants attached to the government. All about ten to fifteen years older than her. Physical descriptions were all different, but humanoid and handsome, educated, well-traveled, willing to spend money on her."

She glared at Hans as he spilled her weaknesses to the world in general. It was just annoying enough she could ignore Cory's sagging jaw followed by an accusatory glare.

"It was always men willing to cater to her and her whims. If they tried to dominate her, she walked. They all had to kowtow to her," Hans said, his eyes sparkling. He knew her, too.

"So, my dear," Gunnar pulled her back around to face him, "you will not be calling the shots here. In fact, if any part of the plan annoys you, that's the direction we go, because he'll least expect it."

Now her jaw dropped. "I won't—"

Gunnar's finger was firm as he pushed her mouth shut. "You will. And you'll like it." He whispered the last words, his forehead resting against hers. And damned if a thrill didn't run through her body.

Staring at him made her eyes cross, so she closed them while she tried to make her mind work, but could only see him moving over her, bringing her to heaven and her body swayed, aching for his touch, his command. With a tiny sigh to hide a smile, she dropped her shoulders and murmured, "Yes, Gunnar."

"How shielded are these rooms?" Gunnar turned to his father-in-law.

"Very. This whole floor is shielded, not only by the gods, but the walls, floors and ceilings are lined with a special mesh," the king answered.

Gunnar nodded. Hollis had said she was well guarded. "Good, then we can stay here for a few hours. I need a bath and time to think. I was unconscious most of the time."

"You also need a good filling meal," Nory said.

He couldn't help himself; he pulled her close again, pressing his scratchy cheek to her smooth one. Could he let her out of his sight for even one second? Somehow, he didn't think so.

"They're going to be useless until they get some time alone," the king said gruffly. "Can we trust you two to not break any more showers? No injuries or emergencies?"

Gunnar grinned over Nory's head. "I think so. I won't even boil her."

"Thank Freya for small miracles. Okay, one hour. We'll meet for tea in my study."

With that, they were left alone.

"Now, what are we going to do with one whole hour?" Gunnar cupped her cheeks.

"I have an idea." Nory kissed him quickly, then stepped away. She picked up the sandwich tray with one hand, took his hand with the other, and led him to the bathroom.

* * * *

An hour later, dressed in soft woolen slacks and sweater, Gunnar followed his wife again, this time to her father's study. One appetite temporarily appeased, he was ravenous for more food. Eyes on her gently swaying hips, the first hunger simmered. She glowed, her body softening and rounding with her pregnancy. Mesmerized, he didn't want to give up a moment of time with her and felt a wave of anger at the four days he had missed.

The off-worlder would pay for those four days and the worry he'd caused Nory. As happy as she was to see him, and Gunnar had no doubt about her joy after they had swamped the bathroom with their enthusiasm, the shadows under her eyes indicated the strain she'd been under.

She turned to him, a touch of concern in her eyes until he smiled, then her face lit up. Still a few steps from the door, he stopped and pulled her into his arms.

"Nory, I love you so very much."

"I love you, too, Gunnar."

Heart overflowing, he rested his palm against her cheek, the pale skin still showing a hint of whisker burn under a light layer of makeup. Blue eyes, as deep as a mountain lake under a clear midsummer sky, stared back at him swimming with emotion.

"We're good together," he said.

"We're getting there," she replied, an impish light in her eyes. "I think we need some more practice."

"Don't worry, we'll get lots of practice," he promised and lowered his lips to hers, which were already red and swollen from hot kisses. This one he kept sweet, soft and tender. Soul-deep satisfaction flooded him when she melted against him. At least soft and sweet was his idea until she pulled his hips tight against her. With a groan he turned until he had her pinned against the wall. Fingers dug into his hips, urging him closer as she straddled his thigh, rubbing herself against it.

"Oh for Thor's sake, can't you two give it a rest?"

Lungs huffing for breath, Gunnar pulled back at the sound of the king's voice. Laced with amusement, impatience was there nonetheless.

"Ja, sire, we'll be there in a minute," he told the king.

"I think I'll wait here. Just to make sure you find your way into the study."

"Oh, Pappa," Noreen sighed.

"None of that now. Get yourselves into the study."

Gunnar cleared his throat of the chuckle bubbling up. Nory just sighed and, with a blush and mischievous twinkle in her eye, straightened a lock of his hair, then they turned to precede the king into the study, where the queen, Cory, Al and a few security people waited. His stomach rumbled at the scent of coffee, soup and sandwiches.

Hearing the rumble, with a wink Noreen served him a plate and settled down beside him on a comfortable sofa.

"So, any brilliant ideas come to you in the bath?" the king asked, settling back into an armchair.

"We proceed according to our original plans. Tonight we move to the Summer Palace. Issue the Lidarian an invitation to the wedding."

Elke raised a regal eyebrow. "Invite not only an off-worlder to the wedding, but one who wants to steal the bride?" Her tone indicated she thought he was off his tracks.

If only she knew. Not just the bride, but the groom and the off-spring as well. The off-spring destined to be the new rulers of Nordia.

With more confidence than he felt, he answered the queen. "Seriously, we want him where we can watch him. If I'm correct, the moment our wedding vows are said, he'll evaporate back to his warship and order the attack from there. That gives us what we want—him firing on the location of the grotta. He can't mess up the coordinates from there, now can he?"

At his side Noreen shook her head. "There is still so much up in the air. Too much could go wrong in too many ways. If he is a shapeshifter who can teleport himself through rock or even up to his ship, then what is to stop him from teleporting us—you and me—right out of the grotta then blasting the planet?"

"His sense of justice. His own rules of the hunt. We need to figure out more of those."

"This is why I should meet him for dinner as planned, only we'll dine with the family. Fader and Al can question him within an inch of his life. You can watch from behind screening and, since you and I can speak telepathically," she grinned at him, "you can feed your questions to me and I can forward them to Pappa."

Gunnar considered her words. There was no denying her quick mind. But they still had the problem of out-witting Traxelgard.

"How close can you and Coreen play the twin card?" he asked.

"I don't know. It's been years…"

He watched as the women exchanged a glance, and probably a deeper communication as well. "I suppose we could manage something." A wicked twinkle struck her eye. "I have just the pair of dresses to do it, too."

Gunnar nearly laughed when Coreen's eyebrows disappeared under her fringe of bangs.

"I will not wear that!"

"Oh yes, you will," Nory laughed. "I wore it my last night on Lidaria and have a second in a slightly different color because I loved it so much. In order to 'twin' him, we have to dress alike. Come to think of it, Hollis rather liked that dress as well. It will throw off his concentration."

"But—but…there's hardly any fabric to it!" Coreen protested.

"That's the whole point. Fader, you will have to turn up the heat in the dining room for the evening. I'm willing to practically bare my body for Nordia, but I'm not willing to freeze it."

"In case you've forgotten, you're starting to show signs of your pregnancy," Cory tried once again to find a point of objection.

"No worries, we'll just leave it loose around the waist. We do our hair the same, our makeup the same and wear the same jewelry, or none at all, and the only way to tell us apart will be by the color of the gowns. They're close enough we'll keep him confused. The other benefit is, by dressing like me, you'll act more like me."

"You have got to be kidding."

The look on Cory's face was merely an underline to her tone. She was aghast at whatever her sister had transmitted to her. Gunnar exchanged a curious look with Al who appeared very interested in seeing the dress in question. If it made Cory blush, it had to be good.

"At least we can't fault the alien for his taste in women," Gunnar said. "Nory, do you have another similar dress for your mother to wear?" he asked and bit into a sandwich made with spicy reindeer sausage.

Funny, he didn't realize the queen and her two daughters could gasp in exactly the same way. Only Nory's shaking gave her away. She thought it was just as funny as he did.

Chapter 27

"You'll just have to put a little cotton wool in there. That's all there is to it," Noreen said.

"I will not stuff my bra!"

Noreen, Sophia and Cory's maid all stood back and shook their heads.

"What bra?" Noreen took a step closer to her sister, cotton in her hand.

"That is entirely beside the point. It isn't my fault this dress doesn't have room for a bra."

"I can't help if the pregnancy has made me more busty. In order for this to work, we have to enhance you just a bit. Besides, the dress looks better with a little padding anyway. It isn't as if you have to prove to Hollis at the end of the night just how deceptive the look is. Open up," she ordered her sister.

Cory slowly unbuttoned the fabric at the front of the dress.

"Will you do it or do I have to?"

"I'll do it." Cory snatched the soft cotton pad and slid it under her breast, wedging it in between flesh and fabric.

Shaking her head, Noreen stepped back. "Sophie, you know how it's done. Would you please instruct my sister in the art of female wiles?"

Five minutes later, they stood side by side and gazed into the full length mirror of Noreen's dressing room.

The dresses were the same design, but one was a blush pink, the other a deeper shade.

"Why did you buy two the same?" Cory asked.

"I usually buy two of anything I really like. I just couldn't decide which color suited me better. More of a mood item, we decided. And current skin tone." She wore the more pale shade this time. She would have preferred the darker, but they'd decided against it as a personality marker. Hollis would expect her in the deeper shade. The lighter would throw him off. Maybe.

A band of linen fabric closed at the front with three large shell buttons, leaving the shoulders bare and their individual cleavages displayed nearly down to the nipples. The skirt, just barely thick enough to be opaque, fell from below the bust to the floor. Soft pink silk slippers covered their feet, only the toes peeking out from under the full and flowing skirts.

"Because we want to hide my baby-belly," Noreen rested a hand over the swell so unlike her sister's flat stomach, "we'll leave the sashes hanging down the back."

"But they drag on the floor," Cory pointed out.

"Okay, Sophie, try tying a bow, but leave the tails long," Noreen instructed. The wide sashes were meant to wrap from the back between the shoulder blades to the front and cross under the breasts, return to the back, cross and back to wrap across the stomach to return and tie at the back. The effect made the dress look wrapped on the body with tantalizing hints of skin through the not-quite-transparent under skirt.

"I'm not sure I like the bow, but it does take the sashes up off the ground," Sophie said and let Noreen turn to see the change.

"Then wrap it once then tie a large bow in back," she suggested.

A few minutes later her maid frowned and shook her head. "Not much better."

"No, it works. Just fluff out the bow a little more..." She stood still while her maid tugged and fussed. "There! That works just fine."

"Jewelry? You two have diamond chokers which nearly match," Sophie suggested as she laid a contrasting length of soft netting around her shoulders.

"No!" Noreen declared. "I can't wear the choker without gagging." She held a hand to her throat. "Either a simple chain or nothing. The earrings alone are just fine." Diamonds on the dangling earrings caught the light and threw out rainbow colored sparkles.

"You certainly are making this difficult," Cory complained and adjusted her own contrasting wrap. Pale pink to go with her gown, darker pink to go with Noreen's.

"I know this man. Diamonds won't dazzle him. Pink flesh will."

"I don't want to hear it," Cory groaned.

"I don't suppose you want to hear about how good he is with his tongue, either, do you?" She gave her sister a wicked smirk. Who knew Cory could be such a prude?

"How can you say such things with your husband sitting just on the other side of that door?" Cory angrily stabbed a finger in the direction of the sitting room.

"Oh please. Did you and Al never kiss before he asked for your hand? Did his hand never stray, just a little?" Noreen tucked a stray wisp of hair into her elaborate braided crown. "Sophie, just a touch more hair spray, please." She glanced at her sister's red face. "Come on, Cory. Al is a man, and men of his age must find release. Tell me he came to you a virgin and I'll know you're lying. I'm sure you were a virgin, but it's impossible to believe he was. It just isn't healthy for men to hold back all those physical urges."

"But—but—Gunnar? Wasn't he supposed to be...pure?" Cory whispered the last word.

"How can you be so naïve? He was pure in the sense he used barriers to keep from spilling his seed in or on another woman. That's about as virginal as my boy was. Of course, I still had my maidenhead when we joined." She ignored Sophie's cough and regarded her fixed hair style. "Didn't you make use of any of the techniques I wrote you about?"

"What techniques?"

"How to make love and keep your virginity. Didn't you try out anything? How many dates did you go on anyway?"

"I never got those letters."

She decided that if Cory's eyes opened any wider they were going to fall out.

"What do you mean you never got the letters? You answered them. Granted you never told me how my advice worked out but you answered each letter." She turned to stare at her sister and their dropped jaws were identical.

"Oh, no..." Cory covered her now bright red face.

"Fader and his damn security teams." Noreen snapped her mouth shut with a frown. "I bet you anything he saw every single one of them. That sly old fox. We'll have to get him back."

"What do you mean?" Cory took a pair of long pale pink gloves from her maid and started pulling them on while Noreen did the same with darker pink gloves.

"I'll have to think about it, but I'm sure we can come up with something good. Oh well, I just hope Al knows what he's doing with a twenty-six year-old innocent on his hands." She tugged at the stretchy cotton, pulling the left glove up to her elbow before starting on the right glove. "We don't have time to talk about it now, but we have more, much more to discuss on this issue. For now, shoulders back, yes, thrust out those things proudly, chin up, and let's go devour some men. Just follow my lead."

Nose in the air, Noreen took her sister's arm and they glided from the dressing room. With satisfaction she watched the stunned faces of the men as they stood to acknowledge their wives. Gunnar was still dressed casually, Al dressed for a formal dinner.

"*Don't give it away,*" she warned Cory quietly. "*If we can fool them, we can fool Hollis.*"

"*But that's not right!*" Cory's protest rang in her head.

"*Stop being such a prude. Where is the girl who used to steal from the kitchen? Where is the girl who would provide distraction by making the guard tie her shoe? What happened to the mouthy wench who would do impressions of that horrible governess?*" She relaxed with a wide smile when Cory giggled. "Judging by the looks on their faces, they're currently noticing the enhanced cleavage and not paying one ounce of attention to our faces," she said aloud.

Gunnar's blue eyed gaze flew to her face, but she looked at Al instead and mentally instructed Cory to look at Gunnar. This was their one chance to see if they could still pull it off.

Ah, maybe they could do it. Both men stopped in their tracks, looks of confusion on their faces, until Gunnar started laughing.

"Nice try. Looking at the wrong husband almost made it work," he said and lifted Noreen's hand. "I'd know you anywhere. Not that you two won't fool anyone else, but," he pulled her into his arms, "I know how devious you like to be. You should know that Traxelgard is aware of your penchant for disguising yourself, so you and Cory will need to stay linked to keep up the deception."

"I intend to coach her with my normal responses and she'd better do the same for me." It really was too pleasant to melt into his arms. "For now though, we'd best send you on to your hiding place, and Al can escort both of us to dinner. Cory will just have to pretend he is you tonight and not snuggle up to him like a newlywed."

"I don't know if I can act that well," Cory whispered.

"Yes, you can. What happened to that famous back bone you use for facing down Parliament? Just don't get gushy when you're with Al. We have to play act for now."

"Just don't get too good at it or you'll get to watch me kiss your sister senseless when this is all over," Gunnar murmured.

"Do that, and I may knock you senseless," she whispered back and nipped his lower lip.

"Nory," Gunnar's eyes turned serious on her, "this isn't a game of seduction. This is a game of politics with much higher stakes."

"I know. Tonight our goal is to throw him off the scent just a little. Enough to make him pause for a few days."

"I don't like it."

"Neither do I. I'd rather have dinner here with you."

Gunnar held her close, forehead to forehead, their breaths mingling. "Don't be reckless tonight. It isn't just your life in the balance."

"I know, *älskling*, I know."

"By the way, you look very beautiful. And if you ever attempt to wear this dress in public again, I'll pin you to the bed and slice it off you."

"Promise?" She dropped her voice an octave and ran a finger over his lower lip.

"Yes, that's a promise."

"I can hardly wait to see what you think of my other gowns." This was one of the more conservative.

"Sounds like we'll have to have a fashion show soon."

She held him close, the rumble of his voice sending deep dark thrills through her. The sessions of lovemaking since his rescue weren't nearly enough to make up for the days he'd been missing. Dinner with Hollis was the last thing she wanted to do right now. Even dinner with her family was a barely tolerable idea.

"M'lady, unless you want to spend another hour dressing, I suggest we move on now," Sophie interrupted.

"Yes," she sighed and lightly kissed Gunnar. "Yes, we need to go."

* * * *

Arms securely linked, with Al following them, Noreen sailed into the dining room with Cory, their chins held high. Minds linked, it felt as if they were Siamese twins.

"*Smile, darling,*" Cory reminded her using the false tone of snobbery they used for play acting as children. Cory had been the better actress, able to better imitate the Lords and Ladies who came to the palace on official visits.

"*Together now,*" she returned the coaching.

"My dear Hollis! So sorry to have kept you waiting!" they cooed in perfect unison.

It was very fun, watching his eyes darken as he took in the two of them bearing down on him. He'd been speaking with Fader and Moder, but now held his beverage glass as if his grip would shatter it. At the last moment his grip relaxed and his white teeth shone out against his dark skin in a blinding smile.

"Ladies, you overwhelm me with your beauty. I've heard but whispers of the twins so alike no mortal can tell them apart. I fear I have my work cut out for me." He bowed over first one extended hand and then the other.

Noreen made her smile stay in place when his grip tightened on her hand. "My dear sir, is everything all right?"

"Perfectly." His easy tone and smile sent a shiver down her spine. His charm could be devastating. Sharp eyes looked deep into hers and she lowered her lids coyly. An act he'd seen dozens of times, if Gunnar had his facts right. Thankfully Cory paid attention and acted the very same way.

"At the end of the evening we'll test your powers of observation. If you can tell which of us is Coreen, and which is Noreen, we may reward you with a kiss. But guess wrong, and Duke NyDunfiddich here may have words with you." They pulled Al forward between them.

"And why is that, Your Highnesses?"

"Coreen is newly wed to the duke."

If she'd been watching from the sidelines, the twin simper and giggle would have made her gag.

Hollis threw back his head and laughed. "A test to my observation skills indeed. My ladies, you are on. I will dare much to taste the sweet lips of my true love once again."

"Dinner is served," a footman announced.

Fader came forward and offered an arm to each of his eldest daughters. "I'm surprised you dared show up dressed like that," he muttered.

"But Fader, this really is one of the more conservative styles we have," Coreen protested, mimicking the words sent to her.

"You, my child, need to be re-educated about what is proper apparel for state functions. Dragging your mother into the charade is going entirely too far. Now which of you is sitting where?"

* * * *

"Nory, my love, he isn't falling for it. He has you pegged," Gunnar sent the thought down to his bride. From his angle, hidden behind a tapestry high in the dining room, he could nearly see down to her stomach, the very edges of her nipples barely contained by the brief bodice of her gown. *"I'm also fairly certain he knows I'm here and no longer trapped."*

The alien's eyes had taken to wandering along the wall across from him. The same wall where Gunnar stood in shadows, looking down on the diners. More than once the unnerving black gaze had stopped on the tapestry he stood behind.

"Then how do we stop the game and get out? I don't know what to do anymore, Gunnar."

Think. He just had to think like a hunter.

"What do I do when he identifies me?" Nory's soft voice was a comfort inside his head.

"Kiss Al and beg for your sister's forgiveness. Don't admit to anything."

A few moments passed before Nory came back. *"She agrees with you."*

"Cory knows her political intrigue. She's sharp."

"And I'm not..."

"Nory, don't. You both are smart in different areas. For example, that dress I hate you wearing for anyone but me, has his attention front and center on the two of you."

The women sat across the table from Traxelgard, with Al between them. Aunt Alice and another, equally aged dowager duchess sat next to Hollis.

"Yes, all I'm fit for is to be the heir-bearing heifer and fashion consultant for off-world tramps."

"Nory, please, that isn't true and you know it. Please focus on what needs to happen tonight."

"You're right. I'm sorry. I shouldn't indulge in self pity. I just feel out of my element here. My response was infantile."

"Considering you are carrying infants and we're both out of our element, your reaction is understandable. We just have to stick together, älskling."

Gunnar's use of the endearment was like a caress, and calmed as much as if he were holding her hand. Under the tablecloth, Al pressed his knee against hers and Cory sent a mental hug.

"Al is touching you for me."

"Thanks, sis."

"What does Gunnar say?"

Pretending to enjoy the story Aunt Alice told Hollis, Noreen repeated the comments. This juggling of so many mental conversations was really getting to be too much. She turned her attention to Hollis and found him staring at her.

"You know, Princess Noreen, this elaborate play has really been most intriguing and a pleasant diversion, but it grows tiresome. Everyone knows I'm here to negotiate to complete the marriage ceremony we began on Lidaria, nearly three weeks ago. My patience is growing short."

She found his gaze most unnerving. All night he'd stared at her and called her by her name, addressing Coreen by hers. How did he know?

"My dear sir, how can you be sure you address the correct princess?" She fluttered her eyelashes in an exaggerated fashion as she'd never done off-planet. If this man knew her, he'd know the action was false.

"I know you like I know each wart on my heart, my lady."

"Now there's an odd expression."

"What do you know of love, my lady?"

"According to you, and nearly everyone around me, I don't know much about it," Coreen injected, but it didn't matter. Hollis was still focused on just one woman. Unfortunately, the right one.

"I agree. You don't. But, I can tell you something of love. You say there is a man here who loves you and will not give you up. But where was he, while you traveled so far from home?"

"We hadn't met. We were destined for each other, but I left before we met."

"You left because you were afraid to meet him and fulfill all that the gods had decreed your life would be. A mother, a queen, nothing more."

Noreen shrugged and felt Coreen do the same through their connection.

"And yet, you left to create a new destiny. How ingenious of you." Hollis's eyes sparkled at her, reminding her of a deep chocolate carbonated beverage she'd fallen in love with on Andromeda IV.

"Cowardly is the word most associated with my defection."

"Was it a coward who faced down each strange world and conveyance to get there? Was it a coward who faced the government of Kookor and talked them into importing your wool and turning it into one of the more sought after textiles on this side of the Universe?"

"I had assistance."

"Me."

"You," she laughed. "I'm sorry, Hollis, I didn't know you then."

"You've known me on nearly every planet where you've stopped more than a month, my dear."

"No, I would have remembered…" she paused as Hollis faded and Count Draxalsan appeared before her as if she'd only seen him yesterday. "How did you do that?"

Hollis returned and lifted his coffee cup as if it had all been an optical illusion. "I've followed you, when I could, from world to world and eased your negotiations at nearly every turn. I introduced you to the right people and made sure they were willing to listen. Once the ice was broken you sold your products yourself. You didn't need my help there. Just the initial networking."

"*Cory, ask him about Lesbos,*" Noreen sent her sister an image from the planet ruled by women.

"What about on Lesbos, Hollis? Were you there as well?"

Noreen felt her face pale as Councilwoman Seribethena replaced Hollis across the table. She could feel Cory's face burn as much as she felt cold. The cough from Hans sitting to her right brought a smile to her lips. Yes, Hans had enjoyed that planet more than just a little. Did this mean he'd slept with Hollis? No, that thought wouldn't go over well at all. Hans didn't cross that particular street. Not knowingly or willingly.

"The point is, Noreen," Hollis appeared before her again, his black gaze locked intently on hers, "because of love, I've followed you, watched your growth, helped you, and plain just enjoyed watching you take on the universe at large. On your terms. No one dictated anything to you. Where was the man who should have been by your side, according to your prophecy? I only saw your bodyguard there to watch out for you." Hollis nodded at Hans.

"He was here seeing to duties I shirked."

"What duties did you shirk? As far as I can tell, you've done more to further the economy of this frozen rock than any ten of your ancestors combined."

"As has he, in his own way. He built up the cargo system to support the economic growth. We each played our role in the improvement of our world. But we're not done yet," Coreen declared.

"Ah yes, Princess of The Profetia, you still have to save your world, by bearing the heirs, the gods of the next generation. I say you already have saved your world. You've saved their economy from stagnating and turned them into a universal name. But tell me, Princess, where is your prince?"

"He is away on business."

"Are you sure?"

"Yes. He is seeing to Crown business." The silence at the table was eerie. Why didn't her father jump in and help with the conversation? He wasn't so far away. She glanced down the table and saw him watching, his sharp blue eyes intent on the discussion, but not interfering.

"*Pappa?*"

"*You're doing fine, Noreena.*"

"*But now what?*" she wailed internally and turned her gaze back to Hollis.

"*Invite him to the wedding.*" Her mother's dulcet tone melded in with the conversation in her head.

"*You invite him.*" Never mind that Moder had never spoken to her this way before. What was going on?

"Minister Traxelgard," her mother said, drawing everyone's attention. "We're all leaving for the site of the wedding in the morning. Why don't you join us? We can continue this discussion along the way."

"Your Majesty," Hollis inclined his head toward her end of the table. "I would be most honored." His gaze swung back to Noreen. "Still, I believe someone owes me a kiss tonight."

"I'm so sorry, Hollis," Coreen laughed. "You guessed wrong. Coreen, give your husband a nice big kiss."

Chapter 28

"All right, Alice, what are you up to?"

Noreen looked around at her father's words. Aunt Alice settled on a settee in the family drawing room with a serene look on her face. Carefully arranging the long skirt of her simple wool gown, she took her time answering.

"Whatever are you talking about, Bjorn?"

Hollis and the other few handpicked guests were being seen on their way to the guest quarters of the palace while the family met for an after-dinner council. Gunnar had been waiting for them, holding a cognac, staring at a newly hung portrait of the royal family showing both girls. The portrait looked like it had been painted from a photo taken on their sixteenth birthday. The last time Noreen's family had seen her in the flesh until recently.

Noreen's gaze met Gunnar's across the room and she went to him. With Al's kiss still tingling on her lips, she wanted to feel Gunnar again.

"You didn't have to be that convincing," Gunnar murmured and took her into his arms.

Breathless when he released her, she rested against his strong chest. "It shut Hollis up, didn't it?"

"Maybe, but—"

"I just pretended he was you."

Gunnar stared down at her, the look in his eyes deep and moving. They were pulled from the moment by her father's voice directed at Aunt Alice still.

"You were flirting with what's-his-face. Don't deny it. I haven't seen you bat your eyelashes at anyone. Ever."

Curious, Noreen turned in Gunnar's arms and sharpened her focus on Aunt Alice. Her father held a cognac glass the same as Gunnar, but he held it out, a finger pointing directly at the older woman.

"If you know something, I want to hear it," the king ordered.

Aunt Alice, her long white hair gracefully coiled on her head, smiled serenely at the room's occupants, her faded blue eyes sparkling from the folds of softened skin around them. "Bjorn, stop getting your knickers in a twist and sit down. It is very clear he isn't interested in an old woman when he has the prime of Nordian womanhood before him." She waved a gloved hand in Noreen's direction.

"Oh, I don't think your day is over," Noreen said and moved over to the adjacent settee. "I bet you could teach all of us a thing or two."

"And don't you forget it." Aunt Alice patted her hand.

"Alice," the king growled, towering over Noreen and the old woman.

"Bjorn, behave yourself. I can still tan your britches, even if you are the king. Now sit down and enjoy your drink. Don't worry about Hollis. I've got his number and will make him behave."

Noreen stared at her and wondered. Who was this woman, really? She'd always been Aunt Alice, but was she really a relation? Always there, always in the background, helping with functions and obligations. A voice of encouragement, a ready ear to listen to dreams. One supporter with a cheerful ear whenever Noreen doubted herself for running off. Never judgmental. She leaned closer to the older woman. "Aunt Alice?"

The clear blue eyes turned to her and Noreen was stunned by the depth of them. These eyes held ancient wisdom and knowledge of the ages. An old soul, or... Noreen gulped.

"Be easy, my dear," Alice murmured. "Hollis won't be a problem. Hurt my girls? I don't think so."

A strange feeling of peace, and a sense of right settled over her, when Alice's hand covered hers. Strong and firm, with no hint of old age weakness, Noreen had no doubt Alice could keep her word.

"Will you tell me?"

"I will, but not this moment. When the time is right. Now, tell me about your time on Lidaria. The mint brandy is as good as ever. How many distilleries are there now?"

Following the older woman's lead, Noreen accepted a cup of herbal tea and leaned into Gunnar's arm when he sat next to her. It was impossible not to smile when he wrapped the shawl of netting across her chest and held her tight. Not allowing it to interfere with her conversation, she answered all of Aunt Alice's questions.

After their departure time for the next day had been determined, people began drifting away. Coreen and Al were the first to excuse themselves. Finally, Gunnar yawned and Noreen realized only her father and Aunt Alice remained with them. Even Olaf and the old bishop had retired.

"Now, Alice." Noreen's father poured another measure of cognac and carefully set the bottle on the table next to Gunnar. "What is this all about?"

Noreen found herself not only smiling, but leaning forward in anticipation.

"It's rather simple, Bjorn. You've suspected for some time I'm not really a relation, but you've been kind about not letting on." She patted his knee while he snorted.

"I just know you haven't aged a day in fifty years. Our cosmetic surgeons aren't that good."

Alice merely smiled, and the warmth of it filled Noreen's heart. Fader was right, not a hair or soft wrinkle had changed in all the time she could remember. "And you wonder why I won't pose for your silly portraits."

"Come on, my daughter needs her rest for the trip," he muttered into his drink.

"Oh all right. So much for one last surprise." She paused and Noreen blinked. Then blinked again. She was staring at Coreen. Or a mirror image of herself. It was hard to tell.

"Are you…" Noreen stopped before she started spluttering and frowned.

"Yes, my precious. I'm the same as Hollis. Only his name isn't Hollis," she said with a touch of sadness. "He's just as stubborn as you, even more so. He's had many more years practice," she sighed. "Anyhow, in case you ever wondered why I supported your decision to run off for a few years, you should know I did the same thing. Only I've been gone from home for close to one hundred Nordian years. It is time for me to slap Hollis into shape and make a proper husband out of him."

Noreen felt Gunnar's surprise as she sat back with the force of her own. "You? And Hollis?"

"I must say he has good taste to fall in love with you. After all, you are a wonderful child, but he's old enough to not be so foolish. So, this is what we do…"

* * * *

Gunnar still shook his head as they entered their dressing room. "Can you believe the old girl?" he asked Nory.

"Right now, I feel as if I could believe almost anything."

She gave him a soft smile and he saw the shadows of weariness under her eyes.

"Lars, Sophie, we'll take care of ourselves tonight," Gunnar told the equally tired looking valet and maid.

"Sir?" Sophie began to protest and Gunnar shook his head.

"I promise to help her. You two get some sleep. The next few days are going to be busy at best, instead of harrowing. I think we'll also sleep in until at least the seventh hour. M'lady has had a very late night. We leave right after the midday meal, so everything will need to be ready an hour or so before."

"Yes, Your Highness." Sophie dropped a short curtsy and left the dressing room with Lars close behind.

As the door closed Gunnar turned to his wife. Pink was good on her.

"You'll have to help me undress," she said, her hand reaching for the hem of his sweater.

"I can do that." He lightly gripped her wrists, stopping her. "I'll be your lady's maid tonight."

"You can't ruin my dress. This one I had to pay full price for," she warned him.

"But you wore it with…" Gunnar couldn't bring himself to say the man's name.

"No, I wore the other one."

"Ah. I suppose that makes some difference." His fingers found the buttons at the very brief front of her dress. "I could almost see this," he traced the edge of her areola with the tip of finger, "from my hiding place."

"Ah," she moaned at his touch. "I thought you were helping me to bed? I still need to wash my face and brush out my hair."

"Oh, but I am helping you to bed. Either you're dense or I'm doing a terrible job of it."

He loved her husky chuckle, which caressed his nerves like a warm breeze on bare skin. Another twist of his fingers and the second button was released, showing even more soft skin forming a creamy cover over soft mounds.

"Release the last one before it bursts open, if you please." She rubbed her hips against his.

"You have grown, haven't you?" The last button eagerly popped through the button hole, releasing her ripe breasts, the nipples a deeper pink than he remembered. "So many changes, in just a few days," he said and rested a hand over her rounded belly. The fullness nearly filled his hand and he had a sudden longing to feel his children moving. "Can you feel them yet?"

"Sometimes, I think I do, just a little flutter, but the doctor tells me it's too soon. She expects I will feel them for real, very soon because there are so many. Far sooner than if there was only one."

"You'll tell me? I mean as soon as you're sure?"

The smile she gave him was tender as she cupped his cheek. "You'll be the first to know. I promise." Deep and swimming with emotion, her gaze locked on his and he felt himself drowning.

Whatever this woman wanted of him, he'd give it with his dying breath. A sudden wave of emotion gripped him and he curled a hand around her neck, pulled her to him, hungry for the taste and feel of her.

Gasping, she lifted her mouth to his, meeting his hunger with her own, her desire pushing his higher. His other hand found her breast, bare and warm, the nipple pressing against his palm. It was impossible to tell which of them moaned. Maybe it was both of them. Either way, he felt it to his toes, along with a mad desire to be free of all restrictions. Tearing fabric brought groans from her, but he deepened the kiss, stealing her attention from the ruined dress settling at their feet. Both of his hands slid into her hair, searching for pins, letting them drop as soon as they were free of her braids. In a matter of moments he combed his fingers through her soft locks, loosening the braided strands.

All the while their tongues danced in a sensuous duel. Long, soft hair tumbled in riotous curls around her body before Gunnar finally released her, letting her lift his sweater up and over his head. Shoes were toed off, then he lifted her in his arms.

"Soon I'll be too big for you to carry," she murmured, lips teasing his earlobe, arms around his neck.

"Never." He silenced her with a kiss and shouldered the door to the bedroom shut behind them. Using infinite care, he lowered her to the bed, pulling away only long enough to shed the rest of his clothes, dropping them in a heap upon the floor.

"You know they'll never let you undress us again after a formal function, right?" Her soft laugh sent a bolt of heat through his blood.

"I don't care," he said and reached over to snap the thin sides of her panties. "Might as well do a really good job of it." He pulled away the destroyed scrap of fabric and tossed it over his shoulder. A squealing giggle answered him when he crawled up on the bed until he lay over her, resting between soft thighs, which cradled him perfectly. Gazes locked, he slowly lowered his forehead to hers.

"I'm so sorry—" The words started to tumble from his mouth, but she shushed him with a finger on his lips.

"You have nothing to be sorry for. I'm the one who is sorry."

"For what?"

"Whatever it was I said or did that made you want to leave that day."

"Oh Nory," he sighed. "I'm such a fool. I love you so very much. I know you have no reason to love me. I was forced on you, but I swear, I'll do everything to take care of you and our children."

"What are you talking about?" She pushed him away until she could look up at him, brow furrowed in confusion.

"I… I…" He rolled off her, falling back on the bed at her side. "I came looking for you at the grotta and saw you, cuddled up…"

"With my staff." She finished his sentence with a sigh. Her hand waved over him. "Pull," she ordered.

Tugging on her hand helped her roll up against his side. She made him move his arm and snuggled under it.

"Gunnar, you have to understand—"

"I know. They were your family all those years. Nearly one third of your life, all of your adult life to date, they were the ones you leaned on, depended upon, as they depended on you. I can't compete with that kind of closeness."

"You don't have to compete with it. You're my family now. My husband. Yes, they're still family too, but you have the higher level of importance. Do you understand? I love you as my husband. I love them as my friends, closer than friends, in many ways closer than family. You're right, we only had each other to depend on. Necessity made us close. But you have top priority, and they understand that. It's the way it should be. Just like things will change when the children are born."

Gunnar stared at the canopy of the large bed, his heart thudding against his ribs. "Nory…I love you," he repeated. "I love our children. I won't let you down."

"You haven't let me down yet, and I know you won't ever."

Little fingers pressed against his jaw and he turned his head to look at her. Deep blue eyes stole his breath. Soft, and swimming with salt tears, he saw a summer ocean in her eyes. "Nory," he whispered and rolled to face her.

"Gunnar, just love me. All I need is your love and you beside me. If we stand together we can handle anything."

"Always," he gave her his oath.

Their lips met and he had the sensation of being tossed about, like sliding over the edge of a thermal pool and twisting while sliding into the next. Is this what it felt like to be tossed by ocean waves?

"*Yes.*" Nory's answer whispered in his mind. "*Open to me, let me show you.*"

"*How can this be?*"

"*Don't ask, enjoy. I don't know if it will last beyond the pregnancy, now pay attention...*"

Like living a movie, he felt the caress of warm breezes, heavy with humidity, and sweet with the scent of flowers and the tang of salt, brush over his skin, her hands furthering the illusion. Catching her to him, he rolled to his back, pulling her on top of him. Closing his eyes, it was as if he saw through hers, felt the sensations touching her skin and, when she settled down on him, the intimate connection intensified the mental connection.

"*Nory...*"

"*Together now.*"

Sensation took over and it was if they swam like seals, their bodies clasped together, diving and twisting through blue crystal clear waters. The vistas awed him as she showed him coral reefs and friendly fish in a dazzling array of shape and colors.

"*Sunfish.*" She identified a fish that looked like a large plate to him "*Dolphin.*" She pointed to a sleek gray creature he'd only seen before in books and movies. Yellow and blue, small fish darted around them, in amongst the fingers of coral reefs.

She moved against him, her soft breasts pressing into him, her *fitte* undulating around him like the underwater current she shared with him.

"*Gunnar, someday we'll feel this together, for real.*"

He felt the sweet longing of memory, her desire to experience it again, and he tasted her passion for travel and seeing new worlds.

"*Yes, Nory, my love, yes. We'll do it, I promise.*" How they would he didn't know, but somehow, some way, they'd find the opportunity to travel.

Joy burst from her and, moving together, bodies joined, they rolled and melded, their souls joined in the most perfect bliss.

Chapter 29

"Relax, princess. All will be well."

The voice of Odin in her head wasn't the least bit reassuring. Not even Freya's soothing tone could help dispel the feeling that she'd swallowed a liter of Muldariat worms. Thin, wiggling, twisting, turning...

Deep inside, below her stomach, a flurry of what felt like butterfly wings erupted, causing her to stop pacing, hands flying to cover her abdomen.

"What?" Gunnar's sharp question made her look his direction as she tried to breathe.

"Nory?" In two long strides he reached her side and gripped her shoulders. "What's wrong?" His blue eyes flashed with worry and alarm.

"Nothing," she found her voice. "Can you feel?" She pulled one of his hands down and held it over her womb as another flutter rippled through her.

A frown and sigh of frustration told her he couldn't, not from the outside. She stared into his eyes, mesmerizing both of them, pulling his awareness into her body in time to feel another, softer, flutter as if the babies were settling down to sleep again. The frown transformed into wide-eyed wonder, his pulse melding with hers.

"The babies?" he asked, enjoying their ability to share a private moment amidst the bustle of last minute wedding preparations.

"Yes!"

His face relaxed into a wide grin and a rush of love made her feel as if she glowed. The babies moved again, this time in a slow, almost lazy, roll, and she had a vision of them, each in their own placenta, bouncing off one another like beach balls. Teeny, tiny beach balls playing in a capsule of warm water.

Gunnar laughed and bent down to kiss her. *"Cheeky little guys,"* he declared.

"Or girls." She pouted playfully.

"*Or girls,*" he agreed with an even wider grin. "*Odin save me from a litter of all girls.*"

With no force, she slapped his shoulder. He didn't mean it. A boy or two would be nice, but Gunnar loved all his children, boys or girls. *Litter*, she snorted in disgust, much to Gunnar's amusement.

"Have they confessed yet?" Her father's question pulled the two of them from their private moment.

"No, they aren't giving up their identities yet," she told him with a sigh. "Then again, their little brains have only been putting out the very smallest of waves a week or so. The doctor says we may be able to tell in the next week just what we have."

"I hope there's at least one boy," her father muttered and she rolled her eyes.

"Odin will take care of us," her mother interrupted. "Now, time to go. Places everybody!" She clapped her hands.

Because of the non-traditional style of ceremony, the traditional walk down the aisle was scrapped completely. How could you have an aisle in the thermal pools? The queen had tossed her hands in the air.

So a small island had been raised in the middle of the largest pool. Just large enough for the bishop and the two of them, they'd be standing in hip-deep water. A step down, her parents and sisters would circle around them in waist-deep water, the ledge wide enough for their husbands to stand behind them, before dropping another step so the rest of the guests would stand around them in chest-deep water until they fanned out to the edges where the pool gradually shallowed. Taller guests had been encouraged to stand in the deeper part of the pool. It would be a very tight fit, squeezing close to a thirteen hundred people from the ruling families into the cavern, much less the water itself. But that, according to Odin and his minions, was what they wanted.

They'd proven physical contact was the key over the last few frantic days. Noreen was able to draw in more power and focus it when standing in the mineral rich waters of the thermal pools. Using the members of her family for testing, she'd been able to instantly draw on the powers of anyone in the water and touching her by only a fingertip, turning her body into a conduit of pulsing energy. Gunnar's arms, wrapped around her, had doubled the power, encasing both of them with energy, their minds meeting and melding, working together. So powerful a combination, they'd been able to seek out the comet headed their way and track its trajectory, confirming its impact if they failed to shift the planet. It wouldn't take much, just a few meters would push them into an orbit that would avoid the collision, which would otherwise occur in three weeks time.

Noreen had been tempted to try and nudge the comet aside, but Gunnar and what seemed like the entire host of *ByalbOgBeLun* had rushed in and shouted her down, breaking up the connection.

"Why did you do that?" she'd shouted in frustration.

"You're not strong enough," Freya's voice had told her.

"And the orbit of the comet is too unpredictable. You just can't jump in and start deflecting rocks." Gunnar had backed up the voice. "These things must be carefully calculated."

"If you'd adjusted the course it would have swung back this way in another year and the impact would be unstoppable," Odin had admonished.

"Fine, fine, fine," she'd capitulated. "Let's just get this show on the road."

"All in good time," Freya had soothed, then put a compulsion of sleepiness on her.

Alert now, Noreen pulled on her disguise. To make the ruse work, all the sisters wore headdresses with veils. Aunt Alice, in the shape and form of Noreen, wore a tiara and dangling earrings. Gunnar wore a simple gold circlet. Once the robes were shed, nothing else would be worn. Moder was still a little scandalized. Not that nudity in the thermal pools was a big deal, but to be married that way? Unheard of. In the pools, people politely looked the other way, concentrating on a person's eyes rather than their body. With the wedding, all eyes would be on the couple on the raised island. And not only that, everyone would be touching. Unheard of. Faced with extraordinary circumstances, the queen merely forged ahead, planning what she could.

"All right now." The queen recalled everyone's attention to the ceremony at hand. "Gunnar, you and, uh, Noreen, off you go and we'll all follow."

Fighting the nerves in her stomach, Noreen fell into line with Hans's younger brother posing as her husband. For all intents and purposes, Noreen was posing as one of her own half sisters, and the veil covering her face made her blend in with the other women. The old bishop looked back and was waved onward by the queen. Leading the way, he was followed by Gunnar with Aunt Alice on his arm, Fader with Moder, Coreen with Al, Noreen and Mikkel next. The rest of the sisters and their husbands fell in behind them as the line, two wide, left the side room. Robes were dropped at the door, and all proceeded down the aisle cleared by the guests to the center of the pool.

Accompanied by the music of the *ByalbOgBeLun*, they slowly filed into the water and walked out to the island. Noreen made sure she stood close to Aunt Alice, next to her mother with Mikkel directly behind, women to the inner part of the circle. Cory stood to her right. Hollis stood on the far side of the circle as a guest. He stood where Alice could look into his eyes, pretending distress at having to marry the duke. According to Alice, he was primed to rescue her, and only her, at the last moment, transporting her to his ship where she would then urge him to fire upon the grotta. It would be easy to aim, as directly over the small island stood a glass gazebo, with a glass floor, providing an open view from space into the thermal pool. It also provided a touch more focusing power for the energy that would be needed to shield from the weapon's blast. The perfect target for both sides.

Drawing in a steadying breath, Noreen focused on Hollis through the gauzy veil of sunshine yellow the queen had finally compromised on. Hot pink didn't seem dignified enough and orange was out. Brown too dull. Yellow answered the requirements of all.

Posing as Noreen, Alice had spent more and more time in Hollis's company the last few days, leaving Noreen free to spend time with Gunnar. Each was loathe to let the other out of sight. Because so few details were needed, they'd been allowed to retire to their suite in the palace and let others see to the final arrangements. The time had been spent resting and communing with the babies.

A few sentences into the ceremony, Hollis made his move. Noreen barely saw him blink, and then the old bishop was pushed aside. Hollis stepped up onto the dais, shoved Gunnar aside, wrapped his arms around Alice and, in the next blink, they were gone.

Seizing the moment, Noreen stepped up while others helped the bishop back to his feet. Gunnar righted himself, wrapped his arms around her and she clung to him. Hands reached to touch them, the bishop's hand on their heads as he intoned the binding words of the marriage ceremony.

"Go, *älskling*," Gunnar whispered as Odin instructed the gathered people to make sure they touched the person in front and behind.

Practiced precision made the connections unite in the next heartbeat, gathering energy as she drew in air. With each surge she drew in, her senses extended out, focused on the foreign ships orbiting over the planet.

"Can you sense the activity on the warships?" Gunnar asked.

"Not...yet...wait..." There was a sense of growing energy, the *ByalbOgBeLun* singing in her head, as the power continued to gather in her.

"Gunnar! Hold me!" She turned her face to the glass overhead and the power burst from her.

"*Shield!*"

Did she shout it or did someone else?

Eyes squeezed shut, she pictured a thick beam of white hot light shooting up through the gazebo. A roar shook her as it raced for the outer edge of the planet's atmosphere just as an equally thick beam of red light aimed at the Summer Palace came from the five warships. Their beams merged and screamed toward the gazebo as well. Meeting at the corona surrounding Nordia, the white light spread outward like a blanket, or balloon, pushing against the destructive energy aimed at them.

"They are firing," Freya said calmly. "They are confused by your beam and are trying to change their frequency, but we have frozen their instrument panels."

Too focused on maintaining the shield, Noreen dug deep within herself, the power from her children merging with the power she already wielded, and the shield strengthened.

The rush was incredible. Unlike anything she'd experienced before, the closest she could come to comparison was the bliss of orgasm with Gunnar, and yet, it still didn't compare. No longer a body, she felt fused with Gunnar, the children within her, and every person in the cavern. Absently, she was aware of the bishop still embracing them, his chanting voice invoking the marriage rituals followed by the coronation rituals, his assistants placing the state crown on her head, a lesser crown on Gunnar's. It barely registered.

"Hold it, *älskling*," Gunnar practically shouted in her ear. "It's working!"

"Almost there, Princess," Freya sounded strained. "Just a few… more…meters…seconds… Get ready to send the final blast… Now!"

A surge of power, blindingly hot, gathered deep inside, then, like a geyser, burst forth from her, pushing the red beams from the ships back, and then all stopped.

Turning off like a plug pulled from an electrical socket, Noreen collapsed in Gunnar's arms and he slipped to his knees, holding her, his grandfather falling with them. Warmth enveloped her as she sank up to her neck in the water that buoyed her, protected her, another layer beyond Gunnar's arms.

"I present to Nordia," the old man gasped, "Queen Noreen Elke Josephina Angelica Tibbetts Audelhuk and Prince Consort Pehr Gunnar

Tore Hunter Harris Zaren Audelhuk. What the gods have forged, let no one rend asunder. May they rule the planet wisely, imparting love and care upon the royal subjects of the crown. Long live the queen."

Only the sound of water spilling from the upper pools broke the silence for a long moment, until Noreen heard her father choke out, "Long live Queen Noreen and Prince Pehr."

Weakly, the cry was taken up, and Noreen had just enough strength to lift her head and look at her husband. "Pehr?" With a sigh she slumped into his arms and blackness.

Clasping Nory to him, Gunnar reached for the tiny reserve of energy he'd held back. As he'd suspected, she'd held nothing back, drawing the full complement of power from the gathered nobility, all of whom sagged, resting against one another, letting the water help support them. It was probably a good thing they were packed so close. As the planet shuddered and groaned, they held each other up, insulated against the upheavals and ground shaking going on. He could detect the shimmer of what looked like an energy shield encapsulating the grotta. Securing Nory in his arms, he simply let go of the worry. There was nothing he could do to stop the shaking, and the gods had promised to secure the chamber. Until the planet settled down, there was nothing else to do.

"Prince," the soft voice in his ear roused him to answer with a mumble. "Mmm?"

"You need to lead," the voice continued. "The worst of the shaking is passing. Rouse your noble class. Damage control time."

Not sure exactly who spoke, he merely nodded. "Right." He forced himself to take stock of his surroundings.

Nory stirred sluggishly in his arms.

"*Älskling?* Nory?" he whispered. She did no more than nuzzle her face against his neck.

"*Nory.*" he tried the mental approach

"*G'way. Sleep.*"

Relief poured through him. She was okay. "*Nory, we must get moving. If nothing else, we need to get you to the bedroom.*"

Her sigh was like a gale sweeping through his head. "*Damage?*"

"*Don't know yet.*"

"'*Kay.*" She lifted her head and the effort made it look as if it weighed fifty kilos. "*Did it work?*"

"*Don't know yet. Need to get to a communications port.*"

"*Right.*" Her eyelids didn't want to work and he watched them flutter.

Around them he heard the sounds of people stirring. The faces looked dazed, eyes blinking as they tried to take in the current situation.

"*Stand, älskling.*" Gunnar helped her to her feet, then reached down a hand to help his grandfather. The king, no, Bjorn, helped first Elke, then Cory to their feet, the brothers-in-law helping the sisters.

Moans and murmurs began to fill the cavern. He needed to speak now, while he could still be heard.

"Attention," he called out and the general hubbub subsided. "We seem to be alive." A general groan and chuckle whispered around them. "Please make sure the people closest to you are okay. We have medics standing by to help. Do not panic, but simply raise your hand if you, or someone next to you, needs assistance. In a few minutes we hope to begin receiving reports of the result of our recent move." Another groaning chuckle answered him. "It may take a little time to get the satellites back online, but we'll start with our immediate surroundings and take stock from there. If the palace is still standing, there should be food in the ballroom along with plenty of coffee. We have a long night ahead of us as we assess the damage."

"Would someone explain what just happened?" A voice in the crowd called out.

"The short explanation? We just moved our planet out of the path of the comet threatening us," Gunnar called out.

A shocked silence fell on the cavern.

"What the hell?" another anonymous voice said.

"We put up a shield which protected the planet from the weapons of the Lidarian. It formed a barrier, so the force of his blasters pushed Nordia a few kilometers or more, into a new orbit around the sun. One that will avoid the comet for many eons if not forever. We're safe. Well, aside from the side effects of moving. We have a few natural disasters to deal with, but nothing along the lines of the annihilation we faced if hit by the comet."

"And Princess—uh—Queen Noreen, did this? She made this shield?"

"She drew in and focused the power you all, we all, supplied. The children she carries, our children, boosted the power even more. Not just your queen, but each and every one of you, helped save this planet." Gunnar lifted Nory in his arms.

"So it's true? She's pregnant? How many?" a woman nearby asked.

"Five," he answered shortly.

"Holy Hell! Get that woman to bed!" an older duchess called out. "Out of the way you ruffians. Can't you see she's exhausted? Put the child to bed and don't endanger the heirs! Five! At once! Unheard of!"

An excited murmur rippled through the nobility and a path to the edge of the pool opened up. With Bjorn leading the way, Gunnar carried Noreen to a waiting medic, her doctor standing by.

As Gunnar tucked a blanket around her, she stirred. "The people... damage? Everyone okay?"

"We're checking on it. We all got knocked around a little. You need to rest now," he told her.

"Your Majesty." The Duchess pushed her way through the crowd and curtsied next to the gurney. "We'll see to you. Let the men look after the planet."

"Yes, Amelia." Elke wrapped her arm around the duchess. "We will see to her indeed. You're so good with organization, would you help Coreen, Loreen and Doreen see everyone gets a bit of sustenance in the ballroom? They'll all need warm food while they dry off and dress. If you could help see to that, Moreen and I will settle Noreen with her doctor to watch over her."

"Of course, Your Majesty."

Gunnar was once again impressed with the quiet authority Noreen's mother wielded when the larger woman retreated. He shared a smile with his mother-in-law before bending to kiss Nory's cheek.

"We'll rally the troops. I need to get to the communications center and see if we still have contact with our world. Do as you're told, and tomorrow you can join in the fray," he told her.

"Kiss me properly. The wedding vows aren't sealed until you kiss me," she said with no hint of guile in her gaze.

"Yes, my queen."

The smile she gave him made the air around them sizzle with energy and his heart knew peace. It was a new day and they were new people. Whatever happened now, they'd see it through together.

He bent and kissed her, long and deep, until the cheering of their audience echoed off the cavern walls.

Someone shouted, "Long live the queen!"

"Long live my prince," she whispered, then nipped his lower lip.

"Absolutely. Now go put my children to bed. I'll join you when I can."

"Yes, Pehr."

"Uh, Nory, we need to change that."

"Right, you be Queen Noreen. I'll be Prince Pehr. Wanna trade?"

"On second thought, let's shoot your father."

"Good plan." She kissed him one last time before the medics rolled her gurney away.

Chapter 30

"Prince Hunter, Prince Tore, Prince Harris, Princess Darren, and Princess Skye."

Braced by pillows, Noreen used her chin to point to each bundled infant nestled against her in the large bed. Hans held the camera transmitting the live feed to the communications satellites, which then sent the signal back to each household on the planet. Rumor had it every pair of eyes on Nordia was tuned in to see the newest members of the royal household.

Gunnar sat beside her on the bed and picked up Hunter. The little guy wiggled enough he nearly fell over. Only a day old, all five were unusually alert according to their nurses. With little experience pertaining to infants, Noreen had no idea if they were or weren't. She was just glad they now did their wiggling outside of her. The last few weeks had been most uncomfortable as the babies grew more and more crowded within her.

"There they are, in order of their birth," she said with a sigh and leaned back.

At that moment Skye let out a belch, then yawned. Tore turned his face to Noreen's breast and started mouthing, looking for her nipple through the soft cotton of her nightgown. She couldn't believe it. He'd just eaten! They'd fed the babies on purpose hoping they'd be content to look cute for five minutes, and already his hunger was making itself known mentally even as he rooted for the source of nourishment.

"We'll give you updates from time to time so you'll know how they fare, however, their lives will not be open books. As you value your privacy, know we do as well. Thank you for your hard work and support these many months. Hopefully within the year we'll be able to resume life as normal, more or less, as we adjust to our new orbit and the new opportunities unveiled by the change. For now, enjoy the beautiful Summer Solstice day and celebrate life. Without heavy sweaters for once!" She smiled at the camera and the recording light went out.

"All right, Tore, all right, we won't let you starve." She nodded to the nurses standing by to take up the other wiggling infants. "I'll feed him, if you'd see to the others please."

Six nurses to care for five babies. A minimum of three were always on duty in rotating shifts. Bucking conventional tradition, Noreen insisted she wanted to attempt nursing each child once a day. She wanted to nurture the bond with her children, so their nursery, for now, was next door to her sitting room. Once they grew a little more and were weaned, they'd move to the traditional nursery.

"I'll hang onto Hunter for a bit," Gunnar told the nurse who reached for the heir. He smiled and she nodded with a tiny curtsy before carrying Harris away on the heels of his sisters and the other nurses.

"Not showing a preference already are you?" Noreen awkwardly unbuttoned her gown. She supposed it would soon be second nature to settle a hungry one to the source.

"No, but he was handy." Gunnar grinned and watched his other son latch on, a grimace contorting his wife's face. "Sure you want to nurse? Looks rather painful."

She sighed as Tore settled in to suckle. "At least he knows what he's doing." The pain settled and her milk began to flow. "In truth, it is almost more painful when the milk lets down like it is starting to do."

Gunnar stretched out on the bed and settled his son in the crook of his arm. Serious blue eyes stared up at him. "Can you tell what they're thinking?"

"Their thoughts aren't articulate enough. Hunger, wet, cold, tired... these things I can sense. Contentment," she said softly, gazing down at the infant in her arms. "Deep contentment. Stronger when they're latched on, but I can still sense their impressions. Skye is sleepy, Darren wants to snuggle. I hope the nurses put them together...ah, there we go, the other three are cuddled up, warm and dry, drifting off to sleep. That one," she nodded at Hunter, "is most curious about this outside world. His little mind is trying to take in the bright colors and the unmuted sounds. He's quite content with his pappa."

"Do they know? Do they sense how special they are?" Gunnar smiled at the tiny fingers grasping his index finger.

"No. This just...is. They don't know different, of course." She watched as Bertrand leaned over the bed and a frond stroked Hunter's head covered with soft blond fuzz. Hunter's eyes followed the green leaf and he tried to reach for it.

"Would you look at that!"

Noreen looked up at her mother's entrance into the bedroom.

"How smart he is!" She clapped her hands in delight. "I'd like to hold my grandson, if you don't mind." Her smile softened the implied order given to Gunnar as she held out her arms.

"One heir, coming up," Gunnar joked and carefully lifted Hunter toward his grandmother.

Bjorn sat down on the far side of the bed and rested a hand on Tore's head. "Boys, at last I have a few more allies in this household."

"Oh fy," Noreen scoffed. "How are the hinterlands?" When they'd arrived the previous night she'd been a little too busy for greeting her parents graciously.

"The people are adjusting quite well. The emergency supplies are holding out nicely, not to mention a few above ground experimental crops are planted and also showing signs of doing well. We'll know better come the harvest in two or three months, but for now, we'll hold onto our optimism. And no one is complaining about the longer, warmer days."

Noreen certainly wasn't. Nordian days were now just over twenty-one hours long with much more sunshine. The planet showed signs of acquiring a more circular orbit a few thousand kilometers closer to the sun. Still further than Earth was from its sun, they'd remain colder overall but, during summer, they'd be warmer than they had been, and winters would be warmer by ten to twenty degrees on average, based on current projections. What were a few ground tremors compared to warmth?

"Well, I don't see increasing the official work day hours for the foreseeable future. We've worked hard for many years, let the people live off the wealth they've banked, and put time into their gardens and hobbies." She adjusted Tore a little to ease the cramping in her arm.

Her father pushed a pillow under her elbow. "You'll develop new muscles soon."

Noreen rolled her eyes. "Is this what they call parents' revenge?"

Her father and mother shared a smile before chuckling.

"I thought so."

Moder carried Hunter to the rocking chair nearby. "You are just the smartest little boy there ever was," she cooed. Noreen felt a burst of happiness from her son and rolled her eyes.

"Let the spoiling begin," she muttered.

"As is my right," her mother retorted, not at all put out. "I saw his eyes tracking your plant pet. Newborns don't do that, but our babies are special, aren't they?"

Noreen caught a glance from Gunnar and they shared their own smile. What was it about a baby that turned an adult into a gibberish-speaking monkey? Her attention was drawn back to Tore when he choked around her nipple. She lifted him to her shoulder to pat his back.

"Are you finished little man?" she murmured to him. An uncomfortable bubble seemed to cause him a little distress, and then he let loose with a belch worthy of the one his sister had shared during the broadcast. Hunger immediately followed, transmitting itself loud and clear to his mother. "I guess not," she chuckled and covered the one breast before settling him on the other one.

"Your intentions to nurse are admirable," her mother said, "but not at all practical. It just isn't done, you know."

"It's done by mothers who care. Just as you did. I'll keep it up as long as I can. I do realize I can't meet the needs of all of them for nourishment, but I can use the time to bond a little closer. I want the time with them while the people are willing to indulge me."

"You'll only have a month or so, you know," her father said.

Noreen nodded as Gunnar's hand cupped his son's head nestled against her. There was still much work to do as the planet adjusted to the recent changes. All of them.

"We'll buy you all the time we can," he assured her.

"So how are the people, overall?" she asked again

"The mood is optimistic and they're in love with their queen," Bjorn said with great satisfaction.

"I still don't know why you did that to me," she grumbled.

"You'll see. Heard from Alice lately?" He changed the subject.

"She sent through a message of congratulations this morning," Gunnar said. "She and Hollis appear to be settling in happily enough. She's sending a whole cargo ship of gifts. It should arrive in the next week. Their wedding went off without a hitch. Her only regret was we couldn't attend, but she's sending photos with the shipment."

"I'm dying to see what a Lidarian wedding ceremony is like," her father said with laugh.

Noreen agreed. Alice had briefly showed them her true form, a small creature, almost resembling a caricature of a mouse. About three feet tall with a large head and large black eyes, she was fine-boned and covered with a soft teal-colored fur. A long thin tail helped her balance on two hind legs. Alice had said the humanoid form was easier for moving around. Most of the time anyway.

"Hollis was furious when he found out how she'd hidden from him for so long," Gunnar chuckled. "Funny, I actually sympathized with him over that point."

Noreen stuck her tongue out at him. "I didn't hide for a hundred years."

"No, you didn't."

"And Fader always knew where I was." She nearly laughed when Gunnar shot a speculative glance towards the former king. Fader didn't look the least bit penitent. Slightly abashed, maybe, but overall, rather pleased with himself.

"Too bad he never told me. I would have brought you home sooner."

"Sure you would have," she said slyly. "You didn't even recognize me when we met."

"My mind may not have, but my body did." He leered at her and she felt herself blush.

"Oh."

Gunnar laughed at her, accompanied by her father. She glanced at her mother and they both rolled their eyes.

"Men."

Gunnar lay down and rested his head in her lap, looking up at her as he unwrapped Tore's little feet to kiss them.

Ticklish, like his mother, Tore protested by kicking, narrowly missing Gunnar's eye.

"Would have served you right if he'd given you a shiner," Noreen said as she cuddled the infant closer, drawing the blanket back around his feet. It felt as if her heart melted when Tore sighed against her, closing his eyes in deep, sleepy contentment, his hunger abated for the moment. "I think this little one is ready for his nap." She looked over to where Hunter was falling asleep to the gentle rocking in his grandmother's arms. "I think the kids have the right idea." She yawned, not even bothering to cover her mouth.

"Well, then." Her father stood and held out his arms. "Hand over the little tyke and we'll get them settled in the nursery. Gunnar can settle you here."

"Burp him gently." She kissed her son's little soft head before reluctantly handing him over. Obviously her father had been waiting impatiently for Tore to finish up.

"Don't worry, I remember how to do it," he laughed at her, settling the baby against his shoulder like a pro. "You may have been mostly raised by nurses, but I did spend a little time holding my girls."

Noreen lost her comment to another yawn.

Sophie came in and quietly surveyed the scene. With a smile in Noreen's direction, she moved to the curtains and pulled them closed against the summer sun flooding the room.

"Don't shut the windows," Noreen murmured and snuggled against Gunnar.

"What? You're not worried about being cold?" he teased her and pulled the light sheet over her.

"With you holding me? No chance of that."

Gunnar looked at his wife for a long moment, then looked up to see his in-laws smiling as they held the babies. It was a quiet moment in what would be a chaotic life and they all savored it, recognizing it for what it was. Bjorn's soft chuckle could be heard as he ushered Elke from the bedroom. Sophie made sure the covers were in place then followed, softly closing the door.

"Gunnar?" Nory's voice was muffled against his chest.

"Hmm?" The warmth from the sun created a feeling of languor in him.

"We're creating our own version of heaven, aren't we?"

"Yes, Nory, we are."

"I wonder how long the snow will hold off?"

"What do the *ByalbOgBeLun* say?" He still stumbled over the name.

"They're guessing four months, but I'm losing touch with them. They're going deeper into their own world."

"Are they okay with all the changes?"

"Yeah, they're okay. We won't hear from them so much anymore. They predict we won't face any major planetary dangers, at least not from the solar system or galaxy for a few eons. Of course, they can't predict the occasional meteorite hit, and no one can predict outside hostile forces such as Hollis represented, but astronomically, we're fine. The planet will settle down for the most part, and we can all get on about living our lives."

"So other than the volcanoes and the planet adjusting to the new gravitational forces and orbit, we're in the clear," Gunnar summarized.

"Right."

"So, just enough activity to keep things exciting."

"Right."

"I can live with that." He kissed her forehead. "You?"

"Oh yeah. Kids, ground quakes, volcanoes, Parliament, trade agreements, and scientific discoveries. More than enough excitement to keep me distracted from dreaming about blue sandy beaches and tropical breezes."

"With any luck we'll get to fit those in as well from time to time. Alice and Hollis have invited us to visit when we can."

"Ooh, family vacation in five years or so. We can leave the kids with Alice for a few days and sneak off to this one little beach…"

Gunnar looked down at the dreamy smile on her face. Realizing she'd probably visited that beach with Hollis gave him a stab of unexpected jealousy. And, if she hadn't visited it with Hollis, then she'd been there with her staff. The point was, he hadn't been there with her.

"Or maybe we'll go someplace new. Discover a whole new planet on our own. One you haven't visited before."

"Don't worry, I still have a list of twenty planets or so I've always wanted to see," she chuckled. "If I can visit five more before I die I'll consider myself well-traveled."

"Sounds like we have our life mapped out as best we can."

"The best part is," she leaned back to look up at him, "each day will be an adventure and we'll experience it together."

Gunnar didn't want to be anywhere else but here and now, his arms wrapped around her. He was also glad they'd fulfilled their reproduction duties in one fell swoop. The births had been a miracle but he didn't want to see her in that much pain ever again.

"So does this mean you're ready to settle down on one planet? Other than for vacations and diplomatic missions, that is."

"Yes, Gunnar. I'm home to stay."

"So does this mean I can't tie you up anymore?"

"Give me a few weeks and we can always pretend I'm about to run off…"

"Seems to me I owe you a replay of our wedding night."

"Hmm, now that you mention it…" She grinned up at him. "You also mentioned something about your country house having a playroom."

"Yep, just for adults, but I don't want to think about it right now. You're too sore and beat up from the birth yesterday, and I don't want to disgrace myself. You need to rest for several weeks before you can play again." He tucked her head under his chin, secure against his shoulder. "I can think of at least a few dozen games to start off with. We can go from there."

"Oh yeah? Tell me a story, Pappa. Tell me how you want to put me to bed."

"Well, it would start like this…" He rolled to face her and kissed her nose. "And then…" His lips moved to her eyelids, one by one, teasing the lashes resting against her cheeks. "But most of all, this is the best part because you can always do this…" He slanted his lips over hers and gently teased her lips open.

Nory opened to him, like the newly planted flowers enjoying the warmth of the Nordian sun for the first full season outside. They still had long winter nights to look forward to, but never again would they be cold and lonely. She was the fire that sustained him. He only hoped he provided the same for her. When she kicked aside the covers over them he smiled, then eased back, kisses turning to small nibbles.

"Sleep, my love. The children will wake soon enough," he whispered.

"Yes, Gunnar," she sighed against him. "Just keep that fire burning for me."

"Always, *älskling*, always."

Meet the Author

Morgan prefers to live under her pen name. An everyday woman, she's a wife and mother like many out there. She doesn't feel there is much that makes her stand out from the crowd, with the possible exception of her imagination.

Inside her mind live characters who look normal, if almost a little boring, on the outside. Inside they have passions and hungers that would shock their preachers and next door neighbors.

Kinky? Maybe. Twisted? Warped? Definitely—but in a fun way. Bloodsport is not her style. Leather and lace? Oh yeah. A sexy stare-down, a thorough tongue lashing, bubbles and petting. Champagne and hot tubs. Morgan lives for decadent luxury and love. Ripped abs, smooth warm skin, and tight butts on her heroes a must. Strong arms on strong men with lusty appetites.

Morgan doesn't consider her day successful unless she's had a good belly laugh and warped her teenager in some way. Luckily, both are relatively easy to accomplish. Or is the teen warping her? She's noticed an increasing trend of rap music on her iTunes lately. When does the parent become the child?

Let your inhibitions go and step into Morgan's world. Erotic adventure often mixed with danger-laced action keeps the pages turning.

www.ingramcontent.com/pod-product-compliance
Lightning Source LLC
Chambersburg PA
CBHW020739250626
47155CB00003B/837